Tom Davies, a Welsh
journalist with the *Wes...*
Sunday Times, the *Sund...*
for three years he was
time writer, his previo...
MAGICIAN AND THE PACIFIC COAST HIGHWAY,
STAINED GLASS HOURS: A MODERN PILGRIM-
AGE (both non-fiction works) and the novels ELECTRIC
HARVEST and ONE WINTER OF THE HOLY SPIRIT
(which is published by Futura).

Tom Davies is married and has three children.

Also by Tom Davies

ONE WINTER OF THE HOLY SPIRIT

TOM DAVIES

BLACK SUNLIGHT

Futura

A Futura Book

ISBN 0 7088 2998 8

Reproduced, printed and bound in Great Britain by
Hazell Watson & Viney Limited,
Member of the BPCC Group,
Aylesbury, Bucks

Futura Publications
A Division of
Macdonald & Co (Publishers) Ltd
Greater London House
Hampstead Road
London NW1 7QX
A BPCC plc Company

Author's Note

I went to live in Maerdy, home of the last pit in the Rhondda, to write and research this book and would like to thank Mrs Dilys Evans and Jeffrey for looking after me; the Rev. Andrew and Ros Morton for their companionship; Bob Reeves for the use of his fine poem *Gwaed* (which is Welsh for blood); Tim Shackleton and Richard Evans for their skilful advice; the marvellous miners of Maerdy with whom I spent many happy hours, both drinking and picketing, and my wife Liz who virtually gave me two years off to leave home and learn about the life of the Rhondda miner.

But Maerdy is not my fictional village of Bont and neither is the Valley herein the Rhondda. The characters and Valley of this book are entirely my own creation and through them I have sought to tell the story of the widespread betrayal and sad decline of the South Welsh Valleys over the last twenty years. It is to my beloved people of the Valleys that this book is dedicated with the quiet prayer that, one day, they will find cause to sing again.

Part One

The Ceremony of Innocence

Once I strode the green fields
On steel sprung thighs
My breath was the breath
Of mountains and I
Snorted fire in my pride.

I knew the heat of iron,
I knew the smell of sulphur,
Mine was the way of moles,
And I thought my pick had
Conquered coal when I shed
My sweat a mile below the sun.

Gwaed, Bob Reeves

Chapter One

It was early evening in Bont, the sun just hanging over the rim of the Valley.

A queue began forming outside the Miners' Welfare Hall for the Saturday night hop. The dance was not due to start until eight o'clock but many queued early so that they might claim their favourite seats – next to the bar perhaps, or the one in which they were once lucky in bingo. Madge Williams from the bakery, they said, had won the flyer seven times this year from her seat by the ladies.

From down in the village square came the long pained squeals of the brakes of the Western Welsh bus as it three-point turned around the clock tower.

The mining village of Bont was a raggle-taggle community scattered along the far end of the Glamorgan Valley, the heart of the South Wales coalfield. Completely enclosed by high, rock walls, it might have been sitting at the bottom of a volcano. A dozen or so streets ran at right angles to the main terrace; there were a few rundown streets around by the waste-paper factory, next to the river, and some slightly posher terraces, with foaming lace curtains cascading around coloured plastic flowers, right up the hill next to the severe grey shape of the Libanus Chapel and a row of rackety pigeon cotes perched dangerously on bandy-legged stilts.

About a mile away from the village were a reservoir, sitting right at the end of the Valley, three huge, black tips and the stern black geometry of the mine itself. As the miners walked or drove down from the pit at the end of their shifts they first came to the cavernous Welfare Hall, with its three lounges, four bars and dance hall. Then there was a long row of shops including the Co-op supermarket, a branch of Barclays

Bank (open three mornings a week), a fish and chip shop, a betting shop and Lee Hoo Wonk's Chinese takeaway. Plonked right at the end of the majestic curve of Bont Terrace was the village's small cinema, The Bug.

Beyond them, in turn, was the brown rocky bend in the Valley, which led to the next village, another world altogether.

Just full of itself was Bont in the early summer of 1966. Every morning cockerels could be heard bugling in the voluptuous dawns. As the sun rose high, cats stretched out on the corrugated roofs of the garden sheds, luxuriating in the glorious warmth of it all. Every afternoon was vibrant with doorstep gossip and the chimes of Gazzi's ice cream van dancing down the gullies. The boys on the bench in the square sat out, drinking cider and yarning. Come the night and lovers found their way down to the long grass on the river bank where they kissed and touched one another.

Every three hours, night and day, a pair of diesels throbbed up the railway line, past the tump, towing a brown rattling chain of empty wagons. Some three hours later they laboured back from the pit again, the wagons piled high with the finest Welsh anthracite. There was enough coal down that hole to blacken and heat the whole face of the world, the miners of Bont reckoned. There was certainly enough to keep Bont going for a hundred years and, when that time was up, they would worry about the matter again.

Back at the Welfare Hall, the doors had opened. Everyone duly paid their half crown entrance fee to Dai Fat in the glass kiosk and filed upstairs to the dance hall. The building was a gloomy warren of bubbling, flaking paint with the smell of stale beer trapped in the carpets. There were aluminium foil ash-trays on the tables, many made level with wodges of beer mats stuffed strategically under one leg or another. Down every corridor you could hear the bright, brittle music of the one-armed bandits or the echoing click of snooker balls. Even in the heat of the summer you could sniff the mildewed, slightly mushroomy damp.

Two women were standing on one of the concrete landings of the stairs and talking to one another in low tones of high urgency:

'I told her. And I do keep on telling her. But she gets proper craxy when you tell her anything at all.'

10

'What did you tell her then?'

'Poor dab I do feel awful sorry for her. I told her again last week but there's no shape on her. There's no grain in her washing. No shape on 'er in the 'ouse. No nothing.'

'So what did you tell her?'

'I told her to brighten her ideas up if she wanted her leg varnished with that stuff again.'

'What stuff was that?'

By far the largest room in the Welfare Hall was the dance floor, its curving, art deco balcony festooned with spotlights. Against a stage backdrop of giant gold and silver strips Smokey Evans was even now setting up his disco – Smokey Sounds – which attracted people from all over the Valleys. Smokey, a young and rather fetching Teddy boy from Pontypridd, had firmly set his back on all the Beatles music that was swamping every set of ears in the land. He still served up the driving hits of the Shirelles, the Crystals and the Ronettes.

He knew his audience well; Smokey's music, they said in the Valleys, was the greatest ever recorded. It might also have been the loudest. When Smokey started up his disco they said the miners started jiving together on the face of the Meadow Seam, a mile underground. For much of Saturday night the whole of Bont Terrace would shake to the nakedly primitive pounding of Phil Spector's Wall of Sound. Aunty Phyllis, in No. 3, would stuff up her ears with bits of Kleenex while Bomber Jones, in No. 9, before getting on with the slow business of dying of pneumonicosis on his brass-knobbed bedstead, would take out his rattling false teeth just as soon as the Ronettes started wailing about how awful it was when the one you loved ran off with your best friend.

The hop began, as usual, with five hands of bingo. Some veteran players marked up to six cards, though a few had difficulty with one card and kept calling bogey houses. A group of young miners, above all this, stood together in a pool of fluorescent light around the bar. Most of the bingo players were young girls, many dressed in the careful emblems of the American teenager – pony-tails, bright red neckerchiefs, tiny pleated skirts and white socks. Their brows furrowed in concentration and their mouths were quiet, for a change, as Walford James, the bingo caller, read out the all-important numbers from his tray of leaping, bouncing table tennis balls.

11

Seven and six — was she worth it? On its own — number five. Legs — eleven. Downing Street — number ten. Top of the shop — number eighty. Unlucky for some — thirteen ...

The one doing all the talking in the group of young miners was Glynmor Jones, one nicotine-stained hand holding a pint and the other in the trouser pocket of his mohair suit. 'Look I'm telling you now, boys, and this is a fact, no lie, but on my mother's life, this piece — a smart piece she was an' all — this piece said that his dick was so big he did wash his back with it. Isn't that right Jampots?'

'That's what she said, aye.' Glynmor always looked for confirmation from his best butty, an even smaller youth with a haggard pale face and a taste for ill-fitting suits and rolling his own cigarettes.

'How can you wash your back with your dick?'

'That's a fact that is,' Glynmor affirmed again with a nod. 'She said 'e was the only man she'd ever met who could crawl on all fours and leave five trails. It's monstrous. Just like some bastard python. Isn't that right Jampots?'

'Correct.'

'They said it was so big that, when he had a bad back, he had a doctor's note so that he didn't have to take it out when he wanted a piss.'

'You're having me on, mun.'

'That's a fact that is. Isn't that right Jampots?'

Glynmor was a short, broad-shouldered man with dark, Welsh good looks. His eyes were blacker than the coal he mined and he had thick eyebrows and a square jaw. But it was his smile that always got the girls going, a broad, laughingest smile which was always there, sitting well with the consistent crudity of his language. Rarely without a Capstan full-strength in his hand and a dirty joke in his mouth he approached every problem with an open mouth did our Glynmor. It was said he could talk the robin off a packet of starch. He had, as they say around 'ere, a bell on every tooth.

After the bingo had finished — with Madge Williams calling the flyer *again* — Smokey began slipping on his golden oldies, orchestrating the pace of the dance with the cunning peculiar to many of the natives of Pontypridd, content, for the while anyway, just to let the girls jive together with their handbags placed near their feet for safety. Sparkly coloured lights bounced off the huge mirrored ball suspended from the ceiling, chasing and streaming over the largely empty dance floor in flashing lights of reds, blues and greens. Now the Ronettes were at it. *Why don't you beeeeeeeeeeeeeeee myyyyyy babeeeeeeeeeee* ... Soon Smokey would have the whole place bouncing. He was one of the first disc jockeys to have his own light show too – a weird and wonderful collection of winking orange and red lights, mainly stolen from traffic signals and parking bollards up and down the Valley.

But no matter how hard Smokey worked, the only boy who ever danced through choice, from very early until very late, was Biscuits, who worked in the stores down the pit. He had not, it seemed, stopped dancing since seeing *Rock Around the Clock* (thirty-four times). The girls all agreed that Biscuits was the best dancer in the Valleys. Indeed, he was not overmuch bothered who he danced with either, merely wandering into the thickest clump of girls and grabbing the nearest hand to jive with. Then all eyes feasted on this fabulous dancer who, dressed entirely in black, had all the elegance and slime of a Brylcreemed tarantula, his hands held out carefully as the quiff of his Tony Curtis haircut dangled down on his forehead and bounced up and down to the beat.

It was from her table, three away from the stage and just next to the Emergency Exit, that Maggie Evans sat with her friends watching Glynmor's every move. Even as she sat discussing such important matters as how much of a bra strap it was proper and sexy to show, or who Betty Sugarlump was knocking off that week, Maggie watched Glynmor even more carefully than a hawk. As far as she was concerned he was the only ship on the seven seas. The poor girl was just crazy about him, even carrying his photograph around in her locket.

Glynmor, alas, was not exactly crazy about her. But if he'd had enough beer and no other piece sparkled his fancy, he usually came over for the final few dances with Maggie.

Whether Maggie Evans was really classy or not was always debated hotly by the boys in the bar. Her face was a perfect etching of a Welsh beauty, with long bobbed hair and lashings of black eye-liner and mascara, in the style favoured by the Crystals. Her mouth was as full as the reservoir after the rain and so was her bosom. Perfect, said some; they didn't like 'em skinny and titless in the Valleys. A bit fat, said others, the

13

girls especially. She could lose half a stone easy, they said, and she knew it. She was very conscious of her figure was Maggie.

Such pneumatic arguments aside, many of the boys were very taken by Maggie, largely because of Glynmor's persistent lurid lies of how she was always desperate for it. Tales of how she would tear off her knickers and beg him to ravish her had entered the mythology of the Valley. As the dance went on, and the alcohol flowed ever more freely in the blood, a whole string of randy and hopeful boys would come over to her table offering a drink or a dance.

But she refused all offers. Just like a bloody fool, said the girls. Her eyes were only ever for Glynmor who never so much as bought her a drink before getting drunk himself and coming over for the last few dances, arms wide apart and one of those silly bloodshot smiles on his chops. Then the soft cow was just putty in his hands.

The girls always despaired of this surrender. It just wasn't right. She wasn't a doormat was she? You're not a bloody doormat, are you? They were always advising Maggie to start being a bit of a girl, to try and play hard to get. At the very least, she should dance with some other boy. But she just couldn't do it. The soft cow just couldn't. She just wasn't interested in any other boy and that was that.

The dopey cow was happy to be putty in his hands. She'd wipe his arse for him if she could. When did a girl ever get anyone acting like that? The soft sod deserved all she got, didn't she?

By ten o'clock more and more dancers were crowding onto the floor. Smokey was turning the musical screws a bit but still Glynmor did not seem to want to come over. He seemed happy to let Maggie fret over her vodka and lime. Oh sure she pretended that she was having a great time, laughing loud along with the girls' quips and even making a few of her own, but her belly was the tightest knot of pain and her big black eyes locked like radar onto Glynmor's every move.

See, now he's left his butty Jampots and gone over to talk to that horrible piece from Penrhos. Now he's moved on again, joking with some old slag in an ocelot dress. An ocelot dress! Only prostitutes down in Bute Street in Cardiff wear ocelot dresses. Come to think of it that one looks like a tart on the beat. She's putting her hand around the back of his neck and

14

playing with his curls, the old slag. And look at the way she walks. You'd think her arse was chewing a toffee. Well she'd open her legs for him fast enough no doubt. Perhaps she would have to give in one day. But someone like Glynmor would immediately get fed up and go somewhere else. Boys like him are only ever interested if there was a challenge. Give in and they're off.

She sipped her drink, then brought the glass down hard onto the table. Oh, why did he do this to her? It was true enough what the girls said: he was a right bastard was our Glynmor. But you never went for the tidy ones did you? That wasn't the way it worked at all. You always fell for bastards like Glynmor who treated you like shit and were always playing you up. And to think she could have had that manager of the shoe shop down in Pontypridd just like that. He wouldn't have mucked her around like this. He was a proper gentleman that one, exactly what her Mam had always wanted for her too.

Smokey was playing the slow numbers now and Dave Berry was singing how he knew all there was to know about the crying game. She watched Glynmor go to the bar and buy a drink for the slag in the ocelot dress. When did he ever buy anyone a drink? She must have promised him a bit of a rub. Now they were laughing secretively together. Making jokes about her no doubt and how she was so fat an' all. He was probably telling her the story of how her backside got wedged in the hand-rails of the slide on the children's playground. He was always telling people lies about her like that. Glynmor must have been the biggest bastard that ever drew breath. *I knooooooooow all there is to knooooooooooooow ...*

The girls were talking of the days when they had live acts here – Maggie, do you remember the night David Whitfield came and we had to go out and get him some chips? – and now the flames of jealousy and betrayal were burning big holes inside her. She stood up, indicating to the girls that they should pick up their handbags. It was time to convene a special emergency conference in the lavatory.

Maggie you've got to stop acting like this init? If he knows what he's doing to you he'll only make it worse. Dance with Biscuits. Try and make Glynmor jealous isn't it? No, not Biscuits. When did anyone ever get jealous of Biscuits? Give us a squirt of that will you? What about Danny? Oh him. He's with that piece that works for Polikoff's in Ynyswen. He won't leave her now. I think that piece in the spotty dress is from Porth. A right goer. Maggie they do say that some man once lost his horse and cart between her legs. Took him three weeks to find it, it did. Lennie. Tap Lennie. Well I think Biscuits is all right. He is the best dancer around 'ere isn't 'e?

But all such counsel did not work and the pain was still playing Maggie up like a renegade ulcer. She returned with the girls to their table. All the conflicting advice had made her brain go funny and Glynmor was still with the same old slag. Now he was even buying her *another* drink. He was going to lose more than his horse and cart the way he was going. She fished a lump of ice out of her drink and flung it at him. But he was so engrossed, leering down the slag's cleavage, he didn't hear the sharp crack of the ice cube against the wall by his head.

He was asking Ocelot Dress where she lived. She shared a flat in Porth with her friend? Well, that was promising enough. Got two bedrooms have you in this flat? Three actually. Oh aye?

Glynmor had heard stories about this one; this was the legendary Phantom Gobbler of Porth who liked to be tied up, then she'd suck you in and blow you out in bubbles. He had always fancied being a bubble, and those were a mighty pair of knockers and no mistake. He would have an awful lot of fun getting lost in them. The sap was rising in him – right up from his toe nails it was rising.

'You come up here this way much, do you?' he asked.

'I've been here a couple of times. I've seen you before too. I remember asking myself what you had between your legs. I'm like that you see. What I want I ask for.'

Uncharacteristically stuck for a few words Glynmor shifted his weight from one foot to another. Something explosive attempted to break out from between the buttons of his tloshes. He had struck gold. He took a swift glance over at Maggie who seemed happy enough with the rest of the girls. It didn't look as if he was going to be with her for the last few dances. He was fond enough of Maggie. He wasn't crazy about her or anything like that but he was fond of her, that figure and all. The boys agreed that Maggie was a good laugh but you couldn't screw a good laugh could you? All he ever got from

Maggie was a knee trembler; a dry run which, apart from messing up his underpants, gave him lover's nuts, an ache so fierce that, the next morning, he had to walk bow-legged to the pit, like some old cowboy.

But tonight, as long as he played his cards right, he had a real goer. He was not going to give it up either. After all – as he had always told Jampots in that merry, poetic way of his – a fuck's a fuck.

It was turning half past ten and the Shirelles were singing of the unutterable pain of being stood up on your first date. Smokey was presiding over a crowded, largely drunk, dance floor, all swaying around with groin pressed to crotch, lips locking against others and fingers feeling bra straps. It was all like a great bed of flowers in a tropical storm.

Glynmor sniffed Ocelot's perfume as he brought his mouth close to her ear. 'Shall I see you home? I've got a car,' he whispered.

'There's a problem,' she said. 'I've come with my friend.'

He studied the inside of his half-empty pint. Whenever you were ever getting anywhere with some piece around here there was always this bastard friend; usually some cock-eyed bint with a stammer and a brain the size of a maggot's.

'Where's she to?'

He looked up and followed the direction of her pointed finger. The friend, slumped unhappily over a glass of orange squash, looked even more slummocky than he had feared. She had pebble glasses and her name was Thelma.

'Well I've got just the boy for Thelma and that's a fact,' Glynmor declared. 'My best butty Jampots will look after her. I won't be a minute. Here. Hang onto my glass.'

'One thing. Thelma's got a thing about bad language. Tell him he'll have a lot of fun as long as he doesn't use bad language.'

Glynmor went over to the other side of the bar and cornered Jampots. 'You fancy a nice bit of snatch tonight, do you Jampots? That one's mine. The other's the friend. You've got the friend. She's weeping for it she is. She was saying she doubts she can last another minute without it.'

Jampots snorted into his beer; his reply was drowned by the shattering, erupting noises of tumbling tables and breaking glasses from up the balcony. The Treorchy boys were fighting

17

again. Committee men, whose job it was to keep law 'n' order in the club, came running in from all directions to smoke them out. *I'm gonna loooooooove you foreeeeeeeever ...*

'You're well in there, Jampots,' Glynmor went on, oblivious. 'I know she doesn't look much but she's desperate for it. Desperate mun. Don't take any notice of her specs. You don't fuck her specs do you? She's been saying she doubts she can wait a second longer.'

'She's got crabs, mun,' said Jampots noncommittally.

Glynmor wasn't listening. 'The piece I've got says you'll do all right as long as you don't use any bad language. Thelma's her name.'

'You hear me did you Glynmor? Watch my lips now. She's got crabs.'

'Who's got crabs?'

'That piece in the spotted dress. She gave them to Punchy last month. Had to shave himself all over he did.'

'Crabs eh? Crabs.'

'Aye mun. Bastard millions of the little fuckers there were. Fred Dwarf got them off her as well. 'Orrible those crabs are too. 'Orrible. And there's this husband of hers. Plays prop forward; built like a brick shithouse. He comes down her flat in Porth now and then – usually in the middle of the night – to beat her up. Never got over her leaving him. And what he does to her is nothing to what he does to any man he catches with her.'

Glynmor looked sadly over to Ocelot Dress, still holding his pint. Tough. A fuck's a fuck but a dose is a dose and he didn't fancy the husband much either. Oh well, win a few, lose a few.

He decided against going back to retrieve his pint and went straight over to Maggie instead with one of those silly bloodshot smiles on his chops. All the girls looked at one another and shook their heads in genuine despair but Maggie stood up to dance with him immediately. The soft cow deserved all she got. Maggie knew all this, of course. She knew that she was little better than a bit of putty but there was nothing she could do about it. If you were crazy about a boy you were crazy about him and that was that.

Not that any of that mattered now. When you were dancing with Glynmor nothing else mattered. Fires of joy lit up inside her as she jived to the voice of Marvin Gaye who had just heard it on the grapevine. Coloured shivers of light went flashing through the brilliantined darkness with her Glynmor smiling at her as they danced through the jammed bodies and ricocheting elbows. Just now he was hers and that was all that mattered.

And all this was as nothing compared with the final few smooches when Glynmor held her tight and the Righteous Brothers told how she'd lost that loving feeling. Not her. She could feel the electric warmth of his touch on her arms, the warm and vital jointing of his groin pressed into hers, his face nuzzling into the side of her neck. She thought she might even swoon in the ecstacy of it all. She felt warm, complete, alive.

A full moon gazed down on the Valley as fat, washing-day clouds went sailing fast overhead. Police Constable Watkins patrolled the gullies, his torch slicing up the darkness as he looked for the trouble that never came. Down on the dark, twisting floor of the Valley the river gushed and sang, the brown trout darting past the moonbeamed pebbles and waving weeds. Occasionally the fat black shadows of sheep crunched around in the ferns and their sorrowing bleats slipped out into the darkness.

In his Ford Consul in a lay-by next to the top of the tump Glynmor was laying siege to Maggie's body. Except that the ecstacy of the dance floor had long since deserted her and she was now making a firm defence of her virginity against his octopus advances. Oh, she fancied it well enough but, when she succumbed, it was going to be on her wedding night with crisp, white linen sheets and an orchestra playing on the wireless. There would be flowers in the room and a maid bringing them breakfast in bed in the morning. It was all going to be like in one of those Mills and Boon books that she loved to read so much. That's how she wanted it, not in the front seat of Glynmor Jones' Ford Consul. That's not how she pictured it at all.

She allowed him to play with her breasts. But now that he had got her bra off, he had tired of fondling them. Now he was trying to get his hand up her knickers as usual. But, at the top of her stockings, she had firmly clamped her hand on his wrist as usual. He could go back but definitely no further. The very windows of the car were misting up with the frustrated passion of the encounter.

After a bit more huffing and puffing he finally sat up

19

straight, putting both hands on the steering wheel. 'Anybody'd think your body was the crown jewels,' he complained angry.

'Well they are. They're my crown jewels, aren't they?'

'It's a wonder you haven't got a headache all day with that bastard halo of yours being so tight an' all.'

'Did anyone ever tell you what a lovely talker you were, Glynmor? You should write love stories with that lovely way you do talk.'

'Bollocks to love stories.'

'But you're so charming Glynmor. That's what they all say about you don't they? Glynmor Jones could charm the very ducks off the lake.'

'Bollocks to the ducks.'

She bit her lip, noticing by the whiteness of his knuckles on the steering wheel that he was very angry indeed. Men were such babies when it came to sex. And her Glynmor was the biggest baby of them all.

'I'm sorry Glynmor,' she said, more placatory now. 'But you can't put your hand up there anyway.'

'Why not? What's so special about up there?'

'It's my period. I'm on.'

Rather than calm him down, as she had hoped, this bit of news made him explode with rage. 'You're on. You're *on*. That's nice init? That's bloody nice that is. Why didn't you tell me you daft twat? Saved a lot of trouble, that would've.'

'What did you expect me to say?' She was getting her hair off as well. 'Did you expect me to say "Oh hello Glynmor. It's so nice to see you tonight but you can't go putting your hand up my skirt because I'm having a period." That would be lovely wouldn't it?'

'It might not be nice. But it would have saved a lot of trouble.'

'Perhaps I should have put an advertisement in the *South Wales Echo*? Maggie Evans of Bont Terrace hereby announces that she is having her period so any person intending to put his hand up her skirt had better wait a few days. Or we could have got Smokey to announce it at the disco? Is that what you wanted?'

'Oh shut your gob. You're getting so that your mouth is getting bigger than the Severn Tunnel.'

'Is that so now? That's rich coming from the biggest

mouth in the land. They do say that you're the only man around here who eats bananas sideways.'

Glynmor blew out a stream of exasperated air. It was a considerable thorn in his side that she could always give as good as she got. There was a part of him that quite liked and even respected that but, for most of the time, he found it a right old pain in the arse.

'What about that bit in the ocelot dress?'

There it was. She was winding him up again. Pains in the arse just didn't come any more painful than her when she got going.

'What about her?'

'They do call her the Boat down in Porth 'cos everyone has sailed in her.'

'Don't be so crude.'

'Me! Crude! Glynmor they do say that you're going to get a special coal board pension for crudity.'

He flicked on the ignition and started the car first time. 'I'm taking you home,' he said flat.

'Oh let's have a wank,' she said, changing her tone.

He turned the ignition off again, hardly able to believe his ears. 'What did you say girl?'

'Let's have a wank. I'm starving. Lee Hoo Wonk. Let's have a wank. That's what my sister calls the Chinese takeaway. Haven't you heard that one?'

He laughed softly and started the engine again. Some, but not all, of his good humour had returned. It was true what the boys said. Maggie was a good laugh well enough. But it was also true that you couldn't screw a good laugh. That was the trouble with going out with Maggie. Perhaps he should have run the risk of catching crabs from the piece from Porth. Even as he drove past the tump he could feel that his balls were already aching from a savage case of lover's nuts. That was the other trouble with courting Maggie Evans.

Chapter Two

Then the month of May came and took up lodgings in the Valley and, with her, she brought the rain. Lots and lots of rain.

On some mornings you could actually see pillars of rain building up over the reservoir and then walking down the Valley in giant strides, washing against the patches of green fern and grey granite of the steep slopes, hissing softly on the dry stone walls of the farm which curled over the grass foothills, sheeting down on the piled pit props and rusty iron drams dotted around the pithead, soaking the wandering sheep and pit ponies alike as well as pattering down on the grey slate roofs of the terraces.

The rain filled up the cattle grids, making the rubbish trapped inside them rise up and float against the thick round iron bars. It made black rivulets pour out of the piles of concessionary coal dumped on the roads. It made even bigger rivulets come pouring out of the sides of the tips to dance and leap down the slopes to swell the already swollen river in the Valley bottom. Nothing escaped the rain; even the sodden blackbirds took shelter in the hissing eaves where their dirty white droppings gave a little splash of colour to the wet grey walls of the houses.

Such persistent dampness invaded Bomber Jones' lungs as he lay in the suffocating warmth of his bedroom. Every part of his body was fighting for breath. Any day now the Grim Reaper would be calling out his number for him to row his boat in and it would not be an hour too soon. His face had gone as old and withered as a blind cobbler's thumb. His nails had blackened and his eyes had sunk into dark sockets. His whole body had gone as thin as a sprat on a hunger strike. Much of the time he just sat propped up by a couple of pillows as his mouth searched around in the air for some relieving oxygen. He was, as they say around here, dying by inches. His tools were on the bar.

He did have oxygen bottles next to his bed, which sometimes gave his squealing lungs some relief but he did not like having the mask on for long. And blindly, madly – or so the family kept telling the silly old bugger – he refused to give up smoking his beloved Woodbines.

Even when he had a terrible bout of coughing and it looked as if his frail body was going to break in two under the jolting strain; even when his guts were bringing up great globs of blood-stained sputum, one of his hands would soon be reaching out for a fag. 'Health be buggered,' he would say, his pink eyes watering and mouth dribbling as he began to cough his guts up again. 'My health went the day I went down the hole. I can't get out for a drink so my fags are the only pleasure I've got left.'

He shared No. 9 Bont Terrace with his nephew Glynmor who never lost an opportunity to insult the dying old miner. 'You're a silly old wit-wat and no mistake,' Glynmor would say, fag in his own hand. 'You know we're going to bury you with two hundred Woodbines in your coffin. But we're not going to put any matches in there. Think of it you old goat. Lying there for all eternity with two hundred fags next to you which you can't light. Now that would be a real hell for you wouldn't it? Worse than any of those chapel flames an' all that.'

'I'd find a way to light them,' Bomber would declare between coughs.

'I – I – I – That's all you think of is your bastard self.'

Glynmor was peeved because he was the one who had to share their three up, two down house. While the family took it in turns to come from far and near to look after Bomber and then go home again, he was the one who had to listen to all that terrible coughing day and night. On and on it went. The night was the worst, the honks and heaves amplified by the big enamel bucket into which Bomber was for ever coughing his guts. This had gone on for nearly three years now. On some nights – particularly when he could hear the rustle of a cigarette packet and the dry flare of a lighting match – Glynmor really felt like going in there and holding a pillow over the old miner's head. And he would have done so if it wasn't that he could almost hear Bomber laughing in his coffin as Glynmor stood in Cardiff Crown Court on a life sentence for murder.

'Still hanging on then, are you?' Pauline, Glynmor's younger sister now in Taffs Well, would say to Bomber, again almost as if it was a matter of the utmost regret. 'You're like some bloody weed you are. Every time you get chopped down you spring back to life again. Isn't it time you gave us all a bit of a rest?'

'Well he's going to give us a very long rest quite soon and that's a fact,' Glynmor would add with some venom. 'The only time I can get some sleep now is around the back of the washery in the pit. It's noisy there but not half as noisy as being in 'ere with that old swine coughing his boots up all the time. It's not that pit that's done this to his lungs either. It's those bastard Woodbines of his. Coffin nails that's all they are. Why don't you give them up, you dopey twat?'

'Aw, why don't you go and boil your head?' Bomber would say. 'Talk, talk. All your talk just gives me a headache it do. I'm really looking forward to getting planted if you must know. Then I won't have to listen to you lot all the time.'

There was still a bit of fight left in Bomber and that was another source of aggravation. Even though his body might have been all washed up, the old reprobate had never lost the great sexual urges he had known all his life. Like his Woodbines they gave him his last tenuous hold on the world and he would grab hold of the district nurse when she tried to take his pulse or else whip his hand up the skirt of the Meals on Wheels woman as she handed over his roast beef and two veg.

'We're going to be tying boxing gloves on those dirty paws of yours the way you're going,' Glynmor scolded him again. 'Leave the poor woman alone, can't you?'

'It's only a bit of fun, mun.'

'Bit of fun! Who'd want a bit of fun with some randy old swine who dribbled all the time? Tell me. Do you get a hard on, do you?'

'There's still a bit of life down there.'

'Bit of life! When are you going to die and give us some peace?'

'I'll die when I'm ready.'

'I – I – I – Just thinking of yourself again.'

24

These days the Meals on Wheels woman had now taken to putting his meals just inside the bedroom door rather than risk a mauling at Bomber's hands. And it had been ages since the district nurse had taken his pulse.

But it was that rainy day in May, when Pauline was cleaning the front room, that, hidden down the side of the sofa, she discovered all Bomber's pension books.

Now it was always assumed that Bomber lived on CID – compensation, invalidity and dole – but the truth of the matter was that no one had ever thought much about it. Yet these slim books in their different coloured covers, tied together with elastic bands, told another story. He had got a hardship pension from the N.U.M.; an old age pension from the Post Office; two private endowments with the Prudential and Hearts of Oak *and* an invalidity pension from the N.H.S.S.

It took Pauline ten minutes of scribbling on the back of an envelope to work out that Bomber's total income was well over a hundred pounds a week. But Bomber's stinginess was a legend, even in the pubs of Cardiff. He was far, far tighter than a crab's arse was Bomber. He sold his concessionary coal, he split his matches into threes with a razor. He had learned that trick in prison, locked up for thirty days he was for, appropriately enough, refusing to pay an alleged debt. He was always rummaging around for empty pop bottles to take back to the shop and he would walk a mile to avoid facing a flag seller. From all this miserly behaviour everyone – chiefly Glynmor – had always assumed that Bomber did not have a pot to piddle in. For almost all Bomber's retirement Glynmor had forever been bunging him a few bob for beer or a flutter on the horses.

And now this.

Pauline's sums caused something close to a nuclear explosion when she presented them to the rest of the family. Glynmor had to go to bed for a few hours to recover. So what had the mean swine gone and done with all that money? Where had he·stashed it? What if he snuffed it and they still did not know where all the money had gone? What if he had buried it in a biscuit tin somewhere in the tip? Come to think of it he had often been seen walking down there, hadn't he? What if …

So, ever since the Great Discovery, the family had flocked around Bomber's bed. Just like vultures wheeling around carrion they were. They chivvied him, flattered him, cajoled him, even threatened the stubborn old bastard with eviction.

'We could always send you into that home in Bridgend,' Pauline offered. 'There'd be no smoking your Woodbines in there.'

'We'd even get you a nice new bed-cover,' said Aunty Phyllis, trying a softer tack. 'Look, there's cigarette holes all over this one.'

'Tell us where the money is or I'll bloody throttle you,' said Glynmor – as subtle as a car crash as usual – his cheeks streaking white with fury.

Bomber neither denied nor confirmed their suspicions. In the face of this hurricane of threats and abuse he chose to lie there and say nothing whatsoever.

Finally, in despair, the Jones family sent for Aunty Maude down in Treforest. Notorious for her war-like manner it was assumed that even poltergeists would abandon their ways and go find another calling rather than face Aunty Maude. She came on the next bus, the plastic fruit piled up high on her hat.

She sat and listened gravely to the problem – as outlined by Pauline – and then marched straight into the bedroom and delivered a great Churchillian speech to Bomber. She told him about the need for him to show a moral responsibility to his family; she underlined his Christian duty to provide for those who had the greatest difficulty in providing for themselves; she reminded him of the great strain he had put them all under for the past three years; she implored him to think of those who had nursed him through his dust an' all.

Warming to her theme, she recalled all those nights that Pauline had sat next to his bed mopping his brow when he was with a fever; the way that Glynmor had ferried the family back and fore – without asking for a penny for the petrol – when he had first been taken to Church Village Hospital. She recalled the way that Aunty Phyllis had cooked all those meals without receiving so much as a word of thanks. She even, towards the end of her address, spelled out the awful details of the pauper's funeral he was certainly going to get unless he spilled the beans about where he had hidden all his money.

The canny old sod allowed himself a bit of a smile at that. He was a member of the Royal Antedeluvian Order of the Buffaloes and, if nothing else, you were always sure of a good

26

funeral from the Buffs. Pauper's funeral indeed. But he didn't let on.

When Aunty Maude finally finished her address she went off downstairs for a cup of tea. Bomber needed time for her words to sink in. When she returned he indicated to her to draw near. She lowered her head and he softly wheezed a sentence into her ear which almost made the plastic fruit in her hat melt. 'Go and have a flying fuck on your broomstick you old bag,' he whispered. By way of an exclamation mark he whipped his hand out from under the quilt and sent it up her tweed skirt, giving her crotch a quick squeeze.

This was the first time any man had ever got his hand up Aunty Maude's skirt – let alone given her crotch a good squeeze – and, after they had revived her with smelling salts Glynmor had to drive her back to Treforest. 'There's the thanks for you,' she moaned piteously, all the way home. 'And after all we've done for him.'

In No. 41 Roberts Street, which ran off Bont Terrace and joined School Street down by the river, Maggie was sitting in the kitchen, eating a boiled egg and reading a Mills and Boon romance.

She had inherited her love of reading from her father, William, a primary school teacher who had enjoyed respectability and respect in the community until he had died of a pull while walking up the hill some five years earlier. It was he who had encouraged her to carry on in school and pick up a few 'O' levels but, try as she might, she had never liked studying which always gave her a stiff neck and, after her father's death, she lost what little enthusiasm she had for it.

Her Mam, however, a pushy type with far too many airs and graces for somewhere as gritty as Bont, was desperate to get Maggie into night classes, still hoping that she would go on to uni., but Maggie had firmly resisted this, taking a job as a receptionist in an upholstery factory down the Valley and insisting to her Mam that it was just a temporary job while she got herself worked out.

Maggie's real problem was that she was an incurable dreamboat, which was why she had come to love her Mills and Boon novels so much: this breathless world of eternal fidelity and dreams that always came true. Even as his soft lips were closing in on hers and he was telling her that he would love her forever the yellow yolk was dribbling and hardening unnoticed at one side of her mouth as a new record was playing unheard on her Dansette. A powerful romantic song it was too, bought out of the bargain bucket in Woolworth's over in Aberdare.

Out in the front parlour her Mam was busy dusting the delicate porcelain statuettes in the china cabinet. Everything was polished and dusted once a day in the front parlour – the souvenirs of day trips to Weston-super-Mare and Barry Island; the neat piles of crockery brought out with the tin of salmon only for the annual visits by distant and largely forgotten members of the Evans tribe; the music boxes and gaudy spray of artificial flowers. The red roses, in particular, were the very devils for picking up dust.

There was never a speck of food on the carpet of the front parlour because no one was ever allowed to eat in there. The antimacassars on the armchairs were never an inch out of place either because no one was ever allowed to rest their heads on them. You might, if you were lucky, get to lie down in the front parlour – when you were dead and waiting for the undertaker perhaps – though Mrs Evans did allow the family in there once a year, on the afternoon of Christmas Day, to play Monopoly.

The front parlour had always enjoyed a mystical function in the life of the valleys because no one was ever quite sure what it was for. 'After all, if you only ever got in there either when you were dead, or for a few hours to play Monopoly on Christmas afternoon, it's hardly what you would call an efficient use of space is it?' Glynmor had once complained to Maggie.

Space was the one thing the Valleys did not have. The houses were so small they only made sense for pygmies or storing cabbages. There were no gardens to speak of and the front door was set almost on the road. Even the rooms themselves had barely enough space to swing a dead cat around.

So why was the front parlour, the largest room in the house, kept as inviolable as the most sacred shrine? It was a Valley secret; a cultural hiccup, as devious and unfathomable as the short, insecure people jammed into the crowded villages along its length.

Not that such metaphysical reflections had ever bothered

Maggie's mother. Her front parlour was her front parlour and that was that. It was only young tearaways like that Glynmor Jones who spoke of knocking down the middle wall and making one big living-room. That was just the kind of left-wing twaddle you only ever got out of someone like him. She could never stand the sight of him and hoped that her Margaret would get rid of him as soon as possible. As far as she was concerned that Glynmor was about as welcome as an outbreak of anthrax.

Maggie stood up and changed the record on the Dansette, pausing briefly to look out through the window at the rain washing against the coal shed out the back. Then she picked up her book again. Now the hero, an architect taken by his job to Peking, had sent his love a gorgeous set of Chinese pyjamas along with a note saying how his love for her came up every morning with the sun. Lovely she called that. Just lovely.

All she ever got from Glynmor was the job of doing his Spot the Ball competition each week in the *South Wales Echo*. She was on half shares if *she* won. That was about the extent of Glynmor's love. *Duw*, there was more feeling in a snooker ball.

The front door opened and closed letting in a youngish woman, cussing softly as she took off her overcoat. Yet to lift the latch on thirty she was attractive with a vivid shock of peroxide blonde hair and lots of expensive rings on her hands which had long, intensely maintained fingernails. It was Maggie's eldest sister, Daisy.

'Hiya love,' said Maggie barely looking up from her book. 'How's tricks?'

'Tricks are terrible,' said Daisy, going over and giving the kettle a soft knock with her knuckle. 'I thought that Ivor Llewelyn was going to give me a lift down here but these days he's getting too lazy to get out of his own way. Just wants to stay in the bar of the Hall, boozing all the time. That's the trouble with men these days isn't it? Beer. That's all they think of. Most of them have only got one good one in them and that's holding them together.'

Maggie continued reading her book as Daisy prattled on above the music from the Dansette. You never had to make any conversation when Daisy was around. She just jawed non-stop – about clothes and money but mostly about men. In many ways they resembled one another both facially and physically though their ideas could not have been more different. Maggie still retained a lot of her Girl Guide ideals such as helping others, while Daisy was drummed out of the Brownies before even getting to the Girl Guides. The sole star in Daisy's firmament was Daisy.

When the record had finished Daisy sat down with her cup of tea. She looked a bit lost for words, for once. 'Maggie I'm that worried,' she said finally.

Maggie turned over the page of her book. The sun was rising over Peking and he was writing to her making a solemn promise that he would get back to her arms soon. The oceans between them would be as a stream.

'Did you hear me Maggie?' said Daisy. There was concern in her voice. 'I'm that worried I don't know which way to turn. I need advice.'

'What about?' His head office was now forcing him to decide between his architectural career in China or going home to his wife in Surrey. The problem was he wanted to go and see his love in Paris. He decided to go and see an old Chinese fortune teller.

'Maggie. Don't tell Mam will you? But I'm having a bit of a rub with the man from the Prudential.'

Maggie swallowed and put down her book as she digested this sorry bit of news. They didn't put lines like that in Mills and Boon, she was glad to say. 'So how long has this been going on then?' she asked disapprovingly.

'A month? No, two at least. You won't tell Mam will you? I don't know how it started. I paid him a month's subs in the passageway and he just started kissing me. Just like that. He started kissing me so I started kissing him. Next thing we're in bed. Now he's collecting his subs every week.'

'But you've got a husband and a son,' Maggie pointed out.

'I know all that. Don't preach at me Maggie. Just advise me.'

'Well stop it. That's the only advice I can give.'

'I just can't help myself. It's so fantastic. Fan-bloody-tastic it is. Talk about the heavens moving. After he's gone I'm shaking for hours. I've never known anything like it.'

'You've got to stop it and that's the end of it.'

'Maggie, I can't! That's the trouble. It's got that he's all I

30

ever think about. He's in my head all day long. And he's nothing to look at either. Denzil knows that there's something up but naturally he doesn't know what. I'm so ashamed of myself. I don't know which way to turn.'

Maggie had seen this happen often enough before, of course: the way her big sister had always grabbed, greedy and regardless of the consequences. What Maggie had never quite understood was why she then always came and told her all about it. It was their Dad Maggie had always blamed. He had always spoiled Daisy rotten, giving in to her every whim largely because she could always twist him around her little finger. He had never acted quite the same with Maggie.

Maggie looked down at the cover of her book; at the sunset where the silhouettes of two lovers were drawing close for a kiss. The wife would be hurt there too, if she ever found out about what was going on in Paris. Meanwhile, here in Bont, Daisy was clearly poised to break the heart of her husband Denzil since he was bound to find out sooner or later. There were no secret affairs around here. It was such a shame, Maggie thought. Denzil was such a wonderful man who had always given Daisy everything she had never wanted while their son Bobby – known to all as Gnasher – was one of the great characters of Bont.

But who to turn to, Maggie wondered. They didn't have Marriage Guidance Counsellors in Bont. 'Daisy, go and see that Baptist minister up in the Libanus and tell him all about it.'

'What good'll that be?' Daisy asked with her eyebrows rising into her hairline at the absurdity of the suggestion. 'He'll just tell me to stop it. They don't even like sex *after* marriage in the chapel. I told you. I can't stop it. I'm telling you Maggie that when …'

'No. Not necessarily,' Maggie interrupted. 'He might tell you how to come to terms with it. These chapel people know about these things. They do look a bit starchy but they know it all.'

'All they know about in the chapel is money in the collection plate.'

'But try him Daisy. He's sure to tell you what to do about it. He's been friendly with Mam over the years and she's always sworn by him.'

31

'He wouldn't tell her anything would he?'

'Of course not. I've spoken to him lots of times. He gets a bit craxy from time to time but he's got a good heart. I'm sure it's worth at least trying.'

Daisy screwed up her nose in mock disgust. '*Ach y fi.* You've got egg all over your face you have.'

Later that afternoon the sunshine staged a comeback, forcing its way back into the Valley and driving out the rain. So strong and brilliant was it that it quickly dried up the huge damp patches, making steam drift up from the roofs of the garden sheds and grey slates of the terraces, creating the illusion that the whole village had been set on fire. The marching ferns out on the Valley walls shimmered a bright, rich green. The hurrying river glinted ferociously. A few optimistic housewives were pegging out their washing which was soon flapping soft in the lazy summer breeze.

In the midst of this brightness came a cacophony of whistling and then three, four, five, seven, eight, nine sheep came running down the pavement of Bont Terrace. They were dirty, scabby scavengers who normally butted down gates to get into allotments or curled up into balls to roll over cattle grids. But this now-glorious afternoon they were on the run as they were being sheepdogged along the terrace by Gnasher and his gang – Cocoa, Iffy, Nipper, Dick and Gaffer – running around and waving their arms around like demented scarecrows.

The sheep dodged this way and that but Iffy and Nipper managed to get in front of them. Just as the flock threatened to break loose outside The Bug there was a renewed flurry of whistling and shouting and the boys drove the sheep smartly through into the cinema foyer.

The cashier leaped around inside her kiosk like a startled goldfish as the sheep streamed past her and into the auditorium where some forty people were fanning themselves in the suffocating heat. They were perched nervously on their rackety, broken-springed seats as, on the screen, Janet Leigh was taking a shower in the film *Psycho*. Then, just as Anthony Perkins began going berserk and chopping her up with his knife, the whole cinema erupted with the alarmed bleats of sheep and customers alike. The usherette, chasing around and around with her torch, was hard pressed to say which was which.

'I've got all your names,' the cashier screamed as Gnasher

and the boys scarpered down the road. 'I'll be up seeing your mothers and fathers about all this.' That Daisy Bland especially, she reflected bitterly.

Once down by the waste-paper factory the boys flung themselves down into the long grass laughing rapturously. They had timed it to perfection and it had worked out just great even if nothing like the time when they had flung four of Dai Morris' chickens off the balcony during the climactic moments of Alfred Hitchcock's *The Birds*. That had even got into the *South Wales Echo* that had.

Nipper handed out some Woodbines to celebrate their coup. They lay around still laughing and coughing; now they were a force to be reckoned with in the Valley. Much of their success was down to the imaginative powers of Gnasher, who had a natural talent for devilry. Just a few weeks earlier they had unscrewed a belisha beacon and been chased by the local copper. Then there were all those cats who kept being mysteriously tied together and the tin tacks which kept finding their way onto teacher's seat in the Clay Class.

It wasn't that Gnasher was a bad lad as such. He was just a wild Bont boy like the other wild Bont boys, always running around harum scarum with the terror of the boogie man in his sails. He was just another Bont Boy with scuffed, blackened daps and the sleeve of his shirt shiny and stiff from using it as a handkerchief; just another boy who, if he saw anything marked WET PAINT immediately went over and put his hand on it; just another who, if the putty around the window was still soft, went and stuck his thumbprints all around it; just another lad in the Clay Class (where you were put if you were thought to be beyond hope and therefore given a lump of clay to play with all day long) who, like his other pals, just wanted to get out of school and into a job which would give him money to drink beer, drive a car and chase a bit of skirt.

But the terrorist was sometimes terrorised too. The night he saw *The Beast with Five Fingers* in which Peter Lorre's severed hand played the piano and went about the place strangling people, Gnasher sat outside his mother Daisy's bedroom door and whimpered for her to let him into her bed. She was having none of that, though his father, Denzil, did take him down to the kitchen to give him a cup of soothing Ovaltine and a talk about how films were nothing like real life.

33

Gnasher put a lot of store by his Dad and hoped he would grow up like him.

One of the boys produced a grubby, well-creased magazine. Flimsily-clad housewives hovered in unlikely poses with vacuum cleaners and washing machines. The sights and smells of sex enthralled the Clay Class. It had taken them an awfully long time to recover from their first sight of pubic hair. Indeed it had taken them ages to even understand that such things existed until one momentous afternoon down near the tump when a certain Tinker Harry had pulled his trousers down and shown them a bush of short and curly hairs far bigger and uglier than anything their mothers ever used as a lavatory brush.

On the strict understanding that they told no one Tinker said that you could get such hairs by rubbing certain ointments over the bald bits. After that the Clay Class was forever rubbing ointments over their bald bits – any ointments they could lay their hands on – and all to no avail. The bald bits stayed distressingly bald.

The boys' favourite activity, though, was watching the gropings of the lovers on the river bank up towards the reservoir. There were times when, depending on what was going on, they all but fainted away in the heavy excitement of it all. As summer spun warm evenings on the river bank and midges danced in the shadows of the bushes the Clay Class stood enthralled by the goings-on of the local lovers, sometimes asking for a tanner to go away.

Such games could be very hazardous though. One day Gnasher had spotted a pair of crutches lying next to an unfamiliar pair of lovers on the river bank. He crept up through the long grass and stole the crutches. Then, from a distance, he stood up and began shouting, waving the crutches around in air before flinging them into the river. Now the man may have been crippled but the woman could run like the very wind and very soon she had caught Gnasher by the scruff of his neck and flung him into the river as well.

There were no lovers around this hot weekday afternoon, though. The Class was bored. Trying to put a spark of life into the day, Dick jumped on Nipper and wrestled him to the ground. The pair of them rolled over and over, hands grabbing at ears and hair until, all of a sudden, they tired of the horseplay. Gaffer blew a quick series of smoke rings, a skill which was the source of some envy with the others. Gnasher, bored too, took little notice. He sat on a rock slightly apart from them, one hand dangling between his knees as he gazed down the Valley.

'I'm getting a hundred Players on the weekend,' Iffy announced brightly. He was always getting something from somewhere was Iffy.

'Where're you getting them from?' asked Nipper.

'Think of it. One hundred Players.'

'Where's Cocoa to?'

'A hundred players,' Iffy went on. 'I can smoke one an hour for the next six months.'

'Where's Cocoa to?' Nipper was now getting highly agitated. 'Where's he to? Where's he to, mun?'

'I've got cigars coming as well I have. Hundreds of them. Anyone want any cigars? Put your order in now.'

'Cocoa. Where's he to?'

'Let's go up to the res.,' said Gnasher, standing up. 'There's a naked woman up the res.'

All the boys stood up and dutifully followed their leader up the path towards the reservoir. They all knew there was no naked woman up there but moved along eagerly enough. The promise of a blimp of a naked woman was just Clay Class language it was.

The sun sent a great golden kiss thwacking against the brown walls of the Valley, dipping out of the sky with such speed you could actually see the shadow of the north east wall rising like a fast-moving eclipse. The disappearance of light and the appearance of shadow was always at its most dramatic in the Valley. Here, in the bottom of the volcano, the sun stayed shortest and the snow the longest.

Not that there was any snow around this warm summer evening, just darting swallows yawing above the twisting gurgling course of the river as huge patches of light and shadow built up over the ancient hills of coal.

'You know girl I was up and down all shift like a shithouse seat. Whenever we chocked up the Dosco the face just kept crumbling and falling and we had to jump out of the way all the time. We shored it up. We put in new rings. But then there was another of those bastard squeezes and it all came down on us again like a shower of black shit.'

Glynmor and Maggie, love's young dream, were walking together along the river bank with Glynmor giving one of his poetic lectures about his early shift down the hole. Following a hundred or so yards behind them, Jampots, hands in disconsolate pockets, was kicking around a tin can.

'It's these bastard surveyors it is. They don't know shit from clay those boys don't. I can smell coal, you know, Maggie. But those surveyors are forever setting up their fancy instruments and getting it wrong every time.'

Maggie made interested noises as he spoke about his work. But in truth she would have found slowly dipping her left elbow into a bowl of cold porridge marginally more interesting. But it was nice of him to call and offer to take her for a walk. What she had long found in Glynmor was a whole mountain of vices and virtues. One minute he was generous and the next he was mean; one day he was being cruel to Bomber then he was being as soft as putty with that Jampots who, come to think of it, was getting her down at the minute.

'I don't mind it so much when we hit stone 'cos we can scaffold the face an' rip it out. After the shot-firing I do love to be there with Jampots next to me and just crack it apart with pinch-bars. Plucking the lip we call that.'

'Talking of Jampots, it's lovely us having a walk together an' all but do we always have to take him along with us?'

'He's all right. There's no harm in him.'

'I'm not saying there's any harm in him. I'd just be happy if he wasn't tailing us all the time. He's like some second shadow he is.'

They both stopped and turned around to look at Jampots who was still shuffling along, kicking his tin can, now stopping himself, shoulders hunched and head lowered sheepishly as he watched them looking at him.

The way men buttied with one another and watched out for one another was a strong feature of Valley mining communities, perhaps inherited from hours of fire and flood in the pits when men needed to look after one another to survive. Glynmor and Jampots, like so many other butties, worked together, dressed together and drank together. Sometimes, when they had drunk a drop too much, they even slept together. It was this kind of kinship which made the Valleys so warm, so much like being part of an extended family.

'It's just that he makes me a bit nervous,' said Maggie.

'Oh I'll tell him to push off for a bit then,' said Glynmor walking back down the path towards Jampots. 'He won't mind. I'll be seeing him later anyway.'

With Jampots given his marching orders they sat down on the river bank near the waste-paper factory where, abandoning his lecture on coal mining, Glynmor climbed on top of Maggie for a smooch. At least that was how it started but she could feel that he was getting unusually excited. It must be something to do with the warm weather. She didn't mind all that much either. Just as long as that Jampots was not still around somewhere watching them.

They remained in the grass for some half an hour, their lips sliding wet and warm across one another punctuated by huge sighs and long snorts of breath. She could feel his heart pounding as if trying to break out of his chest. Satisfied now that Jampots was nowhere around, her heart soon began pounding as well. Like some great sledgehammer it was and, with every bash, her resolve to keep her virginity intact for her wedding night was falling away into the carnal quicksands.

She could not keep saying no forever, she reasoned. There were plenty of old slags who had their big cowing eyes on him and were only too happy to drop their drawers. She had to give him something didn't she? He might find it so good he would never then leave her. Might. She wasn't at all sure about our Glynmor. That was the big snag with him.

His hand went edging up her fleshy leg slow and tentative like a spider moving out onto some luckless fly trapped in its web. He waited for the halt sign that never came. Then he pounced. To his astonishment there was no resistance at all – no clamping hands, no angry cries, nothing at all. He worked his fingers around the elastic of her knickers and began trying to disentangle them from her roll-on.

'Tell me it's more than a quick bang, Glynmor.'

'It's more than a quick bang.'

'Sound as if you mean it, Glynmor. Go on. Try to show me you mean it.'

'It is more than a quick bang.'

'Say you love me Glynmor. You don't have to mean it. Just say it.'

'*It is* more than a quick bang.'

'Love Glynmor. Say you'll love me for ever Glynmor. Just be a little romantic init? Just say it once and I'll take my things off. Here. Now.'

'I love you Maggie. I'll love you for ever I will.'

'You're not just saying it are you Glynmor?'

'No lovely. I'll love you for ever.'

'And you do mean it don't you Glynmor?'

'For God's sake girl. You want me to go down on my knees with a fiver in my teeth?'

She moaned soft and wriggled out of her corset with what Glynmor could only describe as unbelievable skill. Left to his own devices he would have been there all month trying to get that thing off. Next her knickers had gone sailing somewhere too and he was fumbling inside his unzipped fly.

She moaned again and sent her pelvis crushing up into his, even actually beginning to enjoy it, she was surprised to feel. One second her emotions were running boiling hot and the next freezing cold. Her brain was waltzing in a fever. Fantastic streams of passion shivered right down her body making her toes curl up in throbbing tension. Oh well … this was it all right … this was it …

Then she watched, aghast, as a row of heads appeared over the top of the grass bank. 'Give us a tanner Glynmor. Give us a tanner and we'll go away.'

It was Gnasher and the Clay Class back from the reservoir. What was infinitely worse was that Gnasher was wearing her knickers on the top of his head like a party hat.

'Bugger off,' groaned Glynmor. 'Bugger off, go on. Bugger off or I'll be hitting you sick. The lot of you.'

'Just a tanner Glynmor. Just a tanner and we'll go away we will.'

'You lot will get the mother and father of a hammering if you don't shift.'

'It's only sixpence,' Iffy interupted. 'Give us sixpence and we'll go away.'

As the argument continued Maggie began giggling, putting Glynmor in an even blacker mood. He rolled off her knowing that once she started laughing she'd be at it for hours.

There would be no fun and games with her that night. He was going to fix that bastard Gnasher for this he was — no matter if he was the son of Maggie's sister. He was going to fix him good.

Glynmor's aggravation turned to fury when he recognised Maggie's knickers on the top of Gnasher's head. He jumped up and gave chase, letting the others go and concentrating on Gnasher. But Daisy's lad had long legs for a boy of his age and Glynmor, struggling into his trousers, had a lot of ground to make up.

He was just about to give up the chase when Jampots flew out from behind an abandoned coal wagon and rugby-tackled Gnasher onto the railway line.

'Right, you little bastard.' Glynmor's joy was unconfined as he ran towards the panting, struggling heap. 'Right, you little bastard. I'll give you a tanner I will. A tanned arse for you.'

Jampots took one arm and Glynmor the other as they marched Gnasher, still with Maggie's knickers on his head, down to the river bank. Savouring his terror for a few seconds, Glynmor then gave him a good cuffing and kicked him into the water.

'I'll get my father on you for this,' Gnasher wailed, alternately standing up and slipping over in the rushing torrents. 'You see if I don't.'

'Go get your father. See if I care. Bring your mother too.'

'He'll get you for this. You just wait,' Gnasher went on, taking Maggie's knickers off his head and flinging them down onto the water. 'Just a joke it was. Can't you take a joke?'

'Some jokes just aren't very funny, are they?'

A knickerless Maggie had left the river bank when Glynmor returned to look for her. Not that he cared now. He went back to the Welfare Hall with Jampots, arms around one another as they walked up past the tump, quarrelling about whose turn it was to buy the next round in the bar.

Just been to that Dr Teifi Edwards with a bad back looking for a note, said one of the boys in the bar as Glynmor and Jampots sat down at the table with them. Oh aye. What did 'e say then? 'E knows bugger all. Always on the piss in 'e? This back, he said. I'll have to have some heat treatment for it, he said. Where's that then? In a bloody crematorium, he said. Aye. In a bloody crematorium.

Chapter Three

From out of the darkness a gunmetal dawn was coming up in a silvery haze to sit on the far rim of the Valley.

The terraces of Bont sat silent and still. Away down by the Co-op came the faint musical rattle of milk bottles. But, even at this grey hour, groups of men were following the road leading up to the pit for the morning shift, their eyes still puffy from lack of sleep, their bellies churning from too much beer. They talked little as they trudged along with their tea jacks and tommy tins.

The growing light sought out the harsh, ugly contours of the pithead; the long, rising oblong of the conveyor leading from the washery to the rail track; the squat Nissen-hut shapes of the canteen and changing rooms; the coal-grimed grease and rust which caked every inch of the wheel-house. The light touched the untidy piles of pit props and the huge spokes of an iron, winding wheel which rested, knackered, against the side of the welding shop. Down in the chocolate brown puddles of water in the yard the light played on the rainbow splashes of industrial oil, making unlikely swirls of colour.

Most dramatically highlighted, perhaps, on that grey still morning, were the moving black lines of the slag buckets being carried up to the top of the tip by the overhead conveyor. Day and night these buckets went tirelessly up the slopes, as if pegged out on a giant iron washing line, always on the move, always rising and rising like a ski lift carrying passengers up to the top of the glacier, until there was the dull click of the bucket hitting the trip mechanism followed by the soft swoosh as the bucket emptied its black slurry out onto the top of the tip. *Click, swoosh. Click, swoosh.* Such were the sounds of the hours and minutes in this Valley of coal.

The men were undressing in the changing room, many already coming to life in the company of their butties. Some stood around belching and farting, a few aimlessly scratched their balls and stared out of the grimy windows. Others began their loud banter which would continue throughout the shift like some endless tennis game with words. Nothing was ever spoken in a speaking voice; everything was shouted in a shouting voice, even between those who were standing next to one another.

' 'Aven't 'eard from 'im f'r ages. Did 'e phone you last Tuesday did 'e?'

'Who was that?'

'The one who said 'e was going to phone you on Tuesday.'

'About what was that?'

' 'E was going to tell you on the phone.'

'What? Last Tuesday you mean?'

'Well aye, mun.'

Glynmor was standing with Jampots, Ponty Williams and Crow Parcel. 'That Maggie Evans is going to wear my cock down to a little stump and that's a fact that is,' Glynmor was telling them. 'The way she's going on I'm going to wake up one morning and find it just sitting on the pillow next to my head. On my mother's life she's after it all the time she is.'

'Isn't she a bit fat to be good at it?' Ponty Williams asked with genuine curiosity. 'I mean I used to go out with that piece – what's 'er name now, oh, what did they call 'er? Big Tit Lu from Taffs Well, that's it. I did used to screw 'er an' it just kept popping out all the time.'

'Maggie's not that fat,' Glynmor objected. 'Nor her sister Daisy – Fatty Arbuckle they do call her but she's just got big ones, is all. They say fucking her is just like throwing a carton of cream down the mine shaft. Or waving a chipolata in the Cheddar Gorge. But she knows a trick or two does our Daisy.'

Glynmor returned to his epic sexual encounters with Maggie as they moved on into the lamp room and the grease room. PLEASE USE GREASE SPARINGLY implored the notice as they scooped up great gobbets of the stuff with a stick and plastered it all over their boots. Almost all the shift had now gathered around Glynmor, like tourists around a cathedral guide.

'The other night we'd got this big pile of cushions on the

41

floor of her mother's front parlour an' she'd got hold of this tin of vaseline and, jonic now, she ...'

'*Duw* mun! Not on the floor of the mother's front parlour?'

'Well aye. We even had her budgie watching us. An' I'm telling you now, boys, it's fucking good job that budgie has trouble talking 'cos when she got this vaseline – no word of a lie now – she plastered it all over an' there was this cucumber an' she ...'

And so it continued all the way to the wheelhouse with Glynmor's fertile sexual imagination firing and sparking every step of the way. The vividness of his accounts suggested that he had lost his true vocation as a writer of dirty books. Not that anyone doubted that his stories were anything but true. They were just too enjoyable for anyone to go casting doubt on them. A morning shift wouldn't be a morning shift without Glynmor Jones giving them all an uplifting talk about sex.

But Glynmor did stop talking – as did the others – when they all crowded together into the tiny iron box of the cage. Even after a lifetime in the pit, men fell silent at that awful moment when the banksman flung his lever lifting the cage off its keps and sending it freefalling down into the very bowels of the earth. That moment when your belly was suddenly sucked up into your throat was a religious moment; a time, perhaps, when you wondered if you would see daylight or taste fresh air ever again; if you would ever hear the *click* and *swoosh* of the aerial ropeway; if you would ever hold a woman in your arms and know how loving made you alive. The Bont miners had something else to think about: the accident seven years ago when the wire snapped and the brakes failed, sending the cage smashing down against the floor below, killing all eight occupants with the shock of an executioner's axe. Three had died of castration.

Not that the silence lasted long on that particular shift. They could scarcely have dropped a hundred yards when, without a word of warning, Dibber Jones began puking his heart up. You dirty bastard, the boys shouted, clinging to one another and moving away from him in mock horror. You filthy cunt, they shouted as he heaved his guts up again, spraying their boots with a shower of stale beer and bits of carrots. Must be that beer in the Hall again, Glynmor cried as they plunged on downwards. They say the steward's got his barrels piped straight into the piss-house.

Down and down they hurtled into the dark hidden kingdom of the South Wales coalfield. Below them lay the No. 4 Glamorgan, a rich fat seam of antediluvian sunlight and compacted forest stretching the length of the Valley and crossing over from the No. 2 Glamorgan which began at Porth and stretched up to the No. 5, a dark still river which opened out at Nantgarw. Each part of the No. 4 was known by its own name: Red Vein, the Four Feet, the Six Feet, Trelewis, Pentre, Meadow and so on. The Bont mine was working the Meadow B2 where, for close on a hundred years now, men had worked and died ripping out a dry and fiery anthracite as their contribution to keeping the world comfortable and warm.

The cage landed with the softest of bumps. Once out of it and on to the main roadway, the shift leaped onto the conveyor belt, turning on the lights of their headlamps as they travelled along, on the singing wheels and sprockets, down towards the B2 face. The bright yellow funnels of their lamps flashed around them, making the girders and rings sparkle as if in a Christmas bazaar, sweeping into the great dark webs of the ventilation tunnels where you could still see the remains of the old oak trees which had once so thickly graced the Valley. Occasionally there was the sudden furious bellowing of the ventilation pumps but, for most of the time, there was just the agitated squeaking of all the tireless wheels and sprockets of the conveyor belt.

The belt took them down to the locking station where a deputy took their registration number as the black, tired faces of the night shift came trudging up the puddled roadway. Everywhere there were the bright cheery greetings of 'All right' and 'How be?'

Now it was their turn to wade through the great sloshing puddles, the constant dripping echoing in the warm, still air. Jampots, as usual, was right behind Glynmor, both of them even going over to the gob for their ritual piss at the beginning of each shift. 'You know this dick of mine is so sore it's a pain to hold it,' Glynmor told Jampots as they both pissed into the big black hole of the gob. 'I'm going to 'ave to start taking iron pills or something if this keeps going on.'

They turned the next bend and came out behind the

Queen Bee of the hole, the Dosco cutting machine which was the size of a small room and whose functions they were all paid to service ... the chargemen, the machine operator, three on the tail gate and seven ramming, chocking and grading. The rest of the shift worked shovelling the coal onto the armoured conveyors of the Panzers and, when the Dosco erupted into noisy life with its chains cracking and dust billowing everywhere, the men all fell to their tasks with a will as the great blades scored and slashed into the coal face.

It was a scene straight from Dante's Inferno when the Dosco was at full bite, everything all around shaking like a jelly in a storm ... the ground, the walls, your feet, your legs, your very teeth ... Added to this was the shocking, earth-shattering noise and the choking dust which kept your mouth permanently thirsty. Then there was the warm smell of stale piss and the way the bits of coal shot straight into your eye. Worse still was the foul brown water which kept seeping in from everywhere, always keeping your feet freezing cold no matter how hard you worked.

Glynmor and Crow Parcel went up a small tunnel on the side of the face where they had been firing and digging an advance heading. 'Better shovel out this duff before we can fire again,' Crow Parcel shouted over the roar of the Dosco.

Glynmor liked to work here on the advance headings. If he was to work down a mine at all he liked to be close to the coal rather than just servicing the Dosco with the others. Here on the advance heading he was right at the sharp end of the industry, intimate with the black gold of the centuries, face to face with what had provided his family with a living for as far back as he could trace his family. A sense of continuity was important to all miners; that sense of shared experience which anchored them in the past and made them confident with the future.

But the problem today was that they had been cutting a heading into a seam which only seemed to want to fall in on them. They'd discussed it many a time: the problem was that this coal was just too loosely jointed and, no matter how many times they shored the roof up, *bang*, down it all seemed to come again. But, so far, it seemed stable enough as Glynmor and Jampots shovelled out the duff. Occasionally the light of their lamps caught in the stampeding coal dust in the air, making it glitter like hovering fairies.

Some hundred yards behind them the pump man, Tom

Laws, tapped the methane gauge which measured an escape of 2 per cent. Slightly higher than normal but nothing at all to worry about.

The Rev. Mordecai Hughes, resident minister at the Libanus Chapel, was in his dog collar and shirt sleeves as he fussed around in his pigeon loft, one minute sweeping down the shelves and the next picking up one of his most treasured birds, turning it over to examine the texture of its white belly before gazing into the veined magical rings around the bird's eyes.

He had eight birds in all. Now he was getting them ready for the Welsh Open, when truckloads of birds would be taken up to Lerwick in the Shetlands, there to be released and race the 580 miles back down to Bont. The Welsh Open, held at the end of every summer, was the most coveted jewel in the pigeon fanciers' crown and this year Rev. Mordecai had the bird he just knew was going to win the title, by a good few minutes as well. Even now he was hoping to be elected onto the committee of the Bont Pigeon Fanciers who met each Sunday in the Starlight Lounge of the Welfare Hall.

Nothing was too much trouble for his pigeons. Each day he fed them twice and cleaned them out once. He would even rush a funeral if the birds' feeding time was approaching; as any fancier would tell you, regular eating is the key to fast flying.

Sometimes he drove them over to a neighbouring Valley in his Morris Minor, releasing them and thrilling to the sight of them whirling around and around the green hills before flying off home. How they found their way home – particularly from long distances – was, he readily admitted, one of God's mysteries. Some sort of radar in the brain, the scientists said, but God alone knew the full story. Being with his birds made Rev. Mordecai feel close to God and the mystery of His ways.

He heard his letter box click and left his pigeons, walking back into the manse and picking up the pile of letters which had spilled over the hall carpet. They looked the usual clutch of bills and advertising leaflets so he didn't even bother to open them, just carrying them into his study and placing them on his desk next to a very old typewriter.

He pulled a sheet out of the typewriter and read what he had typed the previous evening, the great beak of his nose almost touching the paper which, together with his longish silvery hair and small beady eyes, always reminded his parishioners of some great bird of prey. On some Sunday mornings, when he was in full oratorical flight in one of his sermons with a splash of sunshine glazing the great dome of his forehead, some of his flock half expected him to sprout wings and fly off into the very rafters of the chapel.

Not that he had much of a flock these days; about three dozen regulars, mostly women, who still enjoyed such as the knitting circle or the coffee mornings. The writing was on the wall for the chapel, he could see, with more and more of them being abandoned and left derelict throughout the Valleys. He saw nothing he could do about this except to hold fast onto his own flock and wait on the Lord's pleasure. Meanwhile he husbanded his other passions for privacy and silence.

The sheet of paper contained a description of a long service in the Swansea Valley at the turn of the century since, apart from his pigeons, Rev. Mordecai was working on a long evangelical tome – *Reflections On The 1904–5 Chapel Revival : An Informal History* – in which he was charting the great Evan Roberts chapel revival which had so briefly and dramatically shaken the Welsh nation.

Like every other non-conformist man of the cloth he longed to see another revival, of course, but, with the advent of bingo and television, he did not really see how it would ever become possible. The chapel movement had lost its way. He accepted that proposition calmly enough but was nonetheless more than happy to write about it when it was at its full power and height; when the charismatic Evan Roberts had held the whole of Wales in the mesmerising palm of his hand.

Evan Roberts had even once spoken in the Libanus Chapel too, Mordecai had excitedly discovered; a long and tumultuous service which had converted almost everyone in the building.

Just now, surrounded by piles of damp and dusty books borrowed from the Evangelical Library in Cardiff, he had reached the Christmas period of the Revival when half of Wales had succumbed to the magic of Evan's oratory. They were thrilling times for the austere non-conformist soul were those services. Mordecai never tired of reading about them, sometimes actually able to feel the rapture of an era when the

Welsh were renewing themselves in their love of God.

The silence hung heavy in the manse and the sounds of those Revival services were again hovering on the edge of his consciousness when the front door bell rang. He sighed but simply picked up another of his typed pages. Someone was either dying or wanting to get married. There was always something wasn't there? Sometimes he just wished they would all leave him alone. Why didn't they take their burials and weddings to that Methodist upstart down in Ferndale. He could do with the money and anyway he, Mordecai, had a small inheritance on top of his meagre stipend which meant that, in coldly cash terms, he never had to marry or bury anyone ever again.

When the bell rang again he answered it to find the most familiar figure of Daisy Bland standing there with her hands in coat pockets. 'Yes, my child,' he said soft.

'I've got a problem and I was wondering if I could have a chat with you about it, vicar.'

'Certainly, my child. Come into my study.'

He escorted her inside, sitting her in the armchair next to the fire-grate and sitting himself down at his desk before inviting her to tell him about her problem. There was barely an expression on the tired archaeology of his face as she told the story of how she was having a bit of a rub with the man from the Prudential. Only occasionally did the tip of his fingernail scratch the tip of his nose or toy with the ends of his hair.

As she went on his attention wandered onto a familiar moral path. This was all of a piece with the way the village was going, of course. When he had taken up his incumbency he had met warm, honest people full of decency but not any more. Just look what they got up to nowadays! Almost to a man they were gambling mad, forever buying raffle tickets, filling in betting slips, doing the tote in the Welfare Hall, fretting over the Pools or pouring money into the aptly-named one-armed bandits. Crime was even breaking out in the village too where, only a few years ago, the Yale lock was unknown. Every door had been left on the latch then with such as the rent man coming in and helping himself to the rent money, left with the book, on top of the china cabinet in the front parlour.

Now, as if all this wasn't enough for them, they were practising adultery like it had just been invented. It was shameful and what made it worse was that they had the gall to come and tell him about it. Now this brazen hussy was sitting in *his* chair, in *his* study telling him how she could not keep her hands off the man from the Prudential.

'But why have you come to me my child?' the habitual softness of his voice disguised the weary antipathy in his chest. He just didn't understand why they always walked all the way up that hill to tell him about their sins, as if they hoped he would somehow make them feel better about.

'I was told you understand these things. I was told you might be some sort of help.'

'But you used to come to this chapel, my child?'

'When I was a little *dwt*, yes. But those days are a long time ago now. We seemed to understand things in those days but we don't any more. It was easy to understand the rules then. But times have changed.'

Not the times, he thought sharp, getting up out of his chair and walking across the study to stare down at the village. The people; it's the people who have changed.

'I don't really know why I've come up here to see you. It's just ... oh I don't know ... I really don't know.'

'But why come to me, Daisy?' Mordecai asked, unwillingly to make it easier for her. He really didn't want to talk about it. She knew that it was wrong just as well as he did.

'It's difficult to put into so many words so I was hoping you, with all your experience with such matters, could give me some good advice.'

'Well I haven't any better advice than St Paul. He said much about the mind of the flesh and how it was death. When you keep your mind pure and concerned with spiritual matters then you have life.'

'I don't understand, vicar.'

No you wouldn't, would you? he thought. Sex-crazed reptiles like you wouldn't. It made him so angry. He wondered idly if she left a patch of slime on the bed after she'd had a bit of a rub with the man from the Pru? Did the sheets rot and fall to bits? Did they fumigate the bed?

'This course you have taken,' Mordecai continued still staring out of the window. 'These rubs, as you so fetchingly call them, will bring you nothing but pain. You will feel the pain, so will your husband and so will young Gnasher. There's just nothing more I can tell you. These rubs will bring you nothing. They are of the mind of the flesh. Which is death.'

'I was hoping you might tell me how to stop them.'

'You stop them by stopping doing it.' His impatience was showing now and he was making no attempt to conceal it.

'Well, that's not much use is it? But how do I stop them when they make me so happy? That's what I want to know vicar.'

He shook his head and took a long intake of air. He clearly knew nothing that she wanted to hear and life was too short to sit here listening to such silliness. 'Right, my child, if you'll excuse me, it's time for me to feed my pigeons. You can find your own way out can you?'

'Oh well we know why your chapel is so empty, don't we?'

'Please leave me now. If you really want my advice, which you don't, then just try reading the Bible – and particularly Paul who will tell you all you need to know. But thank you *very* much for coming up here to see me.'

There were two sharp raps on the door in the basement room of the Miners' Welfare Hall. The City Tyler opened the peep-hole and asked for the three secret passwords of the year. The reply was soft and insistent. GOLD. BRAINS. MARLOWE. The door was then opened and a blindfold man was lead inside with his hands resting on the shoulders of two men.

Cigarette smoke curled around the thin bright strips of neon light. Here and there tiny blue pancakes of chewing gum were caked into the wooden parquet floor. The crowds of men already inside the room parted ranks as the blindfold figure was taken up to a plinth at the far end of the room where, beneath a huge pair of Buffalo horns suspended off yellow flock wallpaper, Worthy Primo sat on a wooden throne with gavel in hand. He gave three sharp bangs of the gavel – *bang, bang, bang* – stood up, adjusted his elaborately tapestried and tasselled apron and duly began the initiation into the great and sacred mysteries of the Royal Antediluvian Order of the Buffaloes.

Much of the business and secret life of the valleys was controlled by these Buffs; a sort of working class freemasonry, drawn from everywhere from skilled tradesmen to shopkeepers and middle managers of the pits, who met here each Tuesday evening to swop jokes and insults as well as making contacts useful to their work. Largely shunned by the miners themselves, the Buffs wore so many medals and chains of office they might have been the veterans and heroes of every campaign since the Zulu War. It was said that even Field Marshall Goering gasped in envy when he saw how many medals the Buffs had.

This group was the Captain Laggard Lodge of Bont; some forty solemn, bemedalled men whose organisation had so many rules and secrets it might have been hatched up by the Department of Health and Social Security in collaboration with the K.G.B. In this strange world the rule book was both the king and queen. Every brother was expected to know its eighty-six pages inside out; to learn everything from how many trustees the Grand Lodge of England had, right through to how the balance sheet should be forwarded in accordance with rule 31(b).

The brothers crowded around the initiate in a tight circle, their right hands over their hearts. The initiate held a clay pipe to his own heart, promising to keep all Buffalo secrets and passwords. He was then called on to break his pipe, the act by which he was duly initiated into the mysteries of Buffaloism with all the ancient rites and ceremonies, under the authority of the Grand Lodge of England.

Worthy Primo then handed him his membership scroll, making him read out the solemn promise. Hands were raised twice with the tray of juniper held forwards.

Down at the table at the opposite end of the room sat the City Marshall whose function was to keep order. There, behind the bar – known as the royal foundation – was the City Waiter who would soon serve the brothers with their pints of cloudy, flat All-Bright beer. Waiting with lolling tongues, each with his individual chain of office, were the City Chamberlain, the City Registrar, the Alderman of Benevolence and the City Constable who – collection tray in one hand and a small wooden truncheon in the other – had to collect the monetary fines imposed by Worthy Primo on the brothers for such grave un-Buffalo offences as using obscene language, belching, picking noses or being unfriendly to a fellow Buff in the street.

The initiation ceremony concluded with the newcomer, Ray Pryce, a local electrician, having his blindfold taken off

50

and everyone congratulating him. Then the normal Buff session – an uproarious banging of gavels, screaming shouts and instantaneous charges – began.

I want to lay a charge Worthy Primo. Against Brother Wayne. Be upstood Brother Wayne. *Bang, bang, bang.* What's the charge Brother Jeffrey? Brother Wayne did swear at me in the Starlight Lounge. No, I fucking never Worthy Primo. He fucking did Worthy Primo. Aye, he did. An' I heard you. *Bang, bang, bang.* A twopenny fine on Brother Wayne. That's not bastard fair Worthy Primo. Another charge Worthy Primo. Brother Howard is not wearing his jewels. What do you have to say in your defence Brother Howard? Well, when I moved Worthy Primo, I did leave them in the coal shed an' I've not been able to find them Worthy Primo. *Bang, bang, bang.* A penny fine on Brother Howard. Well that's a load of Buffalo bullshit that is Worthy Primo. *Bang, bang, bang.* A penny fine on all those on that side. Why do we always have to drink this beer Worthy Primo? It's gnat's piss that's all it is. *Bang, bang, bang.* Best of order now brothers. You brother Emlyn. No, you Fred. Right, the whole bastard lot of you. City Constable collect a fine off the whole bastard lot of them. Are we going to get any graze tonight, Worthy Primo?

Just then, for no apparent reason or sign, this noisy period of bawling and shouting suddenly stopped. They all stood up in an impromptu choir and proceeded to sing the Buffalo song to all their absent brethren.

> Spirit of Truth, before we homeward wend,
> On Thee we call:
> Assist us each to succour and defend Good Brethren all.
> From all cares and sorrows, ABSENT BRETHREN free,
> Where'er they roam, in air, on land or sea.
> Let thy kind spirit hover round them now,
> And so enthrall:
> That they will keep their Obligation Vow.
> So say we all.
> And when on us the ivy leaves descend,
> Grant we may join Thy link, our Brother's Friend.

When the song had finished, Worthy Primo announced that, as the brothers already knew, passenger services on the Bont railway line were about to be withdrawn. What was the brothers' pleasure? Should they draw up a petition or what? The brothers looked at one another. Do! A petition! More light Worthy Primo.

'Well what does the loss of the rail line mean?' Worthy Primo continued. 'Does it mean anything to us at all or what?'

'We don't want to get mixed up in all that Worthy Primo. Most of the brothers have got cars anyway. And, anyway, we've got enough to do with all the risings in the next month or two without getting involved in petitions.'

'So we take no action on the rail line then?'

An instantaneous charge, Worthy Primo. Against Brother Fred. He did fart while you were talking, Worthy Primo. A big deadly fart it was. One of his silent killers. No, I never did, Worthy Primo. They always say that a fox do smell his own hole first don't they, Worthy Primo? Brother Fred be upstood. *Bang, bang, bang.* A penny fine for farting while I was speaking. *Bang, bang, bang.*

And so the session prattled on. At 10 o'clock Worthy Primo formally suspended the meeting and the brothers all trooped upstairs to the Rainbow Room saying what a wonderful meeting it had been that week and how lucky they were in getting someone like Ray Pryce joining the order. 'I've got a few 'lectric jobs I can put 'is way, aye.'

Even upstairs the Buffs stuck together, as far away from the miners as they could get. There was little love lost between them.

Chapter Four

Two days later, a Thursday, the morning shift were working the B2 face. Unseen, the pointer on the methane gauge rose to 12. As Glynmor walked along the roadway to pick up some cartridges from the stores, the gauge rose higher. But no one was watching it. Just nearby, two pump men were quarrelling. The argument claimed everyone's attention.

'I gave you the message when the van was coming didn't I?'

'Aye. You did. But I didn't 'ave my teeth in.'

'What's that got to do with it? Are your teeth fixed to your brains or what?'

'I told you often enough. I can never remember anything if I 'aven't got my teeth in.'

Coal dust and noise was erupting out of the Dosco as Sam Swambo stood in the advance heading, stripped to the waist. As he clung to his chattering drill the coal face all around his head began spalling and crumbling. He took one step backwards and something fearful turned over inside him like a pregnancy of snakes.

From deep within the coal there were great ripping sounds as if a giant was tearing up calico sheets.

Immediately behind Sam Swambo, Jampots was shovelling away the duff. Ponty Williams, Crow Parcel and Dibber Jones were working on the chocks under the conveyor belts. They worked in torn vests with their trousers hanging low on their massive hips. Respirators were available but always scorned. Only pansies used respirators. Just visible beneath the grime on Crow Parcel's back was the tattoo of a pair of dogs chasing down through his shoulder blades to his waist-line. The brush of the escaping fox was just poking up out of his arse.

'Hey Sam. What's yellow and stupid?'

The heading screamed hard with the promise of murder again. Sam swallowed and dropped his drill, taking three steps back from the dissembling coal and bumping into Jampots.

'Watch where you're going *mun*!'

Now it was as if a whole army of demons was baying and screaming in the coal face. Angry jets were whistling out of tiny holes. Loud cracks ripped through the screams of the demons. The methane gauge shot up to 28 and the pump man banged it with his hand in disbelief. Five to 15 per cent was an explosion but, if this was registering right, the whole mine was about to be blown sky-high.

In the store room, Glynmor was signing for the cartridges when he felt a cold shiver. It was as if someone had just stepped on his grave.

'Run boys,' Sam shouted, his mouth parched and dry something dreadful. 'It's a bastard blower.'

Jampots dropped his shovel and was off faster than a whippet with its back on fire. Sam was quickly after him too but cursing and swearing all the while since his legs were almost paralysed with fright. The screaming became more intense, filling up the brains with pain, slashing against the ear drums with acid. Ponty Williams, Crow Parcel and Dibber Jones were racing down the roadway as well – their huge boots dragging them down as they pulled at one another's arms urging them to go faster. They knew that, at the most, they had ten seconds to reach some sort of safety. 'It's a blower,' another called out in the screaming darkness. 'It's a bastard blower.'

Sam was still struggling with the effort of getting his legs to move at all. His head turned back to look at the screaming hole. A whole gale of hell erupted out of the wall like a great black breaker in the sea. Huge milky balls of fire rolled towards Sam with lumps of coal flying out of it. He could never remember seeing something so colourful or ferocious and was transfixed by its brilliance. Then a huge rock shot out of its very heart, breaking both his legs with the quiet ease that a child might break a lollipop stick. The very last thing he saw in his life was the tattoo of the fox being chased by the dogs down Crow Parcel's back. Those dogs will never catch that pissing fox now, he thought grimly as a romping tongue of green and white fire completely incinerated his body.

By now the whole morning shift was running down the roadway as the gale of fiery methane – suddenly released after centuries trapped in the coal – went sweeping all around them. Some clutched at their throats and fell to their knees coughing. Others pulled their blackened vests up to their mouths to use as a sort of makeshift gas mask. A flying cob of coal split open a man's head but still he kept running the blood running, red on black, down his neck. The metal rings were buckling in the heat; even the dry lagging above the rings bursting into flame.

Jampots was brought down by another cannoning rock. With a soft sob, he fell forwards with his cheek resting on the cold metal railway line. He lay there unable to move as he watched one of the rusty nuts on the sleepers dance about in the flashing colours. His back felt red raw with the heat and he wondered how much he would be able to claim for this. He'd go all the way this time as well. Get some real compensation out of those bastards in the coal board. He thought of his best mate Glynmor and how, only that morning, he had loaned him a fiver. He wanted that fiver back, he thought. Then, in another burst of heat, he died.

Meanwhile Crow Parcel had plunged into a growing pile of dirt and rings, his big arms and body thrashing around, almost as if he was trying to swim in the stuff. More red-hot coal piled up on top of him and now he could not move at all with just the distant cries of his work-mates echoing dimly on the far edges of his mind. Oddly enough in the circumstances, Crow Parcel relaxed and even felt happy. He wondered what his wife had put in his tea jack. He hoped that she had not given him that bloody India tea again. He liked the tea from the Co-op but she was always giving him India tea – almost as if she wanted to show him up in front of his mates. Only pansies with poodles drank India tea. Everyone knew that. He sighed in exasperation as he thought of all her airs and graces. Twenty-nine years he had been married to all those airs and graces. He had only gone and got that giant tattoo of the dogs chasing the fox just to get up her nose. It had worked too. He sniffed a sort of smile as he remembered how she didn't speak to him for ten months after that. Ten months of bliss that was. Just what, he wondered, would she make of all this? Then, with the broadest of smiles on his lips, he, too, died.

Ponty Williams lay, on his side, on the roadway

half-covered in coal, with great swords of flame slashing the air above his head. He moaned soft and tried to turn over. All this running and screaming had given him a right old headache too. At least he'd have no trouble getting a week off with a doctor's note, he supposed. The doctor surely wouldn't quibble about a sick note after all this. The boys would get him out all right. That was a racing certainty that was.

With that the roof fell in on Ponty Williams. In the crushing darkness he thought of his small boy who he loved more than his own life. He prayed to God that his small boy would never have to go down the hole. He prayed that his small boy would never, *ever* have to go through all this. Not this. He groaned quiet and tried not to move as he thought of their walks together around the *cwm* with the sun shining down on their heads. He could hear the boy's voice, his very laughter. *Dada where do baby lambs come from?* His hand reached out to hold onto the boy's shoulder. How he loved to have someone to instruct; someone not yet wise in the ways of the world. *Baby lambs do come from their mother boy. They do come in the spring.*

Why just in the spring Dada?

Because the spring is the time when all things in nature come to life, he replied. A hysterical choking caught in his throat and a terrible claustrophobia swept over the dying miner. *And tell your mother I've always hated India tea,* he added before he, too, stiffened and died in all that black sunlight of an antediluvian forest.

Glynmor shot off down the roadway as soon as he heard the alarm sounding. Only when he had reached the locking station did he stop running. Horror-stricken, he watched them sealing off the B2. 'Oh shit me, oh fuck it, oh …' he cried incoherently and uselessly as he gazed at the rumbling ball of fire which was holding steady about two hundred yards away.

Even so far away he could feel the ferocious, scorching heat of the blazing fire damp. He ran towards it and was pushed back, his eyebrows and cheeks seeming to burst into flames. He glanced away and began running at the fire again – almost like a moth bent on its own destruction.

Now he was crying and so close to the flames that his tears were drying up before they had fallen the length of his cheeks.

56

All he could see behind that wall of flame were all his butties in general and Jampots in particular. Amazingly, recklessly he began running towards the terrible colours of the fire again, almost as if he was hoping to run right through it. Others were gathering around the locking station calling out for him to come back.

'We'll get you out Jampots,' Glynmor shouted as the hooters blared havoc. 'We'll get you out if I have to do it myself.'

And the tongues of fire came romping and flashing down the roadway, all but incinerating his trousers as he continued standing there as if looking for some alleyway in the flames through which he could run. It was, they said later in the Hall, the most stupidly courageous act they had ever seen.

But they did not manage to rescue Jampots, nor Sam Swambo, Crow Parcel, Dibber Jones or Ponty Williams. It was hours before the rescue team managed to get in there at all, digging out the charred remains of what they could only guess were bodies.

'The price of coal they say, don't they?' cursed Glynmor, the tears still running down his face in the changing room. 'The price of that bastard coal.'

He could not face hanging about the pithead. A small crowd had already begun to build up around the main gate so he went, instead, out through the rear of the welding shop and up past the washery. Even as he walked along the river path leading up to the reservoir, his face still black with coal and stained with the streams of his tears, he was surprised how bad he felt at the loss of his butty Jampots. It was almost as if someone had gone and tied a reef knot in his guts. He had not felt as bad as this since his Mam had died some seven years earlier though, oddly enough, he had felt nothing at all when, a year later, his Dad had died.

They had come through a lot, he and Jampots. It had begun in the nursery school and, even to this day, they had shared any winnings on the horses, raffles or one-armed bandits. Even if they weren't together at the time of the winnings they always, religiously, shared out the loot as soon as they met. And how, now, was he going to pay him back the fiver he had borrowed off him? They had always repaid each other's debts as well.

A soft wind ruffled the waters of the reservoir, a few brown ducks huddled together near the waterfall. At least the air was fresh and clean up here. He wiped his nose with the back of his hand. Stan Hughes had killed himself near here, he remembered. He was a local baker and the police had been after him for interfering with children. He came up here by the reservoir, filled his pockets with stones and jumped in. They didn't find him then, but only last summer, with the water levels low with drought, they reckoned a dead sheep was blocking one of the pipes. A diver went down to haul the carcass up. But it was no sheep. It was the skeleton of one sad and frightened baker, whose knee-cap actually fell off as it was hauled up out of the water. He and Jampots watched it all from the very bridge on which he was now standing.

Duw, they had even thrown a bag of lime into the water here and picked up seventeen trout one afternoon and Jampots' Mam had made them throw away in case they were poisonous.

The tight knot in his guts grew tighter as he climbed on up through the ferns to walk along the top of the Valley where there was a forest of Christmas trees, all now dead after a fire. Dotted around on the paths were the black polished olives of sheep dung. You could see the pit from up here, watch the crowds and ambulances thronging outside. But, strangely, you could hear none of the noise. He pressed his fingertips into his belly and was sick, again and again.

He continued along the thick promonotory between the two valleys, the dusty sheep lifting their heads from their endless munching and looking at him curiously. He and Jampots had actually nobbled one of those sheep once – luring it into a shed with a trail of bits of bread before jumping on it and trying to stab it to death with a carving knife. All that got stabbed though was Jampots' leg. The sheep escaped and they went down to the hospital in Aberdare claiming that Jampots had fallen on a bottle.

Even as he stood there looking down on the village, with the thin blue wisps of smoke drifting up out of the chimneys, he could see him and Jampots racing down the gullies up to no good. He could see them together sliding down the tump on dustbin lids. He remembered the way they hung around together after school down the gully hoping for a quick feel off one of the girls. Just how was he going to live without Jampots? Everywhere he went the dopey bugger would be somewhere around wouldn't he? Perhaps he would have to leave the Valley and start again?

There was only Maggie now – but he was hardly in love with her. There didn't seem any point in going out with her any longer. He would put a stop to all that before it got out of hand. Everything was so serious with the girl. And she didn't drop them either. Why did she think she was so bastard special? Whatever Jampots had was yours but not with Maggie. Oh no. What was yours was hers and what was hers was hers.

The sun was dipping out of the Valley and he was getting cold. He followed the twisting, rutted track down the side of the Valley and back to the village. A group of clacking blackbirds were swooping down on the bread that someone had thrown out in one of the back gardens. The 5.35 passenger train to Cardiff went burbling around the bend. There were only three trains a day and they would be stopping soon, he had heard.

A lot of the boys were already sitting around in one of the bars of the Welfare Hall when he got there. Almost all their families had been touched in some way by the accident. The steward had served each of them with free pints but there was not much being drunk or said as they sat around their tables together in their communal grief. Glynmor took his pint and went to sit next to the television. It was switched off for a change. He sipped his All-Bright; it tasted of coal. He wiped his mouth with the back of his hand but still that was the tang of anthracite. He had not so much as looked at a bar of soap since he had come up. That was the thing about coal wasn't it? It got into everything. Your beer. Your sandwiches. Your lungs. Your blood. Aye. Your very bastard blood.

He spat beer between his knees then finished his pint in two gulps. 'Are we going to drink or what?' he asked no one in particular. 'C'mon boys let's 'ave a fucking drink is it?'

'You're right there Glynmor. Let's 'ave a drink.'

The steward began lining up more pints on the counter. Stan Swansea was passing them back when the swing doors to the bar burst open with a whinnying bang and Maggie came rushing in, her big black eyes wide with panic, her face as white as a sheet.

The boys in the bar were to talk of that entrance for some time – 'Duw mun she did come in like a clap of thunder' – since, no sooner had she spotted Glynmor, than she stood stock still, lowered her head and began blubbering into her two cupped palms. She did not move at all, just stood there with her

59

whole body convulsed with shivering, pitiful sobs. Tears and cries just poured through her fingers as the boys gathered around her, unsure of what to do. One of them patted her on the back when Glynmor stepped up and took her by the wrist. 'Come and sit you down,' he said. 'Have one of those port and brandies.'

Even an hour – and several port and brandies later – she was still shivering and crying, holding his hand tight unable to believe that he was still there. 'I'm sorry,' she sobbed. 'They told me you'd got it and I couldn't find you anywhere. They said they'd all got it.'

'Cool head now. Do you want another?'

'I'm getting a bit drunk, I am. How are you feeling?'

'I'm feeling like another pint.'

'Well I'll have another port and brandy then. You don't mind do you?'

'Why should I mind?'

'The money. Those port and brandies are half a crown aren't they? Here I've got a few quid. Take them.'

The girl had a big heart, he decided, taking the money off her. He had to grant that. She would give him her last penny if he had wanted it. Probably make a good mother as well. It was funny how he always felt that much fonder of her after he'd had a few drinks. He patted her hand reassuringly and stood up to go to the bar.

'Tell me Glynmor, do you think I'm too fat?' she asked him when he returned.

'I wouldn't say fat exactly,' he said hesitatingly.

'What would you say then?'

'Well, sort of ... round ... kind of ample like.'

'I've decided I'm far too fat. I'm going on a diet soon. I'm going to stop eating all those chips and pasties, make myself beautiful for you.'

'But you do look beautiful already girl.'

'You're not just saying that are you? I do want to look beautiful for you Glynmor.'

'But you are beautiful to me.'

'I'm not beautiful. I'm fat I am.'

'But you're not fat.'

'I am. You're the one who's always telling everyone about how I got stuck on that slide.'

'Never.'

Most of the boys were sitting around morosely listening to this low grumbling argument which, like most low grumbling arguments in Bont, seemed to be getting nowhere at all. Stan Swansea stepped up to the bar and turned on the television. A chorus of cries told him to turn it off again.

'It's time for *Peyton Place*,' Stan explained.

'Bugger *Peyton Place*. There's been an accident mun.'

'Well, anything's better than listening to those two arguing,' Stan persisted pointing to Glynmor and Maggie.

'You've got an awful big mouth,' Glynmor warned him.

'If you two want to argue why don't you go somewhere else and do it?' Stan went on dangerously.

'Who's arguing?'

'You are. And, anyway, everyone knows she's too fat.'

It was not the moment to get controversial, as Stan Swansea soon found out, since Maggie let out a wail of agony as Glynmor went hurtling up out of his chair running towards Stan with his forehead flying into the startled miner like an avenging cannonball. The way that Glynmor put the head in was famous in the valleys. And it didn't matter how big they were either since Stan Swansea might even have been twice his size. If anyone upset Glynmor he all but turned into a human rocket and – wham! – it was usually a broken nose.

Except that this time he missed.

Clearly all the aggravation of the day had done something to his normally immaculate timing since he didn't even come close to connecting with Stan Swansea's nose and, the next thing, a man in a baseball hat and a woman in a bathing suit were swearing undying love to one another in *Peyton Place* as the two men were both locked together and rolling around the floor of the bar, punching and kicking like a pair of wild cats.

Glynmor managed to work his knee into Stan's groin a few sharp and painful times while Stan retaliated with a few punches into his eye and ear. It was just then that a few of the boys managed to pull off Stan while Maggie grabbed hold of Glynmor in a Double Nelson. She could feel the tremendous rage of his fury as she held him tight. He had a terrible temper to be sure. The boys in the bar swore that Glynmor would fight a brick wall if it upset him. She was even half worried that he might inflict a serious injury on Stan and was still holding on

61

for all she was worth when his feet just leaped forward and, using Maggie's tight hold as a launching pad, he managed to give Stan a fair old kick in the balls.

Next thing Stan had broken loose and they were all rolling around the floor again until more committee men came running in, finally managing to break up the fight through sheer force of numbers.

'Right, your beer is stopped and both of you are up before the committee,' said the committee chairman, Max Million, a man of military bearing as befits someone who lives his life in accordance to the 151 rules of clubland. 'I know there's been accident in the pit but that's no excuse for fighting in here.'

'What a bastard of a day this has been,' sighed Glynmor as he and Maggie were walking arm in arm down by the river which hurried and twisted and dawdled in the starlight.

'Poor Glynmor,' she commiserated. 'Well, you've still got me and I'll make you feel better.'

And she would too, as he found out that night on the river bank. She wanted to take some of that pain out of him, and letting him have all her body was the only way she could think of doing it. She had even foreseen it by leaving her panties and corset behind in the Hall's ladies toilet. They lay down together in their usual spot in the long grass and, without any preliminaries at all, she took his hand and placed it squarely on her soft pubic mound.

He just lay there for a few moments, listening to the laughing trickle of the river. She undid the buttons of his dungarees and began playing with him, quietly kissing the coal streaks off his face and nuzzling her face into the sides of his neck as she opened her legs wider, wanting him to sink right inside her where he could get warm and comfortable and lose some of that hurt.

She began handling him with quite ferocious tenderness, moving him around one way and another, kissing the coal off his cheeks and circling her hand round and round his confused member until she lowered him into her, feeling it ease into her with a surprising lack of pain, gritting her teeth a bit as she moved her body around again trying to get settled.

She gazed up at the stars and even felt happy as he just lay there deep within her. She was glad that she had finally given in. She wasn't going to have any regrets now. She did, after all, love him dearly. There was no doubt about that.

He continued just to lie there in her arms, doing nothing. His real problem was that he did not want to pick up the ball and make a dash for the line. He was convinced that, any minute, she was going to blow the final whistle. Just how had he made so much progress with so little effort? After all, the boys were supposed to do all the running weren't they? It was up to the boys to fight to get their knickers down wasn't it? But it felt pretty good. There was no denying that. He pressed his pelvis into her and, when she did not cry out or push him away, he pressed down again.

Oooh that was very nice indeed, she thought. They didn't get up to this in her Mills and Boon books, but there were plenty of suggestions of it. She could almost feel the way she was draining the pain out of him; somehow she was taking his burden on herself and that was such a great joy to do. She could really get into this.

'Oh yes my lovely,' she whispered and he knew that she was not going to blow the whistle. He scooped up that ball and flew for the line, humping away like mad, almost as if he had just been given the word that all sexual activity was going to be banished from the valleys in ten seconds' time.

'There's plenty of time,' she soothed as he bucked and swerved. 'Take it slow. We've got the rest of our life.'

He came to a sudden cold halt. We've got the rest of our life? Oh so that was it? And what else had she called him? My love? Distant wedding bells began ringing in the far corners of his mind. So she was going to get herself a bun in the oven and get him up the altar with a shotgun at his elbow and a ring in his nose. His head lay on her heaving bosom and he looked out into the dark tangled grass like a hunted fox settling down beneath deep cover.

So what was the matter with him now? She wondered. Men were funny things and this one was the funniest of the lot. You could never quite make up your mind if he was a boy or a man. You could never really decide if he was generous or mean. One minute he was the loving soul grieving about his lost mate and the next he was shouting at you and treating you like rubbish. Just what did he want from her? Was he looking for a mother or a spot of target practice. Who could tell? She couldn't that was for sure.

Paranoid about churches and weddings, Glynmor took a few slow stabs deciding that he would pull it out before he came. That was the way the Catholics did it, he reflected. He really should have got some johnnies from the machine in the gents, even though that was a bit like sucking a sweet with the wrapper still on. Besides he didn't know this was going to happen. It was his Uncle Bomber who had always advised him never to leave it in to soak. Bomber had always told him that it only ever needed one tiny tadpole to start a baby and those little bastards could do an awful lot of swimming when they got moving. There were millions of them as well but it only took one to swim the length of the fanny, Bomber had always said. The old bastard. It was a pity that tadpole swam all the way to make Bomber.

He thought of that old bastard lying in his bed coughing his guts up. He thought of his butties who died down on the B2 face ... of Crow Parcel and Sam Swambo and his great pal Jampots ... the untidy hair and patches of freckles ...

Then Glynmor cried out as if in pain and he was off on a gallop again, wild, oblivious, driving into Maggie like he was trying to find a way inside her; pushing hard and yet harder like he wanted to disappear within her and leave this valley of pain altogether; whimpering in the running stream of his sorrow when he felt the base of his belly about to explode ... and he pulled it out hurriedly, his whole body leaping upwards as if he had just been electrocuted and – zoom, zoom, zoom – millions of tadpoles went spurting and slithering all over Maggie's bosom.

Chapter Five

On the day of the funeral high winds whipped fat washing-day clouds over the roof of the Valley. They dashed along the backs of Bont Terrace, rattling on the windows and shaking the doors, blowing gasps of soot and coal smoke down the chimneys into the living-rooms, sometimes catching in the heart of the flues and moaning piteously. If it caught a door open, or a window, the wind would dash through the hallway and up the stairs, whirling and slamming about the place like a demented witch looking for her broomstick. The winds made the sheets flap on the washing lines with the flat boom of guns. Everything was noise and drama with those valley winds.

In the street outside the Libanus Chapel, Emlyn Kremlin stood to attention among a group of some twenty best-suited miners. Sung by the colliery choir, *Abide With Me*, came drifting out of the open vestry doors. Even Emlyn, who had no truck with the chapel, thought that it was a fine hymn, perfect in its way for expressing the sorrows of his battered collier tribe.

He took off his bowler hat and almost made a military click with his finely-polished shoes as the coffins of the men were brought out of the chapel. Undertakers in shiny top hats and black tails circled around, quietly forming the pallbearers and mourners into the procession down to the cemetery. Those undertakers all had the fat, bloated bellies of Tories, Emlyn noted. Only some capitalist Tory would choose to make a living out of the business of death.

Emlyn and his group moved across the road to join in the cortège, just behind the members of the choir. As befitted the top official of the National Union of Mineworkers' local lodge, he was wearing an immaculately pressed black suit with a high starched collar, a grey-striped waistcoat and a gold fob watch. He always dressed with fastidious care for such funerals. It was, after all, the last thing you ever did for them. Turning out at your very best was the mark of your political respect for those who had died in the long struggle to win that bastard coal from the bowels of the earth. Weren't all those hundreds of thousands of others enough for them?

He had huge, gnarled hands, ripped and torn by a life of hard work as a pick and shovel man on the face. His face was beefy and ruddy with the vitality of tremendous power. His back was ramrod straight though he did walk with a slight limp where once, as a boy, he had been dragged by a horse in traces some two hundred yards along a roadway. Four pounds the pit owners had paid him in compensation for that, he would tell you readily. Four pounds was the price of a crippled leg.

Rev. Mordecai walked alone with the Prayer Book in both hands, looking even more like a great vulture searching for carrion in his flowing black hassock which contrasted vividly with the pastiness of his complexion. The daylight showed up the thin blue veins on his cheeks and face while he kept his lidded eyes lowered in suitable piety. Such times were always difficult and frustrating for him since everyone always asked him the same question. Why? To which he always gave the same, slightly unsatisfactory, answer. He didn't know.

The winds dropped as the cortège moved off, making the Valley strangely hushed, as if even the walls were standing stiff and silent out of respect. Crow Parcel's family had chosen cremation so there were just four coffins, piled high with flowers and wreaths, six pallbearers to each. Behind came a drift of black-veiled widows and daughters, the rest of the shattered families behind. What with friends and the colliery choir just about everyone in the village was there. It was the biggest funeral in the Valleys for twenty years, it said in the afternoon Valleys edition of the *South Wales Echo*. Some 800 had joined the cortége; relatives of two of the families had flown in from Canada and Australia.

A few tiny groups of housewives stood around on corners, their faces grim, their arms folded tight. The shops were closed and every curtain was drawn. Even the normally boisterous children stood around in still groups near the clock tower, staring at coffins which seemed to be telling them something about their lives stretching out before them, and the manner of the deaths which might await them too.

Emlyn, a true melancholy Marxist, had a strong and despondent feeling for the lessons of history. And this accident had considerably thickened his melancholia; it had given him a sudden glimpse of that old hated Hades full of lock-outs, explosions and Tory coal barons, long thought dead but clearly still very much kicking. Such deaths diminished them all; they took away a part of everyone. Every family in the village had been affected one way or another by the accident.

He took out his fob watch and checked the time, put it back into his waistcoat pocket and blew his nose. To him it seemed incredible that old Lord Firedamp had come riding his chariot into the Valley again. Emlyn had long thought that they had got the problem of blowers under control. *Duw*, they had even accepted a report at their last regional conference, two years in the making, that had concluded that there were now sufficient controls to detect any build-up of gas. But Lord Firedamp was not going to be beaten so easily. It clearly took more than a report to control that old swine.

Keir Hardie must be turning in his grave. On the day that the Duchess of York had given birth to the boy who later became Edward VIII, 260 men and boys had died in an explosion in the newly-dug Bont pit. And everyone knew what the front pages had been full of that day. Now, a hundred years later, they seemed to have learned nothing and progressed nowhere. Emlyn almost spat at the road in the bitterness of his thoughts.

Emlyn Thomas – dubbed Emlyn Kremlin because of his lifelong connection with the Communist Party – was a man of the most perfect rectitude; an assembler of political ideas and a master of rhetoric. He was committed enough to the cause of the working class to hang the red flag of the hammer and sickle in his window on the occasion of royal weddings and coronation days.

A pick and shovel man, long before the soft days of the totally mechanised face, Emlyn was also a man of memories. Mostly he remembered the colour and detail of that old world of zinc baths and wooden lavatory sheds at the end of the garden; those bad old days of black pats in a collier's sandwiches and rats swarming in the dung of the ponies' stables. He still felt twinges of bile when he remembered the way they stopped money for candles, the oil for the lamps and even the chalk for marking the drams. Tell him any story of hardship and he always knew a worse one. He knew horrifying stories of miners covered in boils from head to toe; of men spending long hours on their sides in half a foot of water trying to dig out the coal. He would tell you about when the women used Robin starch on their babies' bottoms because they could not afford talcum powder. Emlyn Kremlin knew everything about this coal game; this the hardest work under heaven.

But the acid bath of his memories were those dread times when the pit hooter sounded after an accident. Then there came the terrible cleats of the hobnail boots in the streets when the bits of the dead men were taken back to the widow in a sack. At least they had stopped that obscene practice now.

Emlyn trudged along with the cortège, past the Welfare Hall where a woman, with a baby in a shawl, was standing outside the door weeping silently. The Hall looked extremely shabby in the sunshine, Emlyn thought: a real broken-jawed hulk of shattered windows and rotten splintered window frames. Every part of it cried out for a coat of paint. It was, he supposed, a definitive symbol of how low everything had fallen. The committee was even now on the point of selling off the library, one of the finest collections of Marxist literature ever assembled in the country. The University of Wales desperately wanted to buy the books and pamphlets and Emlyn had fought hard against the sale. No deal had yet been struck with the university but, in the end, even he had to accept that the men did not want to read the great texts of Marx and Engels any more. They were not interested in the philosophic heroism of those first early prophets of socialism. They did not want to understand the historic inevitability of the class war. Only professors and students were interested these days, sitting there polishing their library seats as they waited for someone else to start the revolution.

The modern miner, he saw, was no longer a man of culture who wanted to learn how to play a musical instrument, sing Haydn or make furniture. All the modern miner wanted was to rot in front of his television, or play bingo, or drive fancy cars. And now here they all were united again, burying the dead who had not lived long enough; burying the poor who had perished so that the rich might stay warm.

A dog was barking at one of the undertakers as the cortège moved in through the green wrought-iron gate of the cemetery. By now the sun was smashing against one side of the Valley with the shunting clouds sending speeding shadows racing along its length. The opposite wall of high brown rock was already darkening fast. Sunlight and shadow moved in fast and endless interplay in this valley of coal. So did the lives of the people who lived here.

Now the mourners were threading their way past the massed ranks of the tombstones and up to the newly-opened graves at the top of the cemetery. The sunshine caught in the gilt handles as the pallbearers prepared the ropes to lower the coffins into the ground. Rev. Mordecai read from the Order of the Burial of the Dead, the wind blowing his words away.

As Mordecai continued reading, Maggie stood next to her sister Daisy, her arm linked with her mother's. Her beloved Glynmor was standing with an old friend of his, Dai Waterboard, and the pair of them were standing so near Jampots' grave there seemed a danger Glynmor might even fall in. She could tell from the greyness of his face and black bags under his eyes that he had not been sleeping properly again. Even so far away she could see that his body was shaking slightly. She so wished that she could take away some of his pain.

But, since the night of surrender on the river bank, Glynmor had stopped speaking to her. He had developed this alarming sense that he was going to be well and truly trapped if he didn't watch it and, as there were many acres of wild oats that he had yet to sow, he was now avoiding Maggie assiduously. She had even sent notes over to his house asking if they could talk but he had replied in kind saying he had a bad back and didn't want to talk about anything. She had long suspected that this would happen and her suspicions proved correct. In that schoolboyish way of his, she reckoned, he had concluded that she was just some tart who would drop her knickers for anyone. She hardly knew what to make of it.

'Forasmuch as it hath pleased Almighty God of His great mercy to take unto himself the soul of our dear brothers here departed, we therefore commit their bodies to the ground; earth to earth, ashes to ashes, dust to dust …'

The whole of Glynmor's insides were shaking like branches in the wind as he lined up behind Jampots' mother to throw a handful of earth onto the coffin. For a second, fearing that she was going to throw herself down the hole, he steadied her with a grip on the elbow. For what seemed an age she stood there, what was going on in her mind he could not imagine. And when she had moved away Glynmor too took his time over the coffin sitting down there in the tiered layers of clay.

'... Our Lord Jesus Christ who shall change our vile body that it might be like unto his glorious body, according to the mighty working, whereby he is able to subdue all things to himself ...'

Glynmor picked up a handful of earth and flung it down on the coffin. Even as the fine lumps of earth bounced off the polished wood, the mourners could see the rolled up bank-note he had thrown down too. It was the fiver that he had borrowed off Jampots just before he died, given back now, the debt repaid in full for all time.

He then moved on, looking up into Maggie's quizzical stare and nodding at her before walking away with Dai Waterboard. He did hope that she wasn't going to dog him all the time. Everywhere he turned she seemed to lock her big black eyes on him. It was that hurt look that got right to him. Even when she wasn't doing anything she seemed to upset him – as if he wasn't upset enough. Women were always pains in the arse weren't they? They didn't even have to work at it.

Once back in the Starlight Suite of the Hall the mourners gathered around the trestle tables piled high with ham sandwiches, sausage rolls and pickles. At the far end of the table Stan Swansea was already eating a sausage roll, poking the air with it as he spoke. 'Crow Parcel always told me that there was gas down there.'

'Well why didn't you report it mun?'

'I never did speak to him did I?'

'But you said he was talking to you.'

'Aye mun. He was talking to me but I never did talk to him. 'Aven't talked with Crow f'r ages.'

Emlyn Kremlin sat at his usual table near the bar among his cronies. Already he was sounding off again about the terrible cost of that bastard coal. 'Heard did you? The Queen has sent another message of sympathy. Why doesn't she come down here and dig the cowing stuff herself? Eh? Could you just see Queenie sitting down there eating coal dust sandwiches with black pats running around her velvet feet? Could you just?'

'These cowing tips are none too stable either,' he went on. 'That's what's going to happen next. Some of us are going to get killed by one of them one day. There'll be a fuss if it kills someone high and mighty from the N.C.B. but, as long as it only kills miners, we'll just get another message of sympathy from Queenie in Buck House. And sod all else.'

'The pit manager sent some flowers I 'eard.'

'He's a bloody flower himself in 'e? It was his job to check the machinery but, what with that woman he calls a wife and that fancy piece he calls his mistress I can't see that he's got any time for anything. Every time I go into his office he just seems to be kipping like some cat. We go and see him about conditions and he just refers us to the board. Mines were always the responsibility of the managers not the board.'

The sombre mood was lifting slightly with the beer. Cigarette smoke curled sluggishly around the neon lights. People began to talk of other things.

'Hah it's the gentlemen from the N.U.M.'

Emlyn looked up at Mordecai, glass of orange juice in hand looking down at him. Emlyn had little time for old Mordecai but, for some reason, the minister seemed to enjoy coming over and needling him. Not that Emlyn took any of it lying down. He had long learned that it was best to get in the first punch.

'Another act of love by your wonderful God then,' Emlyn told Mordecai. 'A fine father I do call him.'

'Accidents and tragedy are not the work of the holy father,' Mordecai replied evenly and without rancour. 'Everything we receive from the Father is a blessing. Accidents like this come from the opposition, I fear.'

'Accidents like this come from human negligence, minister. That's how men have always died in the pits. Through the negligence of men who put profit before everything. Why does your God allow that then?'

'I can't speak for God Emlyn. You must look on God as a great gardener trying to make sense of a wilderness. He has submitted himself to a long and difficult work. He works in ways none of us will ever understand.'

71

Emlyn took in this bit of theology with a soft derisive snort before sipping his beer with a slow exaggerated care. 'This God who created us all can't think too much of his children if he allows them to be snuffed out like that. He did create us all didn't he? That's what you do say isn't it?'

'He did indeed Emlyn. He did indeed. But there are many in this Valley who have turned their backs on God and, when they did that, He gave them up. That's the real reason for our sorrows these days.

That Saturday the passenger rail line service in the Valley was finally axed. Falling revenue from passengers, British Rail announced. A circular from the South Glamorgan Education Authority was also posted through the door of every home in Bont. It said that due to the rationalisation of the health service, the village primary school would close at the end of term. Each day, in future, all children would be taken by bus, free of charge, to a new school in the next Valley. It was earnestly hoped that this rationalisation would not cause the parents too much inconvenience.

Chapter Six

After the interruption caused by the funeral, the little rituals of life quickly re-asserted themselves on the streets of Bont. Evans the Milk began his rounds at six in the morning and the shops opened at eight thirty, closing for an hour between one and two when the fish and chip shop was frying. At two thirty-five the first edition of the *South Wales Echo* was heaved off the van onto the pavement and, at four o'clock in the afternoon, the Welfare Hall was closed for an hour for the cleaners to sort it out after the afternoon session. The film programme in The Bug began at seven in order to finish at ten and give the manager and patrons time for the final hour for a drink in the Hall. At eleven Lee Hoo Wonk was at his busiest, frying up noodles and chop suey in his vast steaming woks and, unfailingly at eleven fifteen, Ivor Massey stopped behind the Post Office to relieve the strain of many pints of All-Bright bitter on his bladder before getting on his way home. At midnight Police Constable Watkins began the first of his hourly rounds on a bicycle, patrolling the dark gardens and slumbering houses until dawn when Evans the Milk began his rounds again.

In this way the life of a Welsh pit village moved from one day to the next; softly, irrevocably, almost without a join, a little like a snake bent on eating its own tail.

The patterns of life behind those frothy lace curtains were much the same as well. In his lonely, painful bed Bomber's coughing had, if anything, got worse. His neck had shrunk, his chest had become increasingly swollen from his gasping fight for air. He was also getting a terrible stitch in his side and bringing up whole lumps of black spit. Even as they slid out from between his teeth like slimy black sweets they told him that the end would be very soon.

But still the stubborn old bastard refused to give up his beloved Woodbines. Even as his eyes were bulging and watering with the strain of coughing up his insides into his bucket, his fingers, as black as his lungs, still clutched a smoking cigarette.

Even more embarrassingly, the irascible old bugger was still trying to maul the district nurse and work his hand up the skirt of the Meals on Wheels woman. Glynmor had never wanted anyone to die so much. He knew that it was wrong but he really was going to dance on Bomber's grave. A mad dance of the greatest joy it was going to be as well. Except that there was one big bastard of a nigger in the woodpile.

Bomber still hadn't told anyone where he had hidden his money.

And that small fact – or, to be precise, that lack of a small fact – stuck in Glynmor's throat even more painfully than Bomber's continued existence on this earth. He could hardly bear to speak to him any more. There was still no communication between Glynmor and Maggie either. Every day she took the early bus down to the factory just down the Valley. And when she returned she sat in her bedroom where she continued reading her Mills and Boon books and playing Hollies records on her Dansette. She also continued to moon about her Glynmor, but he showed no sign at all that he was mooning about her.

After years of worrying about her weight – probably without reason – she had also decided to do something about it. She'd start on a crash diet which involved stopping eating just about everything she loved – like Walls pasties – and starting on just about everything she hated; a meal of crisp bread, cottage cheese and carrot juice. She weighed herself unfailingly first thing in the morning on the bathroom scales – as advised in the slimmers' book – and religiously wrote down the dates and weights in her little red notebook.

The snag was that, far from losing weight, her little notebook was telling her that she was putting it on. And at an alarming rate as well. She was feeling very tired and weak too, which she put down to her horrible new diet.

She had also missed her period. Twice.

In many other ways the rest of the village was continuing much the same. Aunty Phyllis was still gossiping ferociously with her

74

next door neighbour. The clock in the square was still ticking away the hours and minutes. The coal conveyor still went *click, swoosh, click, swoosh* and the sheep still kept knocking over the dustbins to forage in the rubbish. Daisy Bland was still having a bit of a rub with the man from the Prudential.

This peaceful cycle of work, play and sleep was interrupted on a glorious day in June. The musical cheeps of the blackbirds hung in bright clumps over the roofs of Bont as the twisting spine of the Valley basked beneath a bright golden carpet of warmth. Denzil Bland was driving his huge yellow concrete mixer over to Mountain Ash when he remembered that he had left his sandwiches and flask of tea back home. He drove back to Bont Terrace, noticing a dog piddling over the front wheel of a new convertible car that was parked, with the hood down, outside his own front door. He pushed the door open and walked into the house, calling out Daisy's name. Finding no sandwiches in the kitchen, he went up the stairs. Half-way up the stairs he heard, coming from his bedroom, the unmistakable noises of his wife, Daisy, having a bit of a rub with the man from the Pru.

Cool head now, Denzil.

Without a word he tiptoed back down the stairs, went out into the street, backed his concrete mixer up against the new car outside the door and tipped some ten tons of ready mixed concrete into it. With grey sludge brimming over the car doors Denzil went back into the house and screamed blue murder at the insurance agent who, forewarned by all the noise, had already got all his clothes on before running down the stairs, jumping on the bicycle he'd thoughtfully left a couple of doors down the street and pedalling off into the sunshine.

So who owned the car with the new concrete lining?

Three weeks later Denzil Melvyn Bland of 31 Bont Terrace appeared before the Stipendiary Magistrate in Pontypridd and received three months imprisonment suspended for two years, for malicious and unlawful damage to property, to wit his neighbour Clay Evans' new car which had only been delivered the very morning of The Great Concrete Downpour as it became known in the Hall. Clay Evans had not wanted to take Denzil to court — particularly under the sorry circumstances of his wife's adultery — but the insurance people

– by some sick irony, the Prudential – had insisted on it.

'I just don't know what came over me,' Denzil told the Stip. as it was reported in the *South Wales Echo*. 'They say you see red when you get upset but all I saw was black.' On top of his suspended sentence Denzil was also bound over for a year to a sum of £50 to keep the peace.

Denzil said he'd had enough of Daisy after the court case, said Aunty Phyllis to her neighbour over the garden fence. He said all he wanted was the portable Teas-maid out of the bedroom. He'd told her she could keep all the rest, she said. He'd said that he'd never loved her anyway an' he cried when he said goodbye to Gnasher. I heard he went off to live with his mother down in Tonypandy said the neighbour. I don't know if it's true like. That's just what I've heard.

It was but a few weeks after Denzil went off to live with his sister in Upper Boat that certain things began to go missing in the night. Maggie's Dansette record player upped and walked out of the back door, then one of the Pandy boys lost his bicycle, later found in the river.

A few thefts do not a crime wave make but in a village where no door had ever been locked and crime was virtually unknown such disappearances were particularly upsetting. Maggie did so love her Dansette and the Pandy boy had got his bicycle for Christmas and was on it virtually every hour of the day. The wild finger of suspicion went pointing in all directions, of course, and none more frequently than in the direction of Gnasher and the boys of the Clay Class. Could it be that after years of mindless vandalism the Clay Class had now finally graduated to mindless crime? No one could be absolutely sure but, as is usual when there is an absence of fact, there was plenty of inaccurate and malicious gossip.

That very week a new branch of Lipton's opened in the premises of the old cobbler's in the square and immediately plunged into a bitter price war with the Co-op. Huge posters went up in Lipton's windows detailing what was being cut off staples like bread, butter and fags. The Co-op had the advantage of trading stamps, of course, and when they began announcing treble stamps with everything, Liptons hit back with a vengeance slashing all prices down to the knuckle. With every five pounds of potatoes there was a free small packet of Persil.

These days the Clay Class was roaming about with a restlessness no one could quite understand, absorbing the edginess of the leader, Gnasher, who was becoming more moody, ferocious and watchful with every day that passed. No one ever really knew how much the loss of his father had affected him because he had never told anyone. Only girls ever spoke of emotional hurts deep inside, but a right old hurt Gnasher had now – and no mistake.

Sometimes, after breakfast, he had to run out to the lavatory shed at the end of the garden and bring it all back up again. His voice had broken too and he would stand around moodily, never speaking when spoken to. Stubble began growing on his chin and strange stains appeared on his sheets.

Daisy could watch all these changes in her son but did nothing. In truth, she did not see what she could do. When anyone got grumpy in her view they were best left alone. Sometimes she would shout at him to brighten up his ideas and stop being so shandyvan about the place but he just stared back at her, sullen like a whipped dog. Anyway Daisy had enough problems of her own. On top of the fuss about the concrete mixer and seeing her name in the papers, the man from the Prudential was quietly relocated to West Wales which left her temporarily without a man. But things were always very temporary with Daisy. It was only a matter of a few days before she began having a bit of a rub with Walford Evans, the bingo caller in the Hall.

She had long heard it rumoured that his was a whopper. He also allegedly gave away free strips of bingo cards to the favoured few. It would have been more than Walford's job was worth to have actually fixed the numbers in Daisy's favour – it would have been more than his life was worth come to that – but Daisy was delighted to learn that all those other rumours were absolutely true and so, after each bingo session (when he had finished counting the bingo takings and filling in the forms) they would have a bit of a rub on the polished circular table behind the locked doors of the committee room.

With his bald head and different coloured eyes – one pink and the other a forget-me-not blue – there was something about having it off on the sacred committee table that appealed to the

77

primal part of Walford's chemistry. He found something emblematic, almost sacrificial, about the act. It was a form of religious desecration, a way of sexual protest against the dark influence of the chapel which, he believed, had brought about the closure of the railway line. He was a very strange man with elliptical thought patterns was Walford Evans – even his wife went around the shops saying that he would be best off consigned to a loony bin.

For her part, Daisy found the twice-weekly tryst on the committee table considerably more exotic and pleasurable than the normal communion between the sheets. With her eyes closed and a broad smile on her lips, she imagined the faces of those solemn stuffed shirts of the committee as they sat around this very table on Sunday afternoons, trying to decide who they were going to fine or box for such grave offences as fighting, gambling, using bad language, drunkenness or standing at the bar during bingo sessions. Occasionally, as Walford went galloping away into the distant blue yonder, she would actually burst out laughing at the very thought of them deliberating over what the two of them were up to at the moment.

That night, after the bingo had ended, Daisy had been serviced and the last drunk had stumbled down the last slope, Gnasher, Nipper and Gaffer, made their entry into big-time crime. Carefully they levered open the back door of the Co-op with a crow-bar. The problem then was they were not quite sure what to do next. It was Nipper who decided that the bell would ring if they opened the till looking for money. Then Gnasher almost expired when he noticed that Gaffer had knocked over a rack of birthday cards and was even now down on his knees carefully picking them all up. Nipper made this, the crime of the century, complete when he announced that he had shat his pants and did any of the boys know where, in the shop, they kept the lavatory paper?

Dr Teifi Edwards took his pince-nez off his nose and put it down on his desk with a sigh. He looked at his consulting couch and up at the cornices on the ceiling. He so wished someone would come to him one day with an original complaint. 'When was the last time you had a period, Maggie?' he asked finally.

'Dr Edwards?'

'Your period. When was the last time you were on?'

'I'm not sure. Three. Four months.' Her lips were going dry and panic was decanting in her belly. She could see the writing on the wall. 'But they've never been reg'lar at best though. I went six months without a period once.'

'Well I'm afraid that you're up the spout. Welcome to the pudding club. About five months I'd guess. We'll have to do some more tests to work it out proper.'

'Are you sure it couldn't be something else?' Maggie swallowed. 'A bug? They do say there's something in the air at the moment.'

'The only thing that's been in the air, my girl, is your legs.'

Dr Edwards was something of a specialist in blunt remarks and small savage jokes. Even those who came to him in good humour and fine health would leave his surgery with bruised feelings and a flood of tears. The wonder was how anyone ever went to him in the first place.

'I've suffered a lot with indigestion lately. I thought it might just have been too much air.'

'So who's the lucky father then?'

She shook her head and began crying again.

'You mean you don't know? How many have there been then?'

She kept shaking her head and examining her handkerchief looking for a dry bit. 'It can only be that Glynmor Jones. He's been the only one.'

'Glynmor Jones. I might have guessed. They do say he'd rape a hedgehog that one but, between you and me, I'd say that he's all jaw. Did he do it bareback do you remember? You know ... when he did this to you.'

'He had some clothes on as I remember. His working clothes they were. We were down on the river bank.'

'A contraceptive girl. Did he have a johnny on at the time?'

'No. But he did say he'd pull it out first. He said that his Uncle Bomber had always warned him not to leave it in to soak. Then he sort of went crazy.'

Gnasher's big-time career lasted but a short while. One night, his pockets bulging with stolen tins of salmon, he ran straight into the arms of P.C. Watkins as he darted away from the back of Lipton's which he had just done over.

He ended up with three years' probation, I heard, Aunty Phyllis told her neighbour over the garden fence. Daisy was afraid it was all going to get into the *Echo* so soon after her divorce case an' all. Emlyn Kremlin went down to the juvenile courts with Gnasher. He spoke for the boy and said he was his guardian, being Daisy's uncle an' all. Now they say that Emlyn is going to look after him till he leaves school. Some hope. A proper handful he's become hasn't he?

You can say that again Phyllis.

This is all because his father went away you know. Gnasher looks a hard case but he did love his Dad. That was for sure. Most Sundays they did go riding in that concrete mixer of his down to Porthcawl. Denzil even used to buy the boy beer.

Never.

Now I'm not saying anything but I hear that Maggie Evans has gone and got herself pregnant.

Never.

That's what I heard. I was in the Co-op this morning and Jean from over in the bakery was telling Cynthia that she had seen that Maggie coming out of the doctor's in tears. Now I don't know if it's true but I heard that she's been carrying on with that Walford in the Hall.

Never. Him a married man an' all.

It's only what I've heard but Walford's been going home late and Maggie has been seen out on her own late too. Of course she won't have anything to do with our Glynmor now. He's been carrying on with some piece from Cymmer I heard. He can be as common as muck when he wants can't he?

As muck.

But, funny thing, I heard years ago that Maggie had the hots for that Walford. I don't understand the young any more. How can you carry a torch for someone as daft as him an' he's as bald as a billiard ball too? I don't know. It must be the age we live in.

Chapter Seven

The morning the Juvenile Court first entered Gnasher's name in their records was also the day that the Grim Reaper finally began calling out Bomber's number.

Bomber hardly had the energy to breathe at all. He just lay there with the thin sound of his lungs squeaking so thinly and distantly it might have been coming from another body altogether. His alabaster cheeks were but thin, hollowed-out scollop shells. His gnarled hands were useless claws. His whole chest swelled grotesquely through the final days of fighting for air. He discovered that it was best not to try and move at all; he just lay there motionless, as if already dead, looking out through the lace curtains and down onto the small gardens with their ash paths and rackety make-shift sheds. He had always loved looking out of the window into his Valley volcano home had Bomber; loved just lying there counting the clouds as they moved in fast procession high over the roofs of Bont.

Sometimes, he fancied, the clouds came together and formed the great shape of a man with a scythe on his shoulder. 'It's time to come in Bomber,' he could hear in a voice as soft and loud as the summer breeze. 'Your time is up Bomber and we want you home.'

He was so inert these days that even the Meals on Wheels woman felt safe going near his bed again. He never touched the food, of course, but they decided to keep bringing it regularly in case he rallied and felt like a bite.

'Still with us then are you?' It was Glynmor come up the stairs to rub salt into his wounds. 'Still hanging about keeping the sheets dirty then?'

One of Bomber's tired old eyes ratcheted towards Glynmor – a little like a chameleon's keeping watch on a fly.

He also straightened a finger and beckoned his nephew to come near. After much effort and sighing and licking of the lips he managed to get a few words out: 'Glynmor. I've got to see Guto. Guto. Get Guto.'

'What do you want to see that smelly old bastard for?'

'Guto. Send Guto here.'

Glynmor shook his head in wonder. Guto had been around almost as long as the Valley, a truly horrible man who spent his days and nights scavenging. By night he was worse than the sheep, forever sifting through the dustbins in the gullies for any useful items that he could take home. By day he would journey to all the tips in the Valley towns and spend endless hours poking about in the foul maggot-ridden walls for booty as he called it. Beautiful booty. Anything was beautiful booty to Guto and on almost any sort of day you might spot an old mattress or a couple of old armchairs walking down the path along the side of the Valley. Somewhere underneath would be Guto's legs.

But why now did Bomber want to see Guto?

Glynmor had long suspected that Guto had something over Bomber but had never quite been able to work out what it was. About the same age, the two men had certainly once been butties for a while together in school but then something dark and difficult had happened. Something dark and difficult which no one had ever spoken about.

But even when they had stopped being drinking pals, and Guto had begun looking for the meaning of life down the bottom of every dustbin, Bomber had continued watching out for him. Bomber had once even bailed him out of the nick after he had been caught hurling a brick through the window of a shoe shop in Porth. The police had caught him merely by following a trail of left shoes dotted around the town.

Such acts of friendship and charity were totally alien to Bomber's nature so what had happened between them? Why did Bomber want to see him now? These were questions to which Glynmor would clearly get no answers since, after he had sent over a message to Guto, the old scavenger came and smelt so foul that not only did Glynmor have to leave the bedroom but also had to leave the house as well.

He stank even worse than a rubbish tip on a sunny day did Guto. His raincoat, which he wore in all weathers, was thick and shiny with oil and held together with a length of rope. The bottoms of his trousers were tucked in with bicycle clips and the only thing that quite matched the skinniness of his dirty ankles – since he wore no socks – was the dirty scrawniness of his neck. With his torn flat ratting cap, long bony face and stubbly grey beard he had the strange twisted look of a murderer standing before one of those crazy mirrors in a fun-fair. Neither was strangeness much helped by his lack of teeth. He did not possess a single one and the boys in the bar reckoned Guto only searched the Valley tips and dustbins, with such care all the time, because he was looking for a set of false teeth which actually fitted him.

Guto even examined the skulls of dead sheep, the boys in the bar reckoned, to see if the dead animal might have anything by the way of dentures he could recycle.

'You wanted to see me Bomber?' Guto muttered.

Bomber's beady eyes flickered open again as Guto came near the bed and sat on a chair. 'The money,' Bomber croaked, suddenly becoming lucid and almost animated. 'You looked after the girl. I want you to have the money.'

'What money *mun*?'

Bomber closed his eyes almost as if he was having second thoughts about revealing his great secret.

'Bomber. What money?'

'My money, Guto. All my money. My tools are on the bar. I want you to have the money.'

Guto looked behind him at the bedroom door and then moved his chair closer to the bed. 'So where is this money, butty?'

Bomber's eyes opened sharp at this term of endearment. Just about the last thing he wanted to be remembered as was being Guto's butty but, nevertheless, this old sledgehammer had once done something for which he would be eternally grateful.

A piece of folded up paper slid out from beneath the top of the blanket. 'It's all here Guto. Put it away safe. Don't tell Glynmor. Don't tell anyone. You hear me? No bugger at all.'

'You can count on me Bomber.'

Guto looked behind him again and slipped the paper into his pocket.

'There's one more thing you can do,' Bomber continued.

'There's a packet of Woodbines in that drawer. Light one and put it in my mouth.'

Bomber moved his body and lay face-up as Guto lit a cigarette, putting the packet into his own pocket before placing the cigarette between his lips. A look of the most heavenly pleasure crossed Bomber's eyes as the smoke drifted around his lips and poked up his nostrils. His lips tightened and he took the gentlest drag on the cigarette, taking it down a little before letting tiny wisps drift lazy up towards the ceiling.

If heaven had no Woodbines, then he wanted no part of the place, he decided, when the cigarette tumbled out of his lips and, with a soft wheeze, he died.

Guto picked up the smouldering cigarette and sat smoking it as he stayed with Bomber. Even as he tapped the cigarette half-way through, blowing on the butt-end and putting it away in his pocket, he said nothing as he wondered why Bomber had given him all his money just because of that girl? He hadn't done all that much for her.

The minutes passed. Guto was no nearer fathoming the mystery, not even when he looked at the piece of paper which Bomber had passed to him. He looked at the dead eyes, at the hands on the counterpane.

'Time to go Guto,' came Glynmor's voice from the bottom of the stairs.

'He's dead, mun,' he called back.

Glynmor came scrambling up the stairs.

'He's dead,' Guto repeated.

'Did he say anything before he died,' Glynmor asked, breathless.

'He asked me to light a fag for him.'

'Did he say anything at all about money?'

'No. All he wanted was a fag.'

'You black enamelled bastard,' Glynmor spat at Bomber, still lying there with his eyes open, still with a bit of a smile stitched to his lips and that same look of heavenly pleasure in his eyes. 'Where's the thanks, eh? And after all we've done for you. Well it's no fancy fucking funeral for you, mate. You get the cheapest cremation on offer and that's a fact.'

'Wasn't he a Buff?' asked Guto. 'The Buffs will pay for a proper funeral.'

'No fancy fucking funerals for you,' Glynmor continued,

addressing Bomber's dead body. 'You're going to get a bargain-bucket cremation and then I'm going to turn you into an egg-timer.'

'I'll get you an egg-timer if you want one that bad,' Guto offered.

'No. I want *him* as an egg-timer. Just that old goat's ashes. In fact I'll ask them to put him through the oven twice so that he'll make a good egg-timer. Perhaps he'll be of some use now he's dead. He was no use while he was alive.'

Seems a lot of trouble just to get an egg-timer, Guto thought.

When the Buffs examined their subscription book they found that Bomber had been out of compliance for seven years so they decided not to pay for his funeral after all and Bomber ended up with the cheapest cremation on offer.

Not many attended the old miner's funeral service at Glyntaff crematorium. But there was Maggie circling around the forecourt, watching Glynmor talking to the other members of the family. He didn't know, of course. Technically they still weren't speaking.

Since she had been to the doctor she had sent Glynmor no less than three letters asking for them to meet somewhere. He had ignored all of them. She had even hung around outside the pit at the end of the shift, waiting for him to come out. But he still evaded her and there she was getting heavier and heavier – and more and more frightened – by the hour.

She had not actually been invited to the cremation, though he could hardly have stopped her coming. Now she had finally caught up with him and she was determined to break the news to him while she still had him in her sights. It was hardly the right time but she wasn't feeling in the mood for niceties any more. She paused beneath the spiky curving branches of the monkey puzzle tree, standing stock still, watching and waiting. Glynmor knew, without having to be told, that she was there. He was careful not to go near her. He had seen her waiting for him outside the pit; that was why he'd been smuggled out on the back seat of a car. It was all over now, as far as he was concerned. He had other fish to fry.

Another funeral cortège came filing up the path of the crematorium. The sight of the veiled weeping women made

Maggie's pain worse. But there had been no tears shed for Bomber. Even as Glynmor continued moving from group to group she could see the way they were all laughing when he spoke to them. That was the trouble wasn't it? He was always such a laugh to have around. You could never get bored with a man like Glynmor. He had that lovely way about him with his bright laugh and big joke for everything. She knew now that she was too mad about him for her own good.

And then, as if by a trick of mirrors, Glynmor had vanished. The others were climbing into their cars and returning to Bont but Glynmor was not one of them. Panic mounted inside her as she hurried back to the monkey puzzle tree and looked down the newly-arrived cortège. She peered out over the lawns and distant grey headstones but still the lucky father-to-be was nowhere to be seen.

But he had only gone back to the office to pay for the cremation and to pick up Bomber's ashes. 'We could always scatter them around the grounds if you'd prefer,' said the caretaker. 'The grounds could then become his memorial and you could come here whenever you liked to pay your respects.'

'We've got somewhere special to put him and pay our respects,' Glynmor said, taking the vial and putting it in a Co-op bag. 'He had a favourite spot so we're going to put him there.'

Bravura made him careless. He came striding down the side of the crematorium swinging the carrier bag around and whistling when Maggie came sailing around the corner and buttoned him.

'Glynmor. I want a word with you,' she snapped.

'Mag, it's over,' he said. 'Can't you see? It's finished between us.'

'No it's not. It's anything but finished, Glynmor.'

He didn't see how he could take the argument much further than that. They had stated their positions and that seemed to be the end of it. There was a long silence. 'I've got Bomber's ashes in here,' he said, trying to break the deadlock.

'How interesting.'

'I thought we might scatter them over the floor of the bar of the club.'

'I see.'

'I had this other plan to turn him into an egg-timer. Did I tell you?'

86

'Glynmor, I'm pregnant.'

'He was no use when he was alive so ...'

'Glynmor, I'm pregnant.'

He looked quickly behind him as if she was talking to someone else. 'Are you saying ...'

'It's you, Glynmor.'

'Me?' he mimed silently.

'You.'

'It can't be.'

'It's you. There's been no one else.'

'Fair's fair girl, I pulled it out.'

'Fair's fair be buggered. You can't have pulled it out fast enough then, can you?'

'I pulled it out, didn't I?'

'Not fast enough.'

'Bloody hell.' He looked down into the carrier bag at Bomber's ashes. For one terrifying moment he thought that he was going to be sick all over them.

'Yes, bloody hell. So what are you going to do, Glynmor?'

'I'm not going to do anything. What are *you* going to do?'

'You're the father.'

'You're the mother. Can't you get rid of it?'

'No. We'll just have to get married.'

'Married?'

'Yes. Married.'

'Oh no, Maggie. Not me. You're not getting me like that. Not Glynmor Jones. I've got a lot of fish to fry before I get married. You have the kid if you want it. But you're not having me. This is just one of your bastard tricks isn't it? That's what Daisy did didn't she? Well it's not going to work. Not this time it's not. I'm not marrying you and that's bastard that.'

Guto came running down the side of the neighbouring Valley so fast his legs almost ran away with him. It was a fiercely hot day, full of midges and drifting dandelion seeds, making breathing as difficult as swallowing lumps of toffee.

Sweat poured off Guto's brow as he stood still near a refuse tip and studied Bomber's piece of paper again. It was the simple child-like diagram of a mound with the rough sketch of something like a tree next to it. At the base of the lump was a big arrow pointing to a spot marked X with MONEY written next to it.

The more he studied the map the more he had come to believe that it had the same outline as the Tonypandy tip. He now took a trowel out of his oil-stained pocket and began digging a hold at the spot marked X.

The sun scorched down into the refuse hatching thousands of wriggling white maggots and a smell as striking as a punch on the nose. But Guto, hardened by a life of scavenging, hardly noticed anything. For the first time in his life he had the smell of some real money in his nostrils – money with which he could get a fitted set of false teeth – and just for those teeth alone he would have dug right through a hundred tips.

He had been toiling for about half an hour when his trowel bumped into the side of a carboard box. His excitement mounting, he excavated all around it, finally managing to work it free. It had not even been opened. He ripped open the lid to find, inside it, not Bomber's money but a brand-new tumble drier.

Perhaps the money was in another tip altogether, he thought as he hoisted the tumble drier on his shoulder and began the epic walk up one side of the valley and down into Bont. It was so heavy he could only walk very slowly, the sweat pouring out of him in great fists as he struggled up the stony path. Sometimes he had to put the tumble drier down and sit on it to catch his breath before staggering on again. It was terribly heavy. *Duw* he could actually feel his balls cracking up. The thought of what he might do with it had never occurred to him.

Chapter Eight

The white cards, inviting family and friends to the wedding of Glynmor Jones and Margaret Evans, had gold edging and fancy silver letters. The service would be at 11 a.m. at the Libanus Chapel. The reception would be at 12.30 in the Miners' Welfare Hall. R.S.V.P.

When the great day arrived there were such savage summer showers the sheep huddled together under the dry stone walls and even the retired pit ponies went back into the colliery looking for shelter. They stopped, they started, they stopped again did these showers. You just never knew where you were with them. One minute it was sunny then it was some bastard monsoon. You poked your hand out of the door and it had stopped. You stepped out with your shopping bag and it had stopped. You made your way to the Co-op and – *wham!* – a shower started out of nothing with those raindrops smacking against your cheeks and getting right inside your collar to dribble the length of your fed-up backbone.

Stop – start – stop. Cloud – sun – cloud again. Wet – dry – wet again. It was pure valley weather this. Bont weather. In such weather it was best not to take a chance. In such weather it was always best to stay indoors.

But the trouble was that, this day, Glynmor Jones was marrying Margaret Evans so everyone would have to come out sooner or later.

In Maggie's home her mother and sister Daisy were anxiously pinning and repinning the bride's white wedding dress in some vain effort to soften the romping contours of the pregnant bulge which told its own sorry story of sex before the altar. Everyone knew the naughty news, of course. Getting to the altar without actually being banged up was only something the posh from somewhere like Cardiff did. The villagers even knew the date the baby was due.

For his part Glynmor had finally given in under pressure from Maggie's family and accepted that he couldn't have pulled it out soon enough after all. The previous Saturday morning he had gone off to the Dak's suit factory in Caerphilly where, once a month, they sold off their rejects. For three pounds ten shillings he had got a smashing blue mohair suit even if one trouser leg was slightly shorter than the other. He had also acquired a pair of black winkle-picker shoes, a bright green tie and a pair of pink socks which had all but made his Aunty Maude faint when she beheld their luminous splendour.

'You can't get married in them,' she exlaimed aghast.

'Why not?'

'It's a good job your mother's not still alive. She wouldn't have let you get married in pink socks.'

'They're better than no socks at all.'

'Not that much better, they're not.'

Glynmor's best man, Dai Waterboard, had also gone and bought himself a second. He might even have looked as splendid as Glynmor but for the fault in the suit which he had only spotted too late. Dai did not somehow look quite right with his white carnation, Brylcreemed hair and his fly held together with a large safety pin.

The rain eased off for a second and, at that appointed hour, half the village sprinted up the slope. Most got inside the chapel before yet another shower started. It pounded down that rain did, hammering on the grey slate roof and banging on the wooden door of the vestry like a gang of bailiffs come to take possession.

Maggie exercised her womanly right in getting to the altar five minutes late. However, because of some even obscurer custom, Glynmor and his best man arrived later still. It was going to be one of those weddings, Rev. Mordecai decided, as he watched the two of them dash up the aisle and stand before him, soaking wet and stinking of beer.

After the first hymn Rev. Mordecai said his bit about the dearly beloved being all gathered here in the sight of God but then it all began going wrong when he asked the pair to take their marriage vows.

Glynmor managed to make his reply, but, when Rev. Mordecai asked Maggie if she would have this man to be her wedded husband, she broke down in helpless laughter. It wasn't that she wanted to be disrespectful to the vicar. It was just that she was so overwhelmingly happy that she had actually finally got Glynmor to be her wedded husband she just felt like laughing. And laugh she did. Like a drain she laughed, with her head bent forward under her veil and her shoulders shaking up and down like a pair of see-sawing jelly fish.

This outbreak of mirth confirmed Glynmor's doubts about the whole venture. Even when she did finally get her 'I will' out and he took the ring off Dai Waterboard to slip on her fat finger he wished he was back in the Welfare Hall drinking beer with the boys. He had slipped up badly here and no mistake.

And why hadn't this giggling moron taken any precautions either? That was the woman's job wasn't it? It wasn't the man's job to have to mess about with things like that. It spoiled his enjoyment. She had just wanted to trap him she had.

After the Lord's Prayer the Rev. Mordecai, clearly disgusted by all this levity in a house of God, then chimed in with a few words of his own: 'The Bible teaches us many things about our Lord Jesus but nowhere in the Bible do we read of Him actually laughing.' At this point he stopped and waited for Maggie to take control of herself again.

'This absence of laughter is not surprising when you think about it,' the Rev. went on. 'Laughter makes fun of our most precious things. Laughter is what dirty little boys do in lavatories. Laughter is all jests and dirty jokes. There was no laughter with the holy men of old. As soon as laughter enters a marriage it is finished.'

Maggie had now stopped laughing and just stood there taking hold of Glynmor's wrist and keeping her head bowed. She had just never realised that laughter rated with adultery as a mortal sin.

Glynmor, however, was quite positive in his own mind that laughter and adultery – together with the drink – rated the absolute top of the pops and just stood there glaring at the vicar wondering whether to stick the head into him.

'It is not really surprising that it is raining today,' the Rev. went on in that soft merry way of his. 'All this rain is but a sign of the way God is feeling about a marriage like this. It's His way of showing His sadness at the way young people are not keeping one another for the altar.'

Isolated snorts of suppressed laughter burst out of various parts of the congregation at this point while Glynmor turned around to them waving his hand around and around as if turning a starting handle while giving one of his best dirty shark's teeth smiles. Dai Waterboard had to smother his mouth with a handkerchief.

'The reason why marriage is everywhere failing is because the young now insist on regarding it as purely a laughing matter,' the Rev. continued. 'They think it is all a bit of a laugh for the woman to get pregnant before holy matrimony ...'

Apart from Aunty Maude, whose hat was nodding in agreement with the Rev.'s every pained word, the laughter in the congregation was now becoming louder and more widespread. Many of the men had their heads down behind the pews with the women biting hard on their fingers as their eyes watered and they tried to keep a straight face. Glynmor was now back on his starting handle while Dai Waterboard's handkerchief was fluttering out in front of his face like washing in a high wind.

'They think it is all a bit of a laugh to come to the altar late and smelling of alcohol,' the Rev. began shouting above the increasing laughter. 'They think it is all a bit of a laugh to roll around in the slime of their carnal lusts. And when the woman becomes pregnant they think it is all a bit of a laugh to claim it's something to do with the wind.'

That was it. The vicar's seriousness was all too much for them at that point and, as one, the whole congregation collapsed into helpless, terminal laughter.

'Is this wedding finished or are you going to keep us here all day?' Glynmor asked out straight when most of the laughter had subsided.

'The minister is supposed to say a few words but ...'

'Are we married or not?' Glynmor interrupted him again.

'You are indeed. But God ...'

'Right. Come on Mag.' He took her by the elbow and led her firmly down the aisle as he lectured her. 'You be sure, in the future, to laugh any time you want do you hear? Any time you want.' The further away he walked the louder he made his voice so that the vicar could hear his every word. 'At any time you feel like laughing then you get laughing. When you feel a

92

laugh coming then it's just like a fart. You've got to let it rip. You've got to get it out. And if anyone tells you otherwise then you tell them "Bollocks" from Glynmor.'

As the newly-married couple left the vestry, followed by all the highly-entertained friends and guests, God must have changed His mind about the marriage since bright hard sunshine was bouncing everywhere, glittering on the grey slate roofs, glowing ferocious on the windows and drying up the asphalt on the road in huge steaming patches.

Maggie could never remember feeling happier as they both walked hand in hand down the hill to the reception in the Welfare Hall. Glynmor walking out of the chapel like that had confirmed what she had always felt – that our Glynmor was thrillingly unique.

As they walked ahead of the procession of guests other people came out of their homes, smiling and waving at the happy couple. Blackbirds flew in cheeping bunches overhead. Car horns were sounded. Maggie's eyes misted up and she waved regally when she again began laughing uncontrollably.

The Jones family had always been popular in the Valleys but even Glynmor was surprised at all the local characters who had come flocking from all parts of South Wales for the reception. As they filed into the Welfare Hall they put their presents on a display table in the Rainbow Room and, to date, there were blankets, two bedspreads, four sets of glasses, a tea set, cushions and, unbelievably, a tumble drier given by Guto. It even had a receipt suspiciously attached to it. So what were all those scratches doing on its side then?

Some fool even gave some baby clothes which, fortunately, were spotted before Maggie's mother inspected the presents and quietly removed them.

Dai the Rat had walked over from Porth and it was the first time many in Bont had seen him since he had officially retired as the chief rat-catcher in all the pits in the Valley. He could track down those rats in the pitch dark could Dai the Rat. No rat ever slept sound when Dai was around.

Three Teddy boys from Treorchy, distant cousins of Maggie's side, coming over looking simply wonderful in their multi-coloured Edwardian suits as they stood together combing their hair. Then there was poor Danny Bits and Pieces, his pockets full of all manner of odds and ends with the fork of his trousers hanging so low it was if he was joined at the knees. Even his jacket was so bulky he might have had a few dozen ferrets secreted in the lining.

No one quite knew who had invited Danny Bits and Pieces since he was not quite sixteen ounces to the pound and might at any moment go pot-holing under the chairs while the guests were eating. His latest stunt was to keep his wrist watch in his pint of beer as he drank it – just to show that it was water-proof. 'See, boys, I can drink and tell the time as well.'

Then there was Dan Bag O'Shit who once used to be the drinking butty of the singer Tom Jones' bodyguard down in Pontypridd. Ted John North, a wiry Anglesey man who had been the veteran of many sheep and dog rescues down the steep narrow gullies of the Valley, was there. So was Exactly Jones, a money-lender with crocodile shoes from Church Village, who came with the fancy woman he was living tally with – and their dog.

Everyone was surprised and delighted to see Donny Hughes – Donny the Ding, the young banjo player from Sunny Hill, whose playing had once delighted the whole of Bont. Donny had taken lodgings down in Cardiff as his launching pad for crashing into the big time. No one ever quite knew what had happened to him since he had gone to that infernal city but he had clearly gone as daft as trimmings. Where once he had been a tidy boy, swilling behind his ears every morning and going around delivering *Echos* on his bicycle, he now had long black dandruffed hair with huge sun glasses, and had turned into a self-styled Prince of Darkness in his black velvet cape. His ideas about orgies, drugs and Satan worship all but made the elderly women swoon in terror when he spoke of them over a bag of crisps and a pint of All-Bright.

Donny the Ding's girl friend, Splodge, was very strange too. Not only did she seem to be unable to use the English language, as they do speak it around 'ere, but she also seemed to favour baking flour for her make-up with dartboards of mascara around her eyes and black lipstick, for goodness sake! Black? I ask you. There's no shape on 'er at all. And even so early in the morning she looks out of it don't she? Drugs she's on. Smoking that LSE.

Everyone, of course, was still talking about the Rev. Mordecai's outburst against the sin of enjoying yourself in the chapel. It was further evidence – if any were needed – that he was beginning to crack up. 'And don't you come in here claiming the boy's wind,' they would mimic out loud. 'Next thing you'll be saying that Glynmor's dick is a bicycle pump.'

Maggie moved through all the people and laughter, glass of Pomagne in hand, with all the quiet pride of a gardener inspecting his prize allotment. Sometimes she stopped for a chat or a quick kiss. But most of the time she was keeping her eye on Glynmor, who had barely moved from the bar since they had all come in. 'You'd think he would at least go around and welcome the guests wouldn't you?' she whispered to her mother.

Glynmor was on his fourth pint of the morning and telling his favourite dirty story about the queer who got raped by a gorilla in the African bush when the call went out for everyone to take their places for the meal.

He finished his pint in one gulp and Dai Waterboard bought him a fresh one before going to the place of honour next to the bride on the trestle tables in the Starlight Suite. Some wine was then served and Maggie was alarmed when she noticed that Glynmor was now mixing up the wine with his beer. 'Cool head now, Glynmor,' she said touching him lightly on the wrist. 'We've got all day you know.'

The soup was served and Glynmor gave his first indication that all that wine and beer had gone straight to his head since he soon managed to get his new green tie floating in the Brown Windsor. She shook the drops off it and tucked it inside his shirt, next opening the napkin and placing it on his lap. 'Did I tell you how much I liked your new suit today?' she asked.

'Three quid in Dak's,' he said cryptically.

'Three quid in what?'

'Three quid in a sale over in Caerphilly. It's a reject see. One leg is shorter than the other.'

'Oh I see. Did you get those fabulous socks in that sale as well?'

'Oh no,' he said missing the edge of her sarcasm and picking up his soup spoon. 'I got those new in Woolworth's in Ponty. Five bob they cost. Like them do you?'

'They're lovely,' she said deadpan. 'Just lovely I do call them.'

'I'm glad you like them,' he said, whereupon he started slurping his soup like he had just got his snout into the trough.

He had another swig on his wine followed by another on his soup when he turned to her with a wink. 'I'm telling you now and this is a fact,' he said. 'This soup here is thirty farts to the ounce.'

'Oh that's a fact, is it?' she asked.

'It is. So hang onto your bedclothes when the thunder starts in bed tonight.'

It's a funny thing, Maggie thought, how one second you think you are madly in love with a man and the next second you would quite cheerfully drown him in his own soup. She finished her own soup and wiped the corners of her mouth carefully and theatrically before putting the big question to her new husband. 'Tell me Glynmor. Why is everything some sort of dirty joke with you?'

'You're beginning to sound like that daft old vicar.'

'You just can't say anything unless it's filthy, can you?'

'Bollocks.'

'If you do have a clean thought … *if* … do you throw dirt over it before it gets out?'

'I'll be throwing some dirt over you if you don't watch it.'

'Did your mother ever wash your mouth out as a child did she?'

'Leave my mother out of this.'

Even though they were arguing out of the sides of their mouths in low grumbling tones everyone was now watching them intently as they had their very first married quarrel.

One man who was taking particular interest was Emlyn Kremlin who took out his fob watch and checked the time. Somehow he did not see this marriage lasting long. He liked Glynmor well enough – let's face it *everyone* liked Glynmor well enough – but feared that he was too much of a Valley boyo to make any marriage work. Valley boyos liked the beer too much and loved nothing more than chasing new bits of skirt. The most complicated things they did was to fill in a betting slip. Their greatest exercise was leaning against the wall outside the Labour Exchange. They had no fidelity to people and issues like Emlyn's generation. His generation had always been faithful in their politics, work and marriages. His generation of men had always gone home on Friday afternoons and put their unopened pay packets on the table. He doubted if Glynmor would get home on a Friday afternoon let alone hand over his pay packet unopened.

It was a great shame really, Emlyn thought. His niece

Maggie was a fine girl with fine ideals. She would have made someone a fine and faithful wife as well. But not for Glynmor. He was a firebrand, a leader in odd sort of way what with his fluency with words and ability to make men laugh. When he stopped messing about he might even be able to do something very well indeed. He did have bottle and a certain recklessness. But what he would never be was a husband. Not as long as he had a hole in his arse he wouldn't.

As the chicken salad was being served there came a scream from one of the other tables. Danny Bits and Pieces was yet again demonstrating the ancient custom of pot-holing between people's legs and yet again everyone was asking who had invited the dopey sod. The Evans tribe blamed the Jones tribe and the Jones tribe blamed the Evans tribe.

When the ice cream and strawberries were finished Dai Waterboard, none too sober, read out the usual crop of vulgar messages. 'Today's the day, tonight's the night, we've shot the stork so you're all right,' he sniggered. 'From Aunty Mae and Uncle Ernie in Rhyl.' He also thanked the guests for their presents but wondered aloud who had the nerve to give the happy couple baby clothes. What kind of present was that? What were they trying to say? Nudge, nudge. More lewd telegrams.

Later still the drink flowed more freely and tables were cleared away. The celebrations moved into overdrive. Donny the Ding forsook his banjo for the piano and quite soon everyone was giving a spirited rendering of *Toot, Toot, Tootsie; Old Man River* and *Begin the Beguine*. They all danced the *Breakaway Blues* and the *Royal Rhumba*.

The first real solo was performed by Peter Star – a Bont collier who usually spent an unhealthy amount of time patting and combing his hair – who did *Old Macdonald's Farm*. He took off the likes of Harold Wilson, James Stewart and John Wayne in each verse but, by the time he got near the end, he was so drunk he kept mixing them up with one another.

Biscuits tried to do Elvis Presley's *O Sole Mio* but the sound was so unutterably awful a group carried him off to the lavatory where he was locked in and left to get on with it alone. Dan Bag O'Shit played a rapturous tango on the spoons.

Away with the fairies though he clearly was even Glynmor got up when it was nearly time to go and sang that deathless, tear-stained legend of the man who, when mashed up in a motor bike accident, lifted up his broken neck and warbled *Tell Laura I Love Her*. The applause was rapturous and, by now, Glynmor was enjoying himself so much he did not want to go on honeymoon at all. 'We'll go tomorrow,' he kept shouting as Maggie dragged him out of the hall. 'Who wants to go to bastard Barry Island anyway?'

He was bundled into the back of Penguin's Mercedes hire car and was still trying to get out, with Maggie hauling him in by one arm, when, beneath a hail of rice and confetti, the car took off with a row of tin cans and old boots tied to the rear bumper.

The reception was far from over, however. Now the serious drinking began when Aunty Phyllis passed out Lucozade bottles full of her lethal, smoking, home-made punch. No one ever knew what went into this alcoholic Molotov cocktail. It blew your brains away with a wallop which separated you from the world just as convincingly as death. The very smell of it drove you bananas. All that you really knew about it for sure was that it was best drunk already lying down, preferably in a bed.

It appeared that she had made a special dozen bottles for the occasion and, in no time at all, everyone was as pissed as parrots with the various tribes half-clinging to one another and half-falling about like the dazed survivors of a nuclear holocaust. Donny the Ding pounded those ivories and the women hitched up their dresses to do the can-can. The men, many with the tails of their shirts hanging out, formed impromptu choirs. Even Dai the Rat did a small tap dance until he too fell over.

A large group was shuffling around together in one corner of the dance floor doing some strange tribal dance revealed, on closer inspection, to be the beginnings of a brawl. Biscuits was still in the lavatory doing his terrible imitation of Elvis Presley. Some dirty bastard was being sick over Aunty Maude's new hat.

Unnoticed by the revellers the day bowed out of the Valley. As the blotto throng continued with their celebrations, Walford and Daisy were even now downstairs in the committee room having a bit of a rub on the committee's sacred, circular, polished table. Daisy, very badly affected by Aunty Phyllis' punch, was hanging onto Walford's neck so tight it was as if she was up to her neck in a swamp and about to go under at any second.

The committee chairman's wife, Maisy Million, was on her way to the lavatory when she first heard those suspicious grunts and sighs coming out of the locked committee room. She immediately abandoned the mission at hand and went upstairs to the bar. There she told her husband Max that she suspected that some couple were having it away in the committee room. As chairman, Max took a very strong line on people having such fun in his club. A man of striking, dark features, his brow was always furrowed in a permanent frown. Now it hardened as if encased in cement at this disturbing information.

He called over his sidekick, Stan Prees, another committee man, and they both went below to investigate the matter.

Walford was in full thrust with his hips exploding against Daisy, whose nose was only just poking up out of the swamp, when the committee room door flew open and the unamused faces of Max Million and Stan Rees were revealed.

'Well, well,' said Stan. 'This looks like one for the committee, Max.'

'You can say that again Stan,' said Max.

'Oh blimey,' was about all Walford could manage.

'Oh shit,' said Daisy, strangely sober and sinking into her swamp.

'But on the committee table,' Max said, pained. 'The committee table, mun.'

Maggie sat upright in her hotel bed, her arms folded, and the corners of her mouth turned down. Wearing her new négligée she looked very fetching as the bright lights of Barry Island funfair flashed across the darkened room. It was little after ten.

But where was her Glynmor? Her new husband had somehow gone missing. He had gone into the bathroom but did not seem at all keen on coming out again. She heard the shower going and decided that he had just gone in there to sober up. But now he had been taking a shower for over an hour which seemed excessive even by Glynmor's excessive standards. A sudden thought came to her. That Hitchcock film – *North by Northwest* – when Cary Grant pretended to be taking a shower so that he could listen in on something while out of the room.

Maybe Glynmor's up to something, she thought with a twinge of alarm.

She slipped quickly out of the bed and opened the bathroom door. But there he was, still taking that shower, still fully clothed in his new Dak's mohair suit and horrid pink socks. Even more alarmingly he had somehow managed to get hold of a Lucozade bottle full of Aunty Phyllis' punch. Standing under the running water with his head bowed, he would occasionally lift his head and take another swig of that lethal punch. She had never seen anyone so ratted. And this was her new husband! Cary Grant he wasn't, that was for sure.

'Glynmor! Get in this bed!' she cried.

He looked up at her with eyes which were but tiny dead spots. 'As of tonight,' he shouted as if he was trying to be heard in the Butlin's Holiday Camp on the other side of the island. 'Asoftonight,' he repeated. 'I am never going to drink again. Neverdrinkagain.'

He was about to take another swig when she grabbed him by the wrist and yanked him out of the shower so sharply she sent him whirling across the bedroom like a spinning top. He collapsed on the floor by the side of the bed with the bottle still miraculously glued to his hand. Then he began to weep inconsolably.

Maggie stood over him with her hands whirling around uselessly. Just what was she going to do now? 'Come on Glynmor. Let's get you undressed.'

With that he began to wail so loudly she began to worry that he was in real pain, sitting down next to him and putting a comforting arm over his shoulders.

'Just promise me one thing,' he blubbered. 'Promise me one thing.'

'Anything my lovely.'

'If the baby's a boy ...'

'Yes, if it's a boy.'

'If the boy's a baby ... we'll call it Jampots.'

'Jampots. Yes.'

'If the baby's a baby. Jampots. Not if it's a girl mind. If the girl's a boy. Jampots. Right?'

'Anything you want my lovely. You are the father after all.'

'I'm not the fucking father. Not me.' He scrambled to his

100

feet like someone had lit a fire under his bum. 'Not me. No sir. Not this boy.' He took another swig from his bottle and, for a moment, Maggie feared he was going to brain her with it. Indeed he looked just like a murderer in a Hammer horror film as he swayed dangerously, bottle in hand with the multi-coloured fairground lights flashing all over him. She was going to get that Aunty Phyllis for this.

'Me! The father? Huh. Do I look like the father? Are you a father? Look at you. A fat father. Fucking fat. There's nothing left for me any more now. You trapped me in pain you did. Yes you. Just pain and that's a fact. That's what I've got. My pain. Here. See? See this belly button? That belly button is all pain.'

Maggie was now crying softly into her palms. He was not making a lot of sense but it was sense enough to her. He would never believe that he was the father. He would always be accusing her of trapping him in marriage – no matter if he was drunk or sober. He would always be going on about it for the rest of her life. She knew our Glynmor.

Glynmor pushed her to one side and hurled himself into the bathroom. He vomited loudly and abundantly. The honkings were amplified by the porcelain pan and Maggie sat listening to him talking to the Lord on the great white telephone with a great strange sense of emptiness inside her.

Something had gone wrong somewhere and that was a fact, as Glynmor himself might have said. He gave another long whinnying heave. They didn't have men like Glynmor in Mills and Boon – thank heavens. There was no puking up and foul language with them. They said nice things, all romantic, in Mills and Boon.

On the drive down here in Penguin's Mercedes Glynmor had stopped belching long enough to pick up her hand and ask her if he had ever told her what his Uncle Ianto had always said.

'No. What does your Uncle Ianto always say?'

'He always told me never to go out with a girl with big hands 'cos it makes your dick look small.'

'Oh that's a fact, is it?'

'Aye girl that is a fact.'

She was stuck with him now, him and his elegant wit, the wonder lover of the valleys, here on his wedding night, soaked to the skin and throwing his guts up into the toilet. She sighed and looked down at her hands. They weren't all that big.

Suddenly tiring of all this she stood up and got dressed, walking out of the hotel and down to the sea-front where the promenade lights were strung out all around her like a giant gaudy necklace. Just behind her was the funfair and over on the prow of the distant hill the giant neon castle of Billy Butlin's, a place she had hoped never to visit on a holiday or any other day come to that. Far away across the Bristol Channel were the distant promenade lights of Weston-super-Mare. A warm wind whipped in over the sand buffeting the sea-front walls with the numbers painted on them. When they had come to Barry they had always gone in front of the Number Three wall. That had always been the Evans spot, that had.

She leaned against the Number Three wall, looking down at the self-same spot where they had spent all those blessed sunshine days. A patch of smooth sand it was with a derelict sand castle in it now, all lit up by the brilliance of the moon. The Evans family would come here three or four times during the summer – or else for the Whitsun treat, with the chapel, when trains from all over the valleys queued up for hours to get into the station and again to get out again in the evening.

As soon as they got off the train she remembered that they would run as fast as they could to bag a place just here in front of the Number Three wall. Here they'd sit together making sandcastles, drinking tea out of a Thermos and eating tomato sandwiches which always seemed to have sand in them. Funny thing but she had always hated tomato sandwiches unless they were out on Barry sands.

She gulped the fresh sea air, feeling a little better now as her mind wandered in the corridors of her most pleasant memories. She could even see her father with a knotted handkerchief on his head and trousers rolled up to just below the knees as he paddled around in the dirty, brown waves. And there was Mam sitting next to her buttering yet more bread for yet more tomato sandwiches.

But Mam had never wanted to come to Barry any more after Dad had died. A lot went out of their lives when he left them. Some nights she could hear her Mam lying in bed still talking to him in her sleep, still asking him to do things about the house.

102

Maggie swallowed hard, remembering how she and Daisy used to make buckets out of old baked bean tins, how they'd spend hours building sandcastles which were then swept away by the tide. Then there were the donkeys which took you down into the water, and the Salvation Army band which played to try and save your soul.

They'd been wonderful hours out on these sands, aye they had. They had been gurgling days which had gone in and out as regular as the tides; the world outside was gigantic and hostile but that did not matter because, for the moment, you were safe and protected. And urgently happy.

That was why she had wanted to come back here for her honeymoon. She had wanted to reap a few of those golden hours again. She wanted to savour those great days once more. But you could never do that, could you? Those you loved went and left you. Those you didn't love came right into your life and made you unhappy. Sometimes those you loved didn't love you and that was worse than anything. That was her big problem wasn't it? Her Glynmor was just too selfish to know anything about love. That Glynmor who she still loved more than life itself.

She walked up through the terraced gardens and over the road to the funfair. The smell of frying hot dogs mingled with and dominated that of chips and candy floss. A woman in a stall offered her some hoop-la rings. 'A nice prize for everyone, dearie,' she called, but Maggie had already won one prize too many that day. The dodgem cars went banging and swerving around her, the people on the scenic railway screamed out their delicious fear at her. She stopped and looked up at the lights of the giant big wheel as it bore down on her from high above.

But, instead of hauling her out of the dumps, all this noise and laughter made her whole body ache with sadness. She began crying again; from a nearby loudspeaker the voice of Otis Redding sang of how they called him Mr Pitiful.

She stood outside the Haunted House with the noise filling up her mind, and the coloured lights glittering in her tears. Just over there she had once caught her Dada watching What The Butler Saw in a peep-show. Him a teacher and doing that! Just here Mama had held her when she was crying her eyes out after bumping her nose while driving the dodgem cars. She wanted her Dada to come and hold her again. She wanted her Mama to

103

come over and kiss away the pain. She wanted simple love, that's all she wanted. She knew that well enough. What she didn't want was to be married to a man who hated her. She just wanted a few of those golden Barry hours back again. Dear God, that wasn't too much to ask for. Well was it?

Back in Bont the wedding reception was winding down. Groups of guests had broken up into a dozen competing choirs. Ragged versions of *Sospan Fach* fought with off-key renditions of *Bread of Heaven*. Hymns grappled with drunken arias. Everyone, just everyone, was as drunk as skunks. They fell over one another, they held one another up. Dai Waterboard's feet could just be seen poking out from beneath one of the tables. Biscuits was still locked in the lavatory, singing his Elvis Presley numbers. Emlyn Kremlin was done for too, sitting there in his shirt and braces conducting one of the choirs with a bread roll. Even Exactly Jones' dog had got into Aunty Phyllis' punch. He was a depraved pisshead at the best of times, with a perverse taste for goosing cats. People swore that they saw him stagger out of the Hall, lift a leg up against the lamp post and collapse flat on his back, pissing himself.

As they came out of the Hall, stepping over the comatose dog, it was Dan Bag O'Shit who opened the traditional assault on the village clock by hurling an empty flagon of cider at it. Next to step up was Donny the Ding who flung a rock. His girl friend, Splodge, threw a milk bottle. Others stepped forward to take a shy at the luckless clock; but, it being late and their eyesight blurred, most missed by a mile. Rocks, bottles, plates, shoes … anything that could be thrown at the brightly-lit Roman numerals.

No one had ever worked out where this strange custom had come from and what, if anything, it signified. It was never planned either; it simply happened about three or four times a year when the whole village expressed its communal happiness by flinging things at the clock. It was a time when even the ubiquitous sheep stayed well clear of the area.

Fortunately the flat-bed clock had been built in an age when they built clocks to withstand a siege. No matter what hit it, the hands kept going around and around, marking out the hours and minutes in the life of this Valley of coal.

104

Chapter Nine

It was one of those days in the Valley which was neither sunny nor rainy, neither hot nor cold. It was just a nothing day, reflected P.C. Watkins as he stood in his living-room ironing his uniform. As befitted the long arm of the law in the village, his flat was immaculately polished and tidy. Police school certificates had been framed and hung on the wall, silver soccer trophies bedecked the mantelpiece. P.C. Watkins, forty-six years old and a confirmed bachelor, took an intense pride in order and tidiness. The way a man lived on the outside, he believed, was a sure sign of how he was inside.

The actual police station downstairs was a model of polished cleanliness as well. P.C. Watkins was not too proud to go down on his knees and scrub the floor himself. He was given an allowance to hire a cleaner but none of them ever seemed to do the job to his exacting satisfaction. No one seemed to take a pride in their work any longer, he reckoned. So he did it himself.

Just behind the reception area was the cell, so warm and sunny he kept his tomato plants in it. There never was much of a call on his cell unless Curly had been thrown out by his wife again and wanted somewhere to get his head down for the night until she had cooled down. Such crime as there was had, by and large, been trivial and easily detected. It was difficult to have a quiet fart in Bont without half the street knowing about it and, sooner or later, P.C. Watkins, who had been blessed with a fine and ferocious sense of gossip, would get to know about it too.

For a long, long time the only incident that had stayed in his memory was when a whole rack of sunglasses had disappeared from the chemist's. P.C. Watkins had soon tracked them down, since the culprit, Danny Bits and Pieces, who was never sixteen ounces to the pound, had been selling them for a penny each in the Hall. P.C. Watkins just walked into the bar and found virtually everyone sitting there wearing sunglasses with tiny gold stickers on them.

For the rest of the time it was the not unpleasant routine of old pit ponies dropping dead in the street, the odd domestic argument that had got out of control or a spot of after-hours drinking that had gone on long enough even by the boozy standards of the Valley.

Things changed when Gnasher and the Clay Class began performing in earnest.

When P.C. Watkins saw them coming out of the shop weighed down by salmon, the shock of actually apprehending someone in the act of burglary and the prospect of locking Gnasher up with his tomato plants had been so great that the constable had begun to wonder if the Mafia had finally decided to set up their headquarters in Bont – or worse. This was real breaking and entering, he told the old-timers on the bench near the clock. Imagine Bont lads making off with loot in the middle of the night. Kids whose parents you grew up with. And then all they got was a bit of probation. They didn't seem at all ashamed either. It was the parents he blamed. It's the telly, said the old-timers.

The bell on the station desk rang and he went down to find Mrs Muriel Davies there with a query. If a dog did his jobs outside her door was it illegal to scoop it up and take it to the dog owner's home and post it through his letter box?

P.C. Watkins shook his head from side to side. 'The long and short of it Mrs Davies, is that I just don't know.'

'You're the policeman here, aren't you?'

'That is correct.'

'Well why don't you know then?'

'It's a problem I've never come across before.'

'Well I done it. I posted the dog's jobs and he's coming to see you. I'm turning myself in first. I done it.'

'Who's coming to see me?' P.C. Watkins asked trying to keep a straight face. Mrs Davies took herself awful serious when she got going.

'Percy Pugh. He says he's going to have me locked up so I'm turning myself in. I done it.'

'Well I'd better check what law you've broken first Mrs Davies. Will you come and turn yourself in again after I've checked with headquarters?'

'What time would that be?'

'Come about five and I'll know by then.'

Mrs Davies left and P.C. Watkins was about to close the station door when he spotted the Clay Class all heading down to the railway sidings. He watched them intently as something sickly turned over inside his belly. They were up to something that lot. That was a racing certainty that was.

He was fairly sure that they were not up to anything criminal but was highly suspicious at the way they seemed to be so happy all the time. He saw them at odd times of the day, gathered on the swings in the playground or down on the river bank, all forever laughing their socks off. He had never known anything like it and wished it would stop. He far preferred them when they were moody and scowling. That was the way he preferred the Clay Class.

Not that they laughed much when he was around. Their smiles froze at the very sight of his uniform and they stared cold at him and ran away. Come to think of it there'd been reports that a load of hospital ether had been stolen from Tonypandy hospital. He had read that funny things happened to people when they sniffed on that. He wondered if a bottle of that might be accounting for all this riotous laughter.

He closed the station door and picked up the telephone, dialling headquarters in Pontypridd. 'Hello sarge. It's Trevor Watkins in Bont here. Tell me now. What do you know about the law relating to dog shit?'

That same afternoon, in the basement of the Welfare Hall, the committee was also worrying about matters of crime and punishment as they prepared to consider the latest crop of infringements of the sacred rules of clubland. You name it and they had a rule about it. If any misbehaviour was not quite covered by one rule they could usually get you with a sub-section of another. Every smallest corner and cupboard of the club was penetrated and fully covered by some clause or another and, as befits the chairman, Max Million knew every one of them. He wielded the rule book with the ferocity of a tomahawk; those neatly numbered lines of fine print even staked out the parameters of his thoughts and he might even, right in the middle of the night, wake up and begin reciting out loud, say, rule 16 sub-section II; *No payment shall be made from the Welfare Hall's banking account except by a cheque signed by the chairman and treasurer.*

'So what if the chairman and treasurer are sick?' his wife might ask, merely trying to wind him up.

'Then the cheque will not be paid until chairman and treasurer are fully recovered.'

The committee took their duties seriously. Even as they sat around their great polished table, some scratching their balls or clearing out their ears with a matchstick, you could tell from the starched immobility of their features, that these were men come together to do serious business. There was no laughter in committee meetings under Max Million's chairmanship. When he was in the chair it might have been the annual general meeting of some secret police controlling a Caribbean banana republic for all the laughs he allowed.

These chapel-solemn men were the very fabric of the Welfare Hall. All posters were signed by order of the committee. The committee patrolled every room during opening hours. The committee could elect honorary members. A committee man could refuse admission to anyone at such times as they deemed it to be of interest to the club. They could expel, suspend or issue a lengthy reprimand. They could issue beer cheques for favours done to the club or, conversely, stop someone drinking there for any offence, like being caught pinching a lavatory roll. The committee had the right to call any member to appear before them to explain themselves at their disciplinary meetings on Sunday afternoons. If a member chose not to turn up then so much the worse for them. Under CIU rules the minimum was a one-year ban from using the Hall which, since it was the social centre of the village and only provider of strong drink, was death.

Most of their disciplinary sessions were spent adjudicating on and punishing matters relating to fighting, swearing or the bingo sessions. Today, however, it was all far worse. Today they had to deal with the sad and sorry case of Walford Evans and the incident with Daisy Bland.

Even to think about that horrific sight made Max Million sick to the very core. Was nothing at all sacred? The limit of the committee's sanctions was to expel a member for life but he wished that there was something far worse that he could impose. Fornication was bad enough but when it was right here on the committee table? He lifted his elbows up off the polished mahogany at the very thought of it.

Neither was Daisy at all repentant, he was mortified to see, when she was called to explain herself. She just sat down in front of them with a cigarette in her hand and smiled.

'Have you anything to say about this alleged incident?' Chairman Max asked. Even when cases like this touched his bare nerve so deeply he always tried to be fair. What you had to say about Max was that he was always fair.

'Well there's nothing alleged about the incident, is there Max?' said Daisy taking another puff of her cigarette. 'I mean you caught us bang to rights, didn't you?'

'In committee we call Max, Mr Chairman,' said Max's lieutenant, Stan Rees.

'Oh do we?' asked Daisy all sarcastic. 'That's nice for you then init?'

'Would you mind telling us how long this has been going on?' asked Max.

'No.'

'No what?'

'No Max.'

The men sat glaring at Daisy who crossed and uncrossed her legs in great shiverings of rustling nylons. She had deliberately not put on her brassière and her nipples stuck out like walnuts. She enjoyed the hold that she had over men and even now knew which of them would be mentally pulling down her knickers and getting twinges in their sad little worms. Daisy wasn't like the rest of the women around the Valleys. She wasn't scared of these oafs who saw the wife as little more than a doormat who cleaned the house, cooked the food and got fucked, if she was lucky, late and badly on a Saturday night. Daisy was only like Daisy and that was the way she was going to stay.

'You see Daisy,' said Max holding up his hand carefully and theatrically while examining the surface of the table, presumably for any signs of scuff or stains. 'This is a most serious matter. Most serious indeed. If you must have affairs with men it is not normally our business. But this was with the bingo caller, who is in our employ, and on the committee table, which is our property.'

'Damaged then, is it?' asked Daisy, leaning forward and

studying the table along with the rest of the committee.

'There's a long scratch up here,' said Geraint James.

'There's a burn mark down here,' said Brian Thomas.

'Now hold it just there,' said Daisy. 'Now I don't know what the committee does when *they* have a fuck …'

'Your language,' they protested almost as one.

'Listen. I've heard you lot talking so don't tell me anything about *my* language. As I said, I don't know what *you* do when *you* have a fuck but my bum doesn't make scratches and neither am I so hot I scald holes in the polish. Just tell me what's going to happen to me, will you? I've got a date soon. There's these three black seamen coming up from Cardiff and we're having a party.'

A sagging silence enveloped the committee as they stared down at the surface of the table. So much activity on so little polish. Max caught Stan Prees' eye. We're not going to get anywhere here, are we? he pantomimed.

'Well that just about sums it up I suppose,' the chairman said finally. 'Unless any committee man has any further questions I shall ask Daisy to step outside while we consider our verdict. Any questions are there?'

'One thing though,' Daisy added half-rising from her chair. 'I would be grateful if you would go easy on poor old Walford. You can ban me for however long you like but poor Walford's dead upset he's going to lose his bingo job over all this. It's that Aunty Phyllis' punch that I blame.'

'Just leave it with us Daisy,' said the chairman. 'You can always rely on this committee for its sense of justice.'

'Aunty Phyllis shouldn't have handed out her punch in this club,' said Stan Prees. 'These are proper licensed premises. How can we run a club proper with her handing out all that jungle juice all the time? It's enough to drive any man crazy that stuff.'

After Daisy had withdrawn, Shonny Roberts began one of his wandering perorations before the chairman gavelled him into silence. 'In my view,' the chairman continued, straightening his back as he imagined a judge might when handing down the death sentence. 'Daisy Bland in is breach of most of the rules concerning good behaviour in the Hall and should accordingly …'

'But what rule has she broken, Mr Chairman?' It was

Vinny Price, a fierce dialectician when he got going, who was clearly signalling the start of an argument.

'You name it and she's in breach of it,' the chairman blustered.

'In breach of what though precisely?'

'"Offensive behaviour shall not be permitted in the Hall." Rule 9 – sub-section 1.'

'But, with all due respect Mr Chairman, fucking behind locked doors is not offensive behaviour.'

'Well the doors weren't locked were they? I opened them didn't I?'

'You opened them with your own key. As far as the rest of the members were concerned they were locked.'

'There's others with a key to this room.'

'The key went with the man who came to service the one-armed bandits,' Shonny Roberts chimed in with his uncanny sense of the irrelevant. 'You couldn't even get a cherry after he fixed those bandits. Not a bastard cherry you couldn't.'

'Look, Vinny, fucking is offensive behaviour,' the chairman insisted. 'What is it you want, Vinny? You want people fucking all over the Hall. Is that what you want?'

'Well it's better than people fighting all over the Hall isn't it? Perhaps if we had a bit more fucking around here there'd be a lot less fighting.'

'Now you're really mixing your drinks.'

'Who's mixing his drinks, Mr Chairman? I'm talking about fucking. You're talking about fighting. Two entirely different things. Anyway I seem to remember that you used to enjoy a bit of fun fucking down in the cellar when the bar was locked. Rachel Bennett. Now we all remember her don't we?'

'That was a long time ago. And before I married Maisy let's not forget. At least it wasn't on the committee table.'

'Ah so that's what's getting up your nose is it Mr Chairman? But the table's all right. There's nothing wrong with it is there? I'm tired of all this bastard hypocrisy on this committee. It's getting worse than the chapel in here. The Hall can't afford to lose a girl like Daisy. We can't sit in judgement on women like her. We need characters in this place. The Valleys were built by characters – not moralising committees.

'It's Aunty Phyllis who should be up here for dishing out all that punch.'

'Leave Aunty Phyllis out of this.'

'Why don't we get another contractor for the one-armed bandit?'

'Why don't you shut your face?'

In the end it was decided to let Daisy off with a reprimand; that Aunty Phyllis should be sent a written warning not to dispense her punch on the premises in the future and that Walford be duly given his cards and sacked like a dog. He was always getting his numbers mixed up anyway.

'Spunky girl that,' observed Vinny Price. 'A shame about her sister, though, being married to that Glynmor Jones.'

'What's that?' asked Max Million, all ears. 'They're still on honeymoon aren't they?'

'They went on honeymoon Mr Chairman, then they went straight to the divorce court.'

'Can we have a little less of the jokes and get on with it?' said the chairman gavelling the laughter into the table. 'So then? Where is Glynmor? Is he in Bont or what?'

'He's home Mr Chairman. He's been home f'r ages. They had a big fight on the first night of the honeymoon, I heard, and came home. He came home by bus and she came back by taxi. It's awful terrible it is. Her so far gone in the pudding club an' all.'

'What happened then?'

'It was murder all the way, I heard, Mr Chairman. It seems he got hold of a bottle of Aunty Phyllis' punch ...'

Committee rumbles and erupts with cries of 'Not that bloody punch again.'

' ... and on their first night together he went and took a shower with all his clothes on. Then he started crying about losing his best friend Jampots and telling Maggie they had to call the baby Jampots – no matter what sex it was. Then, the next thing, she goes out for a walk and he's down in the bar in the hotel, still in his wet clothes an' all, trying to pick up some horrible piece who turns out, Mr Chairman, to be one of those sailors dressed up as a woman. But Glynmor is so pissed he takes this queer up to his room, shoves his hand up her skirt like and, the next thing, he's grabbed a big handful of knackers ...'

Horrified cries of 'Oh no' from the committee.

'Whereupon Glynmor goes absolutely potty and starts kicking the shit out of this sailor who's screaming blue murder.

At one stage he's trying to shove him out of the window, then he breaks one of those big bedroom mirrors over his head ...'

Committee clucks with choruses of approval at this.

' ... an' then the police come who arrest Glynmor and the sailor and take them away in one of those sit-up-and-beg police vans in which Glynmor starts hitting the sailor again. Then they're both flung into separate cells and Maggie goes down there in the middle of the night with some fags for Glynmor an' saying that it's their wedding night so can she sleep in the cell with her new husband.'

'Had she been drinking that bastard punch as well?'

'Well, they won't let her sleep with him so the next morning he's done three pounds with two pounds costs in Barry Magistrates for being drunk and disorderly and gets back to the hotel where they're wanting him to pay for the mirror he broke over the head of the queer boy. He refuses natural and next thing they're trying to get Maggie to pay for the mirror.'

'Bloody great honeymoon this is init? Made in heaven they said that marriage was an' all.'

'Well you haven't heard the best part yet. Maggie says she's not paying either and only then does it come out how the mirror got broke in the first place. She just thought it was one of Glynmor's fights 'cos she hadn't, in fact, known that the man was dressed up as a woman. So after they scrape her off the ceiling she's throwing things around in the hotel foyer -- everything she can lay her hands on and the manager rushes off to call the police again. Anyway, by now Glynmor has got his hair off so much, blaming the hotel for all his troubles, he picks up a great bunch of the hotel's keys, walks over the road and flings them over the cliff and down into the sea.'

'What did he do that for?'

'Well, you know Glynmor. Always does the first thing that comes into his head.'

'When the police arrive they chase him through Barry funfair but he's too fast for them and, after hiding under the scenic railway, he finally gets a bus home. They detain Maggie in the lock-up for a bit but don't charge her for anything 'cos she's so upset by the early collapse of her marriage and is saying that all she wants now is a divorce. They've still got Glynmor's suitcase at the hotel. They say he can have it when he pays for the keys.'

'Do you know boys,' said Alec Central Heating after hearing this story of thwarted love and passion, 'that must be the most romantic story I have every heard. The wife was down in Cardiff again last week to see *The Sound of Music* but Glynmor's story licks Julie Andrews' by a mile.'

Everyone agreed that it was one hell of a story. They just didn't write scripts like that any more. Even the chairman had put his gavel on hold as the sorry saga unfolded.

'So where is Glynmor now?'

'Maggie went back to live with her mother, Mr Chairman, and Glynmor is living where he's always lived, in Bomber's house. He's not been seen out at all – except late some nights in the Chinese takeaway. They do say there's been a lot of knocking and hammering coming from the house, so he's probably knocking the wall down to make a bigger living room.'

'Doing away with the front parlour is he? Always the rebel eh? You know I've been thinking of doing that f'r ages. Can you just knock the wall down?'

'You need an R.S.J. Twenty quid that's all. They do them in the new Do-It-Yourself shop in Porth.'

'Deliver them do they?'

The gavel came down with a resounding crack and the committee moved onto the next case: that of Danny Bits and Pieces.

'I really don't know how to approach this one,' said the chairman. 'But approach it we must since Danny is going around upsetting everyone with his daft behaviour. He was never sixteen ounces to the pound, what with his pot-holing under the seats during the dances, but, after his brother, Sam Swambo, died in that pit explosion, Danny has gone right round the twist. Speaking for myself I would just like to ignore it. As you know he has always been putting his watch in his beer and leaving to show that it's waterproof ...'

'Harmless enough Mr Chairman.'

'Yes that is harmless enough but now he's actually started washing his socks in the beer in the Starlight Lounge and upsetting the ladies no end.'

'He says it's because his feet do smell something terrible.'

'You know, boys, it might be something to do with the beer as well. It's not been too good of late Mr Chairman.'

'But what can we do? His brain can't be any bigger than a canary's.'

'That might be insulting to a canary Mr Chairman.'

'Well we've got to do something or else we'll be having everyone doing their laundry in the beer,' the chairman insisted. 'I suggest we stop his beer for three months and give him a stiff warning. Any disagreements? Right.'

The gavel came down twice signifying the end of the committee meeting.

Later that night, with the Welfare Hall closed and just Curly there in the queue waiting for Lee Hoo Wonk to make him some chicken fried rice, the sky over the Valley was a light blue canopy with the odd dark smudges of frothy clouds. Here and there the street lamps shone like matchless diamonds in the drifting mists. In such deep darkness even the pit looked like a gorgeous Indian temple, with shafts of light breaking out of its canteen and the white mists wrapped around the black girders like a ghostly ivy.

In the wheelhouse the banksman was reading the *South Wales Echo*. The news of the day was that there had been another night of violence in Ulster.

Down in the gulley behind the Hall a couple of sheep were trying to knock over a dustbin, the one with his shoulder on the one side of the bin and the other with his shoulder on the other, rather like a pair of Pontypool front row forwards packing down for the big push.

These Valley sheep were nothing like the fluffy balls of loveliness found in the nursery books. They were temperamental and not above biting you. Their coats, more grey than white, were criss-crossed with scabby scratches where they had been rubbing themselves on barbed wire or picking a fight with some local mongrel. In their eternal quest for food they would even climb up on one another's backs to scale a garden fence. Some desperate gardeners had even taken to putting the sharp end of nails through their garden doors to stop the sheep butting them down and getting at the cabbages. But the sheep's bony black heads were so hard that all that happened was that the nails were bent in half and the door opened anyway. When there was a funeral, sheep came from miles off for a good scoff of the flowers after the mourners had left. One animal-hating florist in Aberdare had recently taken steps to forestall such graveside banquets by offering to supply plastic flowers to all funerals. Like empty pop bottles, they would be returnable after the burial. But, most of the time, the sound of the sheep's munching gnashers was one of the authentic sounds of Bont.

That night Bont found itself a few more night sounds too. Danny Bits and Pieces, in despair at being boxed from the Welfare Hall, began potching about the gullies, singing hymns on the top of his voice. Like some bloody coyote in the middle of a vasectomy he sounded, said the boys in the bar, the shrieking off-key wails drifting up over the slate roofs of the terraces and down the walls of the Valley. Windows were opened and boots flung and oaths unleashed but still Danny wandered on in an unmelodious cloud of hymns and arias.

Meanwhile there were unfamiliar bangings coming from No. 9 Bont Terrace. Hammer in hand, Glynmor was busy knocking down the partition wall between the living-room and the parlour. Glynmor had always hated the idea of parlour but Bomber wanted the wall left intact. This bit of renovation was another way of dancing on the old bastard's grave. The house had been turned upside down and inside out but still they hadn't found the money.

Just over the road, in the doorway of the Co-op, Maggie was standing in the darkness watching Glynmor work. She was worried about his behaviour. People just didn't go knocking down walls in the middle of the night. Just what was she going to do with him? He made her heart ache when he was around and it was even worse when he wasn't. She was sorry now that she had left him in that hotel in Barry. After all, if she couldn't put up with a bit of drunkenness from a man she couldn't put up with much, could she? She hadn't been much of a wife, had she? She had just walked across the funfair, hopped on a bus to Cardiff and spent the night in the bus station there before coming home to Bont the next morning. The gossip, she'd heard, had somehow created some monstrous story of Glynmor fighting and wrecking everything. How she hated all this gossip with everyone forever gunning one another down with their lying sentences. This gossip was never correct, always cruel and spiteful. How she wished she could get away from it all and live with some dignity and privacy with her Glynmor again. Somewhere away from all those gossiping, lying tongues.

116

And there was another problem which was weighing on her mind and was going to hurl her right into the middle of a storm of gossip if she didn't watch it. After further examinations by Dr Edwards her pregnancy, it seemed, was much further advanced than she had thought. According to the doctor she was now well over seven months pregnant which hardly tallied with the time when she had lain with Glynmor on the river bank. Perhaps he really had pulled it out as he had claimed all along but then, if so, how had she got so far gone? That nasty doctor had even been asking her if she had been seeing any other men before Glynmor. As if she'd do such a thing. Well, she wasn't going to be seeing that doctor again. That was a fact that was. Oh Lord, she was even beginning to think like Glynmor.

P.C. Watkins rode past on his bicycle, glancing over at Maggie in the doorway, but not stopping to talk to her. He knew the troubles she had with her new husband. *Duw* everyone in the Valley had heard what had happened on that honeymoon. Handful of knackers indeed.

Maggie crossed the road and tapped on Glynmor's window. He came over and lifted the lace curtain. His face was dusted with white plaster from his labours but she could see straight that he was happy enough to see her. He wasn't exactly smiling but there was a sort of amused twinkle in his eyes. 'Hello lovely,' she said through the window, her lips almost miming the words. 'Having trouble sleeping are you?'

He shrugged and looked down at his hammer.

'What are you doing, then?' she asked.

He looked behind him. 'I lost the key to the front door.'

'Oh I get it. You lost the key to the front door so you knocked down the wall. Typical.'

He was back studying his hammer again.

She tapped the window. 'Have you been eating at all?' she asked. 'I've been worrying about you. Look, can I come in, can I?'

'Why should I let you in? Eh? Why should I? I have a few drinks and you leave me on my honeymoon. Who wants a wife like that? There's some gossip I went off with some queer in Barry as well. You know anything about that do you?'

She shook her head. She didn't. 'Glynmor. Just let me in. We can't talk through the window.'

'The door's not locked. It's your house as well, remember?'

She walked in through the hall and they stood facing one another over the pile of rubble. 'I've always liked one big room,' she said.

'Well, that's as well. I wouldn't know how to start building it up again.'

'Safe is it?'

'I suppose so. We'll soon find out won't we?'

She eyed the ceiling and took one step backwards. 'Are you going to put some sort of arch in here, are you?' she asked.

'Haven't thought really. What do you think?'

'Some sort of glass doors perhaps?'

'Perhaps. Are you staying with me tonight or what?'

'I could.'

'What do you mean "I could"?'

She smiled at him and he fell on her like the ton of rubble that came crashing down from the ceiling.

Chapter Ten

Autumn came stomping into the Valley like some harridan queen with a hangover. Screeching with cold showers of rain and belches of freezing wind she was, opening wider fissures in the high Valley walls, spitting hard on the terraces and even making the river break its banks, flooding the allotments and chicken runs and making Mrs Pryce's cockerel climb onto the roof of its shed where it strutted about angrily snorting at the effrontery of it all.

Occasionally the rain would stop and allow a brilliant column of sunshine to go marching the length of the Valley, infusing everything with a warming buttercup gold, making the asphalt in the streets steam. But then the dark clouds would gather again and disgorge yet more freezing rain. It was something and nothing weather, aye; fine and wet at the same time. Real Valley weather this was. Bont weather.

It was on just such a day that Rev. Mordecai was standing in the backyard of his manse with his binoculars, anxiously scanning the leaden, windy skies for the return of his pigeons in the Welsh Open. The birds had been released the day before in the Shetlands but where they had got to now was anyone's guess.

On fine days they always flew in up the Valley. On bad days they came in down the Valley. But, on such days as this, he just couldn't make out which way they would come. And they were very late. He checked his watch for the umpteenth time. They had to get back before dark or else the clock would be stopped at 4.30 p.m. and he would have to get up at dawn again. Pigeons did not fly in the dark.

Such days were a terrible strain on the other pigeon fanciers as well. Despite doctor's warnings, John Abdabs kept

119

racing his birds; and he frequently ended up in hospital during the racing season since all the excitement aggravated his angina. Even the pigeons would get tense too, sometimes flying around and around their lofts and refusing to come in. At such moments Mordecai would dance around below, frantically rattling a tin of corn.

His binoculars scanned the rim of the Valley again and again. Then his heart leaped when he spotted a whole group of them coming in fast and low over the outcrop on the south east wall of the Valley. Any second now he would feel the familiar, throbbing excitement as his birds peeled off from the group and headed home, flying at 1200 yards a minute, to have their rubber rings plunged into the timer.

But instead of unutterable excitement he felt unutterable dismay.

The pigeons headed straight to John Abdabs' loft built against the side of the cinema. If a man could have foamed at the mouth then old Mordecai would have done just that. So it was true then, the rumour that Abdabs was experimenting with the new Belgian method. All based on sex it was. The cock was kept in the next cage to his favourite hen and was thus encouraged to fly home fast so that he would be allowed to mate with her. If he flew home very fast indeed he was allowed to mate with a few more hens as well – as many as he could really. As a man of God the good Rev. could not condone the idea of offering to set up sex orgies for his pigeons in return for flying home first. Just the very thought of what was now going on in Abdabs' loft made him feel very ill indeed. Uncharitably, for a man of the cloth, he hoped that Abdabs' angina would play him up again.

It began pouring with rain.

I'm not saying a word but I heard that Glynmor and Maggie are getting a divorce after all.

Never. I thought they'd patched it up.

They do say he's cracking up with it all. He's always got his rag out about something and she's been going up to the cemetery late at night to talk to her father.

Her father's dead isn't he?

'Course he's dead. He's been dead for years but she always got on with him and goes there when she's upset. Sometimes her sister has had to go up there and get her to go home.

What's the matter with Glynmor then?

It's his nerves, they do say. He's been getting pills from the doctor and they're making him worse. Eats them like sweets he does.

When's the baby due then?

Well I'm not saying anything but it's due any day now. Two months three days before time an' all.

That baby's never his.

That's what he says as well. But a boy like Glynmor would wouldn't he? Common as muck.

That morning it was market day down in Pontypridd, the rain beating down on the tented stalls strung out along the twisted cobbled streets, all so tightly crowded together around the market hall it only needed a couple of prams and a wheelbarrow to start a traffic jam which would take an hour to unravel.

Maggie, heavily pregnant and loaded with shopping, had eaten some faggots and peas in the market before struggling to the exit. Smells jostled one another: mountains of fruit and china were piled high in the multi-coloured stalls and indefatigable traders were offering their never-to-be-repeated bargain. 'Today, 'cos it's Wednesday,' shouted one. 'I'm giving the stuff away, asking not ten pounds or five pounds but, look, three pounds – no, 'cos I'm feeling barmy today and it's raining, one pound four shillings for this, that and that over there ...'

Maggie hesitated, but only briefly, before forcing herself to walk on. Those traders had the gift of the gab all right. The last time she had stopped in front of one of them she had ended up with enough black shoe polish to last a lifetime. And she didn't own any black shoes.

Outside the market it was still raining heavily. Cigarette packets and bus tickets were swirling down the overflowing gutters in disorganised armadas, making their way to distant battles at sea. Even such torrential rain, however, did nothing to wash away the stink of rancid beer which hung around the doorways of the pubs. A jukebox inside the club was playing Martha and the Vandellas' *Rescue Me*. Oh yes, Maggie thought. Come on baby and rescue me.

When she got to the bus station the driver had no change for her pound, again, so she had to go to the newsagent's shop, change it there and wait for the next bus.

The engine of the Bont bus chattered and groaned and whined its way up the great winding gulch of the Valley, past the aerial ropeways and spinning wheels of the mines, past the rows of pigeon lofts and the colossal black pyramids of the tips. The air in the bus was as warm as the inside of a baker's oven and, when a man in the seat in front of her lit a pipe, Maggie thought, for a second or two, that she was going to faint. The mist on the windows was so thick you could barely see out. She rubbed a small hole with the ham of her fist and saw a dog sniffing at the base of a lamp post.

The bus stopped and started through the townships scattered around their closed mines. The lines of the terraces were as formal as drilling guardsmen, their dripping greyness relieved only by the odd dirty-white smudges of the starling shit nesting in the hissing gutterings. The Valley had long been shorn of all its trees; they had been used as pit props when foreign supplies of wood stopped in the Second World War. Here and there on the roadsides at the end of the terraces were gaudy coloured advertisements for Hovis bread and Guinness Stout. Water tanks stood on small plateaus of the Valley walls just above the towns like giant fawn mushrooms. A poster on a chapel noticeboard announced: JESUS HEALS ALL BROKEN HEARTS.

The journey wouldn't have been nearly so uncomfortable if she didn't have this huge bump to contend with. It was as if there were now two of her. Where once she had felt fat, she now felt positively elephantine. Glynmor was no help, of course, forever calling her Michelin Man and now refusing to so much as touch her. It was as if she had become defiled. It was a shame really, for in those all-too-brief weeks after they had got together again, she had found their love sessions a great source of pleasure and relief.

Even Glynmor seemed to enjoy them for a short period, until he was overtaken by the glooms again. No more jokes or dirty stories either, none of his bragging lies followed by the inevitable 'That's a fact'. He just went to work down the pit as usual before coming home to eat. Sometimes he'd go straight to the Welfare Hall and miss the meal, which Maggie then flung straight in the ash-can. She thought it a great pity that the committee hadn't boxed him instead of Danny Bits and Pieces who was driving everyone daft about the place as he potched about singing his head off. At least Glynmor would have stayed home more if he had been boxed. As it was they had barely got to know one another and he was forever prowling about the place like a bear with a sore arse. Oh how she hated him when he got like that.

The bus laboured past the clock in Bont Square and Maggie got off outside the chip shop, the misery loaming thick inside her as she lugged her shopping over the road. All her life she had dreamed so fervently of breaking free of this vulgar place with all its nasty gossip but now, married and pregnant, she was stuck in this hole forever. Perhaps Daisy had the right idea after all. Fun. That was all Daisy had ever cared about.

She pushed open the front door to find Glynmor stretched out on the settee, snoring with his mouth open, next to the electric fire. She shook her head and took in a long breath. There he was, a miner with free coal, and he was too lazy to make a proper fire. She had got in the sticks too, which is probably why he hadn't touched them. *He* liked to get in the coal and sticks. That was the man's job and everything else in the house was hers. Huh! Judging by his snores he's been having a long session in the club – the more beer he had, the louder were the snores. What was even worse was when he got his nose stuck into the whisky and those snores sounded like the first rumbles of an earthquake.

She took off her coat, sitting down in the armchair and turning the electric fire towards her, warming her damp hands as he turned over on his side whimpering and chomping his lips. She sniffed a soft snort. Although so young he already had a few of those small tell-tale scars of the miner on his face and there were still coal rings around the inside of his eyes. That was pure Glynmor that was. He did not like to soap his eyes in the pithead showers since too many uncomfortable things happened when you were temporarily blinded. They pinched your soap for one or else someone grabbed your big toe and began yelling 'Rat, rat'.

But, even with all his present moodiness, he was still handsome. That was undeniable enough. His looks had been her downfall hadn't they? In the fight of love she had fallen for

123

the real sucker punch. Like an idiot she had gone and fallen for his dark Welsh good looks. Just like an idiot. She had liked his impulsiveness too; the way he went straight into a fight when he got his rag out. He was said to be the fastest and deadliest head-butter in the valleys. A Glasgow kiss, Glynmor called it.

There was always something attractive about being a bit of a lad but these days he was far from being the star of the party. He had got unusually withdrawn and seemed scared of something. To make matters worse he didn't want to seem to talk about it either. Sometimes she worried that he might be in some sort of trouble with the police. But, whatever it was, he was keeping his mouth well and truly shut. He had been getting such a pain to live with she'd been on at him to go and see a doctor but he wouldn't.

She got up and went into the kitchen to make a cup of tea. On the window sill next to the pantry was the egg-timer that Glynmor had made out of Bomber's ashes. They had never found his money so Glynmor had insisted on him becoming an egg-timer. 'He'd never been any use while he was alive so let him be some use now he's dead,' was his cryptic explanation.

Every time she looked at the egg-timer she let out a soft sigh. What a sense of humour.

She brought the tea back to her armchair stirring it thoroughly as she let the cup and saucer sit, steaming, on her pregnant bump. Her thoughts about him got blacker. Looking around she noted that he had not even finished knocking down the partition wall properly and there were jagged lumps of bricks poking out from the broken plaster. It was strange being married to a man who had given up on all the normal activities of marriage even before it had begun. It wasn't so much that the romance had gone out of their lives so much as it had never come in. There was more romance in a dartboard. She sighed and sipped her tea again. But she was stuck with this snoring bastard and, to make matters worse, she had his child inside her. She would not mind if the child had his looks but prayed that was all it had. Living with two like Glynmor really would be a fate worse than death.

'Any chance of a cup of tea is there?' he said waking up.

'There's one in the pot.'

'On bloody strike again, are we?'

'Glynmor. I've had a long day shopping in Ponty. Now

124

I'm having a rest. If you want a cup of tea there's one in the pot.'

'There's one in the pot,' he mimicked. 'There's one in the pot. Can't you do anything at all woman?'

'I'm not your slave you know,' she said, half-rising and spilling her tea which splashed in small venomous hisses on the bars of the electric fire. 'I didn't marry you to be your slave.'

'Slave! Slave! That's a laugh that is. A great bloody slave you'd make and that's a fact. The other boys get sandwiches in their tins. All I had yesterday was a poxy Mars bar. Then I got some cream crackers and you didn't even bother to take them out of the packet. Some bloody slave you are.'

'You were lucky to get them.'

'Lucky!'

'Yes. Lucky. Pregnant women are supposed to rest. A normal man would make his wife stay in bed at times like this. Not send her shopping and asking her to make him sandwiches.'

'How did you get pregnant? That's what I'd like to know.'

'We're not back on that one again are we?'

'Yes. We are. That bastard bump of yours has got nothing to do with me.'

'I'm not listening to any more of this,' Maggie shouted, standing up and flinging her cup and saucer against the wall. 'I just can't take it any more.'

'Well go then.'

'I will,' she stormed picking up her coat. 'I'm off for good.'

'Goodbye.'

'Goodbye.'

The front door slammed and Maggie, half-ran, half-walked down through the rain which was gurgling out through the drainpipes and washing across the pavement in hurrying rivulets. She was so angry she could have screamed out loud; at the sheep, at the houses, at the Welfare Hall ... Screamed abuse at anything, all because of the sheer unfairness of being stuck in this dump and being married to someone like Glynmor.

She turned past the Welfare Hall when she saw the Cardiff bus standing at the stop, blue puffs of exhaust chugging out into the sheeting rain. That was it, she thought exultantly. She would go and stay with her Uncle Jack down in Cardiff for a bit. Luckily she had her purse with her; she had just enough to buy a ticket and sat down next to a young girl reading a paperback.

Just the very movement of the bus, as it pulled out of the square, made her feel better; just the knowledge that she was putting some distance between her and Bont in general and Glynmor in particular had an amazingly soothing effect on her anger. Oh, she hated the place so much and, just seeing all those tiny houses and that ugly pit slip away from her view, into the tadpoling raindrops across the window, she decided that she would not care if she never saw it again.

Even as the bus was hurtling beneath the Pandy viaduct she was working out a plan. She would stay with her Uncle Jack in his council house out in Llanedeyrn estate until she had the baby. Then she would find a job with some sort of live-in accommodation so that she could work and keep an eye on the baby at the same time. She wouldn't work weekends though. She would set weekends aside for the baby and, if she made enough money, she would buy a car and the two of them would go off for day trips to places like Porthcawl and Barry. No, not Barry. She'd seen all she ever wanted to see of that place.

Rainy allotments chased past pit village and derelict chapels when they stopped in Upper Boat before moving on again, down past the billowing steam and spurting fires of Nantgarw pit, hurtling alongside the swollen black waters of the River Taff and the turrets of Castell Goch (sticking up out of the autumnal trees) and, soon, the very suburbs of Cardiff with its marching lines of semi-detached houses, wide straight streets, lived in by all those strange people. Immediately she began to feel very nervous. Cardiff was nothing like Bont. This was a strange, hostile city that she knew nothing about. This was the city that was always bottom of the league for donations to charity and always top for crime. Here, she had heard, they would rob you and rape you then leave you to die in the street. Nothing for nothing in Cardiff. She spotted the towering white Victorian architecture of the museum, city hall and law courts. Her nervousness began turning into blind panic.

She rang her Uncle Jack from the bus station but there was no reply. Oh well, she thought, I'll set off and walk. He never likes to be out for long. He'll be back by the time I get there.

The rain had stopped as she cut back behind the station and crossed a litter-blown car park where a Chinese man was sitting in a car, looking at her. From inside one building she could hear the shrieks of playing children and, following a high curving wall, she came across the even higher walls of Cardiff prison. Both hands smoothed her bump as her eyes rose up the wall in sheer amazement that anything could be built so high. She remembered that Glynmor had always told her stories about Cardiff prison; of how one of his uncles was once locked inside there for his part in the Tonypandy riots. They were always so hungry in there they had to scavenge for food in the dustbins, Glynmor had said. Just what was she going to do about Glynmor?

She walked back down past the prison and took shelter beneath a huge railway bridge. A deep pool of rain had gathered in the hollow at the bottom of the road and, when the cars raced through it, their wheels threw out huge chutes of water whose noise was curiously amplified by the high enclosure of the bridge. Just past the bridge, on the other side of the road, was a vast hoarding advertising Brains beer. A lorry thundered past, throwing out an even larger chute of water which caught her around the ankles. She turned and turned again, now slumping against the damp hard wall and crying piteously into her hands.

'I can be of help to you, lady.'

Even in her distress she liked the sound of his voice immediately. It had warmth and confidence. More to the point, it was an offer of help which was just what she needed at the moment. But, when she looked up, she began shaking her head and was about to make a run for it since this offer of help had come from some sort of tramp with a bushy brown beard, the large watery eyes of a Boxer dog and dirty clothes which were more like sack-cloth. 'I really could be of help to you,' he said repeating the offer. 'I live over the road. Come and join me for some warmth.'

But then the impulse to run subsided and she just stood there gazing into the stranger's eyes. Quite what it was that he had she was not sure, but he certainly had something which took away her uneasiness. It was something strong yet invisible like unshakeable faith; something which offered hope to the desolate. It was the promise of hope that kept her there and,

127

after he had said a few more words, enabled her to have the courage to go off with a scruffy stranger like this. When there is a promise of hope to the hopeless you can do almost anything, she decided.

There also seemed to be something preordained about the meeting since, when he moved off, he did not even look around to check that she was following him.

The rain had returned, a drizzle with dim shafts of sunshine breaking through as the two of them crossed a main road and walked into the tiny terraced streets of Adamsdown where all the streets were named after precious metals. They came to Gold Street and the tramp pushed open the door to one of the houses which Maggie could tell immediately, by the musty smell, was derelict. He opened another door which led to a small kitchen, inviting her to sit down on a chair next to a small table covered by copies of the *Daily Mirror*. Great holes gaped in the plaster and a few of the floorboards were missing. 'I will make some tea,' he said. 'Make yourself comfortable.'

Maggie sat and watched gravely as the tramp filled up a billy can of water and put it on a primus stove. She just could not understand why she was so relaxed but relaxed she was – almost to the point of sleep. He took two cracked mugs out of a cupboard and just stood there waiting for the water to boil. His oddest feature, Maggie decided, was that he seemed to have no need to talk, even odder since she came from a village where they needed to talk all the time. But, when he did speak, it was in a voice so soft she had to strain to make out the words. 'Would you mind if I read your palm?' he asked.

'Not at all. I've never had my palm read.' She stuck out her hand immediately, like some small boy ready, and even willing, to be caned.

'I will finish making tea first,' he said. 'Put your hand down for the moment.'

On the wall, next to a shattered mirror, there was a calendar with 21 October 1966 marked with a cross. There was also no light, she noticed, wondering how he managed when it got dark.

'You are with baby,' he said bringing the steaming mugs of tea to the table. 'When do you expect birth?'

'I don't know. Soon though. I feel him moving around inside me a lot.'

'How does he feel?'

'Feel? He feels like any normal baby I suppose.'

'No. I mean is there pain with him? Or does it feel like, say, a smile?'

'A smile? Oh that's very nice,' said Maggie warming to him more. This was no Woolworth's tramp, that was for certain. Straight out of Marks and Spencer this one was. His brown eyes were fierce with intelligence and there was, somehow, a fragrance about him; not a soapy or perfumy fragrance either but something wilder and yet more subtle; something of rivers, trees and sunshine.

'Yes,' she went on, 'on some mornings, I do lie in bed and feel this lovely smile inside me. I don't tell Glynmor, that's my husband. He wouldn't understand anything like that. Tell me, what's your name?'

'John.'

'Been living here long have you, John?'

'Long? Yes, long. How often do you say your prayers?'

She smiled and blinked a lot but said nothing.

'You must say prayers Maggie. From now on there will be corners in your life only prayer will help you understand. Prayer will help you understand lots of things.'

'Would it help my marriage, would it?'

'Prayer helps everything and this baby of yours must be soaked in prayer right from the time of his birth. Let me look at your palm.'

He took her right hand with both of his hands and studied her palm with care, splaying out the fingers, shaking them and sometimes rubbing along her life lines with the tip of his forefinger. He seemed to take an age about it, and she began getting impatient asking if she could drink her tea. He nodded, letting her hand go.

'You must go home on the next bus and go to bed,' he said leaning forward slightly. 'You have the star at the beginning of the middle line. Lot of people have been waiting for the star. Baby is coming tomorrow. It will be a boy and you must always cherish boy because it will be a boy like no other boy.'

Her mouth went dry and she swallowed hard.

'Boy will be very different but never worry about that. He will also be under threat.'

'Threat?'

129

'Do not worry. There will be unseen eyes watching out for him. I will always be here too. Come down here if you need my help. Now, drink your tea. You must get home as soon as possible. Tomorrow will be our longest day. It will be long for everyone. When boy is born every eye will be weeping and every heart will be breaking. Every Valley will run with tears tomorrow.'

Maggie could feel a tremor in her hand as she drank her tea and looked into John's brown eyes. There were so many questions she wanted to ask but could sense that he wasn't going to explain anything even if she didn't have the slightest doubt that everything he said was true. 'Will you be around if ever I need you?' she asked.

'I will be here. But say nothing of this to anyone. Not even to your husband. The fewer that know about the boy the better.'

'John, I want to be a good wife. I want to love Glynmor more and I want him to love me more.'

He nodded and smoothed her cheek with his hand. 'You will find the love you want. After tomorrow there will be more love. But first there will be a great lament.'

Huge cartwheels of rain, whipped along by the winds, came rolling in over the rooftops of Cardiff. Milky, majestic thunderclouds belched over the castle and a shivering fork of lightning slashed down onto the twisted tubular shapes and squat furnaces of East Moors steel works. *Duw* there was wrath in the air that night. The rain was so ferocious they were going to talk about it for weeks and years to come. Another dazzling flash of lightning and, for a second, it seemed as if the very city had caught fire.

It was the second house of the Tuesday night bingo session in the Welfare Hall and the new bingo caller, Eggey Jones, was shouting out the numbers of the ricocheting table tennis balls. 'On its own number nine. Clickety click sixty six. Seven and six, was she worth it? Legs, eleven.' The silence on the tables was total, with some marking up to six cards, their Biros flashing up and down the pink sheets. Even the drinks were left untouched as those all-important numbers were read out. But the trouble was that Eggey's numbers were not very distinct, and there were occasional anguished pleas for him to put his teeth back in.

'You know, at that party, the greedy cow ate sixteen lamb chops,' the doorman was telling two women as they stood together feeding coins into the one-armed bandit.

'Sixteen! But she's no bigger than a whippet.'

'They do say she must have worms.'

'Worms! Snakes more like. Here. Got change of half a crown have you?'

'I didn't get invited to the party, mind. That's just what I heard.'

'Round here they do have a party for the death of a cat. I wouldn't go if they carried me there.'

'They'd need a dumper truck to carry you anywhere.'

'Watch your mouth now.'

From inside the concert hall there was a shout of 'House' followed by a widespread groan. That Madge Williams had called the flyer again. Just how did she do it?

The green baize of the snooker table was dotted with tiny white meteors of chalk. The white cue ball cracked into the black sending it shooting the whole length of the table where it caught in the jaws of the pocket. Bouncing heart-stoppingly from side to side, it finally stopped still just a hairsbreadth away from the all-important drop. 'Black be fucked,' Stan Swansea muttered to his cue. 'That's going to finish me that is.'

At the far corner of the bar Glynmor, his eyes already bloodshot with a few beers, was discoursing on the state of his marriage with his pals. 'You know I can only think it must be something to do with her being pregnant. I just never believed that anyone could be such a pain in the arse. Just everything she does gets right up my nose. Maybe that's what she wants. Who's to say? She gets in the coal and sticks − which is supposed to be my job init? − then she always leaves the coal door open, the rain gets on the wood and you can't get it to light. Then, when I come home, she's always sitting in my chair and, if there's one thing that drives me potty, it's the way she's always squeezing the toothpaste in the middle instead of rolling it up from the end. The silly cow can't even play the one-armed bandit properly. If she needs to hold a cherry you can bet your life she'll hold a pear. It's enough to turn a good man into a pansy.'

He picked up his drink, but put it down again as he thought of something else. 'If I'm not at home at the right time my dinner is straight in the ash-can. No messing about either. Whooosh. Straight in there. Not that it matters much 'cos she can't even boil an egg and that's a fact. Instead of putting sandwiches in my tin the other morning all I got was a Mars bar. Aye. One fucking Mars bar. Then she packed me some cream crackers and didn't even take them out of the bastard packet. Marrying her was the worse day's work I've ever done. She left me this morning, she said. I hope she's gone for good.'

'Well you're hoping in vain, Glynmor boy. I just saw her as I was coming in here. Soaking wet she was an' all. Better be careful. She's due any day now.'

'Shit!'

'You'd better get on home Glynmor boy.'

'I'll get on home when I'm ready. Who wants another pint?'

When he did finally get home he found Maggie sitting in her dressing gown with her hair tied up with a towel. And when she saw him come in through the door she smiled. Smiled! 'Hello lovely,' she said.

He just stood there smoothing the raindrops out of his hair as his eyes jerked around the room. She had lit the fire which was blazing in the grate. There was a pile of cheese sandwiches on a plate on the table and, just next to it, a jar of his favourite Branston chutney. There were a few bottles of beer on the television as well and, even more suspicious, she was not sitting in his favourite chair either.

A procession of emotions ... surprise, suspicion, guilt ... went marching through Glynmor's mind as he tried to absorb what she was up to now. Surprise at this upsurge of domesticity, suspicion about the motives behind it, guilt that he had been out in the Hall again while she had been trying to make it nice for him here. There was even some relief too that she had chosen to wave the white flag rather than push it deeper into some almighty row. It was this pregnancy that was making everything so difficult – without that they could probably just have knocked it all on the head and called it a day ages ago.

'I've just been having a drink with that Graham Pryce,' he said, picking a non-controversial subject as he took off his

132

jacket and sat on his chair just next to the fire.

'I thought he'd given it up?'

'Well you know him. Nothing by halves. But he wasn't rotten drunk or anything.'

'I've made you some sandwiches,' she said. 'I've got some beer as well. But you can have tea if you'd prefer.'

'I'm not bothered about tea. But I'll have a bottle of that beer.'

She picked up one of the bottles and poured it into a glass before handing it over to him. 'Tell me, what happened to Graham's wife? I used to like her. A real tidy sort she was.'

'No one knows for certain. I don't like to ask Graham. Mmm. These sandwiches are nice. Cheddar is it?'

'Do you know I'm not all that sure. I just asked for a quarter of cheese.'

The coals on the fire fell in on themselves in a gentle series of creaks, the small blue flames spurting across the bright red fissures. 'I'm glad I bothered to light the fire,' she said. 'I could watch coal fires forever. They're so pretty the way they glow.'

'You look like some bastard sultan with your hair done up like that,' he said sipping on his beer with his right hand while taking one of those sandwiches in the other. Then he spread his legs apart with the warmth of the fire settling over his belly feeling, perhaps for the first time, that marriage might not be quite as bad as he had always thought. 'I do want this to work out between us,' he said. 'I know it often doesn't look like it but I do want us to stay married. I think it could be good if we made a bit of effort.'

Maggie gulped at this sudden outbreak of common sense. She couldn't have agreed more but said nothing.

'I know I get all these bad moods and I'm a pain to have around but I just can't seem to help myself,' he went on. 'The real problem is that there's things going on inside me but I can't seem to explain what they are and I do get frustrated and bad tempered.'

'Oh I wish you would Glynmor. If you could only tell me about those ... about those things of yours then perhaps I could do something about them. We could do almost anything if only we'd talk about it. I do get fed up with all this rowing the same as you.'

'But I've never been able to talk about anything inside

here.' He gestured vaguely towards his chest with his glass of beer. 'I'm sorry girl but I've just never been able to do it.'

'Well, at least try, my lovely. I'm sure we can do anything if we try. Both of us now. Both trying like mad to pull it together. Because that's what we want. That's all. 'Cos we want it.'

Chapter Eleven

Swirling mists and yet more rain crowded into the Valley the next morning – a morning so thick and dark it was as if the dawn had decided not to turn up. Even Mrs Pryce's cockerel failed to bugle in the day, preferring instead to hang around, warm and dry, inside his hutch.

Glynmor was downstairs in just his trousers and vest, building up the fire which had held well through the night. Outside he could hear the sounds of milk being delivered. He turned on the wireless and Stevie Winwood was singing about how he was so glad he'd made it. You and me both, kid, Glynmor thought.

He held some newspapers across the front of the grate to make the fire draw. When it roared with the sudden inrush of air he crumpled the newspapers into a ball and flung them into the fire. Now he lit one of his Capstan full-strengths and coughed his way into the kitchen where he filled the kettle to the brim and put it on the stove before emptying the tea leaves onto the ash path out the back. After rinsing the pot he spooned in the Typhoo. Then, his eyes still puffy with sleep, he just stood there looking blankly at the wall.

The front door opened with a bang and he knew straight that there was something up. It was Stan Swansea who had never, ever walked into his house before. 'Better get your clothes on mun,' he said looking anxious. 'The call's gone out for men. There's been some big mischief over in Aberfan. Better hurry now.'

Glynmor grabbed his jacket and shouted up the stairs. Outside his door was a car with Emlyn Kremlin and Ted John North in it. Glynmor could tell from the white seriousness of their faces that something very nasty indeed had happened.

'Some sort of accident is it?' he asked climbing into the back seat next to Ted John North.

'A problem with the school we've heard,' said Emlyn as he accelerated up the road. 'Something to do with the roof.'

'It'll probably be cleared up when we get there.'

'It was serious we've heard. The word went around the pit for everyone to take their shovels.'

'Anything on the radio?'

'I heard nothing.'

Sometimes on the winding, twisting Valley roads the car came out on the very roof of the drifting white banks of cloud and the air was surprisingly clear with views of forests and distant peaks. But then, as if on a roller-coaster, they plunged down into the rain mists again, moving past faint outlines of shop, pub and terrace. The four men drove on in silence and, apart from the eager scrape of the windscreen wipers, all that could be heard was the doleful sound of a distant chapel bell.

'There's some very bad mischief up here today,' said Emlyn. 'I can just feel it in my water.'

'I've been dreaming of something bad for weeks,' said Glynmor. 'I haven't had them for a few nights but I've been getting these terrible nightmares.'

'I've heard you've not been treating Maggie very well,' said Emlyn with some real edge.

'Well, we won't go into that now will we?' said Stan Swansea.

'No we bastard won't,' Glynmor added.

They drove through the village of Mount Pleasant and down into the scattered township of Aberfan, a gloomy gathering of grey buildings, flung around a main street and at the base of a long brambled slope. At the bottom of the hill, just before a level crossing, they stopped behind a line of other cars. Men were stepping out of them carrying picks and shovels and hydraulic jacks, running up into the thick mists shrouding the village.

When Emlyn drove over a level crossing a policeman waved them down. 'Park your car over there, boys, and get on up to the Pantglas school. You've got to dig the children out.' The policeman had difficulty speaking his words. His eyes were red with tears.

Emlyn did not even bother to park his car properly and

136

was out and running across the field with a surprising lightness for a man of his size and weight. The other three took the shovels out of the car boot and half-walked, half-ran past a row of shops and along the main road until they came to what seemed like a black wall built high across the road. Figures were running back and forth and Glynmor stopped, his heart pounding, his eyes narrowing with the shock of recognising something both strange and yet very familiar. But what was it exactly?

A tiny woman, with tight grey curls and hands thrust down into the pockets of her brown mackintosh, was standing on the garden wall to get a better view of all the activity. Holding his shovel on his shoulder like a rifle Glynmor asked her what was going on. She did not reply so he asked again.

'The children,' she said. 'They're all in there.'

'How many is that?'

'All of them. Would you believe it? 'Course you wouldn't. Every child in that school is under that slurry there.'

He walked closer to the school and indeed was almost on top of it when he saw that it was no longer there. It had been completely covered by a wave of black slag which stretched right across the road. His vision swam with the monstrous dark shape of the killer tip. His belly lurched and heaved again and again with acid. He was sick again and again. So it was back in their hands again; yet another bill to be paid in the terrible cost of that bastard coal.

A man came running down towards him. 'We need that shovel up there quick,' he shouted at Glynmor. 'We've got to have as many shovels as we can. There's still a chance that we can dig some of those children out. There's word they've been hearing crying coming from up out of the classrooms.'

Back in Bont Terrace yet another shower of rain was washing around the tea leaves that Glynmor had flung out only that morning. The black leaves swirled around, clinging together in tiny black mounds as they were washed deep into the ash path.

In the kitchen, the kettle which Glynmor had left untended was still boiling furiously, the steam chugging up out of the spout and against the lace curtains on the misted windows. The fire was blazing emptily in the living-room, which Maggie had been gradually trying to transform from the

137

dull male stronghold of silly posters and ash-trays. She had thrown rugs over the settee and the mahogany armchair that she had always hated. She had put the odd painting on the wall and a spray of flowers on the window ledge. What she really wanted, when they got some money together, was to furnish the room in G-plan. The carriage clock on the mantelpiece said that the time was 9.25 a.m.

Upstairs in the bedroom where Maggie was still half-asleep the wireless was playing her current favourite, the Hollies' *The Air That I Breathe*, when the voice of the news announcer broke into the music. 'This is a news flash. Early reports from Aberfan in the South Wales Valleys say that a coal tip has fallen on a school there burying up to 200 children. The Civil Defence has been contacted and told to come with all the equipment they can muster. All the miners in the nearby area have been called to help in the rescue operation.'

'Oh God, no,' Maggie cried out, her throat clogging up and eyes swimming with tears. 'Oh God no. Let it not be true. Please let it not be true.'

'The nature of the rescue operation precludes the use of heavy machinery,' the BBC announcer continued. 'So the miners are digging out the children by hand.'

'Oh God please let it not be true,' Maggie called out, instinctively holding onto her bump. Suddenly she was almost doubled up with a shivering spasm of pain. Then she began getting strange bursts of cramp in her loins. 'Glynmor,' she called out, but he was nowhere around, 'Glynmor, where are you?'

'One report says that the tip moved over a mile before engulfing the school just after the children had gone into their classrooms after the school assembly.'

It had stopped raining by now with just thin mists curling over the grey slate roofs of Bont. The shops were empty, the Post Office closed and even the milk cart had been left abandoned next to the clock. The time was 10.05 a.m. Further up the sides of the volcano the mists were thickening up again so that the Valley rims could not be seen from below. With a white sheet of mist bearing down on the village it was almost as if great hands were coming down to wrap up all this grief forever.

With every fresh item on the news Maggie cried out in

horrified disbelief, her contractions coming on more regular now as her hands gripped the brass bed knobs of the bedstead behind her head.

'Early reports say that the tip moved over a mile and was over thirty feet high before engulfing the school. Just in the last minute the bodies of three more children were discovered.'

Glynmor found himself but one of three hundred miners and soldiers frantically digging down into that evil slurry. Matters had been made worse by a broken culvert which sent streams of water coursing down past the uprooted trees, broken water mains and ruined cottages, turning the slurry into a shifting glue which maddeningly stuck to their shovels.

'They do say the poor dab can hear his girl crying in there.'

'*Duw* an' he loved that girl so much as well. Waited for her every day after school he did.'

More men came with offers of even more help. As the minutes turned into hours they might have been a defeated army stumbling and staggering across a Second World War battlefield unsure of what or who they were supposed to be fighting. Their warm breath plumed against the cold air. Wellington boots squelched across the black swamps. About a dozen were trying to pull a tree away while a dozen more were trudging across the black, pocked slopes carrying sheets of corrugated iron on their backs. Yet another helicopter bringing in yet more members of the media came chattering up the valley, its swirling rotor blades making the hair of the workers almost stand on end. Ambulances were roaring in and out, and there was an endless line of lorries turning up from all over South Wales to carry away the slurry which was being loaded into them by chains of buckets being passed from hand to hand. Men were sweating and crying at the same time, their features unrecognisable in their stained dirtiness.

The grind, clash and bustle of the work directly above the shattered school would last for thirty seconds and then everything would stop as a whistle was blown. Each of the pauses was part of standard mine rescue technique when, for just ten seconds, silence fell and every ear listened for any cries for help from beneath their silted-up boots and shoes.

These ten second silences were the longest anyone could

139

remember or would remember. They were like great prayers that there would still be life in the tomb of death. Even Glynmor had the overwhelming sense of all the Valleys down on their knees in these silences, all holding their breath and praying with bunched fists held aloft for just one shriek, just one howl of pain which would tell of life. In those silences he just stood there, listening to the frightened pumping of his own heart. Even in his short life he had seen blood on the coal often enough but, as he looked around him, he knew that nothing could have prepared him – or anyone else – for this. This!

He plunged his shovel down into that foul-smelling black glue again, his whole body shivering and teeth chattering as if he had just caught a dose of 'flu and just couldn't get warm. At one stage his hands were shaking so much he could not even hold his shovel properly, letting it slip out of his hands with the handle cracking against his shin. Jesus, miners always expected trouble but not their babies. Not their babies as they sat in their classrooms only to be buried in slurry and killed before their young lives had even begun. His shivering kept up unabated and he finally had to put down his shovel and hold himself tight. Fortunately the others around him were too busy digging to notice him just standing there. His skin was goose-pimpling with something very strange too.

It was now 10.45 a.m. and the reason for his strange sensation, perhaps, was because he had somehow become aware that, at that very moment, on 21 October 1966, his first son was being born in Bont.

On normal days her sister or mother were always calling round Maggie's house to borrow a cup of tea or to bring a bit of hot gossip. But today was far from normal and no one had called over at all. By eleven Maggie had given up shouting for help and could feel the bump beginning to work out from between her legs. *Duw*, it was as if someone was trying to split her apart. Her fingertips fluttered around and touched the hairy head of her pain. She lay back, trying to keep her legs as far apart as she could. But, with each agonised contraction, she could feel a little more of the baby inching its way forward. And each time it moved, her legs twitched as if being touched by live electric wires.

But still, amazingly in such pain, all her mind could think

about was all those children drowning in that sea of black slurry. All she could visualise were all those small bodies swimming around and crying out with silent drowning screams. She too was swimming around in a sea; she was moving around in an ocean of immense and inconsolable grief. The pain of the Valleys was being driven through her heart like some giant wooden stake.

Now the slime-covered head and bunched fingers of the baby were just poking out of her vagina. Her contractions had stopped. She just lay there, panting and crying softly, for almost twenty minutes, still torn apart with misery as the news continued to wash over her.

'The rescue operation has now been under way for nearly two hours but still no one has been brought out alive. Parents offering help have been told to go away and let the miners deal with the rescue.'

She just kept her legs apart and lay perfectly still. She was not at all sure what to do anyway. The tears ran hot down her cheeks.

A van piled high with jangling new buckets from a hardware wholesaler came slithering and sliding down the main road leading up to the destroyed school. As people came hurrying up Moy Road to help unload them and pass them out, no one noticed the Secretary of State for Wales, George Thomas, walking with an ashen-faced Lord Snowdon. Another body had been found, someone said and the word swept around the village.

'Did the girl say anything?'

'No mammy, she was sleeping.'

The whistle blew again and the policeman with a loud-hailer called for silence as everyone held their breath just listening to the creaking thumps of their breaking hearts. In one of the gardens in Moy Road an old miner stood in the garden looking down unseeing at his cabbages, his eyes wide and transfixed with sheer disbelief. A man of the chapel all his life he was asking himself if they finally were putting the children of the earth to the sword? Was this the start of the age of prophecy when the all the first-born must die first?

Glynmor was now working feverishly with his particular group when a cry went up nearby and they hurried over to prise up a blackboard. As they eased it up children's drawings fluttered in the breeze like dead leaves. When the blackboard finally came clear they found one of their teachers lying on his side, holding two children in his arms. Another child had fallen just near the teacher's feet. He had clearly been using the blackboard to try and shield them from the black tide.

Glynmor averted his gaze, the bile rising in his throat. Even though the sun, with brittle irony, was now beating down on Aberfan his vision was darkening. Even though breathing on the sharp morning air he felt himself drowning in the suffocating blackness. Like Maggie he too could see all those small bodies swimming around. He too could hear all those silent cries as their lungs struggled for air in that terrible darkness.

Blankets were held high as the miners picked up the black and broken bodies before placing them on stretchers. Glynmor stepped forward ready to help but there were already enough willing hands. Miners had long learned how to do the most unpleasant things without flinching; it was only later in the privacy of darkness that they did most of their crying. After the teacher came the children. One of their small hands was holding an apple, still ripe, red and shiny in all that dripping slime.

The sun had now risen high in the sky and Glynmor looked up at it, holding up his dirty arm to create a shadow. Just then something huge and dark seemed to move inside the fiery heart of the sun, growing and growing more until the whole of the sun had gone quite black. In the thickening darkness he couldn't see anything at all, though he could hear the sounds of some singing. But there was no fear in him as there might have been with someone who had lost the use of his sight. He was quite calm and still holding up his arm when the light began growing again and a dark spot was still coming out of the sun except that, this time, he could see clearly that it was another helicopter clattering down from the top of the tip. He wiped his eyes with the back of his arm.

Maggie let out an agonised cry and the baby burst forward from her in a tumbling mass of flailing limbs. Its legs and arms opened like an unfolding flower.

Breathless and close to exhaustion, she sat up and looked

at it, unsure what to do now. Where was Glynmor? Where was Daisy? Where was her mother? Where were these people when you needed them? The thick umbilical cord dangled from the baby's belly like a fat tail. The little sausage between its legs told that it was a boy. She recalled the strange words of John the tramp: 'You will always cherish the boy because he will be a boy like no other boy. There will be unseen eyes watching out for him.'

But she did not pick him up. She knew what every mother knows at such times. This boy was like no other because this boy had been born dead.

'The body of one of the teachers, Mr David Beynon, has just been dug out of the tip which engulfed the school at Aberfan,' said the news announcer. 'He was holding two children in his arms and others were dug out near his feet. It seems he was trying to protect them with a blackboard when the tip burst through the classroom wall.'

Tears spurted from Maggie's eyes and, biting her lip, she reached forward to pick up the ruddy splodge of her dead son, holding him in her arms and bathing him in the salty tears of her total grief. The baby's death was right somehow. Who wanted to bring a child into a world where they poured tips over the schools? Well, you were the lucky boy then, weren't you? Out before you were in. That's the way it should be, isn't it my lovely?

She gazed down at her son with her tears still pouring over his beetroot, almost angry, face, smoothing his thick thatch of greasy hair with her palm and now recalling those words she had first heard in Sunday School. 'Our Father which art in heaven,' she recited softly beginning the Lord's Prayer, 'hallowed be thy name; thy kingdom come, thy will be done on earth as it is in heaven. Give us this day ... ' She smiled and ran her hand under his chin. 'Give us this day a son for us to love.'

She stopped speaking and blew soft on the baby's mouth, now washing his cheeks and lips with her tears. Just then the baby's body gave a sudden shiver and, with his fingers bunching tight, his eyes opened and gazed up into hers with a long mysterious look which made her shiver too.

'Was the girl crying at all?'

'No Mammy. I said – I said she was sleeping.'

143

Outside in the backyard there was a furious fluttering of wings, so loud they made Maggie jump. She looked over at the window and then down at her baby again, feeling no fear. Rather a great gladness had exploded in the midst of her grief and she felt released from all her pain. She was the warm woman now, replete and happy holding her new-born in her arms.

Sunshine breezes were now gusting down the Valley, bustling and vaulting over the backyards and small sheds built of odd planks and asbestos sheets. Maggie's backyard had a small lilac tree next to the broken fence and, just near it, was a cucumber frame which had long lost its glass. A pile of breeze blocks stood next to a zinc bath with the washing line nailed to the roof of the coal shed and stretching to a small metal pulley on the wall of the house. The breezes were making the washing line sway drunkenly when three pigeons came down to perch on it, their wings hovering in a blur around their pink chests as they tried to hold their balance like tightrope walkers. They stayed there for, perhaps, three minutes, then flew away again.

Even as night stole on Aberfan its soothing blackness was denied. The sights which the village had witnessed could not be so easily veiled. They had already erected giant sodium lamps over the ruined school. Moths were attracted to their ferocious glow and sent small shadows dancing over the broken ribs of the school which poked up out of the still, black tide. Men were still labouring on; every part of Glynmor was aching, not so much from a day of shovelling the black glue, as from struggling to move his feet around in the stuff.

But when he did take a break, other men moved quickly to take his place. Legs like rubber, he lurched down a slope where a W.V.S. woman with burly arms served him a buckshee mug of tea out of a silver urn. She gave him sandwiches too so he took the opportunity to walk away from the disaster area and find somewhere quiet to be alone.

The rescuers were still taking the bodies out of the slurry and carrying them down to Bethania, the chapel of death in Moy Road, which was now being used as a mortuary. Nearly a hundred children had been dug out. And some of the teachers too. Glynmor stopped briefly, watching the crowds of anxious parents standing outside the chapel, hoping against all the odds that it was not their little one who would be laid out on the pews; that, somehow, their child had decided not to go to school that morning and jumped on a bus to go somewhere else. In the gilded darkness, still throbbing with generators and ceaseless effort, Glynmor turned around the back of a terrace and climbed up the side of the mountain until he came to a grassy bank where he could sit and sip his tea. At this distance the school had the gaudy, almost raucous atmosphere of a circus or a funfair. At least it had stopped raining. The rescue work would have been hopeless if they'd had to contend with more rain. It had been hopeless enough as it was. None had so far been dug out alive. He bit into one of the sandwiches and spat it out. It was spam; he'd always hated spam. A quick look into the others showed that they were spam also. He flung them all to one side and drank his tea. He had not been hungry anyway.

Another whistle sounded and all activity stopped for another ten seconds of silence. Here and there white smoke was drifting up against the darkening sky and a dog was howling, distantly and incessantly, as if in pain. Further away yet there was the noise of distant traffic in some distant Valley going about its distant business. The whistle blew and the shovelling began again.

By now Glynmor was too tired for anger, too tired for bitterness, too tired to even think straight. He just felt like every other tired rescuer in Aberfan that day; damaged beyond words, overwhelmingly defeated, aye. He covered his eyes with one hand as if in prayer.

'I thought it was you sitting there mun.'

Glynmor looked up startled. It was Emlyn Kremlin.

'Just came up for some fresh air,' Glynmor said. 'You know I fancy you can smell death in the air everywhere down there. It's in the slurry. It's almost like you can taste it.'

'You're right there, boy,' said Emlyn sitting down next to him. 'You get to know death in this game. Death has no mystery for the miner. He lives with bastard death all his life. Some of those old miners could hear death in the way the pit props did creak.'

They both sat looking down at the school in silence for a while. That dog had stopped yelping but now a few men were shouting, their angry voices curiously amplified by the desolate Valley night. There was a rustling of fat shadows nearby.

Sheep had found the sandwiches.

'It's bloody marvellous init?' said Emlyn finally. 'We used to beat children for sleeping down the mines. Now we pour slurry over them in the classrooms. You should get more political Glynmor. You drink too much and have got plenty of filthy gab but you should get more political and fight this sort of thing.'

'How can you fight this, mun? How can you fight all those fucking bastards who've done this? There's a century of neglect lying on that school.'

'Yes, but neglect by who?' Emlyn wondered. 'Those champagne socialists in Westminster? Those twots around here they call M.P.s? What happened to the Labour Party? That party was born in these Valleys, Glynmor. That was the party everyone fought for but then it went and died on us. We need new leaders, mun. Men with fire and guts. I know you Glynmor. I see what you are. You should look at that school and think of doing something.'

'Think of doing what?'

'Of standing forward and doing something, that's what. I'm getting old now. I can't do much any more.'

'Old be buggered. You'll still be fighting the management when Maggie and me are pushing up the daisies.'

'I need to know there's some men coming after me, Glynmor. I want some disciples. Men like me need to think we've got someone to hand the torch on to. You're young and you haven't been shocked enough yet. Be shocked by that school mun. Be desperate and angry about it. Let your guts boil in rage 'cos I'm telling you now there'll be a lot of hot air but precious little else when all this dies down. Now the Labour Party has gone to sleep on us there'll be no one to orchestrate our rage; no one at all to stand up and scream about our pain. In my time there'd be a whole revolution pouring out of the Valley after something like this. But not any more. We've been made sick by all our handouts and lies from Westminster. We're confused and have lost our pride. We've lost our anger, Glynmor. Someone like you should step forward and lift the flag for us. You should become more political and give us lessons in anger and feeling. That's what we need most in the Valleys now.'

Glynmor said nothing for a change. Such words had come

as something of a shock. He had worked so hard at being Jack the Lad it had never once occurred to him that he could be anything else.

Yet another helicopter came in, chattering low over the valley; moving one way and another before taking off again without landing. 'That was the Queen's visit, I s'pose,' said Emlyn. 'A quick rattle of her diamonds and she's gone.'

On distant parts of the mountain, banks of sightseers, many with lamps and torches, were building up like long lines of glow-worms, yellow on black, in the darkness.

'We'd better get back down there,' said Emlyn. 'You know my old body has all but fallen to bits but I'd never be able to sleep if I lay my head down. Not with a ton of sleeping pills and twenty pints would I. All that's keeping me going now is a drip-feed of bitterness.'

Glynmor stood up and followed the old miner down the slope. 'Tell me, Emlyn,' he asked. 'Is it true that you sent a telegram of congratulation to Mao Tse-tung when he took over China.'

'I did.'

'What did he say? Did he ever write back or anything?'

'No but every Christmas I do get a Christmas card from the Chinese Consul down in Cardiff.'

'I didn't know the Chinese went in for Christmas.'

'Neither did I. But, you know, I do send him a card every Christmas too.'

'Well don't that beat all? Two bastard Commies sending Christmas cards to one another.'

When they had walked back up Moy Road there was still a large crowd of parents outside Bethania Chapel, waiting anxiously for their turn to go inside. Many would queue all night until that bitter dawn when the last of the children had been dug out. Emlyn had stopped to talk briefly with a woman he knew when there was a commotion. A photographer was being kicked across the road. Word had gone around that some Press men had broken a window at the back of the chapel to photograph the dead children laid out on the pews.

What they had seen was the broken heart of Aberfan. They had seen and photographed some twenty-eight adults and more than a hundred children lying there on the hard wooden pews; all those small broken bodies with their faces dirty with slurry, their hair blackened, their lungs never to draw on the fresh mountain air again … those beautiful mouths … jammed full with silt … never to … never to laugh again.

Somehow Emlyn and Glynmor managed to push their way inside. The aisles between the bare, shocking pews were black with muddy footprints. A lone figure was kneeling at the altar. Even in the smell of the polish and the dull tang of coal this sense of death hung in the very air, as real and as oppressive as the yoke it would forever become. Even just standing there with his hands trembling and looking at the small heaps on the pews, Glynmor's mind told him to refuse to believe what he was looking at. Until he saw a small hand sticking out from beneath a torn sheet, clutching at a sixpence; until he saw another still clutching a birth certificate; until he saw another hand with small lifeless fingers stretching out and clutching nothing at all. And his throat choked and his eyes misted over and yet his mind still refused to believe what he was looking at. Here on these pews was the ultimate obscenity: the murder of children who were young, beautiful and without sin.

'I need disciples Glynmor. Be shocked by what you're looking at. Let your guts boil in rage. We've lost our anger, Glynmor. Worst of all we've lost our pride. The Valleys have gone on a long walk and forgotten their deepest feelings, lost the love that always made them special, lost the politics of brotherhood that made them the finest. Just look at all these lovely dead flowers, Glynmor, and tell me what's happened to our self-respect. This is how every Valley child will end up unless we rediscover ourselves. Look at all these lovely, dead flowers, my brother, and never forget.'

Footsteps echoed in the chapel rafters as a mother almost marched up the aisle. She almost marched because she could not walk. Had she tried to walk she would not have been able to at all; she would have been like her husband who just lay down on the kitchen floor unable to get up again. So she marched this, the longest march of her life and, when she looked down at the body of her daughter, she knew that she would be broken for ever. All she could do was swallow hard and march straight out again, bumping into the pillars and bashing through the swing door of the vestry as if she was on some sort of automatic pilot where, with her sight swimming, her legs gave way and she fainted, to be caught by two pairs of strong hands before she slumped towards the tiled floor.

Glynmor could almost feel his own legs giving way now. A mother and father had come into the chapel and stood briefly, their arms round one another, before moving shakily up the aisle. They hardly dared to look from side to side. A policeman came and pointed at a pew near the baptismal font. When they looked down on that child their hearts seemed to stop beating too. For that broken scrap was their blood. What broke the children broke the parents too. None of them would ever recover.

There was not one mother or father who stepped into the Chapel of Death that night who would not have, happily and with the greatest gladness in their hearts, been inside that school on that morning of mass murder if, by some bleak transaction, it would have meant that their own children could have been alive and free.

It was speckling lightly with rain when Glynmor returned to the spot where he had been working just above the playground. They were still not using any heavy machinery and yet more men had turned up. He waited patiently, his shovel in both hands, for someone to tire and step aside. Even in such a crowd no one spoke; a constant flow of empty and full buckets circled around.

After more than twelve hours of digging the men had given up their ten second silences. They were just going like hell now. Even in all this noise there was a strange sound issuing from the earth, a car horn which continued blaring, maddeningly, for hours until the battery had run flat.

Two men in front of Glynmor stepped aside and he had only just plunged his shovel into the black glue when he felt someone gripping his arm. He turned his head to see Stan Swansea, out of breath.

'Glynmor, I've been looking all over for you,' he panted. 'It's Maggie. She's been taken to hospital, she has. She's had the baby, mun.'

Glynmor looked down at his shovel. This day was becoming far too much for him. 'She's all right, is she?'

'She's all right, yes. But there's been complications. You'd better get over to the hospital. Don't worry about here. It's the living that need you now.'

'Did you hear if it was a boy or a girl, did you?'

149

'I didn't but you'd better get over there fast.'

He handed his shovel to Stan Swansea and walked down to one of the ambulances, hoping to hitch a ride over to the hospital in Church Village. What a day this was turning out to be, he thought as he pushed his way roughly through a bank of sightseers standing near a glowing brazier. A day without end, aye. He heard something and looked up into the night. It was that singing he had heard earlier ... mellow, gusting ... the hymn of a sorrowing wind.

The following Sunday the Rev. Kenneth Hayes, who had lost a child in the slide, stood in the pulpit of his Baptist chapel in Aberfan. 'Let us thank God that things were not worse,' he began. 'We must not be bitter, but we must approach it with a spirit of love. Let us be thankful for miracles and thank God for those who survived.'

Chapter Twelve

Ever since that day, a century ago now, when Rupert Posthumous Evans bought the mineral rights to Bont farm and a gang of sinkers dug a shaft right in the middle of a wood alive with nightingales and squirrels, there had been grief in the Valley. No sooner had the sinkers brought up that first lump of steam coal when old Posthumous himself fell down the stairs of his house and died of a broken neck, leaving his widow and three sons to develop the mine and an early taste for living in bungalows.

Almost from the first month of its operation the pit had been dotted with disasters. It was the grief these accidents created which contributed in no small manner to the very spirit and texture of the community.

For, in ways difficult to understand and even more difficult to explain, they seemed to help strengthen the community by bringing it closer together. Those who mourned in the Valleys — and there were many — observed this phenomenon at almost every funeral from that of Teddy Davies, the cobbler, to that of Mrs Elme Thomas, the chapel-cleaner: the way in which grieving hands of every persuasion came together to heal the hurt. And strange and wonderful things happened in this healing process. Men became better husbands and women became better wives. There was even a more loving, prayerful spirit in the chapel with many going who had not been there for years. Branches of the family came together with other branches of the family with whom they had not spoken for years. In a positive way grief — as much as joy — was the very mulch of the community: it was as if all those tears sprang from the same wound; as if a pain shared was a pain dealt with.

At such funerals it was as if, deep in their grief, they were being told by silent, if insistent, voices that there was but one life which was as short and as a straight as a bit of rope. And in this life there were no rehearsals. At such funerals, then, it was time to put a poultice over the boils of long-festering insults and reach out to one another – in love. There would always be days for fresh insults but, just for now, it was the moment for putting your arms around one another and enjoying love's capacity to heal.

Except that no such process happened in Bont after the diaster in Aberfan.

Everywhere, from the Welfare Hall to the Co-op; from the washery to the time office; from the back seat of The Bug to the counter of the Chinese takeaway, it was the same. The shock of the loss of those children had turned to numbing sterile grief and the bitterness of acid tears. On the first day they gathered in small groups on corners and outside shops … silent, stricken, full of pain. And on the second they were much the same and on the third, and the fourth. As time dragged by and the winter stripped the slopes of the Valley, the villagers of Bont recovered little of their old vitality and ebullience. Men simply hung around, hands thrust deep down into pockets and shoulders hunched, not even drinking or swearing much, their spirits broken just as surely as if they had been smashed by a hammer on the anvil. The women went about their business and gossiped less, always keeping a particularly watchful eye on their own children, making sure they always got home before dark and giving them a good clip across the ear if they didn't.

Each had to handle the shock as best they could; either taking to their beds, or to drink or, even as Madge Williams did, taking a long holiday over in Shrewsbury – where there were no coal tips – and from where she sent a letter to Cynthia saying that she would never return.

But the most visible and obvious effect on the village was to be seen in the attendances at the Libanus Chapel which almost immediately plummeted from a few dozen to around half a dozen. Never a great success story at the best of times the chapel had now hit rock bottom and even old Mordecai, who had long felt that it was coming anyway, could hardly believe it when he looked out on that sea of empty pews on Sunday mornings. He even lost three of his deacons who just stopped coming. If Evan Roberts had presided over this chapel when it was at its height and strength, then Mordecai was surely now presiding over it at the time of its death. But it was hard for his parishioners. He could see that. He just didn't know how to stand up in that pulpit and make any sense of Aberfan and God's reasons for allowing it. Wisely he never tried but, anyway, it was by now all too late. People had made their decisions and voted with their feet. At least it left him with a lot more time to work on his book about the Great Revival and, his principal passion, his racing pigeons.

Yes, something vital had got up and walked out of Bont after the Aberfan disaster. You could not be sure what it was exactly except that it had gone. Even The Bug, which had been struggling for years in a mortal fight that with upstart television, succumbed and was boarded up. In a desperate ploy to boost attendances they had even managed to get in *The Sound of Music*, which had been breaking all records in Cardiff that year, and Stan the Box confidently predicted that the film would do even better than *Cosh Boy* which still held the box office record. But it was not to be. With so many children dying under a black mountain of sludge no one was in the mood to watch Julie Andrews leading her laughing tribe over the sunny Alps of Austria.

Come bonfire night, and the last performance at The Bug was a melancholy affair. Two couples over from Porth grappled and steamed in the back row while the six other people in the audience tried to ignore them. Then, when it did look as if Julie Andrews was going to get away safely, Gnasher and the Clay Class – taking a break from a nearby bonfire party – dropped Jacky Jumpers off the balcony and for one awful moment it looked as if those Nazi bastards were actually gunning down poor Julie and all her singing brats. Even the grappling lovers stopped to look up as the usherette chased the Clay Class down the street.

The next day, rather than face bankruptcy proceedings, Stan the Box left Bont on the first bus. Although gossip had it that he'd been carrying on with Madge Williams no one was ever to see him around the village again.

With no one coming to him on N.U.M. matters – what was there to complain about after Aberfan? – Emlyn Kremlin spent a lot of time brooding in the Welfare Hall library which had still not yet been sold to the University of Wales. Emlyn found the presence of all those books on the inevitable breakdown of capitalism some sort of consolation and he was going to be very sorry indeed when they did go.

He was always first into the library in the morning too, waiting for Tudor to fit the newspapers into their wooden spines and then reading, with mordant interest, how each paper treated the story of Aberfan. He watched it over the weeks, going from the screaming headlines of page one to the small paragraphs on the bottom of inside pages and then out of mind. 'Well, out of the capitalist world's mind,' thought Emlyn, 'but not out of the Valleys.'

The Press turned its attention to other matters. 'Just listen to this,' said Emlyn to the dinner-time drinkers as he skimmed the mid-day edition of the *South Wales Echo*. 'A 45-year-old man was remanded in custody yesterday pending psychiatric reports. Despite persistent warnings, the man, John Tasbib of Adamsdown, Cardiff, continued immersing children and tramps in the river, the court heard. The man, who has a history of schizophrenic disorder, was remanded in custody for fourteen days. He was said to suffer from paranoid delusions of a religious nature, according to one doctor. He was very persuasive in getting the children and tramps into the water, being observed on four separate days dipping them into the waters.'

Emlyn flung the newspaper across the table. 'The biggest disaster in Welsh history and all they can write about is some fruitcake and his crackpot theories.'

There was always something in the news to make his bile rise. Now there was the royal appeal for toys and teddy bears which had all but engulfed the village again. Archbishops, who would be hard pushed to tell you the actual colour of coal, wrote angry letters to the Press. Then there was the appeal fund itself, which soon attracted a million pounds and was leading to endless internal rows in the village. Even then Emlyn could see it was going to turn out to be a disaster almost of the magnitude of the killer tip.

A tribunal was set up to discover the reasons for the disaster and, again, Emlyn was careful to read the Press reports each day. It turned out in the end to be the longest in history,

154

lasting five months, hearing 136 witnesses and listening to 2,500,000 words recorded on 4500 pages of transcript. Sometimes, in his anger, Emlyn practically stabbed a hole in the newspaper with his forefinger. Here it was again, the endless, cultured braying of many people busy trying to shift the blame onto someone else; an ocean of words in search of a reason which could be swiftly dumped on someone else's doorstep.

The reason was simple enough: capitalist greed and socialist weakness. The rich, who had once plundered the Valleys, were strong and the poor, who had been abandoned after the plundering had finished, were weak. End of tribunal. Discovery of reason for accident. Q.E.D.

If it wasn't raining Emlyn might go to the bench near the clock in the square and sit chatting with the old-timers. They would all sit there together and watch the comings and goings of the villagers or nod a greeting to whoever. Maybe they would just try and work out what old Guto was trying to dig up. A day rarely went by when Guto wasn't wandering off to some distant corner of the Valley where, like some demented badger, he would proceed to dig a sodding great hole in the ground.

'That old Guto do work harder than any miner I've ever worked with,' Emlyn would say. 'What's he trying to find? Is there some gold around here that we haven't been told about or what?'

On some mornings the melancholy quiet of a Welsh mining village going about its lawful business would be suddenly interrupted by a red and white helicopter turning this way and that over the great black tips. The sound of the rotor blades would crack against the rock walls of the Valley and the old-timers on the bench would watch it, saying nothing. After Aberfan the cry had gone up to reclaim the Valleys. It was too expensive to remove the tips, they said, but grass was cheap. So they would grass them over instead. But everyone in the Valley knew that not even radishes would grow on those black slopes – and radishes will grow in pure arsenic. So some bright spark in the Welsh Office went back to the drawing board and discovered that grass grew well in chicken shit. A fleet of helicopters duly arrived and were even now streaming up and down the valleys spraying them with chicken shit.

The very sight of them made Emlyn's boots dance about

in rage. 'Look at it,' he would shout at the old-timers on the bench. 'They drown our children in coal slurry and now they're trying to gas us with chicken shit.'

As if the stink of chicken shit on every corner was not enough the same grey functionaries in the Welsh Office let loose a hurricane of empty rhetoric and documents about the way ahead for the Valleys. Learned papers examined the nature of the communities; orators spoke of the need for the provision of multi-purpose sports complexes. Experts argued new socio-economic strategies; the planners outlined how the infrastructure could be restored.

The result of all this urgent sociological bullshit, Emlyn raged, was that even now a third of the youth of the valleys were unemployed, another two mines, the Bwlch and the Ferndale No. 3, were due to be closed early next year and the valley communities were continuing to disintegrate on every level.

'And what are they doing about it?' Emlyn would go on at the old-timers as if, somehow, they might be able to set up a little parliament on their bench and legislate all the Valleys' problems away. 'I'll tell you. Not a thing. All my miners want is to drive a new car or lie on a fitted carpet or rot in front of a colour tele. Even the ones that *can* do it won't. Look at that Glynmor Jones. With what's happened to him and his family you'd think he'd do something but he won't. There's his baby still struggling for life in intensive care 'cos they couldn't get that doctor to come after he was born. And we all saw old Bomber dying by inches 'cos of the dust. But Glynmor won't do anything. None of them will. They just make jokes all the time and there they are with chicken shit running in over their wellies. *Duw*, boys, am I the only one who can see what's going on in these cursed valleys?'

Maggie brought her baby home from hospital two days before Christmas. Something quite remarkable had happened to her in hospital as well. She had shed all her excess weight and, with a large full bosom and legs like a greyhound's, Glynmor had the gravest difficulty in keeping his hands off her. 'I could barely wait till the nurse got out of the ward,' he told the boys in the bar. 'When I did get on her the nurse actually came back in as well. She just said, "Oh if that doesn't get her right then

156

nothing will." '

To almost everyone's surprise – not the least to Glynmor's – he seemed even dafter over the baby than Maggie, actually taking him out for a walk in the pram on his first day back in Bont. He pushed the pram up the slopes with a cheerfulness that made some of the old-timers shiver with shame. In what he said and did he was almost acting like a man in love. From head-banging drunk he seemed to have changed into a doting, loving father who was a pleasure to know.

In the weeks that Maggie had been in hospital, even the dimmest observers in the village had seen a change come over him. When he had not been visiting Maggie or actually working down the pit he had not been going out at all, staying at home busily plastering and painting the new extended living-room, flinging out that old mahogany armchair that Maggie had always complained about so much and going down to Maskrey's in Cardiff where he shelled out for a new G-plan three-piece suite on the never-never. He also bought a plum-coloured fitted carpet which flooded every corner of the space-age room in a wine-dark tufted sea. He was even doing the shopping. All the gossip had it now that he was really cracking up.

It won't last long you know, Aunty Phyllis told Enid. I know our Glynmor, up one minute, down the next. His father was just like that you know. A devil for the horses he was. One week he'd be riding around on a new motor bike and the next he'd sold it and didn't have enough for the bus fare. Erratic. All that Jones family have been erratic. But where did he get the money from for that G-plan suite that's what I'd like to know? From Johnston's in Swansea he got that. Money like that doesn't grow on trees does it? Perhaps he found all those thousands that Bomber salted away. Yes. It's true that is. Thousands Bomber was worth when he popped his boots. Trefor, up in the garage, said it might have been a million.

December was the coldest anyone could remember. The thick night frosts lingered right up to the middle of the day when it would finally be melted by the thin cold sunshine. In some parts of the Valley the frost never melted at all and the huge boulders perched on the Valley walls seemed to have been dusted with finely crushed diamonds.

157

But that Christmas everyone had made an effort: ceilings were thick with gaudy trimmings, Christmas trees with coloured fairy lights stood guard behind the net windows of the front parlours. The sheep came wandering up the gullies looking for food and warmth. At this time of year they were fed too, instead of being driven back down the Valley slopes. The villagers even threw their scraps out to them and a few even obligingly turned over their own dustbins. Daisy – ever the soft sentimentalist – went so far as to put out a plate of mince pies for them. It was after all, Christmas; the time of the birth of the Lord of love.

The pit was closed down for three days over Christmas. On Christmas Eve the manager laid on a party for the boys on the afternoon shift. Even Emlyn Kremlin went along to the canteen for it and was actually civil to the manager. He could hardly have been otherwise since even a diehard Communist had to make an effort, standing, as he was, with a glass of N.C.B. whisky in one hand and an N.C.B. chicken sandwich in the other.

It was getting dark when the party broke up and some thirty of them, many still wearing their miners' safety helmets, walked along the mile-long road back to the village. The bleats of the sheep echoed out of the dark surrounding tips and, with their bellies glowing with a lot of fiery Scotch, they sang Christmas carols, their warm breath pluming in the shafts of their lamplights, their words somehow amplified by the cold stillness of the bright moonlight and transported high over the roof of the village where the quiet, blue smoke from the chimneys curled in the moon-varnished night.

In the square outside the Welfare Hall the singing miners were joined by yet more villagers, moving now onto some of the minor-key hymns of old. John Abdabs, one of the finest tenors in the Valley, led *Abide With Me* and more and more doors opened as that fatally beautiful hymn rose up to meet, warm and melt the stinging coldness of the night.

Glynmor, who had been sitting with Maggie roasting chestnuts, went out to stand at the door. He was just wearing trousers with a vest and braces dangling on either side but, strong and fit as he was, the cold did not bother him as it might have someone who had not spent all his life working in the damp and cold. Maggie came and stood next to him, holding

158

him around his waist, resting her cheek on his shoulder as the impromptu choir continued to swell. Now they moved into *All Hail the Power of Jesu's Name*.

Maggie just couldn't understand what had happened to Glynmor. He did not even seem to want to go to the Hall for a couple of pints of beer. What was even more puzzling, he wasn't complaining – or bragging – about it either. All he'd say was that he'd got fed up with the Hall and preferred to stay in with Maggie and the baby who, for the moment, they called The Boy since they were deep in an official dispute about his proper name. Glynmor wanted to call him Jampots but Maggie was having none of that and was holding out for Huw.

Glynmor also seemed to have abandoned all that old nonsense of him not being the father as well – even though the dates of the alleged dirty deed up on the river bank and the actual birth had never remotely matched up. In fact he just seemed to be hovering around the cot all the time waiting for The Boy to cry when he would be picked up and taken to Maggie's overflowing breast. He took immense pleasure in watching the baby being fed; in the small red fingers reaching out expectantly, the trickles of milk running down the side of his blotched hamster-like cheeks, the steady chomping of the tiny lips. And when he had been fed it was Glynmor who took him in his arms, as gentle as if he was about to fall to bits at any second, now patting his bum until that bright burp of wind erupted. Maggie always clapped theatrically when he managed that.

The hymn-singing continued, with yet more joining in. Never slow to miss a trick, the boys from the Clay Class were even now out knocking on the terrace doors demanding money. They served to bring out yet more poeple to join the choir and quite soon almost the whole of the village was crowding into the square.

Communities grow around their traditions but nothing like this had ever happened before while Emlyn, in particular, was pleased that they could still respond to one another; that they could still enjoy the carolling ease of good singing. The surging voice of a choir had always been the perfect expression of the Valleys at ease with themselves and happy with its future. There had been little singing lately and particularly after Aberfan. Wounds like that take years to heal. It takes a lot of song and drink to heal up a wound like that, Emlyn thought.

And yet ... and yet he could sense that they were strangely happy about something. These sad minor-key hymns were always the way they expressed their happiness. Miners had always gloried in the glamour of sadness and, if a hymn wasn't sad, then it wasn't considered any good. If they didn't make you cry then they were no fun. Those songs of pain were their way of telling everyone that they were happy.

But were they? And, if so, why?

Emlyn was not sure. He felt something else in the night air; something which was not quite requiem but not exactly aria either. There was a trembling in pit props which was telling of something strange. A cloud passed over the face of the moon, briefly throwing the choir in the square into darkness before the light took over again, making everyone seem either black or white or even ghostly. He held his hand over his mouth tight.

John Abdabs led another hymn when the Boy began snuffling sending Glynmor and Maggie hurrying back indoors, she narrowly beating him to the pram when she picked him up and held him to her cheek. 'I'm so happy Glynmor,' she said. 'It's got that all I want to do is laugh all the time. You remember how I was when we got married. This morning I had to go out to the coal shed and have a quiet laugh. This is going to be the happiest Christmas of my life.'

'The happiest of all our lives and that's a fact,' he said holding out his hands, trying to take the baby off her. 'Here, shall we give him some beer or something shall we?'

'Certainly not.'

'Sherry then?'

'Certainly not. I don't want him growing up a drunk like his father. Speaking of which, why don't you go out for a few pints? I won't mind.'

'No. I told you. I said I'll stay here with you.'

That night they went to bed early and The Boy whiffled and snuffled in his cot as they made love, warm and slow.

'You know that bit when I come,' Glynmor said later in the darkness. 'I always think of a crowd of drunks barging in through a pub door at opening time.'

'Really?'

'The whole lot of them come charging in and then start

falling all over one another – bing, bong, bing – just like skittles.'

'You should have been a poet Glynmor. I bet Dylan Thomas never thought of anything like that.'

'What do *you* feel when you come?' he asked.

'Oh. I don't know.'

'Go on. How do you feel?'

'I feel … I don't know … I don't feel like anything really.'

'I'll tell you another thing as well. I can't decide whether your fanny smells of performing seals or fish fingers.'

'You're such a smooth-talking lovely. You should write all these gems down you know. Glynmor Jones. The great poet of the Valleys. Can't you just see all your collected poems on the shelves of the bookshops?'

'Do you think?'

'No, I don't think. Fish fingers indeed. And stop talking filth in front of The Boy. I don't want him growing up with a mind as filthy as yours.'

'Why can't we call him Jampots eh? Anything you want for his second name.'

'Never. Not ever. And take your hands off me Glynmor Jones. You've had your Christmas ration you have. It's like coming home to some over-sexed animal it is. I'm fagged out with it all.'

'What do you want to call him anyway?'

'I told you. Huw. And it's no sex for you till he is called Huw. So get your hands off me now do you hear? None. No drunks banging through doors. No smell of fish fingers. Nothing. Get off.'

'Stop shouting girl.'

'I'll shout if I want. You really make me mad sometimes.'

'If you don't stop shouting you'll wake Huw up.'

A long silence as she lay looking up at the dark outlines of his face. 'Glynmor,' she said. 'Why don't we have a few more drunks banging through a few more doors? And another thing. Don't compare me to the smell of fish fingers is it? If you must, compare me to a performing seal. I've always liked seals I have. Saw them in a circus in Cardiff once.'

'You're enough of a bastard circus on your own girl.'

Strong winter winds were now roaring off the high rocky screes of the Valley, sometimes dislodging a stone and making it bounce and dance off the rocks until it fell onto the road. The winds rattled against all the windows too, shaking them endlessly in their putty surrounds or else pushing up and down on the gutterings of the terraces, like a plumber looking for weaknesses, or even sometimes managing to work free a slate and send it crashing down into concrete patios in the back gardens. The winds seemed to be busily at work in every single corner of the village, if not down in a gulley bumping around a few empty chop suey cartons then up at the Post Office whistling in the mouth of the red postbox or else simply dashing across the very heavens, shipping the dark clouds before them through the moonlight.

The winds were so cold they had even driven the impromptu choir into the Welfare Hall where even now they were carrying the sounds of the continuing hymn singing into every part of the night. But you could only ever pick up the odd phrases as they were blown across the roofs or blown sideways up the slopes. There was no continuity in the sorrowing melodies but there was sweetness in abundance and, as they drifted into Glynmor's bedroom, they even woke up baby Huw whose eyes opened and looked at the ceiling.

The colour of his eyes was not visible in the darkness but, on closer inspection, there was something else; something strange and even magical. There were faint shooting lights in those eyes; sparkly lights that changed colour from purple to orange and green. They were unbelievable colours, almost like a tiny firework display seen from a great distance away.

There was a soft puttering noise too – the racing beats of his heart and the occasional soft sigh which, when listened to closely, sounded like the sigh of an old man.

But then both the lights and the sounds disappeared and all that could be heard were the breathings of his mother and father with, on occasion, Glynmor lifting an elbow into the air and then letting it fall again. Outside the winds were still bustling the length and breadth of the Valley as if looking for a way out.

Christmas Day was a joy; muted, perhaps, but a joy nonetheless. The strong winter winds had wandered off to ransack another Valley while great spinning tops of sunshine came whirling down from the reservoir, dancing gold on the hurrying river, slipping through the gaunt, black shapes of the silent and abandoned mine and running amok around every corner of the village where almost all of the children were up and about the pavements, showing off their new toys, pedalling their new cars down the slopes or wobbling about the place on shining bicycles far too big for them.

Back indoors, the elders were staring into the grey painful dawn of mighty hangovers. The rich aroma of roasting turkeys and cooking vegetables seeped out into the backyards, making even the wandering sheep slaver at the mouth. Some had gone to Oboe Parry's house for a quiet sherry while others, looking for the hair of the dog, were even now waiting outside the Welfare Hall, ready to fall in the door when it opened for the midday session.

The service at the Libanus Chapel that morning was the oddest ever. Rev. Mordecai, as was his custom, waited in the vestry to welcome his parishioners except that, this morning of mornings, only six old ladies turned up – each wearing flowery hats and carrying huge handbags. At one point he was almost tempted not to continue with the service at all but, when he did, his sermon was something of a classic of defeated bitterness.

He began by explaining that the valleys were clearly going through a long dark night and that it seemed to him that the disaster at Aberfan was merely a prelude to all sorts of other troubles which were going to engulf the people and make them cry out for mercy. It was, he continued, clearly a just and fitting punishment for a people who had given up on God and taken to adultery, bingo and the drink. A just father could not allow such behaviour to go unpunished; a just father was a disciplinarian also and what we were seeing was merely the beginning of a long chastisement which was going to be unbelievable in its fury and intensity.

There were few real options open to us, he went on, except to wait on the Lord's infinite and tender mercy. There was no point in even behaving like Moses who prayed that God would change his mind. We now had to face what was due to us and, when it became too bad, the only possible way of salvation was for us to have another great revival when, with glad hearts, the whole nation would turn again to God.

In the absence of that, he said, we can only stay good and keep our faith as best we could. Anyone who read the Bible would know of God's marvellous sense of timing and so we had to believe that the right moves would indeed be made at the right time. Mordecai added that he would now be withdrawing though quite from what he did not explain.

Afterwards, in the vestry on the way out, Mrs Muriel Price told the Rev. that she did not think much of the sermon. She went further. She added that it was the worst sermon that she had ever heard.

'I'm sorry to hear that Mrs Price,' said Mordecai. 'It was a sermon about the complexities and mysteries of the ways of God. You clearly didn't understand what I was saying.'

'I understood well enough. You were telling us that God sent us Aberfan to punish us for all the adultery you say is going on everywhere. Well, let me tell you there's no adultery going on in my house. If you'll pardon the language, vicar, you were talking a load of old balls.'

'Well I don't pardon that language Mrs Price,' said Mordecai, a man of the most spectacular piety when he wanted to be. 'I don't use that kind of language in my father's house so I don't see why you should. But, if you'll excuse me, I want to lock up the chapel now.'

'The trouble with you vicar is that you've got sex on the brain and that's not a very good place to have it,' Mrs Price went on, undeterred. 'The only one to enjoy the sermon was Mrs Pandy and we all know she's as deaf as a post. Well, someone's got to tell you haven't they? This used to be a great chapel – all my family went here they did – but you're driving them away with your daft remarks. Well someone's got to tell you haven't they?'

The Rev. retreated into the chapel, unwilling to confront this outbreak of nastiness any further. He had never understood why there were so many idiots in Bont; even more puzzling was how Mrs Price, the biggest idiot of them all, kept coming to his chapel when everyone else had clearly decided to stay away.

'People don't want to hear about your cruel and unjust God,' Mrs Price shouted after him in the chapel. 'They want to hear about a God of love who forgives all.'

'Please don't talk like a turnip Mrs Price.'

164

'Who are you calling a turnip? That's a tidy language from a vicar, isn't it? That's bloody tidy that is. Vicars are supposed to speak proper and there you are calling me a turnip.'

'It's perfectly simply,' Mordecai rallied again. 'If you don't like what *I* say in *my* chapel then stay away. Do you think I would cry if you didn't turn up here again? Can you see that? Can you see me in my pulpit crying into my handkerchief because a bunch of turnips haven't turned up to hear a sermon they are too thick to understand.'

'You'd better watch who you're calling a turnip you had. If you weren't a vicar I'd hit you sick with this handbag I would. I've never liked you either. None of us have. Ever since you came here with your bloody pigeons you've been nothing but trouble.'

'Look, I want to lock up this chapel. There's things I have to do.'

Meanwhile the Hall had filled up quickly. It being Sunday opening hours on Christmas Day most of the men were trying to get down as many pints as possible before the bar closed at 2 o'clock sharp. There were a few women piking coins into the one-armed bandits but most of the wives were still back home putting the finishing touches to their turkeys or thickening up the gravy with the backs of spoons.

The crowd at the bar suddenly divided as Guto walked up to the counter asking for a bottle of Guinness. He only ever came in once a year, did Guto, as filthy as ever, and had one bottle of Guinness. The way all the other members moved away from him, as if he had some new African pox, did not bother Guto in the slightest. He got his Guinness and went to sit out in the library to drink it alone.

Here, Dai. Did you hear what happened to Gnasher this morning did you? He got this airgun off Daisy for Christmas he did. Went out this morning and Trevor the Copper took it off him in the street. If you're out on probation then you're not allowed to carry a gun, Trevor the Copper said. I'm not saying he's right. I'm just saying what he said. An' Gnasher is going mad over it. Daisy has gone to the police station asking for the gun back.

That old Snipe Wilson is going to need a police station

before he's through. Heard have you? Do you know what the daft bastard went and done? He went to Aberdare yesterday to get the Christmas meat like. He goes an' 'as a few beers in the pub and someone gives him a tip for the 3.30 at Newmarket. Absolute cert it is.

Never.

Anyway the dopey sod goes into the betting shop and bets his Christmas turkey on a horse that's got three legs and is still running around the track. Hang on now. This is the best bit. Snipe decides to confess all to Doris so she asks him what happened to the pork chops. You know what he did? He used the pork chops for the betting tax. I ask you. Pork chops for the fucking betting tax.

Dopey git.

Aye. He did. Doris flipped her lid an' he's gone off to live with his aunty the last I heard.

Well I'll tell you something else boys. We're going to have to do something about this bastard vicar of ours. He's got duck eggs in his duck eggs he has. There's practically no one going there and this morning he was calling the women a load of parsnips.

Go on with you.

He was. He kept on calling them a bunch of parsnips all the time. Muriel Price was real upset with it all she was. He threatened to hit them too. On my baby's life. I heard she said that the sermon was the stupidest sermon she had ever heard an' he threatened to beat the shit out of all of them.

He used those words? Him a vicar an' he used those words? You're pulling my leg mun.

On my baby's life. Mind you he'd have to grow a few feet before he started beating the shit out of our Muriel. Have you seen those arms of hers? But that's what he threatened right enough.

Why are you pinching my bastard fags all the time for? Buy a bastard packet will you?

What's the matter? Poor are you? I'll go out singing carols for you with a tin mug.

You don't have to go singing anywhere. Just buy a packet of fags. Where's Den anyway?

I don't know. How should I know? Last I heard he'd gone to a party at Sandra's and no one's heard of him since.

166

Tell me Dai. Just when is this school closing anyway? One minute it's the school, then it's the railway line.

Well it's both, I heard. But they haven't fixed any dates yet have they? They say they're going to keep the junior school and send the seniors to Tylorstown.

It was the other way around, I heard. They were doing away with both schools and sending all the kids to Treorchy.

Treorchy! How are my kids going to get all the way to Treorchy?

Well they can walk like every other kid can't they?

Not the ten miles to Treorchy they can't. They have enough trouble walking out the back garden for a piss. If our Billy goes to get something in the shop he's got to come home and have a lie down for an hour after. There's more life in a bottle of pop than my lot.

You know, boys, I really am very surprised that Glynmor hasn't come in for a few pints. Today of all days.

A chorus of ayes and sighs.

I really miss him when he's not around you know. He was such marvellous company too, a real bad bugger. And fight! You know, Dai, he'd fight a brick wall if it upset him. He was even banned from the Chinese takeaway once for fighting in there. An', as it's Christmas Day, I won't even start telling you what happened to that Pole's bollocks when they got down to it in the pit once. He reduced them to a tiny pile of jello he did.

The Pole still walks about the place like Hopalong Cassidy you know. He's so bow-legged you keep looking around for his bloody horse.

But he's really fond of that new baby of his mind you. Look at the way he went down to the hospital every day while she was in. An' he's been out taking it for walks. When did you ever think you'd see Glynmor wheeling a baby in a pram?

Well I'm not saying anything but I heard that Maggie has won some money on Spot the Ball in the *Echo*. Glynmor's just being nice to her till the money comes through.

Never.

It's true that is.

Never.

That's what I heard anyway. She's picked up about four grand from The *South Wales Echo* so he's not saying boo, bah, bob's your arse till the money comes in. He's been getting into trouble lately. I'm not saying anything but I heard he's put some piece up in Penrhos in the pudding club.

Get away.

Well you know what he's like. A leopard doesn't change its spots well does it? Glynmor always said that he'd fuck a frog if it stopped still long enough. So he'll be needing Maggie's money to pay the girl off won't he? It's only commonsense init? He doesn't want some bint standing outside the pit, at the end of the shift, holding a baby in a shawl an' shouting it's his. Well does he?

They do say Glynmor has had more nookey than Tom Jones. How many women do you think Glynmor has fucked in his life?

Well he always said he wanted to fuck a million before he dropped. I shouldn't think he's too far off that. Aye. A real bad bugger. I really miss him, you know. Him and his stories. You remember the one where he fucked that piece up in the big house on the corner. I still laughs when I think of that. Anything from eight to eighty he said he'd fuck. Him an' all his bastard stories. There was never any truth in any of 'em you know. He could never open his mouth without telling a lie.

Dead pigeons, all with their necks pulled, lay around the floorboards of Rev. Mordecai's loft. Already their eyes had filmed over with the milky blue gauze of death. Some of their beaks were slightly ajar as if about to pluck a worm out of the grass. Their wings were crumpled with the feathers sticking out untidily so that you could never have guessed that these were once great flying machines of the air, ready and willing to fly through thousands of miles of sky to return home. Home here. Home sweet home.

Now they were just lying there, a defeated army in the aftermath of a total rout, amidst the muddy white splashes of their droppings. Their wings were still, their eyes blank, their radar cut off. All dead now. Here in home sweet home.

Inside the chapel the Rev. Mordecai was standing on the altar all twirling elbows and wrists, polishing the communion silver with a white cloth, occasionally holding it up to the light to ensure that he had taken off all the fingerprints and wine stains. It was the fingerprints that worried him most. Those hands that had defiled the sacred silver. Satisfied, he then put them away in the corner cupboard beneath the board announcing the hymn numbers. He tidied the sheet music on the old harmonium before picking up the few hymnals dotted on the pews and placing them in a neat pile on the table next to the vestry door.

His movements had an exaggerated sense of slowness about them, all somehow as if he had to do everything at the right moment and in the right way. There were lots of tiny white feathers attached to the sleeves of his jacket, a dribble of bird droppings on the front of his trousers.

He stood on the backs of the pews near the walls and went around drawing each of the thick curtains, blocking out the thin light of Christmas afternoon. When he had finished and the dark shadows had huddled together in every corner of the chapel he took the large metal key out of his jacket pocket and locked the front door from the inside in a series of soft revolving clicks. Now he returned back down the aisle, stopping for a moment, as he held the key out in front of him, to look up at the pulpit where the Bible sat closed and shrouded by darkness. He had spoken many words from that pulpit.

But no more.

'Lord come back to us,' he prayed aloud, holding up the key towards the pulpit with both hands. 'We your servants are weak and everywhere your enemies are strong.'

He stayed still as if waiting for a reply and, when there was none, he shook his head in some secret sorrow before putting the key into his pocket and shuffling out of the chapel and back to the coal-fired warmth of his manse.

The body of one of the dead pigeons in the loft shivered suddenly as if being touched by a live electric wire and then it fell still again. A wing on another pigeon lifted slowly before collapsing down to the boards again. Even so early in the afternoon the light was breaking up fast with thick cold shadows stretching down the valley walls.

And so, that Christmas Day in 1966, the Libanus Chapel, set high up on the south east face of the Valley, just on the edge of the village, became a place of death and long winter shadows. The damp darkness inside the building became so musty you could practically eat it. Mould grew on the hymnals and cobwebs fanned out on the windows. Most of all the place missed the sun.

When it was sunny the sun glowered on the opposite face of the Valley all morning. Then, as the sun moved around on its high wide circle, it did briefly shine on the grey slate roof of the Libanus but never for longer than an hour since it quickly dipped behind the outlying pile of jagged brown rocks of the *cwm*, plunging the chapel into yet deeper shadows. The sun came late to Libanus and then left early.

And that was on sunny days. Most of the time it just rained.

Part Two

The Song of the Cave

Now the steelworks are silent
Cenotaphs, memorials to a nation's
Earnings but not its wealth,
And the dead pits, graves that
Echo with the ghosts of young
Men's laughter and flood
With widowed mothers' tears.
My grandsons will not inherit
My blue scars nor the coal that
Has filled my chest and chained me.

Gwaed, Bob Reeves

Chapter Thirteen

The hard yellow vein of sandstone just appeared in the black coal face, as welcome and inappropriate as a streaker at a funeral. The cutting blades of the Dosco sparked and stuttered; the engine sent out high-pitched squeals of frustration. There was just no way those blades were going to eat into that sandstone with the men having difficulty getting their handpicks to chop around it to loosen it a little.

It was the way it had been for days with this Meadow seam. The shift had been asked to make forty feet in a week and, indeed, got off to a flying start, getting out ten feet on the first Monday. After that everything that could go wrong with a heading went wrong. First the seam changed its gradient and began moving upwards turning the working floor into the texture of puddings. Then they had to use special hydraulic jacks to shore up the sloping roof which slowed them up yet again.

Now they were working a one-in-seven slope on a 200-yard seam and this thin yellow yawn in the face had come and dashed all hopes of meeting the shift target.

Such coal as they had been winning had not been up to much either. Some of it had even looked like ash, as if it had already been in the fire-grates and was about to be thrown out. By the time it had gone through the sieving process at the washery there would be very little left to burn.

The engine of the Dosco was cut off and the men changed the positions of the chocks to see if that would help. But it was no use. Again the blades began chattering into the sandstone, slashing on the vein again and again but barely making any impression at all as the engine howled and screamed dementedly.

This lack of progress was spelling out a lot of trouble for the already troubled shift. In their ceaseless search for higher quotas the N.C.B. was now asking for 1800 tons a shift a week out of the pit and, over the past two years, the Bont mine had developed three faces: this one, the Meadow B2; another face on the Six Feet and another running down to Trelewis. These faces had been productive enough at the beginning, maintaining high quotas and keeping the Bont mine open as the other mines in the Valley were all closed, one after another. (Danny Kettle from Porth reckoned that he went through three mines in 1969 while he was still on the same bar of soap.) But last year a squeeze had developed in the Trelewis face and, no matter how many rings they put into it, the roof seemed to insist on coming down, buckling everything in sight until the work there was finally halted and the face abandoned.

So now they were only working the Six Feet and the Meadow B2. Plenty of coal was coming up out of the Six Feet, but hardly enough to keep the pit viable, so a lot was riding on the Meadow, with Emlyn Kremlin, hardly an N.C.B. lackey, telling the men that they must make their quotas.

And now this.

The Dosco was pulled back again and the men stood around in a group with the lights of their helmets shining on the obdurate wall, revealing in the bright blackness the long yellow sliver running through it like a map of the Ganges, perhaps, or even a vein of gold. Except that there was nothing precious about sandstone.

'Why don't we drill it and blow it up,' suggested Tom the Nutter.

No one said anything because no one ever took any notice of anything that Tom the Nutter ever said. Indeed no one had ever figured out how Tom the Nutter had ever got a job down the mine in the first place. You didn't need a degree to work down here but even N.C.B. officials could see that the Nutter was very thick indeed. He had always been called Tom the Nutter because he was nuts and never showed any sign of improving either. He had, however, become Glynmor's new sidekick and they spent most all of their working time together, if not actually studying the topless model on Page Three of The Sun then sharing the contents of their snap tins. Glynmor had found long ago the Tom the Nutter's missus was marginally more creative with a snap tin than his Maggie.

'We'd better call up the manager,' said Glynmor.

'What do we want that silly bastard for?'

'Well we're going to have to see him sooner or later.'

'Perhaps we could pick it for a bit to see if it improves?'

'We could cut it out there,' said the shift foreman. 'But we're going to have to call the surveyor.'

'That won't improve it,' said Glynmor. 'Not that. This fucking rock is only going to lead to more fucking rock.'

His boot kicked out in a gesture of futile bitterness. How he had come to hate this bastard coal. He had been working down this mine for close on eighteen years and he could still remember the times when it had been like a family with its own customs and soft jobs for the disabled. They had been good days too, with men always covering up for the others and familiar with the routines of a friendly management. He could still remember those mornings when the men had been happy to go down the hole and work on a heading where all was jokes and laughter in that warm shawl of brotherhood.

But today nothing could be less likely. This was another Britain. This was the monetarist year of 1980; an era of high productivity quotas and economic efficiency. If it did not make a profit then it was to be butchered. If it was ailing it had to be booted hard like a dog. Everyone was feeling the chill monetarist winds – even that morning shift now staring at a sandstone-ruined face on the Meadow seam.

It wasn't just hostile economic and geological conditions that they had to work against either. A 1967 redundancy scheme allowed those over fifty-five and the disabled to make fast and profitable exits. These old miners had been the keepers of the culture but, as they retired and the other mines in the Valley were closed, younger miners came flocking in. These boys knew nothing of the mine's customs and cared even less to learn them. They would probably be driving their new cars somewhere else again next year. These were the young cowboys of the industry, mavericks who would never stop anywhere long enough to learn about the secret language of the pit props. All they were keenly interested in was the size of their wage packets.

But, even with such problems; even with every rotten mine in the area now closed and almost half the Valley youth unemployed, the pressure on the Bont pit to turn out high quotas was enormous. Men with stopwatches and clipboards would turn up suddenly on the face. There was a lot of talk about 'disturbance' allowances; redundancy in disguise, the old guard called it. They'd seen it all before too. This was nothing but the old hated piecework scheme, believed eliminated in the National Power Loading Agreement of 1966 but now back again and raring to go. Even more insidiously, junior managers with English accents kept making random checks on places like the stores looking for anyone trying to get their head down under a blanket.

Yet, happy or not, the boys did get down to their work, knowing that, if the new quotas were not met, it would be the dole queue and the end of their working lives. Most were unwilling to face the prospect of ending their working lives so soon – most, but not all. Some were forever calculating the likely amounts of their redundancy and wanted to get out any way they could. These were the ones who were often accused by the others of willingly and even happily putting the boot into the pit.

Where there was once brotherhood there were now multiple divisions in the family.

The young were pitted against the old. Sections of the face workers were pitted against the management. The pit deputies were at permanent loggerheads with the electricians. Glynmor had noticed of late that even the face workers had been quarrelling with one another, something unheard of only a few years ago. Somehow – and no one was quite sure how – a lot of laughter had seeped out of the old mine.

You could see the strain in a lot of their faces. You could see it in Glynmor's for certain. Where once there were bright laugh lines there were lines of middle-aged puffiness. The flesh had closed in around his eyes too and there were grey streaks in his hair. He had grown a bit of a beer paunch too and could not even remember the last time he had butted anyone. Somehow he had lost his puff. He made no secret of the fact that he would dearly have liked to have got out of the mine. But to do what? He was too old to be retrained for a job in one of those banjo or pop factories that were sprouting up here and there. He had become yet another slave of the lamp like his father and grandfather before him. He accepted that well enough. It didn't

176

stop him from dreaming though.

'Why don't we blow it up?' the Nutter asked again.

'You'll get blown up if you're not bastard careful,' Glynmor replied.

Just as they were all still staring at the face, like a defeated family gazing out of a boarding house window on a holiday pouring with rain, there was a soft plop as a lump of coal worked loose and brown water came pouring out of a hole the size of a fist. Well I'll go to bastard Africa, Glynmor thought. A vein of sandstone that does not want to be cut and now a pocket of water that had to be pumped. All they needed now was a blower of gas to make the party complete.

'I think this face is knackered,' said Danny Kettle, the shift foreman as the water continued to gurgle out into every corner of the heading.

'Where's your crystal ball?' asked Glynmor.

'One thing's for sure. This shift is knackered till they get the pumps in. Knock off that conveyor Jim.'

The sudden gush of water introduced an unexpected taste of freshness into the turbid, coal-speckled air. It was the taste of a lollipop on a hot summer's day; a taut little reminder of the life that still bloomed above the earth and beneath the skies away from this troublesome seam of coal. Glynmor took a deep breath on it before turning and walking away through the sloshing puddles that were already building up everywhere. 'There's more coal in my shed than down here,' he muttered to Tom the Nutter. 'And, come to think of it, I've got sod all.'

'You can have some of mine if you like,' the Nutter offered brightly. 'I'll let you have it cheap as well.'

'That was always your trouble wasn't it? All heart and no brains you are. It's a wonder you haven't given away your house before now.'

But Glynmor's taunts were always lost on the smiling Nutter. He accepted such comments as gestures of friendship which was perhaps why they both got on so well. Most people misunderstood Glynmor's little ironies and sarcastic flights.

Up top it was a day of bright sunshine. The young heather was poking up out of the dead brown bracken and waving in the breeze as the boys from the morning shift walked back to Bont. Those in cars whizzed up the mountain road while, high up the

177

side of the Valley, a farmer on his horse was rounding up his sheep with the help of three dogs. His whistles and angry shouts carried on the breeze as the sheep themselves tumbled over the rocked face of the *cwm* in fluffy white avalanches.

Glynmor walked along the pit road with Danny Kettle. 'Just look at that bloody mess down there,' he said. 'Sometimes I do feel ashamed when I do look at that dump and know that it's my home. We live in that shithouse mun. What's happened to us eh? A thousand pounds for the first bright bastard who explains what's happened to us.'

Even viewed from as far away as where they were both walking, just past the pit main gate, the buildings and terraces of Bont told their own story. It was the sad story of a village that had died before its time: the railway station long closed, the weeds shunting over the roof of the waiting room; the streets themselves but loose collections of holes held together by tarmac; the outlying fields scattered with litter or the odd abandoned car. A few of the shops had closed too, with planks nailed across the windows. Those still in business had wire grilles over theirs.

There had been other significant changes in detail. The roof of the derelict cinema, The Bug, had fallen in on itself and Lee Hoo Wonk had finally sold enough Chop Suey to save enough to return home to Hong Kong. Walford James, the former bingo caller in the Hall, had left the Valley to seek his fortune but had now returned somehow having got shot of his wife in the process. Walford also had a trail of fluttering affiliation orders in his wake, said the gossip. He seemed to have found a bit of money, however, since he opened one of those new video libraries in the premises of the old Chinese takeaway where, for £1 a night, you could rent all the latest video cassettes. You could also, if Walford knew and approved of you, rent videos of a very different kind; plain, discreet cassettes in which various people of several sexes tied themselves into various reef knots lasting an hour or so before they tied themselves into yet further knots for another hour. Such entertainments were very popular, particularly up in Giro City, the small, award-winning council estate which had sprung up just outside the village.

The school had also closed. There just weren't enough pupils to justify the cost of its upkeep, said the education authority. Now the children were bussed over to Aberdare and the old school had become a garage. There was a high wire fence where the playground used to be and alert Dobermans ran around the dumped cars, their bonnets agape and engines ripped out. Motor parts were now stored in the old school lavatory.

Even the police station had long been closed, with the windows boarded up and clumps of weeds growing out of the gutterings. Graffiti announcing nothing at all had been sprayed on its walls in huge aerosoled whorls of purple and yellow. The Glamorgan police had closed the station in a bid to improve crime detection, finally withdrawing the local man, P.C. Watkins, who was given a desk job in headquarters in Cardiff in favour of a wide network of Panda cars which would cover the five Valleys and enable them to speed to any incident within seconds of it being reported. Ho, ho, said the rude boys from Giro City.

These days, where once every door had been left open and every window unlocked, an unprecedented crime wave was sweeping up and down the Valley with things, large and small, walking out of the houses, day and night. If a housewife wanted to clean upstairs, she first had to lock the front door downstairs. If it was fine enough to peg the washing out to dry on the line it was also fine enough to sit out in the back and keep an eye on it to see that it was not pinched.

The Welfare Hall had not escaped this steady dive into dereliction either. Even as Glynmor and the boys went into the bar for a few pints to wash down the coal dust, you could see its decline in the broken window frames and unpainted doors; in the filthy lavatories and peeling wallpaper. In its whole dusty decay there was the same melancholy music as there was surrounding the rest of the village; the same sad tune of a building that had given up the ghost.

The loss of the library there – together with the closure of the reading room – had, to this day, been one of the bitterest blows in Emlyn's Kremlin's life. He had campaigned long and loud about the committee's decision to turn the library into yet another bar but, in the end, had to give way. So now, where once there were the sacred texts of Marx and Engels, there were now one-armed bandits, a colour television and a pool table – the inevitable notices signed by the committee warning against

179

the doing of this or the forbidden doing of that.

The scale of betrayal was almost Tory in Emlyn's eyes. A group of committee Hitlers – many of whom had nothing to do with the mine anyway – had pulled the plug on a century of miners' learning and quest for self-improvement. They had come and pissed on the very altar of the working class, had deprived them of one of their few hopes of ever gaining political control.

Nevertheless Emlyn nowadays conducted most of his business in the Hall, sitting at his own little table in the corner of the bar, just next to the telephone. From this convenient seat of office he would make himself available to anyone who might want help or advice on the usual issues; claims for 'dust', widows' concessionary coal or some fight for injury compensation.

'So how's the red revolution coming on this morning?' asked Glynmor, going over to the table with two pints in his hands and putting them down next to a pile of papers.

'The red revolution has turned blue – just like everything else in this Valley,' Emlyn replied, straight-faced.

'I think the Meadow seam has turned blue too,' said Glynmor. 'We've hit sandstone and water there this morning.'

'Aw, that does it then.' Emlyn seemed genuinely dismayed by the news. 'They're going to come after the pit with the biggest axe you've ever seen if that face goes.'

'You almost sound as if you care, mun.'

'Care? 'Course I care. When that pit goes this Valley is finished. Dead.'

'It looks pretty dead to me already.'

'It's dead 'cos there's no economic muscle in it. No factories, no roads, no railway, no nothing. When are you going to do something, Glynmor? We need another man on the lodge committee. It's time you did something. Well, isn't it?'

'Not me Em. This place is dead 'cos the people in it are dead. You can't fight with death, mun. Not even the lodge committee can fight with death. Death is death and every bastard one of us has got one foot in the grave.'

'Well wake them up. Someone like you could do it. You could carry people with you if you only tried.'

It was the way the two of them had been with one another over the years. Emlyn Kremlin, the old N.U.M. warrior, forever trying to get someone young and talented to lift up the spear. But, fond though they clearly were of one another, it was no use. In almost every way they were in fundamental opposition to one another. When Emlyn looked at the floor all he saw were principles. When Glynmor looked at the same floor all he saw were fag ends. Emlyn was the defeated idealist looking to others to light the flame. Glynmor's ideals had never been defeated, because he had never espoused any. The pair of them did not even agree on why the Valley had slid into such ruin. Emlyn blamed the economic order and the continued butchery of the pits. Glynmor threw much of the blame on the people and pointed out that the Bont mine was still open.

As if that philosophic chasm was not enough there were many in Bont who did not believe that there was anything wrong with the place at all. It was, they told one another repeatedly, the finest village in the world.

'So how's my favourite niece keeping?' Emlyn asked after taking a long ruminative sip from his pint.

'She's great mun, and Huw is as daft as ever. What's the news on Daisy?'

'Don't ask.'

'Go on.'

'She's gone and run off to Greenham Common. Went last night.'

'You're pulling my pisser surely? That women's peace camp thing? And what about the boy? Who's looking after him?'

'She's asked me to keep an eye on him. Aye. Me! Came to see me before she left. But there's not much I can do with the skinhead bastard. He won't get out of bed all day and roams the Valley at night. I wrote to his father the other day but he doesn't want to know. He said anything to do with Daisy was bound to go rotten.'

'*Duw*, well what a turn up for the books that is.' Glynmor was almost stuck for words looking down into the foam-curled throat of his half-finished pint. 'What a turn up. Daisy can't control her own son so she runs off to Greenham Common to save the world instead. Maggie will go potty when I tell her.'

'Perhaps you'd better not tell her. She's got her own problems with young Huw after all.'

'She doesn't have any problems with him. She bastard

idolises him. Makes me sick sometimes it do. The way she slobbers and drools over him you'd think we had a fucking pop star in the house.'

'It's good that one of them looks after their kids proper.'

'What! If anyone laid a finger on Huw she'd kill him stone dead and that's a fact. I'm not even allowed to shout at him let alone give him a clip across the ear. Here. Do you want another pint of this piss or what? You do? Well get up there you mean bastard. It's your round.'

Several pints later, the afternoon sun was still singing in the rooftops of the terraces as Glynmor, in a cheerful alcoholic haze, walked home. But his good mood soon drained out of his very boots when he saw that his portable television had been put out on his doorstep again, along with the empty milk bottles. It was that cowing son of his again. Every time they took their eye off him he unplugged the television and put it out on the doorstep. Just what was the matter with the nutcracker?

Glynmor picked up the television and carried it back to its place in the living room before going out into the kitchen where Maggie was sitting next to the stove looking through into the bathroom where their son Huw Bungalow, now 14, was splashing about in the bath and shouting noisily.

'Do you think you could stop putting the television out in the street?' Glynmor shouted at Huw. 'He's been at it again,' he snapped at Maggie. 'Leave the thing just where it is,' he shouted again at Huw. 'You hear? Just leave the thing where it is.'

'There's no need to yell,' Maggie said, unconcerned. 'You should know by now he can't understand anything you say. And he still can't understand it if you shout either.'

'Well, why doesn't he leave the television alone?'

'Why? I don't know why. I think it gives him a bad belly.'

'How can television give you a bad belly?'

'I don't know. It certainly gives me a bad head sometimes. So why shouldn't it give him a bad belly?'

'Just watch your step you,' Glynmor shouted at Huw again. But the boy simply splashed him with a shower of soapy water and began laughing uproariously. With soap suds dripping down his face Glynmor just had to sit down on a kitchen chair and smile. It was, he had to grant, impossible to be serious with an idiot in his bath-tub.

He was lucky to be alive at all. Huw was seriously handicapped, his whole body twisted at the spine. His facial features were fine, even handsome though with huge black eyes and a Beatle haircut, a style which had long been abandoned by other boys in the Valley but which, somehow, seemed to suit him. Apart from making loud noises he could not speak either. But he could laugh like a drain and, for most of the day, just wandered the streets of the village in a continual gale of laughter which, in its turn, made everyone else laugh as well.

Loved by everyone, he was known throughout the Valley as Huw Bungalow – on account of he had nothing up top.

At first Glynmor found it difficult to come to terms with having a son who was as thick as a canteen mug. When the severity of the handicap became apparent he even stopped taking him out for a while, blaming the doctor for not coming promptly enough to the birth. In a way he had blamed Maggie too. She surely could have shouted out of the window and got someone to come in. Only Chinese coolies, as he had once seen on television, gave birth to babies on their own.

'Can't you shut the bathroom door when he's having a bath?' Glynmor asked irritably.

'Don't be silly. He might have an accident. Anyway, I like looking at him.'

But soon Glynmor came to accept his son. Right from the beginning, Huw Bungalow let it be known that he might not be able to talk so he was going to laugh his head off. Even when he was still in his pram the sounds of his laughter would drift to every corner of the Valley, be it the pit canteen or down by the river. Ah, the miners would look at one another and smile. It's Huw Bungalow it is.

All this laughter soon undermined Glynmor's hostility. With Maggie in one hand and Glynmor in the other, Huw Bungalow would take them on long walks up to the reservoir on afternoons when it was as if their childhoods had been handed back to them.

'Look at him now,' said Glynmor. 'He's farting like he's in some sort of bubble bath.'

'He does fart a lot,' said Maggie, taking a bath towel over to him. 'It's those Heinz baked beans he loves so much. And it's got to be Heinz as well or he won't touch them. He'd have them morning, noon and night if he had his way.'

'The beer can't help either. The boys are always slipping him a pint or two.'

'Yes and they do slip him a few too many as well sometimes,' Maggie said wrapping the bath towel around Huw and taking him over to sit on her lap in the armchair. 'You came home as pissed as a parrot yesterday didn't you my lovely? He even fell over and got his best suit dirty. *And* they've been teaching him dirty signs. I'll give them dirty signs if I catch them.'

Huw began stroking her hair as she continued rubbing down his body. They were always making physical displays of affection towards one another like this and Glynmor had to look away feeling slightly jealous. He did indeed love the both of them but the blunt truth was that, over recent years, he was coming to feel increasingly envious and excluded.

'Any tea in the pot, is there?'

'Well if you get up and have a look you'll find out, won't you?'

Very soon into their marriage they had discovered a terrific love for one another. They had been talking one night about a line in a popular song – 'the love you take is equal to the love you make' and then stumbled on one of love's sweet secrets: you only ever get out of it what you put into it.

From that night on, Maggie got down to the business of marriage with a clear resolution: cleaning and tidying the house (not so easy with smudges of coal everywhere); having a meal ready for him when he came home from the mine (which went straight into the ash-can if he was more than five minutes late) and, with the help of Spanish red wine and saucy French underwear – together with a sex book which they kept in a brown paper bag under the wardrobe – having some steamy joyous sexual sessions which gave a whole new meaning to the Valleys' expression of having a bit of a rub. Emancipated she wasn't, but happy she was.

For his part, Glynmor shook off many of the old valley habits of his work-mates, coming home sober (if he went to the Hall at all) bringing her a cup of tea in bed in the morning after he had lit the fire; handing over all his wage packet unopened on Friday afternoon and, as often as not, bringing her a bunch of flowers from the grocer's or a bottle of wine which, he had soon come to learn, meant that the sex book came out of that brown paper bag faster than a rabbit being chased by a ferret. He was a very quick learner was our Glynmor.

And, simple as it all was, it had worked beautifully.

'I thought we might all go to the disco tonight,' said Maggie as she pulled on Huw's blue drainpipe trousers. 'I heard they've got Smokey and his Sounds on there tonight.'

'He's still playing the same old rubbish is he?'

'That's not rubbish. They're great records. We fell in love when he was playing those records. The Supremes – You remember Babbeeeee loooooove ...'

Huw began laughing out loud, putting his arms around her neck and hugging her.

'I'm not bothered about going,' Glynmor said moodily. 'It was a hard shift this morning an' I've got to be up early too.'

She looked at him curiously but said nothing. He had always said that he loved Smokey and his Sounds so she was sure he'd be very keen on going to the Hall. But she knew what the trouble was all right. He was getting more and more jealous of Huw and wanted just the two of them to go to the dance on their own. She could see that was why he was getting so edgy all the time but didn't see that there was much she could do about it. She wasn't like her sister Daisy after all. Huw *was* allowed out on his own but she always liked to know where he was. He never usually stayed with them in the dances, come to that, wandering off to sit in with the band or, if it was a lady singer, trying to get a look up her skirt. But Maggie always knew what he was doing every second of the evening. She was just that kind of mother.

Glynmor had no objection to this as such, he said. He just wanted more of her for himself. It was a position in which Maggie just could not win.

Huw Bungalow stood obediently as his mother dressed him in his favourite Teddy boy suit, one of three given to him by a retired rocker from Pontypridd whose girlfriend had nagged him into the somewhat cooler fashions of the early eighties. Huw loved the suit so much he just would not go out of the house unless he was togged up in his blue suede shoes, pink socks, blue drainpipe trousers, long pink, draped jacket with black velvet collar and bootlace tie.

'There you are my lovely,' said Maggie smoothing down the velvet collar with the palms of her hands. 'You're going to have *all* the girls chasing after you now. Just the same way they used to chase after your father.'

'What do you mean "used to"? I can still pull a bird or two you know. An' I don't have to dress up like a Piccadilly pimp to do it either. I'm not past it yet.'

'So why don't you come to the Hall with us tonight?'

'All right. I'll come then. An' I'll show you how a real master picks up women, don't worry about that.'

'Oh Huw boy, we're in for a real treat tonight. The master is going to show us all how to do it. You'd better tell him to get his dinner out of the oven and have a lie down first then. Old men need sleep before they go out dancing and picking up women.'

There was men in suits down at the chapel vicarage again this morning, Aunty Phyllis told Enid over the back fence. I don't know what they're after but they do say the vicar may have to leave after all.

Never.

That's what I heard anyway. He hasn't paid any rent for years either and he's never open is he? Therese in the bakery was saying she hears him singing hymns on his own in the chapel sometimes. Or he might give a Bible reading for all spiders in the cobwebs. As mad as a hatter he is. It's a wonder they've left him there that long if you ask me. I can still remember when it was full every Sunday. And that other chapel where the school was.

Bingo. That's all they worry about now. And that Tote thing. Got your tickets, have you?

Aye. What was the name of that other chapel?

Soar. It was Methodist as I remember.

Soar. That's it. He was such a good vicar too that one. Not at all like old Mordecai. They do say he drinks a lot you know. Whisky and gin mostly. That's right. He spoke to me the other day in the Co-op you know.

Never.

He did. He said that he just couldn't get over the price of butter, he said. He said he was giving up on butter and starting to buy Stork, he said. You could tell the difference no matter what the ads might say, he said. Stock was much cheaper, he said.

What did you say?

I didn't say nothing. What could I say?

186

Guto's new mine working, even by N.C.B. standards, was an impressive piece of work, let alone by Guto's. After years of trying to transform the Valley into a large-scale hunk of gorgonzola, Guto decided that he had not been digging his holes deep enough for Bomber's missing millions. He had, so to speak, just been scratching the surface. So, for this hole, he had gone back to the site of his very first excavation just near the tump, down by the waste-paper factory. He decided to make a proper job of it this time. He had cut into the earth with a hand drill and bow, using the old mining wall and box method, so that he would cut his own natural pit props as he tunnelled inwards, searching out the secrets of the darkness. He had been a miner as a lad had Guto but was kicked out of the Ferndale No. 3 for reasons he had never divulged and no one had ever found out about for sure. Wanking into the shift foreman's sandwiches, the boys in the bar reckoned.

He had been working on this particular heading for close on three months now, shovelling the earth, rock and shale into a wheelbarrow and carting it all out where it was dumped, in a growing mountain, next to the tump. Occasionally an N.C.B. inspector came wandering around to see if Guto had struck some unknown outcrop of coal. But he never had and it didn't bother the N.C.B. anyway since it was the best-known secret in the Valley that Guto was interested purely in the quest for Bomber's millions.

It was a rare day indeed when no one came to watch Guto at work in his new hole. It was as if they were hoping he might one day emerge triumphant, with all Bomber's loot in his hands. Then, the general idea was, someone would crack him on the head and run away with all the dosh, just as invariably happened to those nutty old gold prospectors in the final reel of those rotten cowboys films they always showed when stuck with an hour or so to fill on television.

Guto emerged all right. But usually waving a mandril around in the air threateningly, with sweat and snot flying in all directions and telling any nosey-parkers to 'Bugger off out of it.' He had seen all those films too.

Village gossip marvelled at how hard Guto worked. After all those years of tunnelling, the boys in the bar calculated, even if he found a million pounds, it could only at best work out at something like a shilling an hour. But, by and large, they just decided that Guto had simply forgotten what he was looking for; that the search had become such a rampant bee in his bonnet he had forgotten the purpose of the operation.

It didn't take an Einstein to work out that Bomber's millions, even if they existed, could not be buried very deep in the earth. Even when he had his cushy surface job as a labourer in the mine Bomber's lungs were so dicky he only to dig down into an inch of sand to go into a swoon and be rushing down to the doctor for a paper. Towards the end it got that Bomber could not even lift a heavy pint of beer in the Hall. Guto chose to ignore this irrefutable logic.

That fine Spring evening he was stripped to his waist and bringing out his final load. The sun dipped out of the Valley, suffusing its high dark edges with a buttercup gold. The first swallows of the year were already swooping and yawing through the twilight, black on yellow, as they chased insects. Up at the mine a huge flame of gas spurted and waved in the lengthening bars of darkness and, just by the breeze-ruffled reservoir, two foxes came down together to drink.

He upended his barrow and walked down to the river where he washed himself carefully before putting on his shirt and coat. The ribs on his long body rather resembled the keys of a xylophone but his muscles were clearly strong enough, lean and sinewy without an ounce of fat anywhere. Once he had dressed he flicked two handfuls of water onto his hair and slicked it back on both sides. In fact he was preparing himself for work since, needing money to buy capital equipment for all his excavations, he had now acquired himself a proper job with a proper wage packet. By night he was in charge of security in the new supermarket in Giro City. It was not much of a job but it was a job nevertheless.

Giro City — so-called because its economy depended on Giro cheques from the S.S. (Department of Social Security) and its days were worked out in Giro days or double Giro days — was a development of 142 council houses built under the aegis of the Welsh Office on the north edge of Bont in 1972. The next year it won a gold award from the RIBA and, early the following year, the main support walls of one of the houses collapsed, killing a young mother and her baby.

Investigations revealed that mining subsidence had made

many of the houses unsafe, so most of the tenants had been rehoused in other parts of the Valley. Such houses as had been left empty were soon squatted in, largely by families who had been evicted from elsewhere for non-payment of rent. Quite soon Giro City began winning further awards for dereliction and lawlessness. The council relied on the rain to clean the streets and the sheep to cut the grass verges. Exploded bags of rubbish lay in every corner, graffiti swirled around broken windows.

The supermarket itself – despite security which would have been the pride of Fort Knox, from the thick steel shutters to a grille over every orifice – had been done over repeatedly, with even a guard dog poisoned. Finally, in desperation, Evans the manager had hired Guto to sit in a deckchair guarding the long silent rows of soap powders, frozen meats and high piles of vegetables.

This, as it happened, had been the most inspired bit of casting ever, since the break-ins stopped immediately. The skinheads of Giro City – who had been responsible for most of the break-ins – had a healthy respect for old Guto and his strange tunnelling ways. Somehow they had learned that he had a black belt in Kung Fu and had done time in Dartmoor for murdering two little boys with knitting needles. No one quite knew where this nonsense came from, since Guto could not have fought his way out of a wet *Echo*, though the smart money was on Evans the manager who had discreetly mentioned it to one of the skins one afternoon near the biscuit counter, all in the *strictest* confidence, of course.

This reputation for Kung Fu carnage with knitting needles ensured that no one ever bothered Guto. Together with the fact that he never seemed to need any sleep, it made him an ideal guard for the besieged supermarket and, behind him in the manager's office, was the hot-line for making an appointment with the police.

Twilight was thickening as Guto locked himself into the grey, boarded-up supermarket. He peered out at a gathering gang of youths beneath a street lamp which coated everything with a sodium orange veneer. Yet more youths were coming now. At first there had been three then four ... six, seven, eight ... all skinheads, all gabbling to one another in skinhead language – short uncompleted sentences seasoned with lots of 'fuck this' and 'cunt that'. When they weren't talking to one another they liked to spit in long dribbles or rocket-like flobs.

Occasionally one would walk up to the other and kick him, wrestling him to the ground and trying to stuff some grass into his mouth. Another would walk over and kick out at the two of them as they rolled over and over on the ground. Then suddenly and for no apparent reason the fighting would stop as casually as it had begun, with the three of them brushing themselves off and walking back to their position under the lamp.

Their heads were as shaved and stubbly as sides of bacon. Their jackets were a variety of torn denim or camouflaged combat jackets with tight jeans shorn off just below the knees, showing bright luminous socks and high laced Doc Marten boots. All had rings in their ears, some had them in their noses. They had a weakness for safety pins too, dangling in long chains down to their shoulders. Crude tattoos had been pricked out with a needle and black lead, HATE was favoured on many fingers. SCUM was another. MAM got a look in while one hand MADE IN WALES tattooed right across his forehead.

Here was Iffy and over there was Nipper, Dick and Cocoa. The Clay Class had finally come of age. All now in their mid-twenties, they had never known a job. Just recently they had all gone as a gang one night and trashed the Job Centre in Treorchy, kicking over the notice boards and throwing the filing cabinets out through the window. Everyone in the Valley knew who had done it but, since the Job Centre had signally failed to come up with a job of any description in its two-year history, the police were not called in, nor was any kind of investigation ever launched.

Iffy began running down the road, kicking a tin can. The others chased after him. They kicked it around and around in circles, tackling one another hard until the can was lost in a pile of garbage. They trooped back, with their hands in their pockets, to take up their position under the street lamp outside the supermarket.

'Better get some fucking chips init?'

'Who's got the money? You twat. You borrowed it.'

'What money's that? Haven't got your money. Haven't got your fucking money, mun.'

'Who the fuck's got it then?'

There was a yell in the darkness and a lot of low whistling. Another skinhead came running up the road shouting that the Penrhos lot were coming. They began running helter-skelter down the road, dodging behind fences and hurdling over bags of rubbish. There was yet more frantic whistling, with a few doubling back around the supermarket and tearing down the gulley. A short silence followed and then all the whistling and shouting stopped.

It was a false alarm. There was no mob coming from anywhere.

Hands thrust back down into pockets, they came drifting back, now standing with their backs to one another and flobbing out into the orange darkness.

'Just let them fucking come here that's all.'

'We'll have the cunts. Aye, we'll 'ave the bastards.'

'Just let 'em fucking try that's all.'

Guto watched all such comings and goings through the supermarket letter-box, but said nothing. The skins were aware of him well enough but they always stayed well clear. They were very impressed by all those stories of the knitting needles and, even if false, they were taking no chances.

Nipper produced a tube of glue which he duly squeezed into a plastic bag. They took it in impatient turns to grab the bag and sniff on the glue in deep draughts. Soon they were dancing and giggling and falling about drunkenly. Sometimes they snorted on Butane lighter fuel or they painted solvent on their upper lips. Then there might be sulphates or, if they were lucky, some whaccy baccy or magic mushrooms. Anything that damaged the brain was acceptable.

Another skin rolled up to join the gathering tribe. It was Bobby Bland alias Gnasher except that there was nothing bland about him now. He didn't so much walk as move in a slow-rolling swagger, with his long ape-like arms dangling at his side, his bull-neck squatting in the middle of his shoulders reaching straight up into his brawny shaven head. When he had reached puberty he had just started growing and growing. But no one detected much growth in his brain since he was almost always in trouble with the police.

'Gis that fucking stuff,' he said, snatching at the bag of glue from Iffy and taking a big sniff. 'Gis it 'ere,' he mumbled on before inhaling again, holding his breath as if he was underwater. 'Terrible this,' he exhaled in a long puncturing hiss before going over to the supermarket door and giving it a good kicking. Where once he was once the roaring young lad, afraid of the boogie man – the mythical nightmare figure of the Valleys who came and took naughty boys away in a sack – now he was Gnasher, chief of the skinhead tribe of Bont and gossip had it that the boogie man was even afraid of him. He began kicking the supermarket door again. He wasn't afraid of Guto and his fucking knitting needles.

'I'm going to call the police!' they could hear Guto call from within. 'You'd better stop that kicking, you had.'

But his words only served to animate Gnasher further, making him kick at the door again and again, rattling the bars of the grilles with stubby hands like a gorilla trying to get inside his cage.

A veteran of numerous remand homes – and two brief spells in Cardiff prison – Gnasher might have been reared in the company of Genghis Khan and Tugboat Annie. Whenever anything went wrong or missing, the CID always lifted Gnasher first. As far as he was concerned there was nothing that was too hot or heavy. One of the main reasons why his mother Daisy had finally run off to Greenham Common was that she was fed up with answering the door and making so many cups of tea for visiting policemen. Gnasher was so notorious there were usually at least four cars surrounding the house before the police, unannounced and always without knocking, came steaming in through the front and back doors simultaneously.

Since leaving school Gnasher had never known any form of employment. He burnt off his ferocious energy bustling around the village with the rest of the dole boys or perhaps occasionally organising a raiding party and steaming over to Penrhos, a huge new council estate over in the next Valley where they could usually get a good fight going with the skins over there.

Just anything Gnasher did was all right with the skins of Bont. He was their undisputed leader, the hard man, who, somehow, was going to lead them out of all this and into the promised land with plenty of naked women and whaccy baccy growing in every field.

Neither television nor bingo had ever come near to closing the dances in the Welfare Hall. Indeed the dance floor was jammed solid the night their old favourite, Smokey and his Sounds, was back.

Smokey had become something of a cult figure throughout the nightclubs of South Wales, even had his own late-night programme on a Saturday on Cardiff local radio. Neither was he cheap any more, as the committee discovered to their shock. Once it had been a tenner and a pint or two of All-Bright. Now it was two hundred pounds in cash and a bottle of Bell's whisky, plus ice cubes, in his dressing room. But even the most frugal members of the committee had to admit that Smokey was always well worth it; a queue had formed long before the doors had opened and no one could remember when that had happened last.

And sure enough Smokey was still fabulous, taking them all back through a time warp to those hot, luscious nights when their hearts were full of teenage longing for some boy or girl and they danced and danced till they could dance no more. The Shirelles, the Ronettes, the Supremes. The music was still the same. One part of Smokey's act had changed though: instead of a rackety system of stolen traffic signals and parking bollards he now had an incredible light show – one of the most advanced in Europe, it said in his advertising brochure – with laser effects which could explode starbursts over the heads of the dancers, light up any corner of the Hall in any colour or else make the very dance floor vibrate and shiver as if they were on some magic carpet ride through the distant cosmos. *Why won't you be my babeeeeeeeeee ...*

Even as they had come as teenagers they still came now. Biscuits, looking like a slightly overweight tarantula these days but still in the same all-black gear and shifting about the dance floor, all limp wrists and wobbling pelvis, as if he had just been given a lesson by the ghost of Elvis Presley. And Peter Star was still as mean and magnificent as ever, holding up that great haughty nose in the dancing lights like it was Concorde coming down into Bont to land next to the pit.

But it was the girls who had turned out in force, almost as if all those years had never gone away. The same groups were still friendly with one another, still danced with their handbags at their feet. They still all smiled at one another and snapped their fingers to the beat, still sang those golden words to one another, still did the same steps they had done together when the music had first come out and they were being torn apart by the unutterable pains of being young and in love. *I'm going to wait for you for ever ...*

Huw Bungalow, the Teddy boy peacock, strutted through this bright musical mayhem as if he owned the joint. The girls practically queued up to give him a hug. He danced with whoever he pleased, and whenever he went near the bar the boys bought him drinks. Then, as he stood around getting a bit tipsy, one of the boys might tickle him or one of the girls take a brush out of her handbag and give his hair a quick once over if looked slightly out of place. Strangers in particular almost cried when they saw the way the spirit of the community still worked through Huw Bungalow; the way they absorbed his handicap and cared for him; the way he, in his turn, went among them and brought them joy. It was as if he had become their talisman, the one bright focus of their dark lives which brought them together as one. Even though the chill winds of dereliction and lawlessness were blowing hard through the Valley, Huw Bungalow gave them warmth for all kinds of reasons. They rejoiced in his infectious laughter and the incredibly vivid colours of his gaudy suit. They warmed to his helplessness and uncluttered happiness. He told them something of their lives which had left the Valleys for ever; something warm, loving and innocent which had once made their communities vivacious and tremendous forces to be reckoned with.

As he jived, he was a shoulder-padded poem of coloured movement was our Huw, his hips swaying around, his head nodding along with the beat, his pink socks and blue suede shoes shuffling back and forth, his long drapes flying one way and another, his neat strong hands always there to catch his dancing partner's hand as she whirled breathless around and around like a beskirted spinning top. But then it was time for the raffle to be drawn, for Smokey to take a break and all the dancers to return to their seats. Huw went and sat with his mother, putting his arm around her shoulders as his big black eyes looked around the dance floor. Maggie felt inexpressible joy whenever Huw was near her and they were forever touching one another even when she was talking to someone else, as she was now, sitting at her usual table with the girls.

They were all having a good laugh about how old Jackie

Davies and her boy friend Ian had taken their sickly dog down to the river to drown it. The trouble was the dog escaped out of the sack and ran back to the house before they got home. Now Ian didn't know what to do about the dog and just hadn't the heart to take him down to the river again. Jackie said that it was a sign that the dog was going to get better.

Then Thelma told them that Mrs Walsh was going at her boy Peter again for playing rugby. All right go and play rugby then, she had shouted after him as he walked down the street. But, when you break both your legs, don't come running back home here to me.

The girls roared with laughter at that one, brushing tears out of the corners of their eyes with their finger-tips or else holding a steadying side of a hand to their chest as if it was going to burst. If you break both your legs ... Thelma laughed louder than any of them.

The raffle was drawn and, no sooner had Smokey started up his wondrous sounds again, than Huw went loping off, looking for a new dancing partner. Maggie was looking anxiously over at Glynmor who was sitting morosely with a few of his mates on the next table. She could see that he was sulking; jealous of Huw again probably and uptight about her sitting chatting with the girls. He had never liked the girls; never really liked anyone who took her attention away from him.

Glynmor had a right cob on, he knew. And a large part of this was because he was depressed with himself for the way he behaved. He remembered well enough how he had been a free soul when he had first got married but that had disappeared quite soon and he was astonished at how soon he had come to rely on – and need – Maggie's body. If they didn't make love for three days he began feeling physically sick with large parts of his insides wobbling about in frustration. When she wasn't around he actually missed her – even sometimes when he was working down in the pit. Of late he had even begun to resent the way Huw was around all the time; the way she always showered affection on the boy when she could have been showering it on him. He would have quite liked a bit of the attention that the rest of the village always gave Huw too.

He disliked finding all this in himself, of course; resented this childish jealousy which flared up inside him. But his jealousy was a fact and there wasn't much he could do about it. He knew the way jealousy destroyed all it touched. He knew all that but there was this bright green glow inside him; right in the very pit of his belly. It made him sick it did. But there you are. You can't help the way you're made can you?

He picked up his pint and went downstairs to play the new one-armed bandit in the foyer but that didn't improve his humour much either. He put about two pounds' worth of coins into the machine and hadn't seen so much as a cherry when, lo and behold, he got a line of grapes worth a lovely ten pounds. Then the heavens must have farted since, instead of pressing the COLLECT button, he pressed GAMBLE and, in so doing, lost the lot.

'It's a bastard electronics degree you need for these machines and that's a fact,' he complained to Dai Fat before giving the machine a kick.

'They must have fixed it because it paid out over a hundred pounds last week,' said Dai Fat. 'The chairman went mad and ordered the plug to be taken out.'

'What'd you mean taken out?'

'He had it taken out, mun. Took it home for the weekend and used it for his electric kettle.'

'What's the point of that?'

'Saving the club money. He said the club couldn't afford to pay out another hundred pounds on the bandit. It'd be finished, he said.'

'It's his brain that's finished.'

The colours of Smokey's light show were spurting and flashing over the tables when Glynmor walked back into the dance and Maggie grabbed him, hauling him back onto the dance floor. As though a decade and a half had never passed the Righteous Brothers were still going on about how you had lost that loving feeling and she pulled him close to her, nibbling at his ear and rubbing her crotch up and down against his leg in the glittering darkness. She knew what he liked and had been getting worried about him.

She knew that he was jealous of Huw but, as she repeatedly pointed out to the girls, she felt that there was nothing she could do about it. It wasn't her fault that Huw just loved to stroke her hair all the time and, despite Glynmor's suspicions, it wasn't her fault that Huw kept on putting the portable television out with the milk bottles. Anyway, it was clear that Huw was totally dependent on her so that was that. It was a burden which she shouldered joyfully.

'So what chapter do you fancy doing tonight?' she asked in a low sexy whisper.

'Oh I'm not too fussed,' he replied, cheering up for the first time that night. 'We could try seven again.'

'You know I do sometimes get the stitch something terrible when we're doing seven.'

'Well, let's try eight then. I do most of the work with that.'

'You're on,' she said, giving his crotch another sexy rub. She knew her Glynmor. She knew exactly how to cheer him up.

The trouble was that Glynmor could see through Maggie's little ploys, sometimes feeling like a spinning plate on top of one of those wobbly bamboos in a circus act. When he looked like falling off she gave the bamboo a bit of a shake with her wrist and he went spinning on happily again. Mind you, it was worth it, he reflected, as he picked his way back to the bar. When Maggie was in the mood of an evening he was more than happy to play along.

'Hello Glynmor,' said a husky voice in the dark corner just next to the bar. 'I've got a nice little push-bike at home. What've you got?'

He turned a shade and saw that it was Xenia Prosser sitting alone in the shadows. She had always fancied herself as a bit of a Greta Garbo, had Xenia. As glamorous as a gladioli, she was married to Piper Prosser and the talk was that they were none too happy either. Piper was a pit electrician who was liked by no one. Glynmor wouldn't have pissed over Piper if the man had been on fire.

'I've got a nice little pump if you're short of one,' Glynmor replied, playing along.

He went over to her and offered a cigarette which she refused as she crossed and uncrossed her legs in a shiver of nylons and rustling petticoats. None of the girls could stand her since, at a time when baggy jeans and sweat shirts were enough for most of them, Xenia still insisted on wearing proper dresses with high-heeled shoes and stockings. She also had a full, bubble-blowing mouth and mammary mountains which could have cracked coconuts. She had long tickled Glynmor's fancy – and that of a lot of other boys as well – but even as she took hold of his hand with both of hers, as he held a match under her cigarette, he could feel, by the surges in the whereabouts of his flies, that temptation was the name of the game; that unless he watched it he was going to fall off his married perch. Oddly, in the light of his historic fecklessness, he had not strayed into another woman's bed – by design or accident – in the fourteen years of his marriage.

The dance began again with a multi-coloured explosion of lights over the floor and the very hall seemed to be moving about on great golden waves. The Hollies began singing *The Air That I Breathe* and, despite remembering that this was one of Maggie's favourite pop songs of all time, Glynmor asked Xenia to dance, surprised at how tightly she held his hand as they walked onto the dance floor. She pulled herself close to him and, never one to look a gifthorse up the arse, he decided to continue talking about his bicycle pump since about the only place it was ever safe to talk in Bont was on the dance floor.

'I could come around with my pump if your old man was on nights some time,' he offered.

'There's too many eyes around here. We'd better go up the mountain road one night.'

'Be a bit difficult on a bicycle.'

'A car mun. You've got a car, haven't you?'

'Aye. I've got a car but my car pump is much bigger than my bicycle pump.'

As the Hollies continued singing their golden oldie, Maggie actually began moving around the edge of the dance floor looking for Glynmor. In a way she regarded *The Air That I Breathe* as their record but, quite soon, she saw that Glynmor was indeed dancing to their record but with that fat cow Xenia Prosser. Now she was circling the dancers watching her Glynmor rubbing that cow's backside and her hand around the back of his neck. They were talking awful secretive too. Those bright green flames were exploding inside her. Now it was her turn to cry. She strode back to the girls, even ignoring her beloved Huw Bungalow.

He's only having one dance Maggie. It'll be all right. Even Glynmor will run away when the lights go on. They do say, the only way you could walk down the street with her was if you had a white stick and a Labrador. Who could look at that monster in the daylight? They do say that when she goes to a house all the mice commit suicide on the traps. Snipe was saying her tits are so big she has to put pit props inside her bra.

'But Glynmor's always going on about how he just loves big knockers,' she wailed. 'He's always saying how he preferred me when I was fat.'

'That's just Glynmor. He can never make up his mind about anything can he?'

The record – their record – finished and still Glynmor showed no sign of returning from the bopping scrum so Maggie went off in search of him again, wading past the arms and shoulders and catching him kissing her on the lips. On the lips!

Maggie didn't even think about it. She threw a punch, which might even have brought Rocky Marciano's career to a premature end, connecting on the back of Glynmor's head and, in the nasty collision between Glynmor's teeth and Xenia's teeth, he split his lip and the crown on her front tooth was knocked off. In all that tangled shifting darkness Glynmor was none too sure what had happened to him and was rubbing the back of his head vigorously as Xenia backed away shouting abuse which was not so much abuse as soft whistles through the big hole which had appeared in the middle of her most perfect set of gnashers.

Maggie lifted her fist to punch yet another big hole in her crowns when something very strange happened. It was as if her arm had suddenly frozen in the darkness and her aggression just drained out of her too. Someone might just have slipped her half a dozen sleeping pills, or she might have been bogged down in a slow-motion dream, when, for a split second, the whole of her body seemed immobilised too. It was only freed when all the lights came on to see what Xenia was shouting about. Now Glynmor was painfully touching his bloodied lip with his fingertips while Huw Bungalow was standing by his mother's side, laughing quietly.

'There was nothing in it,' Xenia shouted.

'Just leave him alone in the future,' Maggie told Xenia, surprised at the reasonableness of her voice. 'Come on Glynmor,' she added taking Huw's hand. 'I want the both of you home.'

The silent dancers parted as Maggie led Glynmor and Huw out of the hall. 'What've you been drinking tonight?' Glynmor asked as they went down the stairs. 'One sniff of vodka and it's got that you get fighting mad.'

'I'm not having anyone smooching with *my* husband.'

Glynmor was not entirely unhappy with this behaviour however – even rather approving of it. But what he really could not understand was why now she was being so sweet to him instead of continuing the row as she might have done in normal circumstances. When they got back to the house she made Huw his usual cup of cocoa and packed him off to bed before putting the new Crystal Gale record on their Ferguson stereo sound centre, turning off the lights and not even bothering to get out her saucy French underwear before all but eating him alive on the floor in front of the fire.

Afterwards, they lay back together on the sheepskin rug and she was all but purring with happiness, with a smile spread from ear to ear. But, even in her supreme contentment, her mind continued revisiting that moment when she was about to punch Xenia for the second time. She had just been unable to throw that punch when, at another time, Xenia would have got a few and then Glynmor would have been in for a wallop as well. But no. For no reason at all she was feeling very peaceful and ever since the incident had been throbbing with love.

'Don't go falling asleep now, Glynmor,' she went on. 'We haven't finished yet.'

He let out a mock groan of anguish but was, of course, secretly delighted, now understanding how a spot of jealousy was going to open up a whole new vista of pleasure.

For her part Crystal Gale was busy singing on the Ferguson stereo how it all made her brown eyes blue.

Chapter Fourteen

The village had long been accustomed to Rev. Mordecai's increasingly eccentric behaviour so few took any notice when, on some mornings, he was out and about the streets, shovel in one hand and bucket in the other, searching for animal shit – horse, dog, sheep, cat, it didn't matter – to dig into the earth of his allotment down next to the garage. The Holy Patch, the villagers called it.

With his pigeon-fancying days behind him when, in a fit of spiritual depression, he had pulled the necks of all his pigeons, he now had so much time on his hands after closing the Libanus, he had become an allotment fanatic. Each day he could be found – by those who cared to look for him – tending his vegetables with a loving care. They came up thick and fast did those vegetables, a tribute not so much to his agricultural skill as to his stunning ability to shovel up a pile of steaming shit almost as soon as it had plopped onto the road.

But it was not only the actual shit that got his parsnips so fat. Dead animals went in there too. Sheep, pigeons, goldfish: anything at all which had given up the ghost and fallen dead on the streets got a very swift burial. Talk was that the ground was so rich on the Holy Patch that no sooner had he planted anything in the soil than he had to stand straight back in case the growing plant caught him a fourpenny one in the eye. He was now hoping to exhibit with the Bont Allotment Society but they were being curiously evasive about his application for membership.

This morning he was planting new rows of radishes and onions, down on his knees pricking them out of their seed boxes and placing them in drills. Sunshine blasted down over the high walls of the Valley and sweat dropped off his brow as he worked. He took the quietest of thrills in bringing such life to this valley of death.

For dead he believed the Valley had become and there was no argument about it. Whenever he looked around him he too became increasingly horrified by the spreading dereliction of this poky, dying parish of Bont. Pit after pit had been closed the length of the Valley. More and more chapels had been abandoned and boarded up – even if it had been temporarily closed to the public except in the odd emergency, i.e. when the minister over in Ferndale was unable to marry or bury someone.

The exact position of the Libanus was slightly complicated by the fact that he had never told anyone – least of all the Baptist authorities in Cardiff – that he had actually closed the chapel doors. He told the authorities that the chapel was always opened – and cleaned twice a week – but no one chose to show up for the services. If there was so little call for his services, the authorities had then argued, he should perhaps be moved elsewhere. He wrote polite letters back to Head Office saying that God had, in fact, told him to stay put until further notice.

There was not a lot the Baptist authorities could do about such letters. They could hardly turf him out on his ear after all; that wouldn't look very good in the *South Wales Echo* and, anyway, perhaps God really had told him to stay put until further orders. If that was indeed the case then it was hardly up to them to quarrel with divine commands. There was clearly going to be no turning the Libanus into a bingo hall or a craft workshop while Mordecai was around. It wasn't as if the Libanus was unique after all. These days they had almost as many chapels on their books as members.

But the real reason for staying put with the chapel at the ready – even if the doors were locked – was that Mordecai believed that there was going to be another Revival in the Valley. The Welsh had, after all, had more revivals than any other nation in the world and his deep secret prayers and knowledge of the circumstances which surrounded the last great revival told him that such an outbreak of God's blessings was soon going to happen again. He was going to be ready for it and he saw his life now as one long period of intercessory prayer in preparation for it. It was only the Welsh who could do this and, he was convinced, it was only in the Valleys of South

Wales that such an event could happen again. He still hadn't finished his work on the Great Revival of 1904-5 and, in a sense, didn't see how he could finish it until they had seen in the Valleys the clear signs of yet another great outpouring of the Holy Spirit throughout the land.

And so, until such time as the Holy Spirit let his pleasure be known, Mordecai was going to continue with his allotment. He stood up to stretch his back after pricking out his radishes, looking over at Bont with its bingo halls and video shops, the decayed Welfare Hall and the loss of the train services: it was through just such a landscape, he guessed, that the Old Testament prophets had once moved announcing the coming of the Lord.

He had just resumed work when he heard the loud, almost blood-curdling laughter of Huw Bungalow going about his rounds. These days Huw's laughter had become almost as familiar in the Valley as the melancholy cries of the sheep. He sent his laughter cannoning down the lanes and ricocheting up the gullies. You could almost see the waves of laughter breaking over the very chimney tops as the villagers' own laughter rose up to join it.

Mordecai walked down to the end of his allotment and spotted the loping tea-pot shape of Huw Bungalow walking down the back lane towards the tump. Even the resolute seriousness of old Mordecai's mind saw that Huw was an epic creation of comic and loveable features which were not at all what they first appeared. Mordecai continued along the allotment path to keep Huw in view. Just as he neared the tump three seagulls were now circling over his head and seeming to call out to him. Mordecai was entranced. There was something deeply spiritual about the boy which stirred his old Baptist soul. Even though Huw could not communicate directly with people he generated love and laughter wherever he went. He seemed to have a Franciscan power over animals, too: even the usually nervous sheep came wandering up to him whenever he was around.

It was possibly the way that he radiated joy through the community that was his really unique quality. Mordecai had often noticed that he made everyone laugh in their turn. The shopkeepers, who had little to laugh about in these straitened times, laughed. Mothers, worried about making ends meet, stopped in their tracks and laughed. Children who maybe didn't get the kind of birthday presents they once had, laughed too. Even the old-timers forever moaning and groaning on the bench in the square lit up when he was around.

In the midst of the Valley of death Huw Bungalow had come to them with the gift of life. He had become for the village what the Rev. Mordecai, in his youth, had hoped and prayed the chapel would become; the loving and loved heart of the community.

It was at that moment, with his fingers still dirty from pricking out his radishes, that Mordecai began conceiving a plan which was both exciting and unfamiliar in its initial connections. Somehow – and he was not at all sure how – Huw Bungalow was the key to the new revival that Mordecai dreamed and prayed about so fervently. When the time was right he would use the boy for God's ends and bring an end to the weeping and death in the Valley. Yes, Huw was the key to the Valley's future and, when Mordecai had worked out a plan, Huw would undoubtedly be the one who would help him to restore God to his rightful place high on the Valley's throne.

I'm not saying anything but I heard that Glynmor and Maggie are not sleeping together any more, Aunty Phyllis told Enid over the fence. It seems she sleeps upstairs and he's down on the couch. They do say there might be a divorce too.

Never.

It's Huw Bungalow it is. Glynmor's just jealous of all the attention he keeps getting. I heard that Maggie just follows him around all day like a lapdog. Doesn't cook for Glynmor, wash his clothes nor nothing. I heard in the Post Office that he's been carrying on with that Xenia Prosser.

Never.

That's what I heard. I'm not saying there's any truth in it mind. You know that Glynmor. They said he was carrying on with a hundred women before he got married but no one has ever seen him go near another woman since. He was always saying that Maggie was the only girl for him. I don't think Xenia's husband knows what's going on, mind you. Perhaps he doesn't want to hear nothing 'cos they do say he's carrying on with that piece up in Giro City. But even if he is he wouldn't be very happy with Xenia would he? There's a lot of pride with that Prosser family.

A lot of pride.

An awful lot of pride. You remember the time he caught the milk man with her. They do say that he wasn't man ever again after Piper kicked him. And his milk money bag was thrown over the houses as well. Gnasher and the Clay Class made off with that. There was forty pounds in that bag and he never got a penny of it back.

Never. You know when I look at Gnasher these days I just can't believe it. There's no shape to him at all is there?

He's like something from out of a swamp in'e? I'm not saying that he sets fire to cats or eats babies but the talk is he's gone beyond with everything. Daisy has gone off to somewhere on Clapham Common so he's out all night breaking into places and pinching. The latest I heard was that those skinheads have got hold of some carbide from the pit stores. They do chop it into small lumps and feed it to the birds inside bits of bread. The birds fly off and, the next thing, there's this big bang.

Never to God.

It's true that is. On my mother's life. A big bang, lots of feathers and no more bird.

Even as Emlyn Kremlin held the telephone receiver in the Welfare Hall and listened to the voice of the union official speaking from London he understood that this could be one of the most important calls that he had ever received.

The N.U.M. had got its hands on a confidential list of proposed pit closures, the official had explained. In times of rising unemployment the board couldn't risk making such a list public. So while the officially declared policy was to keep every economic pit going for as long as possible, the truth of the matter was that they were trying to run down the pits on the hit list by a steady process of stealth and attrition.

Bont was near the top of the hit list in South Wales. At the most it had three years to go.

'What we want, Emlyn, is for you and the boys to get yourselves organised now,' the official went on. 'Get the lodge to start a local campaign, organise marches and call in the local media – we'll handle the nationals. What we are doing is asking all the pits on the hit list to organise a fuss and the N.U.M. will do what it can up here.'

'Well you've come to the right lot in Bont to start a fuss,'

Emlyn replied. 'We may not be able to do much but we're marvellous at making a row.'

He put down the phone. He had long expected such a call but he wondered if he really could mobilise the boys now. To a degree what he'd said was true. The Bont boys had once been known as the wildest in the South Wales coalfield but, to be honest, he didn't detect much militancy about them now. All they seemed interested in was the fool's gold of fat redundancy payments.

He picked up the receiver again and called Dan O'Neill, a feature writer on the *South Wales Echo* and an old friend. 'Can you get up to Bont this afternoon Dan?' he asked. 'I've got a good story for you.'

O'Neill, a small cheerful Irishman with an explosively red complexion that told its own story, turned up at the Hall an hour later and they talked together over a stream of pints on the N.U.M. account.

Emlyn had a quiet mastery of the figures and obscure economic forces which were already throttling the life out of the Valley. Patiently he explained that Bont was now the last pit in the Valley. Everyone – even the N.C.B. – agreed that there was still plenty of coal there, some 80 million tons in fact, the finest anthracite in the world which even today was coming up 95 per cent pure. Despite all this the board was claiming that the pit was uneconomic, losing some £140,000 a week. He had just learned that they planned to close it in the next few years.

'Much depends on whether the accountants who are doing the sums are right or left wing,' said O'Neill. 'I've long learned that when you do your business sums you can do them almost any way to suit your purpose or what you want out of the place.'

'Exactly.' Emlyn had found the right man to talk to.

The old miner took out his fob watch, checking the time before continuing his argument for keeping the pit going. Some 750 jobs would be lost in the event of a closure, he said; while there was a ready market available for their coal, there was no capital investment in the pit. Nor, for that matter, was there any in South Wales as a whole. This district was right at the bottom of the board's investment league. Yet it was precisely in a valley like this that work was needed since unemployment for

206

men was now running at 35 per cent with 20 per cent of those between the ages of 18 and 24.

Even as he was relating these figures the image of Gnasher and his skinhead tribe whirled through Emlyn's consciousness. They were enough trouble to the community now but he dreaded to think what they would be getting up to in the future.

'But you see Dan,' he said, dragging himself away from such thoughts, 'we've now got that Maggie Thatcher in No. 10 and a Tory government that argues everything on the basis of profit and loss. This Valley has kept the world warm for close on a hundred years now. Thousands of men have died down the pits. Damn it man, they *owe* us something now. Not only the dignity of work but something better than those new factories as well. We've got to fight to keep our industry here. This coal is our blood, you see. And there are still men prepared to lay down their lives to keep digging it out.'

Whether the men would make such a sacrifice was not at all clear to the old communist. But Dan O'Neill seemed to like it all well enough. In the next day's edition of the *South Wales Echo*, the headlines declared that the Bont miners were drawing up battle lines for a fight to the death. All the figures that Emlyn had related were there as he had given them; there were plenty of quotes from the men and their wives on how they were looking forward to a tussle with the board and the Tory government.

Emlyn folded up his *Echo* with quiet satisfaction, remembering those great days of 1926 when everyone flung themselves into an epic fight which, as he chose to ignore, the miners had lost.

The Valley had been bustling and bursting with small storms all morning. Great black tides of cloud and rain kept bursting over the village in angry formless waves. Spouts of rain sprinted off the slate roofs in blind, mad rushes going nowhere. In the streets themselves nothing moved as the winds drove all before them, sending the sheep looking for shelter, keeping even the bumptious starlings quiet under the sodden eaves.

Maggie was washing up the dishes in the kitchen while Glynmor, dressed only in his trousers and vest, was on the sofa next to the fire doing the Spot the Ball competition in the *Echo*. This week, if he managed to locate the football which had been erased from the picture, the jackpot prize was £30,000 in cash with a holiday for two in the Caribbean plus a new Ford Escort. The second prize was £500 or a Kawai organ. At 20p for thirty attempts the whole picture was now festooned with tiny crosses.

The living-room again reflected a story of growing affluence and changing tastes. The G-plan furniture was still there, even if looking a bit frayed around the edges, but the plum-coloured fitted carpet had been cut up and used for the upstairs bedrooms. Now the floorboards had been stripped down and varnished with thick creamy rugs dotted everywhere. There was a smoked glass table and, on the windows, the patterned curtains of Laura Ashley. When Maggie could give the G-plan the heave-ho it would begin looking like the castle that she had always dreamed of.

Glynmor, still engrossed in his competition, groaned and Maggie looked over at him. She had noticed how he seemed to have lost interest in the pit and was gambling with increasing intensity. He was presumably hoping to win enough money to get out of the pit – even if he never said as much. He was doing two Pools coupons – Zetters and Littlewoods – the spastics draw and the weekly Tote in the Hall. Neither did he seem to be able to walk past a one-armed bandit without piking in any spare coins. She hated all this and said as much.

'Keep your hat on girl,' he would reply, unconcerned. 'There's a woodpecker about.'

The real aspect of Glynmor's gambling habits that hurt Maggie so much was not the inevitable loss of money but the way he had become just like everyone else in the Valleys. They all gambled on something or other around here. The pools, they had come to believe, offered the only possibility of a way out. They had traded in their commonsense for an empty packet of dreams, in Maggie's view, though the real sin of such gambling was that it took away the will to better themselves. That was the way Glynmor seemed to be heading too. And she hadn't married Glynmor because he was like the rest of them.

She walked into the living-room wiping her hands in her pinafore. 'They tell me that if you take a pin and keep prodding the picture you'll find the ball because it'll start hissing,' she jibed.

'That is a very old joke,' he said, without looking up.

'That's no joke. They do say that half of Bont does that. I'm told that your butty Tom the Nutter does it that way, anway.'

'He's no butty of mine any more,' Glynmor exclaimed with real feeling. 'I can't stand being near the sledge. The other day he was around the back of the washery trying to boil a pork chop in an electric kettle.'

'And what happened?'

'The kettle went on fire an' the next thing he's trying to boil a kipper in it and that's a fact. Why there are so many sledges down that pit I'll never work out.'

'Well, you're no different are you? There's nothing very sane about sitting around looking for an invisible ball in the *Echo*, well is there? How old are you anyway?'

'Listen woman. If I find this bastard ball ... '

'If, if ... '

'If I find this bastard ball we're on to £30,000 in cash and a holiday for two in the Caribbean. Not in Barry Island but the Caribbean. You wouldn't say no to that, well would you?'

She walked the length of the room and lifted one of the Laura Ashley curtains to one side so that she could look out into the rain.

'Well would you?' he asked again glaring at her.

'I would. If the holiday was for two I would. We're three remember? I wouldn't go anywhere without Huw.'

'No, I don't suppose you would.' Glynmor got up, suddenly all irritable and flung down his newspaper. 'Being alone with your husband wouldn't do at all, would it?'

She bit the side of her lip but said nothing as she continued staring out into the rain. She knew that Huw would be upstairs in his bedroom watching and waiting for the rain to stop as well. There was nothing quite like the rain for making you feel trapped with nowhere to run or hide. Even breathing became a struggle on rainy days. And that was the way you were in marriage wasn't it? Trapped as surely as if you had a ball and chain clamped on your ankle, just standing around day after day, waiting for the rain to stop.

Glynmor left the room and she picked up the newspaper that he had angrily flung down. Holiday for two in the Caribbean indeed! What next? Who wanted to go to the

Caribbean anyway? She'd far prefer for the three of them to go somewhere tidy, somewhere very smart like the Algarve in Portugal. Now that's what she called a real holiday.

She turned to the front page and read the headlines. A Welsh Nationalist Member of Parliament, Gwynfor Evans, had announced that he was going to fast to death unless the Welsh language got its own television channel. Now who, in his right mind, would do something like that just for a television channel, she wondered. She hated television just as much as her Huw. He was still putting the portable out with the milk bottles and she prayed that one day someone would come and pinch the thing and be done with it. Perhaps Glynmor would talk to her again in the evenings since, these days, what with *Coronation Street* and *The Incredible Hulk*, she couldn't remember the last decent chat they'd had together.

Outside, the winds and rain were shaking the telephone lines up and down. The flowers in the gardens were getting shaken worst of all, their heads battering against the dry stone walls again and again. Apart from the hissing rain all you could hear were the hollow clangs of the huge aluminium beer barrels being unloaded off a lorry by the side of the Welfare Hall. A brown polythene cup was being blown around the doorway of the chip shop, making brittle dull noises a little like a baby's rattle that had gone on the blink.

But then, early in the afternoon, the rain cleared up as suddenly as it had arrived. The smoke from a fire inside the tump drifted down the Valley turning from white to brown to drifting black. One side of the Valley was covered and safe under a dark blanket of shadow, the other side glittering and vulnerable as the sunshine danced in the soft banks of rain mists.

It was the damp from all the rain which made the sun glitter so ferociously. The puddles and rocks and railway sidings all shone brightly, as if they were coated with lacquer. Sunshine burnished the windscreens of the cars coming down the mountain road, almost making them look like celestial objects. Splashes of sunshine hung bright in the clothes pegged out on the lines.

Everywhere you looked on the one side of the Valley this glitter was so hard, so bright like, you had to squint or shade your eyes as you looked around you.

It was into this great swirling symphony of sunshine and shadow that Huw Bungalow descended, soon after the rain had stopped, making his way towards the pit, which stood like a gaunt black fist just next to the river. This afternoon he was being followed by a couple of inquisitive pit ponies, retired long ago but still taking exercise wandering around their makeshift Valley paddock.

No one – least of all his father Glynmor – had even so much as guessed what it was that made Huw so happy all the time. After all, said the boys in the bar, your only real option when looking around Bont, would be to burst into tears. There was nothing funny about the place, mun. It was a rundown village with a rundown pit populated by rundown people who drank and gambled too much. So what did Huw Bungalow find to laugh about?

They would never have guessed the truth. Far from being empty up top, as his name suggested, fiery and miraculous visions were forever sweeping through his mind, making his whole body shiver with rapture. Sometimes, if she caught his eyes at a certain angle, his mother did spot an odd evanescent flash or a tiny eruption of brilliant colours. But this was nothing compared to some of the performances that were being regularly staged in the mystical amphitheatre of Huw Bungalow's mind.

Nothing about these visions made any sense, the colours and themes jumbling and crashing against one another like some old Celtic story that was just impossible to understand. On some days his eyes might settle on something like the streams of smoke coming out of the chimney tops, drifting and tangling with one another until they made a great silver cloud. The coats of the blackened scrawny sheep might begin glowing as if on fire, or the walls of the Valley might become veined with gold. Even the winds that whistled around his laughing head might become soft, warm and caressing like a shawl of the most marvellous silk.

Just near the pit he turned and looked down to where a group of white sheep were coming through the dark shadows on one side of the Valley. But, when they crossed over into the bright sunlight, they turned to black. Then other black sheep were coming down through the sunshine on the opposite wall and, as they moved over into the dark shadows, they changed to white. It was all a bit like gazing at a huge canvas in which the artist kept on changing his mind about how to colour his animals. Look and look again and nothing was as it appeared and the colours kept changing at the precise point where the jagged line of shadow interlocked precisely into the jagged line of sunlight.

Not that Huw ever worried about making any sense. He beheld such moments of tribal magic with sheer joy. His mind was very much the repository of what was true, pure and lovely in the ancient Celtic culture.

He stood watching the changing colours of the sheep for perhaps five minutes until his blue suede shoes began taking him down towards the river itself, jerking along the bank past waters hurrying over the rocks and around old prams and dumped armchairs which littered its length. Just near the railway bridge an old mattress was being buffeted around, the rusty springs breaking out of its worn sodden covering like mortal wounds. Then, just above the chuckling sounds of the river, he heard a thin cry of anguish.

A bird was lying forlorn on the river bank. Its body was half in and half out of the water as if its back had been broken. Occasionally it would raise its beak out of the mud and take in a desperate breath of air before its head fell forwards again.

Huw reached down and picked up the bird, laughing softly as he rubbed his cheek up against its head, smoothing down its ruffled dripping wings, now blowing the bird warm and dry all over. Its small blue eyes looked up at Huw's and a small song trembled deep within its throat. He blew on the bird again, smoothing its wings before, suddenly, flinging it up into the air with both hands. He let out a great gale of golden laughter as the bird circled his head three times before flying off over the tip, soaring on up into the sky, high and proud, way above the Valley.

Guto brought another barrowload of rock and shale out of his new working around the back of the waste-paper factory. The late afternoon had become terrible cold and a thin fog was rolling down the Valley. The lights on the terraces flicked on, making the village look like gaudy necklaces scattered about irregularly beneath the mounting bands of grey mist.

But despite this damp cold Guto was sweating profusely. His lamp, tied around his belt, made his whole body glisten. There was no time to rest with Guto. Even with this fog thickening fast he barely stopped for as much as a few seconds before unloading his barrow and trundling back inside his working again. *Duw* his every move suggested that there was simply not a second to lose; that tomorrow all Bomber's money would dissolve, and be no more, unless he found it all now.

He threaded past the natural pillars he had fashioned in the earth for some fifty yards before coming to a face studded with rock and red crumbling shale. It came away easily enough under the continued onslaught of Guto's pick; indeed it was so soft and loosely jointed he was now certain that Bomber must have buried his fortune here. Bomber was never very strong so he must have buried it in soft ground and he had never come across any earth which was quite so soft and damp as this seam.

He whacked the pick into the face and tried to work it loose. Then he felt his boots sinking into the ground. He tried to loosen the pick; his legs sank up to his knees. He still clung onto his pick as fissures began cracking and loosening up all around him. There was a great explosion of air, which sounded more like a tired yawn of a giant, and he could see, in the flickering light of his lamp, that he was hanging above an old and long forgotten mineshaft. So this was where Bomber had stashed all his money, he thought, with an internal shout of triumph, as his pick came loose and he fell and fell and fell.

There is a whole body of mythology of what happens to men when they fall down mineshafts; of the way their hair turns white and they hear the music of their lives. But nothing remotely like that happened to old Guto as he fell, since his only concern was whether at last he had finally, and after all those holes, fallen into the very hole which hid Bomber's missing millions. For maybe ten seconds or so he bumped around before hitting a soft ledge, bouncing off it and tumbling onto his side, gashing his head and smashing one of his knee-caps. Even though in the greatest pain he struggled to get his torch out of his pocket and shone it around him. But there was no big, golden cask with the name BOMBER written on it – just a lot of damp limestone walls and an awful lot of drips.

Unable to move his left leg he had begun dragging himself along by his elbows when there was another loud splintering of opening cracks. He pitched forward through yet another opening in the ground, falling through dark spaces until his body smacked into yet another level. He groaned in pain, rolling over just long enough to see the falling shadow of yet more rock as it rolled onto his legs, pinioning him to the floor as efficiently as a maggot impaled on the end of a fishing hook.

Just after three in the morning, with nothing moving in the village streets except the dark and the cool, you could see, by the number of doors broken off their hinges, that the boys had decided to have themselves a party.

The back door of Walford's video parlour had been smashed in and there was a big space in the top shelf of the back room where Walford normally kept all his extra-blue pornographic films. The side door of the Co-op had been jemmied, yet again, with five bottles of Southern Comfort and a carton of pre-cooked chicken legs having upped off the shelves and walked off into the night.

Meanwhile a window had also just happened to fall off its fixture at the side of the Welfare Hall while, inside, in the Starlight Suite, Gnasher and the skins were sitting around on the floor, eating chicken legs, watching a blue film on the committee's video recorder and getting ripped to the tits on Southern Comfort.

They were barracking some rotten sod for abusing a young woman when there was a long lingering shot of her naked body.

'Tell me one thing,' said Nipper. 'Can someone tell me what your belly button is for?'

A long, stupefied silence.

'Go on. Can't one of you clever bastards tell me what a belly button is for?'

'It's to keep your belly in one piece,' said Gnasher, spitting out a bit of chicken bone. 'It sort of ties your belly together an', if you didn't 'ave one, your belly would sort of fall to bits, like. You couldn't keep any food in it could you? Well, it stands to reason don't it?'

'Isn't it something to do with your Mam?' asked Iffy. 'Isn't it where you were connected with your Mam?'

Gnasher hauled himself up with a sigh and, none too steadily, went over to Iffy and kicked his leg a couple of times.

'I fucking tole yer didn't I? It's to keep your belly together. Anyway you didn't 'ave a Mam.'

'Well I think it's where you were connected to your Mam,' Iffy repeated bravely. 'I think it's where you were joined up to her heart.'

'Who wants to know what you think?' Gnasher asked, kicking him again. 'When we want to know what you think we'll fucking ask you, all right?'

'All right.'

'My belly button has got a bubble in it,' Dick announced.

All bloodshot eyes turned to Dick.

'You wanna look see. It'll cost you a quid.'

They all hauled themselves up, swigging on their bottles and examining Dick's belly button minutely. And sure enough it didn't go inwards like ordinary belly buttons but stuck out in a small bubble of white skin.

'That's the most disgusting thing I've ever seen,' said Gnasher, his back to the orgy that was raging on the video. 'Really disgusting I do call that.'

Just then all the lights came on in the Starlight Suite and everyone looked up from Dick's belly button.

'All right now boys,' said a huge Alsatian dog coming through the swing doors attached to a policeman on a lead. 'There's ten of us so stay right where you are.'

Gnasher dropped his bottle, his eyes darting about him like a cornered panther working out which way to leap. He was the first to stand up and the others followed looking at him for a lead as yet more policemen slowly filed in through the door. There must have been a dozen of them. Gnasher had never realised that there were so many policemen working in the Valley so late. He looked down at the floor and spat defiantly. The others spat too.

All the policemen's eyes were on Gnasher since they knew that, if they got him, the rest would give in quietly. If Gnasher decided to make a stand of it then all hell would break loose. The dog was snarling ferociously as he strained on his lead to try and get at Gnasher except that the brawny skinhead did not seem at all frightened, just standing his ground and spitting on the floor again, clenching and unclenching his fists as he had once seen Sylvester Stallone do when he was in a similar tight corner.

'Are you coming quite then?'

Gnasher shook his head and spat on the floor again so, without further ado, the policeman unleashed his dog and it leaped straight at Gnasher's throat.

Gnasher then executed a move which would even have made Sylvester Stallone gasp with pride since he went down on one knee and caught the dog's forelegs with both hands, whirling the squealing animal around and around. Then he ripped the dog's legs apart, tearing its chest and flinging it back at the police who had watched all this aghast. 'So then. Who's next?'

Then all hell broke loose.

The police stepped forward with all the precision of a Roman phalanx. Truncheons went scything through the air in all directions with Dick going down on the first blow. Iffy was also whacked straight to his knees while Cocoa merely held up his hands in surrender.

There were no thoughts of surrender on Gnasher's mind and it was around his defiant frame that the police largely massed, cracking him on the head and shoulders or working in a kick whenever they could. He sidestepped some of the kicks and indeed managed to get in a few punches of his own, fending off the truncheon blows with his thick forearms and now getting in a head butt before he too finally succumbed after receiving three separate blows on the same spot just above his left ear.

His shaved head was but a battered, bloodied beetroot as he sank to his knees with all those truncheons belabouring him again and again.

'You're killing him, you bastards,' Iffy shouted as a policeman tightened a grip around his throat. 'You're fucking killing him.'

'I wish I could sonny. I wish I could.'

With that Dick gave a terrific shove and small mountain of flailing skinheads and kicking policemen went rolling over and over the floor fighting with one another.

Now yet more policemen were streaming in through the door when there was terrifying scream and one of the policemen stood up with a hand running with blood. One of the skinheads had bitten his little finger off.

'It wasn't me,' Cocoa was protesting through a mouthful of blood. 'I didn't do it.'

Chapter Fifteen

Glynmor was on the early shift. Even as he walked down the pit road, in a misty dawn which was neither day nor night, he knew that it was going to be one of those days. Somehow he couldn't seem to get himself awake. He wouldn't talk to the rest of the boys either. Bleats of sheep slipped around in the air as they tramped along.

'Curly got stopped in the bar again last night, I heard,' one of the boys said in front of him.

'Oh aye.'

'They do say he was eating the glasses again. He's a crazy bugger when he's had a few. It's no wonder he's always getting his beer stopped. I saw him eat a whole pint glass in there one night.'

'Must be better than my old lady's sandwiches though. Jam I've got again.'

'I prefer jam to cheese. Cheese is all I ever get. You'd think she married a bastard mouse.'

'Tuna I really like. But she's always saying she can't get tuna.'

'The trouble with tuna is not that it's difficult to get. It just costs so much.'

Glynmor paused briefly to read the notice on the door of the canteen. There would be a full meeting of the lodge the next night to discuss the impending closure of the pit. There was going to be trouble in that meeting and that was a fact. Some of the boys were saying that they were going to give Emlyn Kremlin's bollocks a right roasting for telling the *South Wales Echo* all about it first. The boys could get very self-righteous when they got going on things like that.

But who gives a toss anyway, he muttered to himself. In

217

an even fouler mood he changed and went down to the Deployment Centre. There he put his plastic check into his pigeon hole before going into the lamp room, where he put in another, brass, check for the lamp. All this palaver was to monitor their time and safety. But it didn't end there. After a brisk frisk for fags, they had to hand in yet another tally to the banksman before going into the cage. Yet they had been going through these little rituals and tally checks for so long they never thought about it at all.

They were, as usual, silent the moment the cage fell but soon Oboe Parry was passing on the hot gossip that he had picked up. 'There were a dozen cops down the Hall last night,' he reported. 'They picked up Gnasher and all those skinhead bastards.'

'Never to God.'

'Everyone got injured I heard. Gnasher thought he was General Custer on his last stand. A terrible fight it was with ten coppers injured and three dogs killed.'

'Three dogs killed! How could three dogs get killed?'

'They even got reinforcements in from Cardiff in the end they did. I heard it from Ted the Milk. Fucking millions of them, I 'eard. Emlyn Kremlin had to go over the police station this morning to bail Gnasher out.'

'They won't bail him out mun. He's already been in the nick a couple of times. They'll throw away the key they will. He won't be sniffing glue for a long, long time.'

Glynmor kept out of the gossip for a change. He had enough problems of his own without worrying about Gnasher's. There was something going very badly wrong with his marriage and it was preying on his mind. There wasn't really anyone he was close enough to to talk about it all but, even if there was, he would have had grave trouble articulating the real nature of the problem. It was not so much one problem as an ugly knot of several. That Xenia Prosser had been coming on a bit strong again and he was getting more and more tempted to try and give her one even if he hadn't actually done anything yet. But then, with his relationship with Maggie at an all-time low, their marital rites were getting worse and worse which, in its turn, was making a tumble with Xenia more and more attractive. The other main problem, of course, was that his nutcracker of a son was standing in the middle of everything.

He genuinely didn't mind that his son was a nutcracker,

mind you. He didn't even mind when he began dribbling and making weird noises to himself. The boys in the bar had even taught him rude two-fingered signs which he now used on everyone he met. He didn't mind that either, or even the way Huw would always ostentatiously sit with his back to the television when Glynmor was trying to watch it.

In fact there was nothing he minded Huw doing except that he so wished that he would go and do it all somewhere else.

They crowded out of the cage and onto the little underground train which took them as far as the locking station, where they were again clocked in and the firemen checked their lamps. Then it was the long hard walk to the new face, a two-mile trudge up slopes which had been squeezed and down slopes which had been hollowed out, through puddles which were shallow and others which were knee-deep, with just the beams from their lamps shining everywhere, swirling like lighthouses when the men turned their heads to talk, lancing the darkness like bobbing beacons as they walked along the roadway, dancing in the puddles which were broken up by marching boots, slicing into dark holes where old pit props lay abandoned and forgotten, catching in the millions of drips which fell all around them, perfect, like jewels full of light.

The walk to the face was no place to be walking when you were down or feeling blue. The damp still air gave off no encouragement to cheerfulness. It was muggy like a hangover; depressing like an old-time Valley Sunday. This walk, deep down in the earth, even gave off its own little whisperings of the death that was certain to come one day. It was the silence that got to you most: this eternal silence, shorn of the street, the Valley, life itself – all locked away down a hole and in a seam that had been around long before the dinosaurs.

The men even gave up talking to save energy for the long march, though the silence was soon shattered by the roarings of the Dosco and the clanking spiked teeth of the armoured belts of the Panzer. This was rip-roaring life in the middle of silent death; this was the fury and greediness of man come with his grasping hands and great machines to plunder the deep secret kingdom of the earth ... *Varoom* ... *clug, clug* ... *varoom* ... *clug, clug* ... *varoom* ...

Thankfully this seam had not thrown up any geological faults lately. The giant teeth of the Dosco were eating into the face as effortlessly as a child eating ice cream. Sparkling clouds of black dust erupted and belched as the men got to work, silently and efficiently servicing the queen of the hole. Some were bashing in a few more chocks to stabilise its level, others were keeping the sides of the roadway clear by shovelling any stray coal into the Panzers which dragged it along on it spiky chains to the waiting drams.

Everything was directed towards the Dosco. When it was eating well the whole future and health of the pit was assured.

Glynmor had been shovelling coal into a panzer when Dai Blades, the shift foreman, told him that they needed some more chocks. Would he wander down towards Trelewis to see if he could find a few spare lying around? It was a job Glynmor was happy doing, wasting a few hours wandering about looking for chocks. If he located them quickly enough he could easily slip into some dark corner and get his head down for a few hours.

He was walking in the direction of the old Trelewis seam when his helmet lamp lit upon a couple of chocks lodged under a pipe. As he pulled them free he dislodged a small, sharp stone. He stepped back to avoid any other falling stones and the light from his helmet caught on his hand. He just held it there and looked at it with all the objective curiosity of someone studying something in a museum case.

Other than a slight burning feeling he had felt no pain, yet his left thumb had been sheared clean off. There on the side of his hand, where once his thumb had been, a white nerve end was moving around slow, like a tiny ballerina dancing under a spotlight. He couldn't believe it. There wasn't even any blood.

He swallowed and continued staring at the space where his thumb had been, wondering at first why had felt no pain. He looked around the ground for his thumb and, unable to find it, stared back at the dancing ballerina again.

This here, Glynmor, a small voice told him, is your long-awaited ticket out of this pit, butty. This here is £35,000 and a pension for life. If that Harry Bando could get £25,000 for his little toe then your thumb has got to be worth a good £35,000 and stuff Spot the Ball. This here is a caravan in Porthcawl and long holidays in Spain. This here, butty, is what you've been long waiting for.

But watch out for those bastard surgeons, the voice added. They can sew anything back on.

He took off his helmet and placed it on a pipe so that he could get a lower angle with his light and locate his missing thumb which he found after a while, about four feet away, lying on its own in the coal dust near some loose rock. It was an eerie feeling looking down at this thumb which he had sucked and bitten and played with all his life, lying there in the coal like a dusty turd, not his own thumb any more. Could have been anyone's really, he decided as he stood up and scrunched the steel-tipped heel of his boot around and around on it. Those bastard surgeons would have to be pretty clever indeed to have been able to sew that on by the time he had finished with it.

Then, quietly and even happily, he walked back to the working face and up to Dai Blades. 'I've had a bit of a bump Dai,' he announced holding up his thumbless hand.

'Gis a closer look,' said Dai holding Glynmor by the wrist, the lights from both their helmets flooding down around the ballerina. 'Does it hurt?'

They both just stood there looking down as the ballerina did a few more pirouettes. 'Hurt, does it?' Dai asked again.

'No mun. I don't feel a thing.'

'Where's the thumb? Did you find it did you?'

'I looked but couldn't find it anywhere. It's up towards the Trelewis.'

Jones the First Aid was sent for and the Dosco was shut off as others came over to examine the space where once sat Glynmor's thumb, each offering bits of advice or consolation.

'Could have been your dick, couldn't it?' asked Oboe Parry.

'Should get a fair bit of compo for that,' said Tom the Nutter.

'It's going to be murder playing snooker with no thumb,' decided Dan Box. 'It's not going to be much help to your love life either is it?'

'You don't fuck with your thumb do you?' Oboe asked.

'I do.'

'Oh that's why you've never had any kids.'

All this talk about what you could and couldn't do without a thumb was making Glynmor as sad as rain. Come to think of it he had often used his thumb when in bed with Maggie and he had always loved playing snooker in the Hall. Perhaps it hadn't been such a good idea doing a tap dance on it. 'Someone go and find my thumb will you?' he asked, miserably.

'Where's it to?'

'It's down towards Trelewis.'

'Where to down towards Trelewis?'

'Just before the locking station,' said Glynmor. 'Just whistle for it.'

'Now what are we looking for? A thumb or a dog?'

'My thumb mun. It always used to twitch when I heard someone whistling.'

'Whoever heard of a thumb that twitched when it heard whistling? No wonder the bloody thing fell off.'

'It's a pity your bloody tongue doesn't fall off. Go and look for it will you?'

But no sooner had Jones the First Aid given Glynmor a shot of Pentathol than he was happier than a small baby, laughing and cracking jokes like he had just won Spot the Ball rather than lost his thumb as they prepared to stretcher him out of the mine. '*Duw* that's some good stuff you've got in that needle Jonesey. I'll have another shot of that any time you like. I'm telling you, boys, that Whaccy Baccy has got nothing on this stuff.'

There was, as usual, a stampede to be in the stretcher party since, as soon as you got the injured man up, you could go straight home as if you had finished the full shift. You were also unofficially free to rifle the injured man's pockets for things like snuff or sweets that he wouldn't be needing for some time. By contrast an injured man would have his pay cropped exactly from the moment of the accident. No free time, no free sweets, no snuff, no nothing. Not that Glynmor was feeling terribly deprived at that time since he was on cloud number nine.

'Hey boys have I ever told you that story about the queer who got raped by a gorilla?' he asked as he bounced along the roadway.

'Did he use his thumb for this rape, this gorilla of yours?'

'No mun. Gorillas have got huge dicks they have. Didn't you know that? They can screw female gorillas six at a time, just like a string of conkers. They've got enormous dicks they have. Like bastard pythons they are.'

'Glynmor. Give your mouth a rest and your thumb a chance will you?'

'Gorillas' dicks are so big they do wash their backs with them. They're so big they do lasso their girls with them and drag them into their caves and that's a fact. You know, boys, they're so long their wives do use them for washing lines when they're sleeping. You could hang a pit cage on a gorilla's dick you could.'

'Shurrup Glynmor. Hey Jonesey. Give him another shot will you? The man's gone mental.'

By the time they got him out of the cage and into the waiting ambulance he had calmed down and was whiffling quietly to himself. When next he opened his eyes the heads of the stretcher party were around him with a hand holding up a black dog turd in an empty crisp packet. Except that this was no dog turd. This was Glynmor's missing thumb.

'Don't worry butty, we found it,' said Tom the Nutter.

Glynmor's brow furrowed into a question mark.

'Your thumb mun. We just all stood there whistling and it came running down the roadway, wagging its tail and barking its head off.'

Glynmor sat up on the stretcher and took the crisp packet with his left hand, laying it on his lap and flicking it around until he could see down inside the packet's mouth. He might have been looking down into it for a full minute when he asked 'Which one of you thieving bastards stole the blue packet with the salt in it? Some mates you are. You'd steal a man's wooden leg you would. I hope I don't get a wooden thumb or I can see you lot will be pinching it all the time.'

'Give your mouth a rest Glynmor.'

'Look here,' said Jones the First Aid as he proceeded to give Glynmor another shot of Pentathol. 'They want you to keep hold of your thumb until they get you to Chepstow where they'll sew it back on.'

'But I don't want them to sew it back on,' said Glynmor throwing his thumb onto the floor. 'They'll only sew it on backwards or something.'

'They might sew it into your mouth Glynmor. You might talk some sense then.'

'Well you never know with that lot do you. They took two legs off one man who went into Chepstow and he only went in for a check-up.'

'Oh shut up mun. It'll be better than new when they've finished.'

223

'But I don't want it better than new.'

'You don't want your thumb?'

'No. I want the blue packet with the salt in it.'

Now no one said anything as they looked down at him. Glynmor so resolutely mixed his jokes with his seriousness you just couldn't be sure what he was trying to say half the time. And anyway they had shot the poor dab full of drugs.

Now one of the ambulance men took charge of the thumb, transferring it out of the crisp packet and into a polythene bag full of ice which he put on a small table before sitting down next to Glynmor as the vehicle sped off, with flashing blue lights and blaring sirens, down the twists and turns of the Valley.

'We had a miner with us yesterday who had lost an arm,' the ambulance man said brightly as if talking about the weather.

'Did they get it back on did they?'

'No. We never found the arm. It got lost down some shaft full of water.'

Glynmor groaned and turned over on his side facing the side of the ambulance. His Pentathol haze was thickening up again though he felt curiously alert. His mind wandered around from Maggie to Huw Bungalow and then to all those years he had spent down the hole.

They came to him, those years, in strange bursts of disconnected music; the sounds and pictures mingling together with no logic or order. He saw Jampots' face laughing at all his dirty jokes. He saw the boys all holding down Danny Rees in the baths and giving him a love bite to go home and explain to his new wife. There were the roars of noisy laughter as the boys played cards next to the Dosco and panzers. There was everyone jumping out of the way in the cage when Dibber Williams began puking up the previous night's beer.

But gradually and again in no particular order, other, darker pictures came winging into his mind too. That coloured fireball just hanging there in the roadway after that blower that killed Jampots. The way you would be eating your sandwiches and have to spit the coal dust out of them. His Uncle Bomber just lying there in his bed fighting for more air after his lungs had been eaten away by the coal dust. Jampots' incinerated remains piled up on a stretcher. *You got that fiver I owed you*

Jampots boy. You remember I paid it back now.

He rolled onto his back and stared up at the ceiling of the ambulance. And after Jampots there had been Aberfan. Who could ever forget Aberfan? Even all these years later he still had black nightmares about that. They had been coming more regularly of late too; the dreams of another killer black tide that was going to sweep them all away to their death. He never even told Maggie about these dreams of course. Just woke up grumpy and blamed the beer.

But he'd had enough of this dark bitter struggle with the coal. Oh aye. Even in his Pentathol haze he was very sure of that now.

'We've got to stop for a bit here to get petrol,' said the ambulance attendant. 'I won't be a minute either. Got to have a piss.'

Glynmor closed his eyes and took in a sharp intake of air through his nose. Typical. They're taking a man in for a serious operation and they'd got to get petrol. It's a wonder there was anyone left alive in the Valley at all, he thought as he sat up and stared gloomily out at the petrol forecourt.

It was then, barely without thinking, that he decided to settle his job as a miner once and for all since he stood up and took his thumb out of the polythene bag and placed it on the ambulance floor. He then took one of his boots and, with the gusto of a cobbler who had not done a shoe repair for a year, proceeded to smash the thumb again and again. When it had been all but flattened he put it on its side and flattened it again, now placing it back inside the bag and shaking it about.

Well, they really would be very clever bastards indeed if they could sew that back on.

'Sorry about the delay,' said the attendant hurrying back and still zipping his fly. 'We didn't get a chance to fill up after the last job.'

'It doesn't matter mun,' said Glynmor po-faced, sitting on the side of his stretcher with his legs dangling down. 'I've got all day.'

The ambulance accelerated up the motorway and, on Radio One, Kim Carnes was singing about Bette Davis' Eyes.

Wood smoke drifted lazily in the clear, cold sky as Emlyn Kremlin stepped off the path to allow a small child to walk past. A tall tepee stood in a clearing surrounded by low bushes. Nearby was a crude encampment of tents, old cars and tarpaulins tied to tree branches. There was a large grey and white caravan with slogans daubed on it. The smell of brewing tea drifted past. He walked on, stepping on the broken cardboard boxes which served as makeshift paving stones in the squelching mud.

In his formal pin-striped suit with waistcoat, fob watch and bowler he looked like a VAT official or a bailiff sent in by the rent man. No one would have taken him for a tired and increasingly bitter lodge official of the National Union of Mineworkers, come looking for his niece, Daisy. Certainly some of the women of Greenham Common, wrapped in Mexican ponchos or embroidered kaftans regarded him with suspicion.

It was a case of hate at first sight for Emlyn Kremlin. Their hostile questions merely added to the antagonism which was now bursting out of him like a bad bout of 'flu. All this muddy adventurism offended his Marxist version of history. What could ever be achieved by a few women squatting in a patch of mud? Revolutionaries had to get inside the working class and *organise*. Only such class organisation would provide the real springs for revolution and change. Even being close to this lot irritated Emlyn.

He hated the unmistakable whiff of these women's piety. He hated the heady air of self-congratulation in these women's hugs; the way they smiled at one another in the clear understanding that they had become modern martyrs out this morning to save the world. What Emlyn saw when he looked around him was a world abandoned; a world where militants had no clear perceptions of their first duty to radicalise the working class. On the contrary, this lot were actually alienating them by sitting in the mud and parroting slogans at the American servicemen. The working class reject all this as the ravings of hippies high on magic mushrooms. But the really loathsome smell for Emlyn was that of academe. He could see that a lot of these peace campers were well-educated and this added, in his eyes, to the unreality of the venture. In his book, academics knew nothing about anything that was important.

The sunshine had become acid-fierce and Emlyn was grateful for the shade of his bowler. Realising that he could be here all day he approached a woman sitting on a log, quietly plucking a guitar. 'I'm looking for Daisy Bland,' he said. 'She's from South Wales.'

'There's lot here from Wales,' said the guitarist without looking up from her strings. 'The Welsh women started this camp. Did you know that?'

'I did. Do you know her? This Daisy Bland.'

'I know her. They call her Daisy Three Balls because she's got more balls than any man we've ever met. Quite a girl isn't she?'

'She is.' He could sense her reluctance to give him any specific information about Daisy Three Balls. 'I'm her uncle,' he went on. 'Chairman of the Bont lodge of the National Union of Mineworkers.'

At the mere mention of the miners – always a favourite with the Greenham women – the guitarist smiled and jumped off her log. 'Follow me. Daisy's in a tent on the other side of that hedge.'

Daisy was down on her knees blowing into the flickering embers of a dying fire when Emlyn, bowler in hand, stooped into her large tent. Even in the half light he could see that she had not quite lost the bloom of her famous beauty. But she was ageing and no mistake. The fireglow caught in the crow's feet around her eyes. The thick rim just above her upper lip had got thicker and there was little softness about her curls either. She was wearing frayed scrubbed jeans and a floral silk shirt busy trying to come apart at every seam. It was her complete lack of provincialism that Emlyn had always admired; she had never allowed herself to be enclosed by the Valleys and its conventional ideas.

'There's no bottle left in that fire Daisy Three Balls,' he said. 'You need some good anthracite coal from Bont to get that going.'

She looked up at the tall shadow framed in the V of the tent entrance. 'Well kiss my aunty's cat's arse,' she said. 'If it isn't Emlyn Kremlin. Funny but I was talking about you only last night. Do you still hang out the hammer and sickle on royal birthdays?'

He smiled and stepped forward for her to kiss him on the cheek.

'Welcome to Greenham Common,' she said.

'What's all this about Daisy Three Balls then?'

227

'Oh it's just a nickname. I've been pinched by the police so many times all the girls do say I've got far more balls than men. Then one of them started calling me Daisy Three Balls and it stuck. I thought it was just the Valleys where they had a nickname for everything.'

Daisy knew immediately why Emlyn had come so far but decided to let him get there in his own time as they sat outside the tent and he gave her all the news on the latest comings and goings in Bont. Glynmor had lost his thumb down the mine, he reported, but seemed unusually cheerful about it with Maggie and Huw visiting him daily in Chepstow Hospital. The pit was under an unofficial axe and the men were already getting themselves organised for a long fight. There had been two meetings so far and he couldn't remember them being so united.

She decided not to let him wander about any longer and asked out straight how her Bobby was keeping.

'He's ... er ... he's keeping very bad, Daisy. It's him I've come to see you about.'

'What's he done now?'

'It's serious this time. Breaking and entering. Burglary. Assault on three policemen. And that's just about half of it.'

'That's serious all right. That's serious.'

There was a muted yelp of pain inside her and her shoulders slumped forward. Emlyn could see that she was very upset indeed. The girl's heart was in the right place even if her ideas were all over the shop. 'I could never do anything with him Em,' she said finally. 'He had more spirit than six stallions that one. The very first time they sent him to an open prison he broke into the canteen. What could *I* ever do with him?'

A woman walked past them carrying a kettle and calling out someone's name. She then stood still holding the kettle up in the air, calling out the name again. No one came so, letting the kettle drop to her side again, she turned on her heels and walked back to where she had come from.

'I've come because I want you to come back for his trial Daisy. He needs all the support he can find for this one otherwise he's going inside for a very long time indeed. It's a real shame with the boy. He's got the brains you know.'

'I can't come Em. I know he's my son but this is my home now. I could never do anything for Bobby. Even when he was a kid he was always his own man, always getting into trouble. I always thought he he was born old. I never had any control over him. His father did while he was with us but, after he went, that was it. Let's walk for a bit shall we?' she added, suddenly growing restless.

They followed a path through the tents and clearings while Daisy explained a little of their fight against Cruise missiles, telling him of the beautiful moments, particularly at nights when they all sat around the fires, happy with the righteousness of their cause. She explained how the whole process had turned her into a feminist and how she had now come to realise that her own personal problems were as nothing compared with the larger struggle to save mankind from its own stupidity. The women were fighting for the right of the whole world to survive.

'So that's what you're all doing here,' Emlyn said finally taking out his fob watch and checking the time. All at once he felt very weary. He was very sorry that he had come. Amateur politicians had always depressed him.

'I'll have to be going now but let me tell you something, Daisy Three Balls.'

She looked away from him, not at all liking the sarcasm that he had invested in her new name.

'You say that you're here so that the whole world can survive but the Valleys of South Wales; your home, Daisy Three Balls, have already died. While you are here having your beautiful moments' – he spat out the two words as if they had been freshly lacquered in syphilis – 'there's fear come to every home. The communities are crime-ravaged. Our leaders have gone away because there's nothing to lead. We are the most depressed area in Britain with just one pit left as our children are standing around on corners. Soon we are going to be taking them home in coffins and your son is one of them Daisy Three Balls. So don't tell me about your beautiful moments at the camp fire girl. Come home to the Valleys. I'm sure you do care but come home and care about what's important. We need everyone we can get just now.'

'No one wants me in the Valleys, Em.' She made it sound like the silliest proposal she had ever been made. 'They never forgave me for finding out that I liked sex. They've always hated that in those preacher-ridden Valleys. All they've been good at is malice.'

229

'The preachers have all gone, girl. The chapels are closed just like everything else. The chapel is not even an issue anymore.'

'They're still around. Wherever the Welsh are, those moralising maggots will always be around. It was them that drove me out.'

'But your son, Daisy. Surely you care something for him?'

'I care. Of course I care, but I told you. I've never been able to control him. Never.'

The argument continued, attracting the attention of some women who, sensing danger, gathered around. 'Your place is in your home,' Emlyn shouted at Daisy provoking a chorus of whistles and ironic cheers. 'My place is in my home,' they mimicked in his strong Welsh accent. 'Peeling potatoes and changing nappies. That's my place.'

Emlyn glared around at them, backing away like a stag at bay, barely able to understand these absurd politics of self-indulgence that had gripped the women in modern times. 'You're just amateur politicians the lot of you,' he barked at them. 'It's people like you the Tories welcome just as the mincer welcomes the meat. You divide the working class. You make decent people hate you. You abandon your homes to sit out here but your homes are the world. Can't you see that? If you let your homes go rotten then the world will go rotten with them. Every revolution has gone wrong when it left the home for the street corner. You don't win anything on the street corner. You win by organisation, argument, through the ballot box.'

Even as he voiced the tenets of his old-fashioned Valley politics he could see that his words meant nothing to them. Women like these were going to stage a revolution and to hell with the practicalities of power. They were all just dreaming in their mud patches.

'Go and jump on your bike old man,' said one. 'Go find another soap box.'

'Fling him out,' advised another.

'Don't you lay a finger on me,' Emlyn warned in tones which left no doubt that there might be big trouble if they tried. 'I'm going to walk out of here on my own now. You just continue saving the world, since me, I'm going for a quiet pint.'

Guto groaned softly and dragged himself a further few yards

230

along the narrowing pot-hole. By the date on his wristwatch he could tell that he had been trapped underground for ten days now, and had taken five of them to scratch and wriggle himself out from beneath a rock which had fallen on and crushed his legs. Sometimes he blacked out for a few hours while trying to release himself. When consciousness returned he would scratch around his legs some more. At times he clawed so hard at the coal and shale his nails had been torn and his hands were ripped and bloodied.

He was so ravenous he had sometimes in desperation sucked on his bloodied fingers. Fortunately he had later located some dripping water which had slaked his thirst. Just occasionally – to conserve his batteries – he would turn on his torch to look around him and it was this single-minded obsessiveness that was keeping him going even now. He only ever used his torch battery just long enough to get his bearings then he switched it off again. From time to time he stopped crawling, listening to the sound of his breathing lungs, powerfully amplified by the dank stillness of the air. But he was going to survive this small setback just as surely as he was still going to find Bomber's missing millions.

When Maggie and Huw turned up, Glynmor was lying in his hospital bed with his hand bandaged up and smiling like he had been given a permanent lease on the sun. His smile dimmed considerably, however, at the sight of Huw's splendid Edwardian suit.

'Does he have to wear that suit in here?'

'He likes his suit.'

'Looks like he's going to some bastard carnival and that's a fact. This is a hospital mun.'

'So how's your thumb today then?' Maggie asked seeking to change the subject.

'It's a Piccadilly pimp he should be in that suit,' Glynmor went on. 'This is a place for the ill. Next thing he'll be making all those disgusting signs again.'

'Well we all know where he got them from don't we? I must say I never thought I'd live to meet the day when *you* would be complaining about disgusting signs. Glynmor have you heard the news? Everything you say is disgusting. So then. Let's start again shall we? How's your thumb?'

'Well it's not anything is it? It's not there any more

remember? I'm thumbless, woman.'

Even Huw could see that his father was in a foul mood so he wandered off up the ward, standing briefly at the end of each patient's bed, making two-fingered signs at them and roaring his head off with laughter. Even the most haggard; even those who looked as if they were about to snuff it any second lit up with his performance, some giving him the V sign back and all joining in the laughter. It was the sheer infectious quality of Huw's laughter that overcame them since it attracted yet more laughter to itself and yet more until the whole ward had become a sort of eisteddfod of giggles with barely anyone knowing what they were laughing about. Maggie shook her head and smiled after him while even the grumpy Glynmor was forced to concede a bit of a smile.

But Maggie was just dotty about her son. The whole village knew it and she openly admitted it. When the women gossiped together in Lipton's they would call her a saint for looking after Huw so well but they didn't understand half of it. Maggie had never ever seen Huw as a burden; had never known a moment when she resented having to do as much for him as she did. There had never been a second when she had regretted having him. He was the joy and justification of her life.

Which is a lot more than she could say about her Glynmor. When Huw woke up in the morning it was always with a whoop and a smile while Glynmor was invariably moaning and bad-tempered in a hangover. Huw always did as he was told as well, always ate his meals tidy and spent a lot of time outdoors, always coming back just before dark, when she would be out on the doorstep waiting for him.

On the other hand there was her moody sod of a husband forever pushing his meals to one side and complaining that there was too much water in the sprouts or that the gravy had dried up. He had also become a devil for staying out late with the boys in the Hall then coming home drunk and banging about the passageway like a deranged snooker ball. At least now that he was in hospital she was having some peace and quiet with her Huw. It's odd, she thought, how, not so long ago, the marriage was doing well when, suddenly, and for no reason at all, it turned sour and just getting from one day to the next became an exhausting and frustrating struggle.

'Emlyn called over the house last night,' she said sitting

232

down on the armchair next to his bed. 'He'd been up to Greenham Common to see Daisy. She won't come home for Bobby's court case though.'

'She wouldn't would she? Not her. Daisy only ever did anything to suit herself. Did Emlyn say anything about the compo for my thumb?'

'Well he said it depended on the reports of a few inspectors. He said there'll be an N.C.B. report on liability and a doctor's one on disability. The inspectors have already been to where you lost your thumb. It seems the lagging was all hanging off where the stone fell so there'll be no trouble about liability, Emlyn said.'

'What did he say about money? Did he mention a figure did he?'

'He reckons about £34,000. More if it had been a right thumb.'

Glynmor smiled broadly and looked up at the ward ceiling. 'Well I'll go to Swansea. Thirty-four thousand smackers. We can do a lot with that Maggie my girl. We'll get a new car for a start then a fortnight's holiday in Butlin's or somewhere nice in the sun.'

'I'd prefer it if you still had your thumb though.'

'Nonsense. The left thumb's nothing. What did you ever need a left thumb for? It's as useless as a foreskin a thumb is.'

'I would though. I wish you still had it. I never understood why they didn't sew it back on.'

'There was too much coal dust in it, they said. Miners are always difficult to deal with because of all the dust. They can't get it clean.'

'But I heard they said it was broken in too many places as well. I don't understand that. How could that be?'

They both sat staring at his bandaged hand like two workmen staring down a newly-completed hole. Just then there was a huge eruption of laughter down the end of the ward and they looked around to see that Huw was entertaining a large crowd with his laughter and crazy whistles.

'Did Emlyn have any idea when I might get the money through?' Glynmor asked finally.

'Money, money, money. Is that all you think of these days? What's the matter with you? You used to like the pit you did but now all you want to do is take the money and run away from it.'

'Used to Maggie. I *used* to like the pit. I used to like a lot of things but not any more.'

'Why're you looking at me like that?'

'Like what? I'm not looking at you like anything.'

'I married you because you were always full of fight. That Glynmor Jones, the girls would say. That boy would fight a brick wall if it upset him. Everywhere you were fighting – even got banned from the cockle stall in Cardiff once didn't you?'

'It was just a misunderstanding about some whelks.'

'But you fought quick enough. Now look at you. All you seem to want to do is run away. That's not what I married.'

They were arguing in low-toned whispers. The visitors and patients on the other beds were trying hard not to look over at them.

'Look. I'm lying here because I've just gone and lost my thumb. You've come here and are having a go at me. Why?'

She looked at him with her fingers playing and pulling on the strap of her handbag. Her eyes were bubbling with tears too. Just what was going on, he asked himself with alarm decanting inside. Had they found out that he had deliberately jumped on his own thumb?

'Emlyn told me something else too.'

'Oh aye.' His eyes darted around shiftily.

'They've put a date on closing the pit. It came through yesterday. A year next October. And they're going to fight like hell to keep it open.'

'We all knew it was closing. So what're you raving about?'

'What it means Glynmor is that all the boys are going to have a big, long fight on their hands and you're just taking the money and running away.'

'I don't understand any of this. What're you trying to say? That I took a pair of scissors and just cut off my thumb like that?'

'I think you smashed up your own thumb after it had been cut off.'

'Rubbish.'

'They're good at surgery here, the best. I was talking to one of the surgeons. He said it was a straight slice but you probably smashed it yourself afterwards. Don't worry. They've had cases like this in here before. They sympathise with men so desperate to get out of the mines. But you did smash it didn't you?'

'What a load of old cock you do talk sometimes.'

'Glynmor, you can lie to the N.C.B. You can even lie to the N.U.M. if you want. But I'm your wife. Don't ever lie to me, your wife, now will you? I've got to know the truth about this.'

He brought his face close to hers and wiped away her tears with his bandaged hand. 'I do and say a lot of things but I've never lied to you,' he said softly. 'All I've ever wanted is the best for you so please believe me when I tell you that some of the boys may have trodden on it accidentally when they were looking for it. But I would never do anything so daft as to smash my own thumb myself.'

Glynmor's coming home in a few days, I heard in the Post Office, Aunty Phyllis told Enid over the fence. They're asking a few questions about his thumb down the pit as well, I hear. I'm not saying anything but the talk is that he put his thumb on the railway line and let a dram run over it. He wouldn't have cut off his right thumb now would he? Stands to reason donit? It's that Maggie I blame. She doesn't seem to have any time for Glynmor. It's all Huw this or Huw that. Maybe Glynmor did it just to get some attention from her. Men always need to be looked after doon' they? If you can't mother 'em, smother 'em I've always said.

Chapter Sixteen

Sunshine burnished the cars parked along Bont Terrace and there was a stiff smell of frying chips in the breeze as Curly, Idris and Snipe sat on the bench in front of the village clock with empty cider bottles beside them, their arms folded in readiness for a lunchtime of amateur philosophy. All three of them were now working out committee suspensions from the Hall – Curly for fighting with one of the barmen, Idris for standing at the bar during bingo and Snipe for using obscene language in front of the committee chairman's wife.

They accepted their punishment without qualm or protest though, content to sit out their time on the bench in front of the clock if it was fine, as today, or in the bus shelter when it was raining. From this vantage point they could kick their heels and watch the comings and goings in the village; the white Sidoli's ice cream van rattling up the Valley in a cloud of golden chimes; the burly men on the Welsh Brewers' delivery truck sweating as they rolled the aluminium beer casks down the wooden ramps of the Hall; the Meals on Wheels van which always chugged past the boys on the bench just before lunchtime leaving a cape of boiling custard trailing in its wake.

'What've you got to do to qualify for that Meals on Wheels then?' Idris wanted to know.

'You've got to be sick mun,' replied Curly.

'Well I'm sick,' Idris boomed, retaliating as if a doctor had just told him that he was going to live forever. 'I'm bloody sick all right. Every morning I get up I'm honking into that bed pan for a good half an hour. That's bloody sick isn't it?'

'That's not sick mun. That's all the rough cider you do drink. That's not sick.'

'Well what's sick then?'

Curly paused, rubbing his tongue around inside his cheek and making it bulge out as if it was filled with air. 'Sick is being really bad like. Sick is when your legs won't take you anywhere and you can't have a pooh without three men carrying you down the back. That's sick. Sick is when you can't tell the difference between a knife and a fork and you have to suck up your gravy through a straw. Sick is when your arms won't move and you even haven't got the strength to lift a pint because it's so heavy.'

'Oooh that's sick all right,' Idris agreed.

'Sick, as far as the Meals on Wheels people are concerned,' Curly continued with his lecture, 'is when you are no bigger than a shoe box and they've got you in a coffin and are about to hammer in the nails.'

Idris pushed his cap up with his finger, marvelling at the awesome extent of Curly's knowledge. 'But Curly, tell me one thing now,' he said, pulling his cap down again. 'What's the point of feeding you, if you're inside a coffin? There's no point is there?'

Curly sighed and clamped his hands on his knees. 'It's a contract between Meals on Wheels and the council,' he explained patiently, as if talking to an idiot which, in a sense, he was. 'It's the law see. Don't ask me why but Meals on Wheels are obliged, by the law of the council, to feed you until you are dead.'

'Right up to the last minute? In the coffin?'

'Right up to the last minute. In the coffin. Even when the death rattle has set in, those women from Meals on Wheels have got to be forking in the food as fast as they can go. By order of the council.'

'But why's that then? It doesn't make sense does it?'

'I don't know. It's the fucking law. I didn't make them up did I? Go and ask down the council offices if you don't believe me.'

Idris looked under the bench to see if there was any cider left in the brown bottles. 'You'll never catch those Meals on Wheels in my house,' he announced after some thought. 'I'm told the food is shit anyway.'

Sunshine continued hosing the roofs of the village and there were isolated cheeps from the blackbirds breaking ambush from around the chimneys, always as if they were about to start a song but never getting around to finishing it. Sometimes a whole group of them started their cheeping calls and then they just all cut them off abruptly, all as if belonging to the same well-drilled choir.

The next vehicle to attract the consuming attention of the boys on the bench was a police car which pulled up outside Lipton's. 'Oh finally made it have we?' the manageress, Mrs P.J. Jones, asked, all sarcastic, as three policemen got out of the car to examine the big hole in her window. 'Tell me, should we make an appointment when a crime's being committed next? Perhaps, when there's a burglar downstairs, you'd like us to send you a registered postcard or something?'

'We're very busy these days Mrs Jones,' the sergeant explained. 'You know there's so many burglars working the Valley at night they now do it in shifts to avoid traffic jams.' He could be very satirical too.

'Well it shouldn't be too difficult for you to catch them then, should it?'

'We do what we can Mrs Jones.'

'You lot couldn't catch a cold,' she sneered. 'This shop has been done six times since Christmas. When we had that Trevor Watkins stationed here he always knew who'd done it before it'd even been done. He was on his bike and picking them up even before they got home. Everyone knew him but you lot don't know anyone now do you? You just want to live in your new fancy bungalows down in Pontypridd.'

'Have you made a list of what's missing Mrs Jones?'

'But what I don't understand,' she went on, ignoring him, 'is that when you came for all those skinheads in the Hall you practically brought a whole army with you. When there's been a simple break-in you can't get a single one of you to come for hours. I was told all the break-ins were going to stop now you rounded up all those skinheads.'

'We thought they were too. But there's a storm of crime in the Valleys these days, I'm afraid.'

'They're not out again, are they? Those skinheads.'

'No. Mrs Jones. They're going away for a very long time indeed. This broken window is the handiwork of someone else. Now what, exactly, is missing?'

That same morning Gnasher, the still small centre of the storm of crime in the Valleys, had been temporarily becalmed in the dock of Treorchy Assizes. In his ill-fitting, torn denims and scuffed Doc Marten boots, the swastikaed fingers of his hands clasping the dock bar in front of him, he stood to attention as the judge addressed him and his assembled co-defendants.

'It has been represented on your behalf that there can be some mitigation for these appalling crimes,' the judge droned on. 'But the law of the land has many attractive features and ...'

Gnasher stood a good head and shoulders above the rest of his pals who crowded around him, looking, with their ear-rings, black eyes and cuts, much like a defeated tribe of Red Indians who had missed the last bus back to the reservation. Practically every one of them had sustained some sort of injury or another, what with bandaged fingers and arms in slings. But it was clearly Gnasher who had taken the worst hiding from the police. There was so much sticking plaster over all parts of his head it was as if he was wearing a turban. His nose had been so flattened and broken in parts he might have been French kissing a dumper truck. Even in such discomfort he still had that special air of unremitting hostility that was pure Gnasher, glaring at the judge with his beady green eyes and occasionally squeezing the bar of the dock until his knuckles showed white.

'The attack on that poor dog was one of the most heinous that has ever been brought to my attention,' the judge went on. 'Then to argue, as your barristers have argued, that this was a clear case of self-defence is also inadmissable in my view. Police officers need the protection of such dogs against the growing viciousness of youths such as you and I want to be very clear ...'

Down in the well of the court the clerk was turning over the pages of a fat law book while a blind stenographer, with hands the size of small shovels, was taking a transcript of the proceedings. Just above him, on the Press bench, a reporter from the *South Wales Echo* was playing noughts and crosses with a reporter from *The Western Mail*. Fronting the well of the court were fourteen of the arresting police officers, sitting in a long blue line facing the judge and occasionally looking up at the defendants who, every so often, would giggle or pick their noses ostentatiously.

One of the policemen had lost his little finger in the mass

arrest but they had never got near to finding out who had bitten it off. Cocoa had been duly charged but they had to drop that one in the end since Cocoa pleaded successfully that he hadn't had his teeth on the night of the arrest and had difficulty eating biscuits let alone a policeman's little finger. He had got all the blood in his mouth from being punched there.

'The crimes committed on that night were serious enough but the far more serious charges concern the repeated assaults on the police officers and the death of that luckless dog. Now the jury have rightly found you guilty on all charges and it is something to your credit that you have not contested that guilt but ...'

In the crowded public benches at the rear of the court Emlyn Kremlin sat with his head in his hands. Next to him were Maggie and Huw Bungalow. The rest of the seats were filled with worried parents, relatives and friends who had come over every day since the trial began.

Bont villagers had always turned out in force when one of their number had fallen foul of the law. For this trial there had been so many of their own in the dock, not everyone had been able to get into the public benches. Those in the dock were, after all, their children – not sensationally good examples of children, admittedly, but their children nonetheless. This, after all, was the Clay Class, with whom they had grown up man and boy and of whom they all had some funny stories to narrate. Time and the calls of the pit a'willing as many came over in Trevor's mini-bus as possible, following the proceedings with the greatest care.

With most of her time taken up visiting Glynmor in hospital, this was the first time that Maggie had been able to come to the trial. She could feel Emlyn's terrible anxieties about the outcome. Huw Bungalow, on the other hand, seemed content just to sit there twiddling his thumbs. He was keeping quiet too but, at such times, Maggie could feel the laughter simmering away inside him. She did so wonder what it was that made him so happy. When Huw did catch her staring at him quizzically he would just give her arm a soft squeeze as if to say, 'It's all right Mammy. I'm just enjoying myself.'

'*Duw*, this judge is so boring he'd put a glass eye to sleep,' Emlyn whispered to Maggie. 'When's he going to get to the point?'

Maggie bit her lip but said nothing. There were many times when she had been grateful that Huw was as he was since she was sure he might even have ended up with the Clay Class in that dock if he'd been normal. It was so sad seeing those young boys, who really hadn't done anything really terrible, get into all this trouble. She always liked Gnasher as well, and was furious that her sister had not come home to be with him in the time of his trouble. She held Huw's hand. She would have travelled the world if she thought Huw had so much as cut himself shaving she would. She had that mother's love within which she was helpless and just couldn't understand why Daisy was being so hard about it. Mothers who didn't love their children – no matter what they'd done – weren't normal in her view.

'Of course the predictable defence is that you have all been unemployed since leaving school. The argument runs that these frightful assaults are not your fault at all but crimes that are somehow commissioned by the government of Mrs Margaret Thatcher. We have even had some less than notable members of the local miners' lodge coming here to this court and declaiming such specious nonsense.'

At this point Emlyn, who had stood in the dock and given a character reference on Gnasher's behalf, leapt to his feet. 'What does he mean by "less than notable" then?' he stormed. 'I'll give him less than notable.'

'Shush,' the court usher shouted at him. 'Shush up there.'

Emlyn reluctantly sat down again.

'So, before I deliver sentence, I'm going to ask you if you have anything to say in mitigation. Is there anything any of you want to say?'

'I've got something to say,' Gnasher announced evenly, in a voice which carried through the court with surprising authority.

'Very well, Bland.'

'You've locked me up before an' now you're going to lock me up again. I just want you to know something. When I come out you're going to have to lock me up again as well. From the day I left school all I ever wanted to do was to work, to set myself up with a car and a bit of money. But there was never any work an' we was left to the street corners where we learned 'ow to pass the time. That became our work; that's where we

241

learned to be like what we are. It's too late for you and yours now.'

'Get to the point, Bland. The point lad.'

'Well the point is – your honour – you might as well hang us all now since we're going to continue tearing this place apart till we get work. Do you hear me – your honour – send us all to the fucking gallows now 'cos we're going to tear this fucking place down if you don't give us more than the dole to keep us going. You hear me? Tear this fucking place ...'

The rest of Gnasher's speech, which was getting on for the first coherent – and certainly the longest – statement that he had ever made was drowned in a terrific uproar as uniformed arms went around skinhead throats, tattooed arms tried wrench other hands free, balding foreheads went butting blindly in all directions as yet more uniforms went vaulting over the dock rail and flung themselves into the ruckus with the whole struggling pile surging one way and another until, miraculously, Gnasher's whole body emerged from the fighting pack with his arms raised like an international line-out forward and the whole court looked up, with their eyebrows raised, half-expecting to see a rugby ball in his hands.

Emlyn's shoulders slumped downwards. 'There's another year on his sentence. But I'll tell you something Maggie. That was the finest speech I've heard many a man make. It had fight, spunk. I only wish I had someone like that in the union. "When I come out you're going to have to lock me up again as well." Fire, Maggie. If only we could get some fire around here.'

After the dock had been cleared and each of the defendants handcuffed to a policeman – two for Gnasher with one standing at his rear – they were brought back into the court to hear their sentences.

'Robert Emlyn Bland, you are clearly the ring-leader of this unhappy gang of thugs and I hereby sentence you to a total of seven years imprisonment.'

Seven years! Emlyn's blood ran cold and he sprang to his feet as some of the women groaned aloud. 'Shush!' the usher kept shouting. 'Shush! or he'll be clearing the court.' Gnasher began struggling with the policemen again before being led downstairs.

'Richard Michael Williams, I sentence you to four years imprisonment ...'

Others on the public benches jumped to their feet as the sentences were being read out, one of the mothers screaming and shouting hysterically. They may have been bad boys but they were Bont boys.

And so, one by one, the Clay Class, who had been schooled and come of age only to be given a handful of glass and a bucket of spit, were led down the stairs to their cells and the start of very long sentences. The villagers were still numb in their disbelief, some crying out in their anguish and shame at such young lives being chopped down at the knees. Finished before they had begun.

'Well he was right on one thing. This fucking place will be torn down. That's for sure.'

Emlyn was shaking with rage and Maggie had to hold on to his arm to try and calm him down. This capitalist system had nothing to offer its children so it just destroyed them instead, he now saw all too clearly. This was Aberfan all over again, this was. Why didn't they just shove slurry into their mouths at birth and be done with?

'Hey, Judge Jeffries, why don't you just do as he said an' hang them an' save the taxpayer some money,' Emlyn shouted, his cheeks streaked white with anger. Maggie had never seen him so livid. 'Seven years for killing a dog. What do you give someone who kills a man then? Do you kill his whole family do you? You would, that's for sure. *You* would. Well, wouldn't you?'

The judge stood up and stared down at Emlyn. 'Clear the court,' he said and walked out.

It was just after eight o'clock and the sun was sinking in a fiery red ball over the west side of the Valley when Glynmor was brought home in an ambulance from hospital.

It was an extraordinary sight as the ambulance followed the winding road up the Valley. The floating, still clouds turned from ice-cream white to candy-floss pink, throwing a brilliant red gloss over the grey and green slopes of the east Valley wall and actually changing the still surface of the reservoir, just above the pit, into a skating pool of fire. A few trout jumped, black on red, near the still, pointed reeds.

Next to the pit, a diesel locomotive, striped black and yellow like a hornet, was shunting some wagons down the line.

John Abdabs was driving a huge ten-wheeled Arctic truck down from its delivery of slurry up at the top of the tip. The old, overhead conveyor had gone now, with the sounds of the labouring Arctic replacing the trickles and swooshes of the old iron washing line. Down below, the river was laughing and hurrying around the abandoned hulk of a burned-out car. But it was the pit itself which looked the most emaciated, particularly at this time in the half-red night; not so much a pit as a giant modernistic cathedral which had fallen on hard times, its windows all broken, brilliant splashes of sapphire light inside rooms without walls and floors on hapazard levels, all just flung together without any shape or symmetry; an industrial ruin sorrowing against a red backloth for the boundless energy of its lost youth.

But this sense of death was belied by the sudden roar of machinery in the washery and the hollow clatter of coal falling down a chute into a waiting wagon. Then silence reigned again in this jagged-toothed cathedral. If you listened very hard you could hear the distant bark of a dog. Even then you could see that the pit, like the village, was already gathering around itself the dark shadows of ruin and decay. In this broken-jawed cathedral the Mass had gone silent and soon the very altar would be carried off to the knacker's yard. In this down-at-heel cathedral the soaring organ notes had finished and the air was alive with the dead music of dripping water and the persistent whine of electric generators.

The red sun sneaked away over the high, rock walls of the Valley and the bluish night thickened as the ambulance finally turned into Bont Terrace. Maggie was quickly off with her pinafore and out onto the doorstep to welcome her husband home. She had got her hair done in Sandra's that afternoon and even put on some lipstick, determined to make a fuss of him since she knew that he would be down in the dumps. Even in the unflattering glow of the sodium street lamp she did look a picture, Glynmor had to admit, after he had stepped out of the ambulance, waving his bandaged hand around at the neighbours who, as usual at the sight of an ambulance or fire brigade, had all come flocking out onto the pavement to have a good gawp.

'Hello there, lovely,' Maggie said, going over and taking him by the arm.

244

'It's all right. I can walk. It's my thumb not my legs. How are you girl?'

'Oh I'm as nice as ninepence.'

'You do look as nice as ninepence too.'

'Thank you Glynmor. You can come to this house again.'

There was a bunch of fresh flowers on the television in the living-room and he could smell stew cooking as he settled himself down into his favourite armchair. He could see that she had already put Huw to bed, since his clothes were on the back of one of the dining chairs, and this made him almost as happy as the glass of beer she put in his hand.

The truth of the matter was that Maggie still felt guilty about accusing him of crushing his own thumb. So much of this cossetting was penance, even putting his slippers on for him and lifting his feet up onto the pouffe. He accepted this treatment with faint agreeable murmurs since he loved nothing more than being pampered. Beneath all his vulgar excesses was just another Valley kid out looking for his mother.

'I went over to the court for Gnasher's case this morning,' she called out from the kitchen where she was plating up the stew.

'Oh aye. Did they hang him after all?'

'No but there was blue murder there was. Gnasher made this terrific fighting speech about the kids in the Valley being out of work and, at one stage, there was such a fuss I thought the judge *was* going to hang him. But then he got seven years. Seven years! Emlyn practically had a fit and I thought from all the shouting he was doing he was going to end up in the clink as well.'

'Oddly enough, I've been thinking a lot about Gnasher and the boys since I've been in hospital. You do get a lot of time to think when you're in there. If you're not going to give them work then prison becomes inevitable when you think about it. If I'd been a lad with nothing to do and no money there'd be nothing else but trouble for me to do, when you think about it. Still seven years is an awful long time and that's a fact. You can eat an awful lot of skelly in seven years. At least the shops around here are going to have some peace and quiet for a bit.'

'No. I heard Lipton's was broken into again last night,' she said handing him his meal on a tray. 'They got off with four boxes of meat.'

'Was it heavy carrying all those boxes back home then?' he asked, looking up from his plate.

'Oh shut up. I wouldn't have the strength to break the window let alone cart off all those boxes.'

'Mmm. Great smash 'n' grab team you and Huw would make. The Bonnie and Clyde of the Valleys. How is he, anyway?'

'He's all right. The boy's all right. They do still get him drunk in the Hall sometimes in the afternoons which makes me get my hair off 'cos it makes him dribble. Otherwise he's all right.'

'Can we have the television on?'

'If you want, my lovely, anything you want at all. I'll get you another beer if you want.'

'Why are you being so nice to me?'

'Because you're my husband,' she said all wide-eyed. 'And I'm glad to have you home.'

She sat at his feet on the carpet as they watched *It Ain't Half Hot Mum* which was interrupted, much to Glynmor's considerable irritation, by Mrs Pritchard from next door who called to see how he was. When Maggie managed to get rid of Mrs Pritchard they both sat watching *The Des O'Connor Show* and it was then that everything seemed to break inside Glynmor and he began crying. She could not remember when he had cried last and stood up with her hands flapping around in alarm. 'What's the matter lovely? We can always switch the tele off if he has that effect on you.'

'It's not that, daft twat,' he said, still sniffling and crying like a leaky tap. 'It's my hand. How am I going to manage without my thumb?'

'It'll be all right Glynmor. There's a lot of things you can do without a thumb.'

'I won't be able to go fishing, will I?'

'When did you ever go fishing? Glynmor, you've never liked fishing.'

'I was going to go halves with Tom the Nutter on a rod. We were going to join the fishing club, we were.'

'Well you can still do that, can't you? Since when did you need a thumb to go fishing? It's maggots you need for fishing, not thumbs mun.'

Des O'Connor was busy singing on the television as the

246

coal fire fell in on itself and glowed in the reflection in the china cabinet. Now Glynmor, still crying, was holding up his bandaged hand like that gravedigger examining poor Yorick's skull. 'Did you know I always used to suck that thumb when I was a kid,' he wittered on. 'My Mam was always complaining because I sucked that thumb and, in the end, it got slightly smaller than the other one. But there's not much to suck now is there? There's not much there now.'

Maggie sighed and stood up, switching off the television and shaking her head. And to think that she had once married the greatest fighter in the pit, the man who knew every dirty story in the world and had been banned from half the pubs in the Valleys for fighting. And here he was crying because he didn't have a left thumb to suck any more. She had never been able to make out if she had married a man or a baby though that, she freely admitted, was a great part of his charm – if ever you could use such a word about Glynmor. Come to think of it, she had long stopped reading all those Mills and Boon novels too. It was just too ridiculous reading about all those flash architects flying in with rare orchids from the continent and then having to face Glynmor covered in coal dust, smelling of the beer and bragging about the size of his dick.

'And how am I going to play snooker? I used to love snooker I did.'

'Glynmor, you're being pathetic now. Do you want another beer or what?'

He started wailing again. 'I just want my thumb back. That's all I want.'

'I know what you want,' she said taking hold of his right wrist and leading him up the stairs. 'And I've got just the thing for this little ailment.'

She had already made a few preparations for his return to the married bed. She sat him down on a chair and poured him a glass of red wine. Now she stepped out of her skirt and blouse, taking her time about hanging them up in the wardrobe. Next off were her stockings and suspender belt, leaving on just the tiny white bra which supported and displayed her lovely firm bosom and the tiny frilly panties of red silk with the black embroidered split in the crotch that always drove him daft with lust.

'So what have we got down here then?' she asked shoving

247

her hands down inside his pants. 'What's this then? Well, I do believe, it's my favourite big lollipop.'

Missing thumb or not he was on her in a flash, driving into her without taking his or her pants off: no foreplay, no kissing, no nothing but, although a bit dry, she let him get on with it, reasoning that he probably needed it now more than she did and, with a little bit more wine, she might get a decent one out of him later.

It all seemed to do the trick as well since, almost the second he had come, he had rolled off her and was talking something like the Glynmor of old. He discoursed for a while about the size of his dick and then asked her, in all seriousness, if perhaps it was just too big for her.

She rolled over on top of him kissing him on the nose, the mouth and licking him on both cheeks. 'Well I do have some trouble,' she mock-crooned. 'But there again you always said that I had a fanny like a council skip so I do manage it somehow. It's a lovely big dick, fair play. It's got to be the biggest dick in the Valleys.'

Now he was like putty in her hands and she smiled to herself. He could be such a boy sometimes. A drop of wine, a bout of slap and tickle and a few compliments about the python-like qualities of his dick and she had him purring with happiness for hours. They had not been getting on too well of late and she now saw that she had better work a bit harder since she could clearly make him very happy indeed when she tried. Over the years she had come to understand him quite well though she had also noticed of late that he was even showing signs of becoming serious about a few issues. He had been talking a lot about the health service while he had been in hospital and hearing him say what he had just said about Gnasher had been very surprising indeed. He normally had nothing but scorn for his wayward nephew.

They drank more wine and then they made love again, softer this time, more considerate, with her even rubbing his bandaged hand around inside her legs, moaning in comic ecstacy just to show him that, thumbless or not, his left hand was still a vital element in the truly fabulous sex machine that was her husband, Glynmor Jones.

'Doesn't hurt, does it?' she asked him. 'Your thumb, I mean.'

'Hurt? No, it's fine. Just itches sometimes but it's fine at the moment. Plenty of sex is clearly going to be good for it.'

'Oh so that's going to be your line now is it?'

Later in the contented darkness of the bedroom they both lay looking up at the shadows and sharing a cigarette. 'If it could only always be like this,' he said.

'But it could Glynmor,' she said, draping her leg over his. 'It's always down to us. We could always make it like this if we tried.'

'You know with all the compensation I'll be getting for my thumb we could afford to put Huw into a home. It would be good for the boy too.'

Even as he said this she slid her leg off his, took away her hand and moved over to the other side of the bed with her back to him. The warmth had gone and the frost was as certain as a winter's morning. Why did he always have to go and ruin everything? And after all the effort she had made to make him happy tonight as well.

'My compo should come through quite fast after the doctors have settled it,' he went on, oblivious to her hurt. 'Thirty-five thousand, Maggie. That's an awful lot of bananas and it would be good for Huw to get the benefits of a home. It's marvellous what they can do with handicapped kids, I heard. Only the other day in hospital I was reading about Remploy and the great work they were doing.'

She said nothing for a while, just stared into her hands which she could cheerfully have wrapped around Glynmor's neck and squeezed very hard indeed. Her belly was a taut knot of fury.

'They could teach him a trade if he went into a home. He'd be able to get a proper job.'

'He's not going anywhere,' she grumbled finally and incoherently.

'What did you say?'

'I said the boy's not going anywhere.'

'It would be good for the boy. Thinking of the boy I am.'

'No you're not. You're thinking of yourself as usual. That boy is not going anywhere. He's not going to any home. He's not going to learn any trade. He's stopping here with me.'

'Don't you want him to learn anything at all then? Is that it? Do you just want him tied to your apron strings all your life?'

'Yes. Yes, I do. You think he's daft but that boy knows more than you'll ever know. Just watch him one day and you'll see. There's things about him that would amaze you if you'd only look. But you don't, do you? You resent your own son and you've never even bothered to look at him proper.'

'All I see is a nutcracker who should learn a trade or something.'

'You would, wouldn't you? You would.' She was practically speechless with rage. 'Well let me tell you something now. He stays here with me. You go before he does. Got it? *You* go.'

Guto had been crawling along underground tunnels for a staggering thirteen days now and only the naked urge to survive kept him going at all. With just dripping water to sustain him he was barely strong enough to move. It might take him an hour to struggle a foot. Where he was going he had no idea. His body was really exhausted and he was subject to hallucinations.

These hallucinations, brought on by his deranged senses and lack of food, had begun as strange lights, some bright and some faint, like a distant firework party. But the more they came, the more elaborate they were. On occasion they were accompanied by their own sounds and smells. The first one was so real he jerked his head up sharp, giving himself a crack on the tunnel roof a few inches above him.

And still the hallucinations kept coming – stammering, vivid and as fleeting as waking dreams. A pack of white dogs with red ears went dashing and barking all around him. Even in his discomfort he struck out at the dogs with a fist, yelling at them to go away when, as if by a series of mirror changes, they all disappeared.

He dragged himself onwards and there was a faint whinny and a lady with gold brocade on her white silk dress went cantering past him on a big white horse. She was being followed by men with rag boots on their feet. Guto called out to them for help but his cries died away in echoes in the empty darkness.

Somehow, the hallucinations galvanised the remainder of his strength and he wriggled forward again still clutching his torch in his hand. The iron discipline, which had made him switch it off almost as soon as he had switched it on, had served him well since it still worked, albeit faintly, throwing a pale yellow stammer of light all around him. In some odd way the very constriction of his underground prison kept him moving along too. If he had been at all comfortable in that suffocating darkness he might even have stopped all his painful movement and just given up the ghost. As it was, he just kept moving, every last fibre of his being anxious to get out of this hellish tomb in the hope of finding some warm, well-lit place in which to end his days.

He crawled blindly on, squeezing past hidden obstacles in his path, inching uncomfortably through black muddy pools. Sometimes his movements disturbed stones that might never have been disturbed before. Then he found some space and he tumbled downwards hitting one side of a tunnel and then the other, feet high above him and arms floating around as if in water, crashing into another jutting rock again before falling with the softest of thuds on to a pile of coal dust and sliding down it, legs and arms akimbo, as easily and gently as a child coming down a playground slide.

Finally, exhausted by the effort, he lay quite still, not even sure if he was dead or not. He did not even try to open his eyes in case he found that he could not. Neither did he move any part of his body lest he could not. His smashed knee-cap was now so painful he could not feel his leg at all. In the dripping darkness all he was aware of was a faint quivering in his belly. This alone told him that he was still alive.

Had Guto not been past caring he might have realised that he had fallen into the Ynysybwl No. 2 shaft, sunk in 1886 and sealed off and abandoned after being swamped by firedamp in March 1889.

Everything around him was as still as it had been a hundred years ago. The gas had long seeped away but there were the wooden wedges and pinch-bars lying around next to splintered pit props. There were the old wooden tubs used to carry the coal out of the pit; even the iron man-rider trolley was still there on the rails. More ominously, there were the perfectly preserved skeletons of eight miners lying where they had fallen after the pit had been sealed off all those years ago. Their jaw-bones seemed to be sagging in frozen laughter at the cruel fate which had befallen them.

One of his old eyes opened and he switched on his torch. The pale yellow light stammered briefly onto the skeleton of a pit pony which lay on its side, its legs sprawled out grotesquely on the floor of the heading. 'Well I'll be buggered,' he said, believing that he was hallucinating again. 'Well bugger me.'

The yellow funnel of light swept around this deserted charnel house, picking out the white skeletons of the miners which glinted, white on black, against the seven-feet-high coal face and rickety structures of the pit props. This really was the eternal silence of the tomb, amplifying Guto's startled breathings and turning them into great shuddering gasps.

Realising that all this could be far worse than a hallucination he turned around suddenly and tried to scrabble back up the small mountain of coal dust down which had first slid. But, instead of taking him anywhere, this flurry of movement merely served to tumble him forward down against one of the wooden coal tubs on which he cracked the side of his head. He swore savagely again and, looking around, his torch beam picked up another skeleton, its skull lying incongruously next to its leg, the wooden handle of a pick lying across its rib cage.

By now Guto had no feeling in his broken body at all. He could sense the remainder of his life draining slowly out of his very legs and yet he felt strangely peaceable about it, his spirit already surrendering itself to the tomb. At least he had a sort of company with the other miners lying around him. Not much company, he thought blackly, but better than bugger all. Anything's better than bugger all init? Moving his arms around a bit to try and get comfortable he lay down next to the man-rider trolley and closed his eyes. He just wished that he could have had one last glass of Guinness.

But there would be no more Guinness for old Guto now. The all-time champion tunneller of the Valleys had sunk his last shaft and it was fitting somehow that he had finally come to rest here, miles below the sun. His forehead crunched down into the coal dust which billowed up in small choking storms all around him. 'Bomber, you bastard,' he cursed into the dust. 'Bomber you great bastard I'll get you for doing this I will.'

Even as he lay there he knew that he was but a heartbeat away from death. In all that perfect silence of the tomb, with smiling skeletons sitting all around him, he could hear his heart puttering faintly – *pa, baam* – *pa, baam* – *pa, baam* – but so faint they were, so lacking in any conviction he knew now that this was going to be the very last beat of his heart. *Pa, baam* …

Right from the day after Glynmor had come from the hospital the marriage went as sour as a crab apple. There was no wine, no saucy underwear, no slap and tickle, no nothing except a thick sulking silence and Glynmor sitting around watching television all day. He watched any old rubbish from *Blue Peter* to the old cowboy films and he liked the volume up so loud it made his son whimper with pain.

Huw would sit on his favourite chair in the kitchen waving his hands around his ears as if someone was pouring acid into them. He would stroke his belly as if he had a couple of dozen ulcers. Most of the time he tried to avoid the sound of the infernal television by going outdoors.

The sight of all that anguish in those big, black eyes was more than Maggie could bear. It usually led to another loud quarrel for the neighbours to cluck over.

'What do you want me to do?' Glynmor would shout. 'Take the bastard television up to the top of the tip?'

'Take it anywhere you like. We don't want it here.'

'What about me? Don't I live here? Don't I have any rights?'

'You don't have the right to upset us.'

'I thought it was his nibs that was getting upset.'

'It is him that's getting upset. But, when you upset him, you upset me too. At the very least, turn the sound down, will you? You could hear that down in Cardiff.'

Huw found the sounds of such arguments even more hateful than the sounds of television. That day, even though it was still raining hard, he loped out through the back yard and took to the slopes of his beloved Valley.

'See what you've done now?' screamed Maggie. 'You've driven him out into the rain.'

'I never done nothing. I was just sitting here watching the box. If he wants to walk around in the rain that's his look-out.'

Huw really cheered up, however, when he took to the rainy slopes, exulting in the thrilling fragrances of the damp heather and ripening blackberries, enjoying the company of the sodden sheep and the rich, green moss squelching beneath his shoes, wandering through the drilled lines of pine trees of the Forestry Commission where squirrels came bounding out of the hissing mists to look up at him.

Sometimes he climbed into the steep crevices of the Valley walls even in the rain; a familiar, if odd, sight in his Edwardian suits and yellow socks crossing crab-wise from fissure to fissure or else climbing yet higher up the steep volcanic slopes with the sure-footedness of a mountain goat. The gaudiness of his clothes ensured that he could be spotted for miles around and children in the village streets would stop and shout out: *Look there goes Huw Bungalow again.*

But today the streets were deserted and the windows misted up with the rain. No one was watching as Huw walked across the sewage pipe over the river and climbed the dry stone walls of the farm as he made his way down towards the Banana Tip. No one, that is, except Rev. Mordecai, who was standing in the opened window of his bedroom following Huw's footsteps with the same binoculars that he had once used to spot and track his returning racing pigeons.

The reclusive minister had developed a bigger obsession with Huw than he had ever had with his pigeons. When possible he charted Huw's every move, noting the times he left his home and the times he returned. When possible he logged the places Huw visited as well, trying to work out some sort of pattern to his movements. The boy was the key to something very important indeed, in the Rev.'s view, and neither could it have been an accident that he had been born on the morning of the Aberfan disaster. Through Huw's life God was clearly trying to tell his people something and it was up to Mordecai to help deliver the message even if he was not yet quite clear what it was.

As Huw walked on, the stiff winds punched hard into the rain, spinning it around and around into small frenzied whirlpools or else fashioning it into huge white toboggans of mist which were driven along the length of the high walls of the Valley as if in some great and endless race.

The winds were driving so hard and the rain coming down so ferociously Huw was forced to take shelter down the side of a deep gulley, an exploded slash of stone from whence a stream, swollen by the rain, was sprinting out beneath some rocks to dive over a high ledge to join the river below. He followed the stream right up into the mouth of the gulley until he came to a small opening through which he could just squeeze.

Inside he came out into a wide cavern, new to him, with small piles of rusty stones strewn over the floor. In the gloomy light he could just see some rusty old mining drams lying next to one of the walls and a neat pile of wooden pit props. There was an old wooden hut without a door and, moving further down into the mouth of the cavern, Huw came across a huge boulder which, in its enormity and presence, transfixed his eyes and made his spirits soar as if set on fire.

He had seen something like this somewhere before. It was on a postcard from a foreign land and something very dear to him which he had pinned on his bedroom wall. In its size and shape it was exactly like the rock in The Garden.

His jaw open in wonder he took a few steps closer to it, holding out his damp hands and touching the stone with the backs of his knuckles. Despite its size it was the softest rock that he had ever touched. He looked very closely at it and, from somewhere out in the storming rain, there was the sound of fluttering wings.

He touched the stone again, laughing this time and smoothing its contours with his palms when he could hear a strange music of organs and women's voices coming out of it. The music surged and faded away again. He saw the very veins of the stone light up with parts of the rock glinting as if they had become diamonds. He stamped his foot and laughed in delight at the beauty of his wonderful new vision. He stepped forward and laid his cold cheek flush against the warm rock, relishing its silk softness. There were those women's voices again, deadly in their pitch, heart-breaking in their sorrow.

Now he took the rock with both his hands and there was the sound of those wings beating again as he moved it one way and the other as effortlessly as if he was handling a fairground balloon. Now he moved the rock to one side and that sorrowing music came surging out again; the pure, crystal music of the tribe. He lifted his face and smiled into the rapture, turning his cheek from side to side as if warming himself in a gusting summer breeze. Now he joined in the sweet song of the cave as well, whistling along with the powerful many-layered sound of the resurrection morning.

Outside the cave, milky thunder rolled over the roof of the

Valley and joined in the music. The rains and the odd slash of lightning added their own voices to that of the women's. Even the sounds of the angry winds came to add texture to this universal song until it seemed that all the elements in the world were at it; joining together in the glorying passion of a wonderful music which penetrated and exposed the darkest secrets of life itself.

Something stirred in the sepulchral darkness. Unsure of its provenance, Guto turned on his torch and, without lifting his head, gazed at a group of black pats scurrying away from this sudden and unwelcome spotlight. The faint noise drifted through the air again and he knocked a couple of times on the iron rail with his torch.

Silence.

He knocked again and had closed his eyes when the sound drifted back through the darkness, clearer now, more assertive, a soft reviving whistle which told even old Guto something of the preciousness of life and made his failing heart quicken. He tapped on the rail again.

The whistle faded away but then became even stronger and, as the sweet notes sailed around him, his smashed body seemed to acquire a new strength. There was a new power in his broken knee and his very fingertips seemed to glow with a new purpose. He rolled over onto his back and could actually feel the blood moving through his ears. Every fibre of his being was humming as he painfully hauled himself to his feet and set off along the track.

As he staggered away from the face and down the tunnel the gradient of the track became quite fierce. Being dragged along on the tightening elastic of gravity, he soon found that he was stumbling along at a fair lick, his mind whirling around and around with that strange whistle still calling him home. Now he was lurching through the shifting darkness almost as fast as if he was on a train, scything through large puddles with enough water to dream of drowning, sweeping into a long curve, now chasing out into a pit-propped roadway where Davy lamps flickered like pale isolated fireflies.

Now Guto was running like a man possessed, barrelling out into an even larger cavern where he plunged straight into a blazing hallucination which made him cry out and keep

256

running faster than ever before.

Skinny children were working the wooden handles of rag and chain pumps. Bilious jets of steam were exploding out of spluttering tappets. Grieving women were carrying wicker baskets full of coal, some in their arms and others with hemp ropes tied around their foreheads. The air was thick with shrieks and obscenities as men in moleskin clothes and trousers yorked with twine below their knees were wheeling barrows or whipping the mange-ridden rumps of the pit ponies ... everywhere, just everywhere, there was noise, pain and frenzied movements as these people, these slaves of the lamp, toiled in their bitterness and pain, mauling and scrawling to win the black gold from the earth.

Some of the moleskin miners shouted out at Guto in a strange language and others waved their Davy lamps as he staggered past, still so terrified he could only cry out loud as he hauled his screaming body through the flame and flood of an old working mine; too terrified even to dare to believe that he was still alive as he chased his own hallucinations down through the fires of hell; too terrified even to notice the great boulder which he had stumbled against.

Guto put down his head and cursed his fate piteously. He just did not understand it all and had no words to even try and explain it. For someone who was expecting and even hoping to die he just seemed to be moving on to fresh forms of torture. Now his escape was blocked by a great boulder. He sank to his knees in a frenzy of despair. 'Bomber, I'm going to have you for this,' he cried out, shaking his fist uselessly in the darkness. 'I'm going to have you, you great bastard you.'

But even in his darkest despair he was released from it yet again by that strange whistle. And yet again his bloodied and battered body sang along to its mesmerising lilt. He cocked his head to one side and spotted a grey shaft of light, thick with drifting mist. A black bent figure, with Edwardian drapes, a bootlace tie, drainpipe trousers was silhouetted in it. Huw Bungalow lifted one of his hands and waved at Guto.

'Get me out of here will you, butty?' Guto called out.

There was a bit more whistling and a faint chortling laugh.

'Don't just stand there,' Guto called out yet again. 'Give me a hand, will you? I want to go home to my house.'

Chapter Seventeen

Summer drifted into autumn, and the air was full of floating pollen and dandelion seeds. The walls of the Valley turned to ragged patches of gold and dark orange. Even the sheep were finally rounded up and taken in for the annual count. The winds became colder too, scissoring through the thin summer clothes and making the people of Bont ransack their cupboards and drawers for the old winter flannels and woollies which had served them so well in so many past winters.

The village continued its way with the tenacity of a life-long believer. The Buffs still met every Tuesday night in the Hall basement to celebrate the sacred mysteries. The Hall committee still met every Sunday afternoon to quarrel and bicker about crimes and their appropriate punishments. Though the pit still kept producing coal, maddeningly the board had withdrawn its earlier closure date and was now saying nothing at all. This move infuriated Emlyn Kremlin and the boys of the N.U.M. lodge since, as the board well knew, they did not have a date around which to orchestrate their anti-closure campaign.

Rev. Mordecai came out of his seclusion long enough to enter his hernia-inducing leeks and cannonball cabbages into the Horticultural Society's annual show. But the bronze commendation for his cabbages so enraged and disappointed him that he returned to his seclusion and his great literary and historical work on revival which was now running to some seven tomes and encompassing every single revival since 1700.

On other levels Snipe Wilson was picked up one afternoon on the bench in front of the clock and taken to the police headquarters in Pontypridd for questioning about a stolen video. Mrs Oboe Parry went into Church Village Hospital for sterilisation and Ted Milk was given instant dismissal by the

Co-op dairy for watering down his milk. The housewives were complaining that he was putting water in his water.

After his brush with death, and the even more perplexing problems of life, Guto temporarily abandoned his search for Bomber's millions and went home to his house where he took to his bed, overcome by what felt like a terminal bout of melancholia.

Meanwhile, the passion in Glynmor and Maggie's marriage had packed its bags and caught the next bus to Cardiff. There had been no fights or ringing arguments. The relationship just seemed to fall face forward, dead in the middle of the road, like an old miner who had finally run out of puff.

But it was quiet enough, until Maggie had her first real inkling of the coming storm when Glynmor went over to Aberdare to have his hair cut only to return with his hair permed and curled in a style that had been made fashionable by the footballer Kevin Keegan. What is more he was wearing a ear-ring.

Huw Bungalow was eating a plate of chips and Maggie was preparing some sprouts when Glynmor walked into the kitchen with one of those broad silly smirks on his face. She took one look at the curls and ear-ring before dropping her peeling knife into the sink and running out into the backyard. There she had to sit in the outside lavatory for a few minutes before she managed to compose herself.

'What's the name of this barber then?' she asked when she came back into the kitchen. 'I'll go over and break his arm.'

'It's the new style,' Glynmor shouted, sitting in his armchair with his feet up against the mantlepiece. 'All the boys in the pit are having their hair curled now. We're not the apes in Wimpey jackets of old, you know. The modern miner has got style ... class.'

'Glynmor, there's more style in a sack of nails. Go and have your hair cut proper will you? I can't go out with you looking like that.'

'I had it done like this because I like it like this.' There was a coldness in his voice that Maggie did not like at all. 'What's more I haven't asked you to come out with me, have I?'

'You'll be wearing one of those gold medallions next.'

'It just so happens woman ... ' He stood up, opening his shirt buttons and displaying a huge gold sovereign hanging on a gold chain. Medallion Man. She looked at it, appalled, but said nothing. Perhaps all these idle days were having an effect on his brain.

His compensation offer was going to come through at any time now, Emlyn had said. He was confidently expecting something in excess of thirty thousand pounds – though the real problem, which had yet to be resolved, was if he was too disabled to go back down the pit. The N.U.M. was claiming a 60 per cent disability on his behalf but the N.C.B. was claiming that it was more like 15 per cent. Somewhere between these two claims there was also the problem of a hardship pension. Meanwhile, he was drawing social security which, in real terms, meant that he was as well off as ever.

Perhaps it was only Maggie who had seen how much it had really affected him; the way he sat around watching television and neurotically trying to gnaw the space where his thumb had been; the way he kept on blowing on his stump and complaining about the pain which got worse after he'd had a couple of pints. *Duw* she could even feel him sweating and shivering in his sleep. It would not be so bad if he would talk to her about it all, but he wouldn't even say boo, baa, bob's your arse.

Now, as if there weren't troubles enough, he was becoming as flash as a poodle with diamond fillings. Maggie sighed and returned to the sprouts. The sooner he got back down that pit the better. To hell with the hardship pension – and any compensation money, come to that.

The next morning he drove off to Pontypridd in their old Cortina car and came back driving a sparkling new Toyota estate car with an enormous dashboard bristling with rows of buttons and space-age dials.

'Glynmor, what've you done?' Maggie asked, coming out of the front door holding her hands to the sides of her head.

'I've been to see the bank manager. He says I can have anything I want till my compo comes through.'

'But this car ... look at it ... it must have cost millions. We were going to save your money.'

'Save for what?'

'Save for a rainy day. You'll need all that money if you don't get your job back.'

'We'll worry about rainy days when they come. You fancy a ride?'

'No, I do not.'

'Please yourself,' he said and accelerated off up the road towards the pit.

Maggie ran back into the house in tears. She could see what was going on clearly enough. Retaliation was the name of this game. He was needling her because she was sticking by her Huw. He was hitting back at her as well as trying to make himself look big and more fanciable in her eyes. But the more he acted like this the more ridiculous he became. She fancied him well enough as he was. If she had wanted perms and ear-rings and fancy cars she would hardly have fallen in love with him in the first place. Well, would she?

But all that week it continued to get far worse since him and his fancy car were now staying out until three, four and even five o'clock in the morning and, what was even worse than that again, he was not coming home drunk and smelling of the beer either. He said he just curled up in the back of the car and slept off the drink rather than drive home, when she challenged him about it.

Although frantic with worry she tried to stay calm, always waiting up until he came home, leaving out little peace offerings like cheese or corned beef sandwiches with Branston pickle, even making tea for him as he chattered on freely – rather too freely? – about what fun he'd had in this unspecified pub in this unspecified Valley, usually with Tom the Nutter.

He was not acting happy enough, that was for sure, so she supposed it wasn't for her to interfere with that. But it was terrible hard for her. She just wanted to make sure that he knew that her love was forever; to make him understand that there really was enough love for both of them and, when he accepted that, perhaps everything would become fine again. As he stayed out she sat staring at the fire and listening to her records with her belly knotted into a dozen knots until he came home again. Then she made him feel welcomed, loved, reassured. But it was terribly hard.

'I'd like to come to this pub with you sometime,' she said as he sat eating his sandwiches. 'I'd like to see a few new faces. And it must be boring for you being with Tom the Nutter all the time.'

'Oh aye,' he said, looking shifty.

'Huw doesn't need to be baby-sat all the time now does he? It'd be nice for me to get out a bit more. It'd be nice for both of us wouldn't it?'

'Aye. It would. Is there another cup of tea in the pot is there?'

Maggie could see that she was losing, though quite how much she only discovered one morning when she was cleaning out the bedroom and discovered that their sex book in the brown paper bag had gone missing from under the wardrobe. She was truly astonished at how much that hurt. It was *their* book and he had gone and taken it to someone else. It was as if someone had punched her half a dozen times in the belly. She sat on her knees on the bedroom carpet, her hands shaking, practically doubled up with pain. Oh Glynmor, how could you do that? *Our* book with all that *our* bodies have done together.

There were a couple of inches of vinegary wine left in the bottle and she poured it into a cup and swallowed it in one gulp. At least he had not taken that to his fancy woman though, come to that, he was probably buying her champagne. But even as she finished it and stood looking at her shocked, haggard face in the dressing-table mirror, she resolved there and then that, painful though it all was, she was just going to sit it out. There were going to be no rows and no bitterness. She had seen far too many hasty divorces in the Valley. She wasn't going to be like her sister Daisy. She'd divorced in five seconds and look what had happened to her – camping in the mud in Greenham Common and a son who had gone rotten and ended up in the clink.

When you were married, you were married for life and that was the end of it.

The next day there was a brilliant autumnal afternoon of bright crisp sunshine and thin shadows. Ghostly, purple mists were sliding along the rims of the Valley when, as the police were to record in their notebooks, there was an incident outside the Welfare Hall just after four o'clock. As an event it shot through the parish precincts like a giant electric shock, adding considerably to the lustre of the gossip for weeks to come.

The 4.10 X6 bus to Upper Boat had been standing outside the Welfare Hall, filling up with about a dozen old age pensioners and mothers with armfuls of babies and shopping. Inside the Hall the driver was having a smoke and catching a quick pint at the bar.

There was a particularly raucous group in the corner of the bar including Snipe Wilson who, only that day, had completed his suspension from the Hall for using obscene language in front of the committee chairman's wife. To celebrate his return to the fold it had been drinks all round with Snipe even doing a turn on his spoons.

When the bar steward pulled down the wooden shutters to signify the end of the afternoon session, Snipe lurched slowly up the Hall's corridor and stood outside on the pavement looking up at the half-full X6 bus. Now everyone knew that Snipe was as brainless as a waterfall – even when sober – but no one could ever work out quite what had wandered through his beer-addled mind at that moment. At 4.05 on this bright autumnal afternoon he just climbed straight up into the bus' driving seat, switched on the ignition and accelerated down the road with a furious roar of cylinders and a long screech of speeding tyres.

At first none of the passengers, all busy gossiping to one another, noticed anything wrong. But, instead of following the road straight down the Valley, the bus turned right by the village clock and began rattling and bumping up the mountain road, flattening the village sign and sending the frightened sheep running helter-skelter in all directions.

Pained shouts of anguish echoed up and down the pavement outside the Hall. Women ran towards the shocked driver shouting dementedly. Sister Betty was expecting a baby any moment now! She shouldn't have come out anyway! Uncle Fred had this heart trouble and couldn't stand any excitement! Snipe had drunk at least sixteen pints and couldn't tell his right from his left at the best of times!

'Well it's no good shouting at me, is it?' the bus driver kept repeating before going back into the Hall to phone head office. Someone else called the police.

Glynmor, who had been dozing in his armchair in front of the television, pricked up his ears at the agitated noises going on outside the Hall. He wandered down to investigate and soon found out what had happened. Snipe Wilson had hi-jacked the X6. Recalling the chase scene in *The French Connection* when

Gene Hackman had pursued the hit man in his car, Glynmor ran back to his new car and was off up the mountain road in hot pursuit.

Even as the Toyota sped past the flattened village sign there was a quick burst of movement in his own house. Huw Bungalow had come in through the back kitchen door and spotted that the television had been left on. He ran across the living room, unplugged it and heaved it out onto the pavement along with the empty milk bottles. He permitted himself a few joyous giggles and promptly hurried out through the kitchen door again.

By now a whole cavalcade of cars, police cars, ambulances and trucks were careering up the mountain road in pursuit of the hi-jacked bus. Wheels were screeching through clouds of dust, the windscreens brilliant blazes of light in the sunshine.

Inside the bus, the mothers were weeping and clutching their babies tight. All bloodshot eyes and hiccups, Snipe trampolined up and down on the driving seat arbitrarily flinging the huge steering wheel one way and another as they crawled along on the old road, bashing the trees on the edge of the pine forest.

'Snipe Wilson, I'm going to tell your mother about all this,' one of the women shouted from the back of the bus. 'She's going to box your ears proper when she gets hold of you.'

The wheels of Glynmor's car went scything through a patch of shale as a police car tried to pass him on the narrow trail. Headlights blazing they both jostled for possession of the mountain road. But it was the Toyota, with the benefit of the curve and the maestro at the wheel, who won. Nose to tail, they scorched along the path of those broken trees until they finally came across the missing X6 bus in a Forestry Commission car park. There, next to a sign warning about forest fires and a wooden paddle to put them out, sobbing mothers were coming shakily down the stairs of the bus and frenzied cries erupting from inside that Sister Betty was about to have her baby at any second. Worse, Uncle Fred seemed to have chosen that moment to have another of his pulls, his face a pilchard red as he gasped for air.

Meanwhile the still centre of this storm, Snipe Wilson, had sobered up enough to take off on foot through the pine forest pursued by Glynmor and a policeman anxious for Snipe to breathe into his breathalyser. Just behind them were two brolly-wielding mothers anxious for revenge and a few kids anxious to see what kind of walloping they gave Snipe when they caught him. Snipe leaped across two gullies and a stream before running out of puff and being caught behind a woodman's hut.

'I think we'd better start with this breathalyser,' the policeman said when he got hold of him to start helping with their inquiries.

'What's that?' asked an out-of-breath Snipe. 'Some kind of new cocktail is it?'

'It's a new kind of brain you're going to need,' said Mrs Palser, raising her brolly and belting Snipe a real brahma with it.

Even as another woman began belabouring Snipe with Glynmor egging them on, yet another crime was being committed back in the streets of Bont. An unmarked blue van pulled up outside Glynmor's house and, faster than diarrhoea with daps on, which is Valleyspeak for very fast indeed, a man leaped out, picked up the television among the empty milk bottles, flung it into the back of the van and drove off.

Mrs Pritchard, standing in her doorway in the next but one house, actually witnessed the theft, but the van was just about out of sight by the time the penny dropped. Maggie was coming back down the road from the shops when Mrs Pritchard broke the news.

'It's *Coronation Street* tonight as well!' was about the height of Maggie's outrage. 'Glynmor do love his *Coronation Street* he do.'

After they scraped Glynmor off the ceiling he was practically speechless with rage. 'It's *Coronation Street* tonight as well,' were about the only words he managed to get out after he returned from the chase to find that his television set had been stolen in broad daylight. 'I'm never going to find out if Len Fairclough gets off with that piece now,' he wailed.

'Well that's not really the end of the world, is it Glynmor. I'd hardly call that the end of the world.'

He looked truly comic with his gold medallion and poncy long curls, standing there, foaming at the mouth about

Coronation Street, of all things. Unforgiveably, she laughed.

'It's funny is it?' he snapped. 'You think it's bastard funny do you?'

She could see by the white fury in his face and the trembling of his fingers that he, at least, did not find it funny at all. Far from finding it amusing he seemed to be alarmingly close to frenzy.

'I've nothing, have I?' he screamed. 'I'm disabled out of the pit with no future and I enjoy television. Where's the harm in that?'

'There's no harm in it Glynmor.' She was trying to stay cool in the face of this storm of self-pity and bluster. 'It's just that Huw can't stand television, that's all. You probably left it turned on when you went out, so he put it out into the street.'

'Well if this goes on he'll just have to go and that's the end to it.'

She could feel her blood pressure rising and actually saw a few spots but managed to control her temper.

'How can anyone live with someone who keeps putting the furniture out in the street?' he went on. 'Next he'll be putting out the beds and chairs. It's time he went away to a home. Do you hear?'

'No Glynmor. Huw's not going into any home. I've told you. I've told you before. Huw stays here with us.'

'He stays here with us,' he mimicked. 'He stays here with us.' His eyes darted around, his face taut with fury. For a second she thought he was going to throw something but, unmoved, she stood her ground.

'I really do think it's time he went into a home,' he said. 'I mean how can anyone live with a sledgehammer like that?'

'If you find it so difficult to live with him,' she replied evenly and calmly, 'why don't you go and live with your fancy woman if you find it so bad living here? Well, why not? She'd let you record *Coronation Street* on a video, no doubt, and you could play it all night as well. You'd like that wouldn't you? You could watch Len Fairclough while she was giving you love bites on the neck. That would be lovely for you, wouldn't it?'

She stood glaring at him impassive, hardly able to believe that she had finally blown her top. So she had done it now. The question was what was he going to do?

He didn't know. Her words had cut into him like darts and

he'd seen the way she had diced him up before. Somehow she had managed to turn his self-righteousness about his loss of his television against him; somehow taken out a completely different hand of cards while he had not been looking. He felt raggedly exposed, unsure of what his position now was.

On the matter of his fancy woman how much did she really know?

'You're talking through your arse again,' he said lamely.

'Oh I am, am I? Well you should know all about that shouldn't you? Tell me, does your fancy woman like *Coronation Street*? Do you talk about Len Fairclough while you're screwing the arse off her?'

'Don't be so disgusting.'

'Me! Disgusting? Glynmor, you invented the word.'

He stood glaring at her for a few seconds then, without saying a word, strode out of the room, slamming the door so hard the noise exploded right through the house. She knew that he was standing out in the hallway and wondered what he was going to get up to next, now really regretting that she had opened her big mouth. He opened the door again.

'I'll be taking my things,' he said quietly with tears pouring down his cheeks. Tears! 'I'll go and lodge with Aunty Phyllis.'

'Oh Glynmor don't. Don't do this to me.'

'I've already spoken to her about it. I'll have the back room. At least she likes television.'

'Glynmor, if we're going to split up let's do it about something proper is it? Not over a bloody television for goodness sake.'

'I'll take my things later.'

'Don't Glynmor. Don't do this to me.'

She heard the front door slam and him start up his hateful car as she sat down on her armchair and stared at the space where the television had been. Oh that damned television. It seemed to ruin and cheapen everything it got near. And who was this Len Fairclough anyway?

Autumn was busy colonising the Valley with long tall shadows and russet-coloured leaves. After the long sumptuous days of summer it was if, just after five o'clock, a hand had been rolling down a curtain of murk. Shadowy figures moved, black on orange, past the brilliantly-lit shops. Figures shuffled through the patches of sodium lights on the pavements outside the terraces calling out 'Good night' or 'All right?' to one another as they crossed paths: a custom passed down, perhaps, from the times when there were no forms of street lighting in the Valley and such greetings provided a form of security insofar as everyone was then instantly recognisable.

The thickening darkness also told Huw Bungalow that it was time for him getting back home. In his usual state of animation, and chewing a jelly baby, he was loping down the hill past the Libanus Chapel when the Rev. Mordecai called out to him 'Huw, Huw! Come over here! Come inside. I want you to look at the chapel.'

Huw just stood there chewing and made no move. Then the Rev. walked out to take him by the wrist and led him up the chapel steps. Inside the vestry he switched off the main light and, still holding onto him, escorted him down the chapel aisle where strange brilliant lights shone in the shivering darkness. In its atmosphere and protective magic it was like nothing that Huw had ever seen and he was immediately drawn to the place. Just being there was like putting on an old and well-fitting glove. As his eyes became accustomed to the strange shifting light he could make out some of the features of the place. Just above the pulpit on the wall, an inscription in gold letters on a green scroll read: 'Enter into his gates with thanksgiving and into his courts with praise,' Next to the pulpit was a hymnary. In one corner an old pedal organ, dead now from mildew in its bellows. But the reason for the shifting light in this deserted place of worship was that the floor had been taken up from the dais in front of the pulpit and the baptismal font had been filled up with moving water with lights submerged just beneath the surface.

It was the light swimming in the font water which was making the whole building tremble with the promise of something new. The very waters spoke of the renewal that is at the heart of the Baptist belief; the statement that, in these waters, it really was possible to have a new start in the cleansing hands of the Lord.

Huw walked up to the water and looked down into it, turning his face to Mordecai and laughing softly.

'Here is where we Baptists perform our most sacred rite,

Huw. If you'd care to come down into those waters with me I could cleanse you of all sin.'

Huw went down on one knee, putting one of his hands into the font and letting the water trickle down through his fingers.

'Water. The symbol of all things holy my beloved Huw. Water, with which the Lord washed away all sin. Water, the giver and sustainer of all life. Water, God's most precious gift to us all.'

Huw stood up again, showing no indication that he had understood Mordecai's invitation to the Baptism, now walking back to the deacons' Big Seat at the front of all the other pews and smoothing it before looking up at the rafters where the lights from the font danced in his dark eyes. Despite the chapel's dank coldness he still felt very warm indeed.

'I thought you would like it in here,' said Mordecai. 'Evan Roberts once spoke in this chapel you know. Have you ever heard of this mighty man of God have you? He stood in this very pulpit.' Mordecai walked up the steps. 'And he spoke to the congregation for five hours and, in turn, to the world. Huw, it was fantastic. All the pews down there were packed, the gallery was packed and out in the streets you just couldn't move.'

Huw, nodding his head and smiling all the while, looked back at the vestry and then up at Mordecai again.

'And the people came from every Valley to be saved Huw. Evan Roberts would work on them with all the powers of the Holy Spirit until they yielded their lives and hearts to God. His lady singers were the greatest singers the world has ever known and, between them all, they brought thousands, no millions, back to the arms of the Lord.

'And all from this pulpit Huw. This pulpit was one of the pulpits from which Evan Roberts launched one of the greatest revivals that the world has ever seen. Can you hear them singing now Huw? *Diolch Iddo*, thanks be to him for remembering the dust of the earth. I can hear those voices myself sometimes. And the people from every Valley were bound up in the great golden chains of love.'

Mordecai came down from the pulpit and held up a key, smiling perhaps his first smile for years. 'God has told me to give you this key Huw. He wants you to come here and spend some time with him.'

He put the key into the top pocket of Huw's Edwardian

suit. 'Look on the key and this chapel as yours,' he said putting his arm around Huw's shoulders and leading him back up the aisle. 'I know that you are not good at understanding but let this house be your house too. I see you out on the hillsides on your walks, so use the key and come in here whenever you feel in need of a rest. Some day, perhaps, you will let me take you down into those lovely baptismal waters since, just like those waters, there are clear marks of holiness on you Huw. You are a child of God and there's something in your soul which is going to save the Valleys.'

You know I just can't understand, for the life of me, what's got into Glynmor these days, said the boys in the bar. All those years he was quiet and faithful to Maggie. There was no other star in the heavens was there? An' now it's got that he's a'willing to fuck anything at all. I heard he was even dicking that horrible Chinese piece over in Ferndale. Aye.

An' I heard that Oboe Parry's wife has gone into hospital for an abortion. That's got to be Glynmor's for sure that has. He's been seen coming out of the back lane when Oboe's been on mornings. It's more than a cup of tea he's been having with that Brenda I'll bet a pound.

Do you think it's something to do with him losing his thumb? He's never been right since he lost that now, has he? He was a wild bad bugger when he was young but he settled down sweet as a nut after he got married di'n'e? But ever since he lost his thumb he's been busy shafting everything that moves.

Well he's going to lose more than his thumb the way he's been performing. I hear that he's been shafting that Xenia in his new car up in the sidings. And you know all about those brothers of hers. Right mad bastards they are when they get moving. They'll tear him apart they will if they catch him at it.

Aye an' Maggie will tear apart anything that's left. That's a racing certainty that is.

Late that night Huw was splashing about in his bath while Maggie made his tea. She was still dreadfully upset. Silent tears continually ran down her cheeks and onto the bread as she buttered it. When she had finished the sandwiches she went and hauled him out of the bath, wrapping a towel around him. He could sense her mood but his sympathetic hugs and touches only seemed to make her worse.

'I'm going to start making you less chips,' she said through her tears. 'That's a real pot belly you've got growing there.'

Lucky to be born alive at all, Huw had spent the first few months of his life in intensive care and then it was not at all clear quite what was wrong with him. He had been to see several specialists and although they all diagnosed a form of brain damage from the moment of his birth they were not at all clear what it was and neither extensive tests nor X-rays brought them any closer either. Since they did not know what it was, they did not know how to treat it though, for a few years, Huw was daily bussed to a Mencap school where he quickly learned how to do such basic tasks as make beds for himself, use a knife and fork and tidy away his clothes. The real puzzle was that, although his speech was impaired and his movements uncoordinated, he often showed signs of having a quick and agile intelligence. He even showed a nifty bit of pace and skill on the rugby field until Maggie put a stop to it after he got a bruise one afternoon. He was also quite good at snooker, all of which continued to bamboozle the specialists who had, by now, given up trying to work out what was the matter with him. If, indeed, as Maggie reminded them sharp, there was anything the matter with him at all.

She got his pyjamas on and he sat at the kitchen table, eating his sandwiches and sipping his cocoa. She ran a comb through his damp hair, patting the fringe into place. 'We should get you a more up-to-date hair-cut, I suppose. The Beatles are a bit old-fashioned now but it suits you, in a way.' He looked up at her and winked.

What she could never get over was how good he was, particularly compared with the other teenage thugs of his age who were always running about the village vandalising things. He was also marvellous to have about the house, getting in the sticks and coal every morning, even managing to go shopping down the Co-op as long as he had a note. Not only did he never complain about such jobs he actually seemed to enjoy doing them.

Everyone in the village seemed to love him as well. He could hardly walk down the street without someone giving him a sweet. He only had to show his nose in the Hall and one of the boys bought him a pint. Even that smelly old tramp who never

271

said anything, Guto, had brought him an old miner's lamp as a present the other day.

So what had Glynmor, his very own father, got against him? He should be proud of having a son so good and so loved, she told herself. All right he didn't look like Mr Universe but, in his own way, he was more beautiful than any person she had ever come across. Often she could not bear to be parted from him for more than five minutes and that, of course, was a large part of the trouble. She did understand that.

There was the sound of some shrieks and argument out in the street so she rushed out to the doorstep expecting that Glynmor had come back and was up to his old tricks again. But it was young Audrey, Mrs Pritchard's ten-year-old daughter, who was standing out on the pavement in the sodium darkness, crying and holding her new puppy. Mrs Pritchard was yelling that the dog had to go and Mr Pritchard was yelling back at her to leave the girl alone. It appeared that the dog had gone and got Mrs Pritchard's false teeth and she was even now screaming that she couldn't go out for weeks until they got fixed.

'Leave him here with us,' said Maggie bringing the crying girl and her puppy indoors. 'You can come and get him in the morning when it's all blown over.'

The puppy was shivering with terror, with its big brown eyes looking up guilty and head lowered, when Maggie took him off Audrey and put him into Huw's hands. 'All the animals love Huw,' said Audrey. 'Even the sheep and pit ponies follow him around. You should get a puppy for him, you should.'

Huw chuckled into the puppy's ear as the dog kept licking Huw's nose and cheeks. He put the dog down on the carpet to let him run around, dashing here and there, yelping as he sniffed out exciting new smells.

'Oh Glynmor would never allow a dog in the house,' said Maggie. 'He never liked dogs since he was a kid and got bit by one when he was scrumping apples over in Mountain Ash.'

'But Mammy said that Glynmor had left home.'

Huw was down on all fours and barking at the dog as Maggie looked straight at the girl's guileless face. Such innocence. There was nothing like a child for getting straight to the heart of the matter. 'Oh he's only gone for a bit,' she said brushing her skirt down with her hand. 'He'll be back soon.'

'But you could have a dog, if Glynmor didn't come back, couldn't you?'

'I could, yes. But Glynmor *is* coming back. Your Mammy got it wrong. Now let's put the puppy out in the kitchen 'cos it's time for Huw to go up the wooden hill. Come and get him back in the morning. Your Mammy will have calmed down by then.'

She tucked Huw into bed and, as was her habit, read him a few verses of the Bible before holding one of his hands and reciting the Lord's Prayer very softly. She had never told Glynmor about the tramp John who she had once met in Cardiff – never told anyone come to that – and how he had asked her to surround Huw with prayer. She had often wondered what had happened to John but had never gone back to Cardiff to look him up. The Lord's Prayer was the only prayer she had ever known but Huw seemed to like it well enough, smiling and closing his eyes just when she reached the end. She kissed his cheek and sat watching him for a bit, the light from the street lamp filtering through the curtain and making him look just beautiful as he lay there like a smile from God.

Downstairs she put a record on the turntable and let the puppy back into the living-room to scamper around. She liked the noise it brought to the empty room, quiet for a change without television and Glynmor. She really did want him back though. She was sure of that. She would never let him go without a fight.

Diana Ross was singing about how she wanted to be touched in the morning as Maggie sat gazing into the coal-fire remembering the way, when they were kids, they used to flick bits of orange peel into the glowing coals and watch their small phosphorescent explosions. She liked old things. She was an old-fashioned girl all right and perhaps it was the chapel in her blood but she would never agree to a divorce. Never. The puppy put his nose near the fire and she pushed him away from the grate.

She had even got on the phone to the Rediffusion people in Pontypridd that afternoon and asked them to send up the biggest television they had. That's how much she wanted him back. Huw would just have to learn to live with it and that was that. They could always bolt it down if necessary.

Out in the Valley, a crescent moon was throwing a bright

fluorescent sheen over the roof-tops with the black lines of the
pit edged in a silvery glow as Xenia Prosser was busy undressing
in the back of Glynmor's Toyota, parked down by the railway
sidings, just above the gurgling river.

Glynmor had never quite seen such a performance and had
to work hard not to laugh as he remained in the driving seat and
she scrimmaged around in the back, bent double as if working a
two foot seam, while taking off her clothes and hanging them up
tidy. With most of the girls that Glynmor had grappled with in
his new passion wagon he usually half-ripped the clothes off.
But not with Xenia Prosser. She always brought a carrier bag
with a bundle of wooden clothes hangers, first hanging up her
coat on the safety belt hook, hanging up her skirt on one of the
passenger hooks, then her blouse and now folding up her
underslip all as if getting some C. & A. shop ready for its January
sale.

'Why don't you just wear jeans and a sweater like every
other girl?' Glynmor asked.

'Because I always like to look smart,' she said, rolling
down her tights. 'Anyway I do tell him I'm going to play bingo
with Jennifer over in Aberdare so I can't go out wearing jeans
and sweater can I?'

'Don't see why not.'

'He'd smell a rat straight away, fathead. He knows me. I
won't even peg out the clothes on the line unless I'm looking
tidy. Anyway I could never wear jeans. My legs are too fat for
jeans.'

'How much longer …'

'All right. Keep your hair on is it? Right. I'm ready for you
now Glynmor. As ready as I'll ever be anyway.'

He sort of vaulted over his seat and grabbed her
goosepimpling flesh. 'Hold on there lover boy,' she puffed.
'After all that complaining aren't *you* going to take anything
off?'

'Aye.' He unbuttoned his belt and pushed his trousers
down his knees before jumping on her and trying to get straight
down to business.

'No, no, no,' she squealed. She pushed him off, dusting her
hands together as if they had become covered in dirt. 'What
kind of behaviour do you call that then? I had a rabbit who used
to act just like that. He jumped on anything that moved. We're

not animals, Glynmor. I want a bit of magic with my sex. What I want … what I want is for you to lick me all over for an hour an' then we can make love slow. The bingo doesn't throw out till half past ten so we've plenty of time.'

'An hour!' He swallowed hard. 'A whole hour?'

'Well half an hour maybe. I do like my nipples to be licked first. Then I'll lick you a bit, if you like, and we'll move on from there.'

He was squatting with his trousers down around his ankles while she was lying in front of him with her legs apart and her pudenda gazing up at him like a cat that had just had its throat cut. He was not at all certain by now if his old boy wanted to perform or not. He was not certain of anything by now. All he kept seeing was his Maggie and all he kept aching for was Maggie's body. He wished he wasn't here doing this, anything but this. He had never enjoyed himself so much as when he was in bed with Maggie so why was he throwing it all away by being here with this bingo bitch now? Word would get out soon and that's a fact. He might have been able to get back with her as it was but if she found out about this, that would be that.

'We girls do love to be licked Glynmor an' I don't care what any of them say. That's probably what went wrong with your marriage you know. Not enough licks. Me? I love being licked. I could be licked all night I could. Did you lick Maggie much did you? Different positions are all very well but the tongue, Glynmor. The tongue's the key to it all.'

Now his old boy knew one thing anyway. It didn't want to get erect after all. If he wanted to go in for all this licking he'd go and buy himself a lollipop. He pulled up his trousers and turned away from her.

'What's the matter my lovely?' He felt sick again. Maggie had always called him that. Somehow it sounded obscene in Xenia's mouth. 'Are you upset about something?'

He nodded. 'It's Maggie. I've gone and left her.'

Sensing a good gossip she sat up and rolled onto her side. She preferred a good spicy gossip to a good licking any day of the week. 'Now what did you go and do a daft thing like that for?'

'What do you care? You never liked her. She hit you once didn't she?'

'Maggie's a girl of passion. Like me. Anyway I never bear

grudges an' I've never liked to see couples break up.'

'So what are you doing here now then?'

'A bit on the side? That's different. That's nothing. That can be good for a marriage that can. But you'll never find another girl like Maggie, you know. I've never known a girl love anyone the way she loves you.'

'It's not that. It's not like that at all. It's 'cos of Huw, really.'

'Huw Bungalow? But everyone adores Huw Bungalow, Glynmor. He's the joy of the Valleys. Why don't you get on with him for heaven's sake?'

His mouth went completely dry and he just stared at her saying nothing. When he saw that she was going to say nothing until she had a reply he finally said 'I can't get on with Huw 'cos he takes Maggie away from me.' His eyes opened wide and he continued staring at Xenia, barely able to believe that such words had actually come out of his mouth. So he had finally admitted it out loud. It was nothing to do with the loss of his television or anything like that. It was because Huw took his wife away. It was because he was jealous of his own son.

'Poor dab,' said Xenia, understanding it all immediately. 'This jealousy is a terrible thing. That's why you're here with me now I 'spect. Trying to get back at her, trying to work the old knife in.'

'I'm here 'cos I want to be here. Not 'cos of her.'

'I've seen whole families destroyed by jealousy I have,' she went on, unconvinced by his feeble protest. 'There was that Tibbs family down in Ferndale. Everyone was jealous of everyone else in that house. If the husband went out the wife would follow him all the time – even down to the pit gates to see him in. Then back at the end of the shift to see him home. The kids were the same and the funny thing was they all hated one another. It was terrible seeing them jostling against one another all the time. Everything was some sort of a competition with them. Freddy Tibbs killed himself in the end. Put a pipe over his exhaust and gassed himself in his car. Couldn't stand it no more.'

'Aye, I remember the story. Didn't he kill himself outside his first girlfriend's house?'

'That's the boy. He had to die making the big gesture. You know how they always love making big gestures in the Valleys.

Here. Turn up that heater will you? I'm getting goosepimples on my goosepimples.'

He leaned across to the dashboard and turned up the heater, making the windows cloud up as she, as unselfconscious as a fanfare, stretched out her long fleshy body. He lit a cigarette and they took it in turns to smoke it.

'Funny thing is I've never felt anything like jealousy before,' Glynmor said, the smoke coming out of his mouth and nose alternately.

'Well you've never found anything you've cared about much have you? But you must fight it. It'll kill everything in time. Not just you and Maggie but everything. It'll kill everything that ever came your way. Everything walks out when jealousy walks in.'

'Quite the little thinker aren't you, girl?'

'We Valley people always have trouble with our emotions. They're stormy, difficult to subdue. Our chance is only through thought, to try and reason our way out of our passions. And with jealousy you've got to get your brains and stamp on it hard. Jump on it like a slug.'

'But it's not always as easy as that, is it?'

'Perhaps not as easy as just saying it. But it's like these fags here. They can be given up if you work on it, convince yourself how bad they are like. It's easy for me, of course. I've never felt a flicker of jealousy in my life. My 'usband could have a dozen women all at the same time an' I wouldn't feel a thing. I'd just be happy that he was happy. Proud of 'im, in a way, if he could get away with it.'

'What about him?'

'If he caught me at it? Oh he'd get upset right enough. He'd get upset all right but he'd get over it. We get over everything in time.'

'You should work for some marriage advice bureau you should.'

'Aye. My friends always said that. I do love chopsing and my Dad always said I was the only one he could ever tell anything to. The problem is I'm into adultery. It's good to get fucked a lot.'

'I like fucking too,' said Glynmor suddenly remembering why they had come there in the first place. 'You know when I come my whole body rattles.'

'You rattle when you come do you? Another of those rattlers eh? It's a bit like a car when the big ends goes I've always thought. Come on. We're here now. Let's try a friendly one is it? Just a bit of a cuddle like.'

'You're not going to worry if my big end goes then?' he asked rolling down the window an inch before flinging out the cigarette stub and rolling it back up again.

'No, but I must warn you that when I come I do sound like an emptying bath.'

'What does an emptying bath sound like?'

'If you stopped chopsing and got on with it you might find out, mightn't you?'

He slipped off his trousers and rolled over on top of her, cuddling for a while as she slipped off his shirt before pushing it in and riding her home slow. She kept making little gasps and her legs moved around gently like long white tentacles. It was odd but he felt a little closer to her now that they had had their little chat. The thought of betraying Maggie wasn't burning into him so fiercely either. Her face was even moving away into the distance for a while as his lips looked for a soft kiss. Then his hip movements became a little quicker and a little more urgent. Quite soon now his big end was going to bust.

'Not too fast now Glynmor,' she said softly. 'Remember the bingo doesn't fling out till half past ten.'

'We'll have six more before then.'

'Oh, bragging are we? I must say that dick of yours was always something of a legend in the girls' bog back in school.'

'A legend in its own nightshift this thing here.'

Outside in the crescent moonlight five men in flat caps and baggy trousers came running out from behind the coal wagons on the sidings. They were not actually talking but pointing their agitated fingers at Glynmor's misted-up Toyota which was rocking gently on its chassis.

Xenia was gurgling like an emptying bath and Glynmor's big end was knocking badly when the five men tipped the car up on its side and rolled it over the bank. With a great concerted heave they then sent it spinning down towards the river.

Carried along on a breaking surf of their surging lusts the two adulterers were not at all sure what was happening. They grunted and gasped and had the vaguest idea that they were rolling over and over – naked limbs, ash trays and clothes spinning around and around as if they were inside some giant tumble drier. He floated upwards and she sailed past him in a swoosh of mammary glands. He hit his side and she gave her head a nasty crack. There was going to be no more playing around for him, he decided as they both landed in an untidy painful heap with the car on its side in the middle of the river, two of its wheels spinning slowly.

Glynmor, fortunately still with his shoes on, kicked his way out of the shattered back window, standing up to his knees in the freezing water with Xenia's brassiere half-wrapped around his neck. Blood was trickling down the side of his head. Looking a little like a half-murdered crazy in a Hammer horror film, he just stood there screaming wild obscenities at the moon.

'What the hell was that?' cried Xenia, trying to crawl out of the shattered car.

'My car! My fucking car! Three weeks I've had this car. Three fucking weeks.'

'Never mind about your car. What about my clothes? This water's freezing. Where are my clothes?'

'Here's your bra anyway,' he said flinging it towards her, only to see it floating off down the river like a couple of mating jellyfish.

'Look, are you going to help me out of here or what?' demanded Xenia her wrist throbbing badly as if it had been sprained.

'Perhaps we should have kept our seat belts on,' he said, reaching down to help her out of the shattered window.

'You can't fuck in a seat belt can you? Oh I've done something awful to my hand, I have. I've broken it, I have.'

Even as they helped one another up the slope a police car, with revolving flashing lights, pulled up in the sidings. 'Now what precisely have you two been up to?' the policeman asked, flashing his torch on the naked, bedraggled pair. 'We had a call that someone was out here pinching coal.'

'I work in the pit and get my coal free,' Glynmor puffed piously. 'We were just out having a swim we were.'

'I see,' the policeman replied with a bright note of disbelief in his voice. 'A sort of midnight dip was it?'

'Aye. You could put it like that.'

'Mrs Jones? I've come to tell you that your husband's been in an accident. There's nothing to worry about, but he is in hospital.'

Maggie could feel the blood drain out of her face and the strength going out of her knees as she looked up at the policeman on her doorstep. It was dawn. Since midnight she had sat dozing in her armchair, the puppy sleeping on her lap. She had woken when she had heard loud knocking on the front door.

'He was in a parked car up by the sidings,' the officer was saying. 'Five men rolled it over and down into the river. We've picked up the men involved in the incident and are questioning them down at the station.'

'Do you want a cup of tea or something?' she asked, ushering him in.

'No thank you, Mrs Jones. But it is my unpleasant duty to inform you of something else since it is bound to come out in any court proceedings later. You might as well know now that your husband had a woman at the time of the accident. We have grounds to believe that it was the woman's husband who ...'

At this point Maggie's knees gave way. White as the milk bottles on her doorstep, she fell into a swoon. The policeman just managed to catch her before she slumped to the ground. He carried her inside and stretched her out on the sofa. 'Better send a nurse or something,' he said on his radio, to the Police H.Q. 'I told her what had happened and she just flaked out on me. Of course I told her about it. It'll all come out in the trial won't it?'

Later that morning, after a visit by the doctor, Maggie felt well enough to make a couple of telephone calls and a decision.

She rang Brian Jones & Co., the Cardiff solicitors, to make an appointment to discuss a divorce. Then she rang Rediffusion in Pontypridd to cancel the incoming television set.

About half an hour later little Audrey, from next door but one, came into the house in a flood of tears saying that her Mammy would never allow the dog back. There and then Maggie decided to keep it. She hoped that it would grow up to be very big and fierce. She hoped that it would bite any Bont miner who came near her. She particularly hoped that it would take a big chunk out of that Glynmor Jones.

Chapter Eighteen

After the loss of his thumb and the car-rolling incident, Glynmor's confidence crumpled like a paper bag. For the next few weeks he rarely ventured from his bedroom in Aunty Phyllis' house. Instead, he listened to the radio, watched the little portable television, or just sat at the window looking at the comings and goings in the street.

It was an unhappy time for him, never more so than when he saw Huw going to the shops or Maggie, with that new puppy of hers on a lead, going down to the hairdresser's. She walked past the house with a cold, distant look on her face but with her heart pounding. But he could not read her mind and her apparent coldness always managed to bring his spirits right down.

The police came one morning and explained to him that Xenia Prosser's five brothers-in-law would be charged as soon as they had decided exactly what to charge them with. Glynmor said that he didn't know what they were talking about. Flatly contradicting what he had said in earlier statements he now insisted that he had just stupidly left the handbrake off and this had led to the plunge into the river. With Xenia coming out with a similar story, the police were clearly going to find it difficult to bring a successful prosecution against the Prosser brothers. After making various threats about the penalty for perverting the course of justice, they went away again.

More worryingly, though, the car insurance man had called about the written-off Toyota. When Glynmor told him what he had already explained to the police – that he had simply left off the handbrake – the insurance man warned that this might affect his claim since, as he only had third-party cover, he was not insured for personal negligence. Glynmor then began to have grave doubts about the virtue of letting the Prosser boys get away with it. Not that he had decided to let them get off scot free. In his own way, and in his own time, he was going to beat twelve different colours of shit out of each of them when he caught up with them. No one was going to roll him and his new car down into the river and get away with it. Not even if he was screwing their sister-in-law at the time.

To add to his woes the stump of his thumb was giving him murder. The doctor gave him a variety of pills which did nothing to soften the pain. And he was having dreams of the black tide of Aberfan. Come the nights, while watching the portable television, he would sit drinking whisky to enable him to sleep. But no matter how drunk he got, those bad dreams came swirling back. Everyone was being swept away by the black waves: Maggie's face was often there, the terraced houses, Huw's teddy boy suit, the insurance agent, the committee chairman ... friends, enemies and homes all being swept away by the same killer tide.

Some nights he woke in the dark, covered in sweat and believing that he was drowning. Then, still shivering, he would sit chain-smoking and looking out onto the empty street, lined with parked cars and silent shadows, when everyone else was in bed, doubtless enjoying great dreams of sex, money and power. Not that he was so lucky. He was a prisoner in a cell which he could not quite understand.

There were some mornings when he did sit with Aunty Phyllis down in the kitchen next to the range fire, but then Enid would come in and they would drive him daft with their continual gossip, usually about ailments ...

Marjorie's found that she has got another lump again and she's ever so pleased about it. Gwyneth has been in twice with the fatty lump she's always been worried about. It's a sort of sprout it is. She says it's a gall-stone but they keep saying they can't find anything wrong. She's off to hospital for more tests next Wednesday. That Brenda Parry has found out she's got bad blood pressure and the doctor can't seem to get it down. They've tried everything on the poor dab but she's on the turn she is. On the turn. You get some terrible things when you're on the turn.

Sometimes Glynmor felt that he was going to drown in all this infernal gossip. He longed for the compensation money for

282

his thumb to come through but nothing came and nothing had yet been resolved with his continuing dispute with the board. Since the loss of his car, the bank manager had stopped 'that overdraft lark' – as Maggie had once scornfully called it – and, since he was still giving Maggie most of his social security money (delivered in an envelope every Friday by Aunty Phyllis), he had virtually nothing for any reckless spending now, even letting his curls grow out. What he had, he spent on whisky, looking for the concussion which never quite seemed to come.

He was quite sure that Maggie would have him back when his compensation money did come through. He would bump into her one night, by accident perhaps, in the Hall after a few drinks, and offer to take her away from all this. They would go to Cardiff and start again or even go to London. She would agree straight away and they would pack and disappear into the night, first signing into a hotel in Porth where all their differences would be settled by a night of warm passion in a soft bed. He missed her body terrible. He was almost physically sick when her lovely limbs crowded into his mind in the lonely darkness.

Such escapist fantasies came to an end when he received a letter from Brian Jones, the posh Cardiff solicitors, informing him that his wife was suing for divorce on the grounds of his adultery with Xenia Violet Rose Prosser of 18 Taff Street, Bont. Who could commit adultery with a bastard flowerpot?

He put the letter into his pocket and promptly took it out again, hardly able to believe the cold, dismissive message of farewell the legal words contained. Surely not after all these years? And just for one night? Well, the one night that she had found out, anyway. How much worse could it all get? He didn't want to play this silly game any more and, plunged into the deepest despair, went upstairs to his bedroom where he wept, silently and copiously, until his eyes stung red.

But there was one incident in this period of desertion and misery which was to turn out to be significant. One afternoon, while sitting staring out of his bedroom window, he spotted the mobile library which came around twice a week. Tiring of the persistent fatuities that seemed to drip constantly from his portable television he went over and signed up with the library, and then looked for a suitable book. The one that took his fancy was *Martin Eden* by Jack London. That book was the start of a long socialist rapture which deepened with every book by Jack London that he could lay his hands on. He wondered at the commitment and humanity of the great writer, the sheer strength and tenacity of his beliefs. *The Iron Heel* overwhelmed him and, together with his domestic misery and a whole new range of ideas, this was clearly a time of deep and lasting change, even if he didn't quite understand it himself at the time.

Unaware of even the possibility of any change, Maggie was surprised at how fast the divorce proceeded once it had been set in motion. She hardly felt a part of it at all, just signing statements sent to her through the post or filling in forms for legal aid. It was like signing things about someone else's life altogether. And when they told her that she had to list all Glynmor's bad behaviour over the past fifteen years and she said she didn't want to do it, she was assured that this was the way the law asked for it to be done. A funny old law that seems to me, she thought. Who would think up a law like that?

The emotional strain of it all had made her go as thin as a lath and, in the process, even more beautiful. All this had not been lost on the boys in the Hall. There was never any shortage of drinks if she went there for a quiet half of lager with the girls. Not that she was interested in any of the boys, as she had to make clear more than once. All she ever seemed to want to do was to sit with the girls and talk about Glynmor. Had they seen him? What did he look like? Who was he with? Had they heard if he was eating proper?

The girls did their best to try and smooth the ruffled waters of her anxieties but then it was 'do you remember' time. And do you remember that night when the two fire engines came when Glynmor was in bed and he was going around bragging about how he was clearly the hottest thing in the Valleys and they had to send out two fire engines to cool him down? And do you remember the time when Glynmor ...

A time of divorce was awful hard for any woman the girls would say to one another when Maggie was not around. But if I hear any more of Glynmor this and Glynmor that I'll scream I will. She was mad enough about him when they were married but listen to her now. And I'm worried she's beginning to neglect poor Huw Bungalow too. She's not been ironing his suits the way she used to. And there were holes in his socks as well. Perhaps she's cracking up. I hear Glynmor's in a terrible mess too. Drinks in his room all night, he does, but you couldn't tell her that could you? What a bloody mess it all is. Still you couldn't expect much else with that Glynmor could you? I've always said he's as odd as a bottle of crisps.

Maggie and Glynmor did bump into one another one sunny Saturday morning outside the Co-op and had their first chat for a month.

'Better be careful you don't fall over with all that stuff in your bag,' said Glynmor, smiling while his eyes misted over.

'What do you care?' she asked with her insides going all funny.

'I've just been for a walk up the pit to see the boys.'

'Really? A nice walk, was it?'

'It was. Nice to see the boys anyway.'

'Nice.' She showed her teeth in a sort of smile though it looked to Glynmor more of a snarl.

They both stood there awkwardly for a few more seconds, she looking inside her bag of shopping, as if she had forgotten something important, and him looking over the road. 'I'd better get on,' he said. 'Aunty Phyllis will be having the dinner on.'

'Well, you'd better not be late for that, had you?'

'No. I'd better not. See you.'

'Aye ... see you.'

She half-walked and half-ran back to her house, bursting in through the front door and letting out a fearful wail as she flung herself on the sofa, with the puppy making her worse by coming over and licking her face. Even Huw got out of his chair in the kitchen to give her some reassuring pats.

'Oh leave me alone,' she snapped at him and, more amazed by her tone than anything, he returned to the kitchen followed by the puppy. Now she felt really awful. 'I'll make you some hamburger and chips in a minute,' she called out. 'I've got some ice cream too.'

It was a damp arthritic morning in November when Emlyn Kremlin and five of the boys from the lodge went in Ted Jones' mini-bus down to the Llanishen headquarters of the National Coal Board.

'How much coal do you think we dug to pay for this place then?' Dai Prosser wondered as they entered the great neon and glass edifice where the smell of polish bounced off every wall.

'How many men's lives more like?' asked Emlyn.

It was time for the six working miners of the Bont lodge to meet over the conference table with six officials of the board, or best-suited capitalists, Emlyn always decided, with tailor-made brains, who sat in unsmiling line, taking out yellow folder after yellow folder and explaining that the pit was continuing to make heavy and unacceptable losses. The usual game.

'So what are you trying to say then?' Emlyn demanded.

And that was precisely the trouble. The board wasn't really saying anything. This murky cloud of statistics was just another of their ways of dispiriting and demoralising the miners, who were not economists after all; another part of the steady process of softening them up and pulling a few teeth before finally putting the boot into the pit.

'The South Wales coalfield lost seven per cent of the market availability last year ... '

'We know all that. So what are you trying to say?' Emlyn asked again, dogged in his pursuit of plain meaning and motive.

'We don't necessarily have to say anything. We just want to make sure that we have painted the fullest picture of where the Bont mine stands.'

'But, if you stopped painting pictures and told us what was on your minds, we'd all know where we were.'

'Well, we're not really anywhere ... '

And so it went on but – apart from suggesting that the miners might improve the pit's productivity, which they might, agreed Emlyn, if the geological conditions were with them – they still wouldn't say what was on their minds. It was all as you would expect, Emlyn thought, from men who drove Volvos, had expense accounts and went to B.U.P.A. hospitals; men who barely knew where the Valleys were, let alone ever having visited them. Such men spent their days standing on shifting sands and, when the sands shifted, they shifted with them. These were the real barnacles on the ship of coal, not the struggling pits and their decaying communities. Emlyn had watched such men become more arrogant and offensive in Margaret Thatcher's Britain. There was a time when the board seemed to be on your side, but no longer; these were steely, plump men with short hair who would knock you down sooner than look at you; yet another part of the Thatcherite enemy dribbling on about economic efficiency while the Valleys and their communities rotted away.

'Next time you gentlemen call us up here,' Emlyn said finally standing up, indicating that the meeting was over. 'Try and make sure you have something to say will you?'

When Emlyn stood up, everyone else stood up too – even the members of the board. The old communist warhorse had some of that old-fashioned quality that inspired a form of respect – even among his enemies. It was always interesting that very few men ever swore in front of him. He was one of those big, learned men, with a quiet committed passion, who, in another life and with different political ideas, might have been a Member of Parliament or even a Prime Minister.

He felt very old and tired when they got back into the waiting mini-bus. What he had really wanted to find out was the date the board intended to try and close the pit. Only then could they get their campaign properly organised; a stratagem which the board recognised all too well which is why they clearly weren't going to give them a date. Instead they kept shuffling around on their shifting sands, speaking their mealy-mouthed platitudes which meant nothing.

And in such a mood they drove silently back to the Welfare Hall, a weary and dispirited group, frustrated at fighting with an enemy who would not fight properly. 'You know, boys, talking to them is a bit like shouting down an empty oil pipe,' Emlyn said. 'You get plenty of echoes but you never get a reply to anything.'

But, after a few pints in the Hall, always the pit rhetorician, he began to get a little rhapsodical. 'You know, I've always hated these new steel pit props,' he said, his back straight and one burly hand clamped on his knee. 'They snap sudden they do and never give you a warning about anything. Now those old wooden pit props would tell you all kinds of things. You could tell if there was water about. You could see in the way they sweated, how hard the rock was coming down. But, most of all, they told you when a fall was coming. They squealed and moaned in a way which told you that you had better make a run for it. And run you did. These days the air is

287

full of creaking pit props. But we just sit here and don't know what to do. We just don't know whether to fight or run. That's the way they've got us now.'

Later still in the afternoon Maggie came and sat with the group. Emlyn shifted around in his seat uneasily and already some of the boys were drifting away. Maggie was becoming notorious for going around the place boring everyone senseless with her talk about Glynmor and, when everyone else failed her, Emlyn's was the one broad shoulder she often ran to for sympathy.

He was good at sympathy too was Emlyn. Even when his very veins were clogging up with boredom he never showed it. Perhaps it was something to do with his natural feeling for the suffering of others, or perhaps it was something altogether different, but many beat a path to his door when they were in trouble.

Barely had Maggie got her behind down on her seat than she was going on about Glynmor. Emlyn wouldn't have minded so much if he could have done anything, but Glynmor had refused to speak to him at all about the break-up and all Maggie really wanted to do was talk to herself. He smiled faintly to himself as Maggie prattled on. What he really ought to do was turn her loose on those men from the N.C.B. They'd all be agreeing to anything, then running down the road crying with their hands over their ears.

'Look I've told you before,' he finally interrupted her and getting quite sharp. 'You've got to call off this divorce thing. He might talk to you then. He might.'

'He doesn't give a rat's arse for me, Em. He never did.'

'What nonsense you do talk sometimes. You were the only star in his firmament. But you can't really expect him to come rushing up to you and kissing you in the street can you?'

'I don't see why not.'

'You don't see why not? Because you're divorcing him that's why not. It stands to reason. Men don't like it when their women divorce them. They get upset.'

'But he doesn't love me any more does he?'

'Of course he does. But he's like all the other men around here. He doesn't like to show it. Valley men never like to show their feelings. They're afraid of being thought pansies.'

'But, if he'd loved me, he wouldn't have gone off in his car

288

with that cow Xenia Prosser would he?'

Just then Emlyn was caught short of air and just sat there for a while, with his mouth opening and closing, waiting for his lungs to catch up with his body again. 'Who's to say why a man like Glynmor does anything?' he said finally. 'Someone like him has got more layers than a prize onion. Beneath all that wide-boy, dirty talk there's a man of exceptional tenderness who lives in a cloud of terror. That's probably why you fell in love with him. He's not a robot and he's different from the rest – childish often – but angry and sharp too; someone who I wish would join us in the lodge. Oh I'd love to have him in with us. I've always wanted that.'

Maggie loved Emlyn and the beauty of his words. It warmed her that someone could speak like this about her own husband and even made her ashamed of her own low opinion of the philandering old bastard.

'Who's to know why a man like Glynmor started playing around with that Prosser woman,' Emlyn continued. 'It might have been because he lost his thumb. It might have been because he thought he was losing his attractiveness to women. I think it was because he was jealous of all the attention that Huw gets. A man like Glynmor needs warmth and praise. He needs to be at the centre of the comedy. He just can't live with any form of rejection, so, if you really want my advice, call off the divorce and see where that gets you. One thing's for certain – he won't talk to you proper again till you do.'

'I've got to go down to the solicitors in Cardiff on Tuesday,' she said through her tears. 'Should I tell them to call it off then do you think?'

'I do. Put it on ice for a bit anyway. Look, if you're going down to Cardiff, take some fags to Bobby in the prison will you? I'll get you a visiting order. I'd go myself but I'm too busy to get there next week.'

The bus journey down to Cardiff to see about her divorce was something of a family affair, since Maggie took along Huw Bungalow and the dog. It was one of those tiring stop-start journeys with the bus filling up with cigarette smoke and body odours as doddery old ladies with varicose legs got on at every stop and took an age to pick the correct fare out of their purses. At one stop, at Llwynypia, an old man lit up a pipe which led to a storm of protest and complaint from the nearby passengers.

'What are you smoking in that, then? Smells like dried shit and bus tickets it do.'

'Leave me alone,' the old man squeaked, putting another flaring match to his pipe. 'Just leave me alone, is it?'

'I'll leave you alone with my umbrella if you don't put that thing out.'

And so another quarrel broke out, giving Maggie a right old headache. Any excuse for a quarrel with this lot, she thought, looking out at the moody day which was neither sun nor rain, a nothing day, almost regretting that it had to make any kind of appearance at all. If you told them black was black they would start quarrelling about it.

Her Huw was enjoying the journey immensely though and, at times, she could feel him quivering with delight as he looked out through the window. Even now he was trembling with happiness as he looked up at the old Thomas and Evans Welsh Hill Works in Porth. What he found so enchanting about an ugly and derelict pop factory, with weeds growing out of the walls, she could not think. Indeed she would have been truly astonished had she known that his imagination had transformed the broken-toothed building into a bright fairy castle with turrets and a drawbridge, all burnished with lots of small bright rainbows. Huw's bright black eyes never beheld such things as ugliness and decay. Whatever he looked at made him joyful.

Duw, even the dog stood on his lap and seemed to be enjoying everything he looked at too. What with Huw's laughter and the dog's squeaky barks the pair had now established themselves as a sort of comic double act around the village and, if ever Huw went into a shop or house, the dog just sat down on the doorstep and waited for him to come out again.

Maggie's belly tightened and headache thickened as the bus roared down past the misty steel shapes of Nantgarw colliery and into the sprawling semi-detached suburbs of Cardiff. She had never got on with the city, finding it gigantic and full of threat. Even as the bus jerked into the sprawling bus station, with its massed queues and shelters, she took hold of Huw's hand for comfort. When they got off, seagulls sailed through the grey skies overhead as whole marching bands of people went crashing through one another in the shops and pavements. *Echo* sellers cried the latest bad news and babies cried in their prams as she skirted around an omelette of dried vomit just outside the Boots chemist shop. The very roads were jammed with traffic of all shapes and sizes while the Castle clock chimed dolefully, telling the populace the dismal story of the passing hours.

She just felt so menaced as they made their way to the solicitor's office in City Road. All this noise! All this filth! She couldn't understand how anyone could live here. Glynmor had often said that he wouldn't mind living in Cardiff but she had never fancied it. She was a mining village girl who liked living in a mining village. She liked one chip shop and one Welfare Hall. She liked people to be where they were yesterday and would be tomorrow. She wished that Glynmor had been there yesterday and would be there again tomorrow.

Huw and the dog were made to stay in the reception room when Maggie went in to see the solicitor who, with his large mahogany desk and fitted carpets, only added to her sense of inferiority. But he was likeable enough and had a smile, which she took to immediately, even if it did waver when she announced that she had decided not to press on with the divorce.

'I'm glad, because I've always hated divorce myself,' he said straight away and she nodded, relieved that he wasn't going to throw a wobbly about it and send her huge bills for wasting his time. 'But if you are still estranged from your husband, by which I mean living apart from him, I must warn you of certain difficulties that may lie ahead for you.'

He then, with great patience and clarity, outlined the problems of her maintenance, living accommodation and the custody of Huw while her matrimonial status remained unresolved. If there was not a divorce, or at least a legal separation, the court would be unable to set a proper level of maintenance and her husband might get away with paying nothing. Although she had certain common law rights to half the house he could legally argue that he had inherited it and that it was his alone – if there was not a legal and proper divorce. Her husband could also claim custody of their son.

'He wouldn't do that. He can't stand the sight of him.'

'Well that's what he might be saying now. But there's always strange, bad feelings when marriages break down.

291

People start saying and doing the oddest things. Huw is due for a disability pension next year. That could be a lot of money and your husband would enjoy certain legal rights over it.'

Maggie was quite dazed by this barrage of advice and legalisms but was considerably unnerved by the thought that anyone — let alone Glynmor — might be able to take over custody of her Huw. 'What do you suggest then?' she asked.

'Keep the divorce process going but look for a better basis for calling it off.'

'Better basis?'

'A better basis would be if your husband came back to live with you. But you are saying that you are not even talking at the moment so, while the prospects of reconciliation are dim, you should — you must — keep the divorce process going, if only to protect your future rights. The best we can do, on our side, is slow everything down which will, at least, give any reconciliation plenty of time.'

'All right, if you say so.' She frowned hard and felt that she was being led somewhere she did not quite want to go. It now rather looked to her as if it was going to be easier to get a divorce than to actually call it off. It was all beyond her. There had been no mention of love or anything like that. 'All right, if you say so,' she repeated, uncertain.

When she left the offices with Huw and the dog she was not even very sure what she had agreed to in the end. She just had a dim idea that she was going to wake up one morning and find herself divorced and that would be it. Emlyn was going to be furious with her. That was certain, that was. And what was Glynmor going to say about it all? Her mind was whirling with so many colliding thoughts and anxieties she was almost sick as they walked down the road towards the prison.

The prison officials were not at all happy about the dog coming inside their high stone walls but finally relented when they saw that Huw Bungalow was do-lally and very reluctant to part with the thing. They were also much taken by Maggie's good looks and there was a fair bit of uniformed jostling to escort her down to the visitors' room. Glynmor had often told her about this and how the screws often knocked off visiting wives, working on the assumption that they were desperate for it with their men locked away inside. That was just the dirty kind of information you would expect from him.

Young Gnasher actually seemed very pleased to see her and even more pleased when she produced the carton of cigarettes that Emlyn had bought for him. Although he was her nephew she had never had a great deal to do with him in the past. Oh, she had done what she could, in the way of meals and spare cash, when Daisy had upped and left for Greenham Common but, like so many others, she had flung up her hands in horror and turned away when he had become a fully-fledged skinhead at war with society.

Not that he looked terribly ferocious now, she was pleased to see, since his hair had grown to a normal length and he looked almost human in his blue dungarees and polished black shoes. Those horrible home-made tattoos were still on his fingers though and she had to keep looking away to stop herself from staring at them in disgust.

'There's talk I might be sent to Dartmoor,' he told her, with a hint of pride.

She looked at him appalled, visibly shaken by the picture of some dark Victorian fortress where they toiled, breaking up rocks all day.

'Oh don't worry,' he reassured her. 'They've got good teachers in the Moor. You can learn things there.'

'Things like what?'

'Business things and trades. I could become a plasterer.'

'That would be good, wouldn't it?' She did so hope he would do something useful when he got out but, again like so many others, she had the gravest doubts.

'Might keep me out of trouble for a bit init?'

The visitors' room was high and wide with plain, white-washed walls and thin strips of neon hanging on chains from the ceiling. The visitors and prisoners sat around small tables, many holding hands as they were watched by the warders who stood near the doors. Odd prison sounds like the hooter or the slam of a metal door, penetrated the room, but this afternoon, most of the sounds were the sounds of laughter as Huw Bungalow and the dog went around the tables entertaining everyone. It was just the sheer unlikelihood of the act that amused everyone; a whistling, laughing teddy boy in bright gaudy drapes with a dog that kept barking and running around his blue suede shoes.

'Still as dull as ever then?' Gnasher asked nodding towards Huw.

'Aye. An' if he had two heads he'd be twice as dull.'

'Glynmor is all right, is he?'

'Yes, he's fine. Are any of your Clay Class butties still in here?'

'Not any more they're not. Cocoa has gone off to an open prison. And Nipper and Iffy. But they wouldn't send me to an open prison would they? After what I've done like.'

'No. I don't suppose they would.' A wave of sadness washed over her. Such a youngster and everyone was treating him like a hardened criminal. But he was still just a kid really, wild and footloose like every other kid in the Valley. Now that he was out of his skinhead uniform, and holding his carton of cigarettes like a baby with a new toy, he didn't even look terribly tough.

'I was talking to that Snipe Wilson in here the other day,' he went on. 'Sitting on the bog eating a bacon sandwich he was. He's in here for pinching that bus. I had to laugh. He said he'd only borrowed it for a little ride and just took the wrong turning. One of the screws was saying that there's always been a fair few of us from Bont in here.'

'Must be something in the air.'

'Aye. One of the screws said it was something to do with us all living at the end of the Valley. He said that they always get madder if they live at the end of the Valley.'

She looked around anxiously at Huw again but now even the stone-faced warders were beginning to laugh at his antics. She shook her head in mock-sorrow. 'It's like living in a circus with him sometimes. I don't know where he learns all his little antics. Oh well, time to go. I'll come and see you again soon. I don't suppose you get too many visitors do you?'

'My Dad came in to see me a few weeks ago. He was my last. He's given up the building and works for Rentokil. The money's great, he says an' now he's the champion rat-catcher in South Wales.'

'Really?' She would have laughed out loud at the thought of Denzil becoming a champion rat-catcher except that she felt an even stronger urge to cry. So she was Gnasher's first visitor for a few weeks. A few weeks! And even that great lover of men, Emlyn Kremlin, hadn't been here for ages. She was going to be sending off some scorching letters – to her sister for one – when she got home. 'I'll come and see you again next week,' she promised.

'It's all right. You don't have to.'

She looked at him with crouching eyebrows. Rough he might have been but thick he never was. He saw things as clearly as anyone. 'I promise,' she said firmly. 'And when you do get out you're going to come and live with us.'

'Glynmor wouldn't like that,' he laughed.

She decided then that there was no point in trying to explain anything to the lad. 'He might, you know. You can never tell about anything with Glynmor.'

Chapter Nineteen

It was the pounding bass guitar of the rock 'n' roll band from Swansea that told the Valley that the Saturday night hop was well under way. It had the throb and authority of tropical thunder did that bass guitar, shaking the flaking walls and rotten rafters of the Hall, filtering out through the adjoining terraces, rattling the dustbin lids and banging into the dry stone walls of the gardens, throbbing through the damp night air as pervasive and insistent as a giant hangover and even making the sheep look up from their eternal munching before they moved off with a jerk and a melancholy inaudible bleat, hoping to find a patch of grass where it was not quite so loud.

As the bass thumped on, the volume knobs of the televisions were turned up very loud. Some jumped into their cars and drove off to spend a few hours with some distant relative in some distant Valley. Others, like Aunty Phyllis, went through their little rituals of plugging up their ears with screwed-up lumps of Kleenex or penning yet another letter of complaint to the committee. But they were all just futile, empty gestures against the world colonisation of rock 'n' roll. Even the bolshiest members of the community accepted that, just like the rain and the rent, they had to learn to live with rock 'n' roll.

The music even penetrated those houses well up the hill, forcing the Rev. Mordecai out of his manse and into the chapel whose walls were just thick enough to make the pounding of the bass guitar bearable. He hated rock 'n' roll with a particular ferocity, seeing it as the dead marching music of a dying tribe.

Most in the village, however, saw that the only way to beat the band was to join them, which was why, as usual, the dance was packed with huge groups standing around near the bar with even more either dancing or sitting at the tables, pens and pencils at the ready, with their bingo tickets in front of them, waiting for the game to begin in the interval.

Maggie was sitting at her usual table with the girls. For some of the livelier numbers she might have had a dance with Cynthia but, most of the time, she stayed seated at the table, singing and clapping along with the others. They were much the same group of girls as had sat together for most of their lives, singing and clapping along to the music every Saturday night, supportive in times of marital strife, despairing over the inequity of bingo, celebrative in times of anniversaries, mournful in times of bereavement. For Saturday nights in particular they were the closest of friends and, in this group, there were hardly any of the ordinary breakdowns of ordinary marriages.

'Don't look now Maggie,' said Thelma. 'But I've just seen Glynmor come in.'

Maggie had already spotted him, talking with that Graham Mainwaring just near the door to the Gents. She had seen him as soon as he had walked into the dance, not as cocky as usual maybe but cocky enough, going over to the bar to buy a pint, smiling at that boss-eyed cow from Aberdare, nodding at Oboe Parry then going over to chat with Graham. He was wearing a white shirt, which seemed to have been nicely ironed, and had just had a hair-cut too, by the look of it from here. He still had those poncy curls with that silly gold medallion around his neck.

Now, pint in hand, he moved away from Graham and sat down at a table with the two Costello brothers and their wives. What was he sitting with them for? He had never had anything to do with them. He had spent much of his youth fighting with the Costellos and not always winning either.

'I wish I'd stayed in the house now,' she sighed, overcome by a feeling of gloominess. 'I just can't seem to relax when Glynmor's around. I do get this feeling he's watching me all the time. You know how jealous he gets.'

Take no notice of the silly sod. Come and have a dance is it? You know I still think that Lenny Fox has got his eye on you. All those years and you're still sparkling his fancy. She doesn't want to be bothered with Lenny Fox. Don't talk soft.

297

He's all right. Lenny's all right. Well go and have another dance with Cynthia.

'I don't want a dance with Cynthia. I just wish Huw would come.'

'Where is he anyway? It's not like Huw not to be here.'

'He'll be along. He fusses around for hours in front of the mirror on Saturdays so he can look lovely for the dance. He's as bad as Glynmor when he gets going.'

'Stop it now, Maggie.'

'Stop what?'

'Stop what you're doing to yourself is it?'

One of the Costello brothers got up with a tray, buying three pints and two gin and oranges. Why was Glynmor sitting with them of all people? Well at least he wasn't out with another woman. She doubted if she could have put up with that. Anything but that. Well he looked as if he was eating proper anyway. That Aunty Phyllis was probably throwing tons of food into him. He was laughing at something one of the Costello boys were saying. She had always fancied him for his laugh with those lovely teeth of his and the way he lifted his head back.

'Stop it now, Maggie.'

'I'm not doing nothing. I wasn't even looking at him.'

She began sipping her Bacardi and Coke morosely when the band began a medley of those great old numbers by such as the Crystals, Shirelles and Ronettes. It was the very music that she had courted Glynmor by – the sounds of their love – and she was almost furious she couldn't just go over there and get him up on the floor. She finished her drink fast with bits of her insides collapsing with the sadness of it all. *Why don't you beeeeeeeeeee my babeeeeeeeee* ...

It was just after nine with the bass guitar still throbbing along the terraces when Huw Bungalow, all spruced up in his Saturday best, and with the dog at his heels, was ambling down the road to the Hall. Five skinheads were playing the new Space Invaders machine in the chip shop and a bus was turning around the clock. Huw stopped walking and looked up the hill.

Normally, the Libanus Chapel, as befitted an empty tombstone on the grave of a dead movement, was dark and silent but tonight its lights shone out like a lighthouse on a sea of black rock, huge golden shafts which sprayed out onto the walls and roofs of the outlying houses. It was almost like some joyous and miraculous oasis of light and Huw found himself irresistibly attracted to it.

Gaudy rock 'n' roll was still thundering out of the Hall as he walked up the hill towards the chapel, the dog still running around his feet, snuffling under stray newspapers and stopping to investigate the odd stale patch of dog piss on a lamp-post. Now Huw stood in front of the chapel, grasping the iron railings and looking up at the light filtering through the dirty windows and over the rotting wooden door and decaying noticeboard with its posters long since faded. At the foot of the noticeboard was a rubble of stained polystyrene chip trays.

He paused, unsure of a certain atmosphere in the air. He was about to return back down the hill when his ears caught the sound of music coming from out of the chapel, a compelling, sorrowing sound that made him walk up to the wooden doors and push them, only to find that they were locked against him. The dog was still snuffling around the pillars of the noticeboard as Huw took out the chapel key that Mordecai had once given him, unlocking the door and closing it behind him.

All street sounds stopped as soon as he moved through the vestry, half a smile on his face, past a table piled high with mildewed hymn books and the dusty pews leading to the wooden pulpit where the Baptismal font had been sealed off again.

Then the sound of many voices singing a hymn broke out of the very air as sudden and striking as blood from a savage wound. It was the hymn of a people singing the praise of God, the many-layered harmonies soaring and breaking over Huw's head in the sweetest waves. He looked up and around the chapel rafters, his smile getting wider and yet wider, as if he had just been made a personal gift of the sun.

> Abide with me; fast falls the eventide;
> The darkness deepens; Lord with me abide
> When other helpers fail and comforts flee
> Help of the helpless, O abide with me.

A man's voice, powerful in strength and resonance, interrupted the singing of the second verse and Huw kept looking around trying to locate its source.

'Though he may send thunder and locusts we will still love God. Though we be thrown into burning bushes or pierced with swords we will still love God. Though misery and darkness and the slime of Satan overtake us we will still love God. Even though we have lost our eyes and ears; even though every bone in our bodies be broken; even though the blood pours from every vein and we have fallen as low as it is possible to fall ... we will still love God. Always love God, my people, and be certain that he loves every second of our adoring praise. Know the world is round and day follows night so that the sound of our prayer and praise will always be in his ears. The only command is to love him.'

The speaking stopped and fell away to singing again, the massed voices of the congregation being lead by the strong direct voices of a group of women. *Diolch Iddo*: thanks be to him for remembering the dust of the earth.

Thank you Jesus.
Praise you Lord.
Hallelujah. Amen. Hallelujah.
Bless you Jesus.

Outside the chapel nothing moved in the village streets except light through shadow. The rock band had given way to bingo. The pale deathly glow of television sets flickered in the blinds and net curtains of the terraces. The orange street lamps shone on the silvery tops of the cars and, down at the mine itself, the great wheel was black and motionless above the huge pool of naked light in the empty windows of the canteen.

In the sepulchral silence of the Welfare Hall the bingo caller was reading out the all-important numbers from his glass box of bouncing balls. Everyone was rapt and attentive, their pens jerking around the blue cards. *On its own number eight: all the threes, thirty-three: old age, number sixty ...*

The bingo numbers carried out into the deserted streets as distinctly as had that bass guitar. Even the starlings dozing in the eaves seemed to heed the numerical progress towards the flyer of fifty-eight pounds. *Five and nine, fifty-nine, two and six – was she worth it: all the sevens, seventy-seven ...*

A police car turned a corner and accelerated down the Valley. The staccato, electronic gunfire of the Space Invaders

300

spat out of the chip shop as the skinheads continued trying to gun down monsters from outer space, kicking the machine hard when they failed. The face of a woman appeared in one of the windows before she drew the curtains on herself. *Top of the shop, number ninety: one and six, sweet sixteen: all the sevens, seventy-seven ...*

In the back room of Walford's video parlour some six men were sipping cans of beer while watching a blue video. Sweating, slithering flesh climbed over yet more piles of sweating, slithering flesh. When they were not actually grappling with one another they were torturing one another in various ways. One of the men sitting in the darkness at the back of the room was masturbating discreetly. *One and eight, eighteen: all the fives, fifty-five: two and three, twenty-three ...*

Around the back of Lipton's shop there was a lot of cussing and swearing in the darkness as two youths tried to jemmy off the back door. Long experience of break-ins had encouraged the management to smother the door with bars and bolts but still the two continued ripping off the steel strips, swearing when their fingers got caught, now scraping and scratching around a long bracket. Even when a window went up and there was a shout they kept up with their scraping and scratching like starving rats knowing that they were on the brink of a load of food.

Down in the floor of the Valley the river continued washing over the unruly rocks and swirling around the dumped prams and old fridges. In the Hall a loud cry of dismay went up when someone called 'House'.

The next house is your snowball accumulator which stands this week at three hundred and twenty-four pounds ...

Thunder cracked like giant cannoning snooker balls over the heads of the Valleys as dark, fat clouds were being shunted together by speeding winds. Sheets of white lightning stammered again and again followed by slashing rips in the skies, all telling of one hell of a storm about to arrive on the doorstep.

Huw Bungalow had mounted the pulpit and was just standing there with his hands on either side of the lectern as the lightning flashed through the windows and the thunder cannoned closer. But, even with the air full of a coming commotion, he could still hear the words and music of older, more precious, times seeping out of the air. 'In the last days, we are told, certain things will happen. I read my Bible to mean that we are coming to the last days when the old men will dream dreams and the young men see visions. There will be bloodshed on the moon, a great darkness over the land and signs writ large on the sky ...'

That singing filled up the chapel again; singing like Huw had never heard. He stood there smiling, still looking around him as the great groundswell of voices came together in scalp-tingling harmony, shaking the chapel rafters with the warmest emblems of power.

> Love divine, all loves excelling,
> Joy of heaven, to earth come down,
> Fix us in thy humble dwelling,
> All thy faithful mercies crown.

A pink slash of lightning tore apart the sky and the Valley walls shook with fantastic hammer blows of thunder as clouds built up into huge mountains of black shadow, now disgorging torrents of rain. But, even in the angry hissing of the rain and repeated rolls of thunder, it was the winds which screamed the loudest; a savage, siren wind, thick with obscenity and hate.

Such was the fury in the sky, the chapel lights dimmed and Huw's eyes darted around anxiously, worried by the dark that was falling everywhere.

'He is coming then and will engulf the world,' a soft voice muttered in the darkness. 'Satan and all his dark angels have escaped from hell. Beware, my people. Arm yourselves with holiness for this hurricane of destruction is coming down on you with a terrible force.'

Lightning the whip cracked again as Rev. Mordecai stepped out of the flashing shadows, stopping at the foot of the pulpit stairs and blocking Huw's way out. Huw looked down at the Rev., his eyes wide with fright.

'This invading force of evil will come as organised intelligence,' the Rev. spat soft, holding up a rope in both of his hands. 'He will come anxious to serve you and even able to convince you that Satan does not exist. But he does my people. The tongues of the old Welsh prophet has been fulfilled and

302

even this very hour he has thrown a cloak of violent perversion all over the face of the world.'

The storm continued to rage, making the domestic lights stutter and dim. Walford's blue video even jerked to a halt and the electricity supply to the Hall itself failed, making the band's amplification whine and twist before it too went dead. There was a short dark silence but then the supply was restored and the hop was quickly back to its normal buzz.

Here Maggie I've heard they've got a great group from Manchester here next week. You remember that one from Manchester? Winston weren't they called? Wasn't he the singer who was always making eyes at you? Gorgeous he was an' all. What wouldn't I give to meet him down a dark alley.

But Maggie still wasn't listening to the girls' chatter, she was still watching Glynmor who had now left the Costello brothers' table and was back talking to that Mavis Nipples, a very fat and totally boss-eyed cow from Aberdare. What he saw in her she couldn't think. She even danced like a hippo with arthritis. He was keeping his left hand in his pocket all the time too. He could never get used to not having a thumb could he? He'd just worry about it for the rest of his life he would. He wasn't the sort who could just shrug it off and learn to live with it. Not Glynmor. He was far more sensitive than most people ever gave him credit for and there was a seriousness about him that he kept well-concealed too. She'd heard about all the socialist books he'd been taking out of the mobile library and had started ordering some of them too. Just to see what he was reading and thinking about. That Jack London was one hell of a writer and she longed to have a chat to Glynmor about it all, longed to discuss that Martin Eden and how he stayed up all night on that boat educating himself. She had cried along with Martin Eden's frustration, was sure that there was enough in Glynmor for him to become a writer too.

But now she was almost crying in frustration about something else too since that fat cow was drooling into his ear and he was responding happily too. He was going to need a new set of glasses as well as a new thumb the way he was going.

Maggie's back stiffened and she took in a sharp intake of breath. The fat cow was going off to get her coat. Now Glynmor was finishing his pint and following her out of the dance. She saw that all the girls had gone silent and were looking at her, curious. She was engulfed by a feeling of total despair and began weeping uncontrollably. She just couldn't see how she was going to cope with all this pain. The band was playing some jubilant rock 'n' roll totally at odds with her mood. 'Where's my Huw?' she wailed. 'I just want my Huw. Why doesn't he come to see me?'

Oh Maggie it's all right. Huw will be along any second won't he Cynth? Do you want another drink do you? Shall we go to the ladies shall we? Glynmor's only going off with that piece to get you all worked up. Just look at the size of her. You'd need a block and tackle to get on top of her.

'Huw. I just want my Huw.'

With everything bleeding and crumbling inside her, she picked up her handbag and ran out of the Hall, leaping down the stairs three at a time and hurrying home in the driving rain. She hardly cared about the storm though and her eye-liner had been blotched and smudged as much by her own tears as the raindrops when she burst in through her front door. 'Huw? Where are you my lovely?' she called in desperation.

The house was worryingly, and obviously empty. She walked out into the kitchen, picked up a tea-towel and dried her face with it before going upstairs. His bedroom was empty too, his best suit and shoes gone. She so hoped he wasn't outdoors in this storm or he'd be getting a terrible cold. She so hoped he would just come home now so she could hold him tight and take some comfort in her wretched misery.

Once back downstairs she stood in the window of her living-room looking out onto the Terrace where the rain was still pouring down on the parked cars and filling up the gutters, making empty cigarette packets and lollipop wrappers dance around. The band had stopped playing now, she could tell, with the people running home fast: the men, with their shoulders hunched forward and their jackets pulled up over their heads: the women bustling along the pavement, with grim lips and eyes half closed, in a clatter of high heels.

After a few minutes Maggie put on her raincoat and braved the storm again, going back down to the Welfare Hall and finding a sort of fight in progress on the stairs, though not so much a fight as a rolling maul with lots of shoving and pushing by some men she did not recognise.

'Boys, boys,' Max Million, the chairman, kept shouting. 'Let's have some order now shall we?'

Maggie sidestepped the maul and hurried up to the dance hall where, already, the tables were deserted with the band shouldering out their equipment and just a few committee men picking up the empty glasses.

'Stan. Have you seen my Huw?' she cried out to someone behind the bar.

'No girl. Haven't see him all night.'

She ran back down the stairs and out into the rain again, her hair by now but long dripping ringlets as she walked to the bus shelter where Curly and Idris were sitting sharing a bottle of cider with Danny Bits and Pieces.

'Have you seen my Huw anywhere, have you boys?'

'I seen him,' chortled Bits and Pieces. 'I seen him a few days ago. In the chip shop, wasn't he?'

'No, we haven't seen him,' said Idris. 'Do you want a swig from this, do you?'

'If you see him send him home, will you?'

'Aye. For certain. C'mon Maggie. 'Ave a drink of this.'

She turned into the rain and began running again – where she was not at all certain. She just ran on in a blind panic up the road towards the pit. She passed a huge tip drainage pipe which was gurgling and foaming with torrential swollen streams when a great roll of thunder stopped her dead. She looked up at the quivering sky, half fearing that it was all going to collapse on her head when lightning lit up the whole Valley, with the mine and surrounding tips looking like some strange wet moonscape with just a few black shapes of sheep moving around. Then everything turned to darkness and rain again.

The rain had seeped right through her raincoat and seemed to have got right into the very marrow of her backbone as she turned and turned again. Perhaps Glynmor had not gone off with that fat cow from Aberdare after all? He didn't have a car these days and that piece was too fat to get into any car of her own. Perhaps Glynmor had taken Huw home to Aunty Phyllis just to upset her. That would be just the kind of thing you'd expect from someone like him isn't it? Anything to get back at her for what she'd done to him.

But she could find no sign of Huw. Tired and out of breath, she strode back to the village, knocking on the door of

Aunty Phyllis' in No. 3. When there was no reply she knocked again so furious it was as if she was about to bash it in.

'Who's there?' Aunty Phyllis called out. She had long given up opening the door at night.

'It's Maggie. I want to speak to Glynmor.'

'He's not here. He hasn't come home.'

'Did he say if he was coming back?'

Aunty Phyllis opened the door and her plump frame, in her dressing gown and curlers, seemed to fill up the whole doorway. 'I'm not sure where he's gone,' she added. 'He did say he might not be coming home.'

'It's Huw. He's gone missing. I've been looking for him everywhere I have.'

'Called the police have you? You'd better come in and do that straight.'

The police could not have been less helpful when Maggie told them that her son, seriously handicapped, had gone missing. They took his name — 'Oh that's young Huw Bungalow is it?' — and suggested she went home and waited for him. If he didn't turn up she was to ring them again in the morning. 'He might just have got drunk somewhere,' the policeman added.

'He doesn't get drunk,' Maggie snorted.

'Or just fallen asleep somewhere.'

'He always likes to sleep in his own bed.'

'There's always the simplest reasons for these things, Mrs Jones. And it's far too soon to put him on the Missing Persons' List.'

'Well a fat lot of help you are, I must say.'

'Do ring us again in the morning, Mrs Jones,' the policeman said, putting down the receiver.

'Useless bastard,' Maggie replied, putting down hers.

'Do you want a cup of tea?' Aunty Phyllis offered.

'No. I just want my Huw. I just want to know what Glynmor has done with him.'

'Glynmor wouldn't harm a hair of that boy's head.'

'Well, you don't know Glynmor then do you?'

'He never would.'

'But you don't *know* do you? You don't know him like I do.'

In a state of high dudgeon she stormed out of the house,

hurrying first to re-check her own before continuing her search in the rain. She followed the gulley along the back of the terrace, peering into the dark sopping places but hardly able to see anything at all. Down by the garage the barking of a Doberman reminded her of something that made her stop still. She had been so distracted by Glynmor's behaviour and then worried about Huw she had quite forgotten about Huw's dog. What had happened to him? And, if they had both disappeared together, should she be comforted by that or worry even more?

Yet more furious dodgem cars of thunder were crashing against one another as she strode on up the hill, past the council houses of Giro City with its broken street lamps and cardboard windows. How could anyone live in houses like that? A dog was howling miserably inside a garden shed and she hurried over, but it sounded far too big and savage to be their dog. Now she had reached the outskirts of Bont and she didn't know where else to go. She stood on a patch of waste ground near the tip, wondering what to do. 'Huw!' she called helplessly into the rain. 'Huw, where are you?'

But, even shouting as loud as she could, through cupped hands, her voice didn't seem to carry anywhere in the rain which just kept falling – steady, determined, inhumanly mocking her human anxiety.

Her stumbling, calling search carried on for the remaining hours of the night, taking her up around the huge forests of pine trees and back around the reservoir. She moved slowly but relentlessly – over brambled fields and dry stone walls, up gulleys and into brown beds of bracken, across the swollen rivers and around the sides of the giant tips. She went down the Valley as far as the next village then crossed the river by the Banana Tip, finally arriving back in Bont unable even to feel her muddied and scratched legs. Not the athletic type at the best of times it was only some dark crawling fear that kept her going.

A grey, weeping dawn finally broke over the village when she returned from circling the reservoir yet again, fruitlessly checking her house once more. By now she was so dirty and dishevelled, Emlyn Kremlin did not at first recognise her when he opened his front door. She was so tired and overcome by shock it took him a full quarter of an hour – and a good three cups of tea – before he managed to extract the full facts of the disappearance out of her. She was chattering and shaking so much she actually dropped one of the cups of tea onto the kitchen floor.

He made her take a hot bath and put on one of his thick, blue-striped nightshirts as he hung her sodden clothes up on the range before putting her into his own bed where, still shivering and chattering incoherently, he promised he would sort it all out, providing she stayed put.

There wasn't a better man in the Valleys to meet such a crisis than Emlyn, the old N.U.M. warhorse, who had spent most of his life leading teams through fire and gas, to rescue those who had gone missing. Where others merely panicked, Emlyn became calmer. Where others dived off in all directions, Emlyn actually sat down, as he was doing now in his kitchen, studying the face of his job watch, thinking the rescue syllogism through from known premises.

He might have been studying his watch for a full five minutes and some would have said that he was just taking it easy. But those who knew him would know that he was thinking it through. There were none of the usual premises here – this was not some unfortunate miner trapped in a known position deep in the bowels of the earth. This was the mentally handicapped child of a broken marriage whose father had gone missing and who, given his love of wandering the Valley, could be almost anywhere.

When he did act, he did so decisively, picking up the telephone and first ringing Ted John North, the mountain rescue specialist. 'Ted, it's Emlyn. Get the rescue team together and down to the Hall now. Huw Bungalow has disappeared.'

'Dai, it's Emlyn. Open up the Hall. We've got to mount a search of the Valley. Huw Bungalow has disappeared.'

'Oboe, it's Emlyn. Get word to the boys of the lodge to get to the Hall. Huw Bungalow has disappeared.'

He put down the receiver and looked up to see Maggie standing in the kitchen doorway. She looked dreadful with her twisting, anxious mouth and black sunken eyes which were even more pronounced on the white mask of her drawn face.

'Couldn't sleep,' she explained feebly. 'Any news is there?'

'None. I forgot to ask but does Glynmor know about all this?'

'Glynmor's not been around. I thought he might have

308

had something to do with it but now I'm sure he hasn't. He's … oh … gone off with some fat cow from Aberdare.'

'Typical. But he could, of course, have gone off with Huw somewhere. You don't know do you? It would make some sense. Just to get at you over the divorce. I told you before. He wouldn't like any of that solicitor stuff.'

'Glynmor wouldn't go anywhere with Huw. He can't stand the sight of him.'

'Well maybe the pair of them'll show up. Let's hope so anyway.'

'Yes. Let's.'

She went home, alone.

It was still sheeting with rain and not yet eight o'clock on Sunday morning when Emlyn had chalked a map of the Valley on a blackboard on the stage of the Rainbow Room as his damp, bleary-eyed troops, still stiff with stale breath and hangover, filed in through the doors and dragged chairs up near the stage. Stan Swansea, Graham Mainwaring, Dai Box, Ted John North … None of them spoke or bantered with one another in their usual manner and just sat there with their arms folded, waiting for the word of command. Oboe Parry, Tony Chef, Tom the Nutter, Dai Prosser, John Abdabs …

Although he never said as much, Emlyn was always proud to be a man among men on such occasions. These were the men who had fought long and hard to save a dying pit and who would even now fight just as hard to find a missing boy. Somehow they always *responded* when they were needed; always faithful to the call of distress; ordinary, decent men, primed and ready to do whatever was necessary.

'This might be a short one since Huw Bungalow might turn up at any minute,' Emlyn told the men. 'But let's tackle it from the start as if it was going to be a long one. Huw was last seen at about seven last night so, first off, I just want to mount a general box and sweep search of the Valley. Everyone is to report back here within two hours. If the general search fails, we'll just have to plan a particular one. Ted, take a few men up to those steep gullies opposite the Banana Tip. Abdabs, take the res.; Graham, the forest; Tony, the mine – just the surface workings, he couldn't have got down below; Dai Box, the tip over on the council estate. Huw's got his dog with him somewhere too. Remember now, a fast search then back here and, if we haven't lifted him, we'll send out more men.'

Even as they left the Hall, the men hurried across the village streets, knocking up their butties to join the search and, within minutes, a small army of men, many in brightly coloured wellingtons, capes and sou'westers was marching out into the drifting rain.

The thunder and lightning of the night had stopped by now – as had the savage siren winds. All they could hear now was the steady hissing of rain. Lots of rain.

John Abdabs and two others jumped into a van and drove up to the edge of the reservoir, which was as quiet and as still as the marbled moat of a ruined Norman castle. Fanning out into a corridor of some ten yards they worked around the brown rocky shoreline, prodding their sticks down holes and into the scummy froth trapped in the small pools. Nothing moved except the odd trout, swimming away and leaving a V-sign on the surface of the rain-speckled waters. Way out on the middle of the lake two abandoned fishing skiffs sat, black on grey, with the muted sounds of a flock of wintering geese gabbling softly to themselves somewhere in the distant mists.

'We used to catch frogs up here when we were kids,' said Abdabs. 'We'd get straws and blow up their arses.'

'What did that do?'

'It made 'em blow up like balloons. Then we'd throw them into the water and throw rocks at them.'

'You were nice as a kid then Abdabs?'

'Nice? Aye. As nice as any of us were.'

The rain had swollen the river so high that Oboe Parry was taking no chances with his river search, holding hands with Dai Prosser and Roger Williams as they waded up it. Actually being in the river was the only way to see what was in it and they could stop together and pull away a mattress or sheet of lino to see what it hid, usually something in the way of more rubbish – empty processed pea tins or Coca-Cola cans.

'We ought to get together and clean up this river one day,' Roger Williams shouted above the swirling roar. 'I do get sick every time I look at it.'

The river charged against their thighs and legs, as relentless as Llanelli rugby prop forwards, hungry to get the ball back. But the trio held solid as they waded up through the

310

railway sidings next to the pit, the two of them standing steady if one of them lost his footing on the slippery rocks. 'If Huw Bungalow has fallen in this he could be in the Bristol Channel before they find him,' Oboe called out.

The trickiest job in the search had fallen to Ted John North who, with Dai Blades and Dan Corduroys, had to climb over the deep slashes of the ravines opposite the Banana Tip. The bright, even fluorescent, colours of Huw Bungalow's suit had often been spotted out in the ravines. It was, of course, unlikely that someone even as do-lally as Huw Bungalow would go out climbing in the dark in the middle of a storm. But, as a veteran mine rescue man and expert at pulling sheep and dogs out of these gullies, Ted understood that any search had to cover the whole area: that you just could not miss out parts of the search area just because access was difficult. The fissures were unstable at the best of times and the rain had opened them up, dislodging small stones and sending them tumbling down the Valley wall. He leaped across one of the gullies with the sureness of the local sheep. Wet rock was always murder to grip.

If Ted had fallen he had been taught to relax and just enjoy the fall. You would only get a few broken bones and they would dig you out soon enough. The trouble was, you never quite knew how deep some of the gullies were. Dislodged rocks seemed to fall down them forever before any sound came back again. Sometimes if you stopped and listened hard, the infernal noises inside some of them sounded even more destructive than the seven furies trapped inside large seashells.

Seagulls always gathered around the village tip in the heavy rain since it made the foraging easier and the maggots more plentiful. They took off in a squawking cloud of flapping wings however when Dai Box and Dibber Williams came tumbling down the rubbish slopes, cussing the rain and kicking out at the exploded plastic bags of rubbish which, even in the freshening rain, released their foul smells of mildew and rot. Dibber, who had already been belching and tasting last night's beer, began puking over a rubble of potato peelings. 'Why couldn't you have got the reservoir or something Dai? These smells mun. You know how I get first thing in the morning.'

'Better you puke up here than in the reservoir. We wouldn't want the village drinking your puke now would we?

It's bad enough getting it over our boots in the cage.'

'I haven't done that for weeks.'

'You did it last Thursday you bastard liar.'

'So I did. I must 'ave one of those ulcers you know, Dai. No one else goes about puking all the time like me. Now do they?'

'No. Thank God.'

'But I've been to see the doctor and he keeps saying it's indigestion. Then I'm taking some of his medicine and that's making me puke as well. How can it be indigestion?'

The mine itself was abandoned and silent this Sunday morning, the roofs of its many buildings and outhouses weeping along with the rain. Tony Chef toured the workshops and changing rooms scrupulously, even looking inside the large refuse bins next to the canteen. The rain pattered on the corrugated iron roofs of the foundry and on the huge ten-wheeled Arctic lorries. The rain danced off the gutterings and fell into the brown muddied pools rainbowed with whorls of oil. The rain washed over the wheelhouse where a deputy was sitting with his feet up and smoking a Woodbine. Who would want to go missing in the rain? Tony Chef asked himself. Why be out in all this when you could be home in a warm, dry bed?

Glynmor was happier than the smallest baby as the first Aberdare bus of the morning came toiling up the Valley. This was more like the Glynmor of old; an old woman kept turning and glaring at him as he sat looking smug. He had spent most of Saturday night clambering over the extremely pneumatic frame – and poking his tireless winky into the various orifices – of Mavis Nipples and it had been like scaling a mountain so big it even made the Himalayas seem like a row of beans. All night his whole body seemed to have been trampolining over those giant tits capped by nipples the size of apple tarts. He had gone snorkelling down into her cabbage patch too before having a rest and returning for air around the whereabouts of those amazing nipples. Even her appendicitis scar was vivid with torment.

And after all this sporting activity – which clearly needed a kind of sexual decathlete – he had, not surprisingly, slept the sleep of the dead. Aye boyo bach, there was gold in them thar hills and that was a fact. Clearly the lakes and mountains of Mavis Nipples were going to be explored again very soon.

Even more unusually his missing thumb was not playing him up either. If it was sunny or rainy; if he was drunk or sober; even in the middle of the night in bed or just sitting quietly on the lavatory trying to get a big one out, his thumb would suddenly start romping with pain and he would spend hours sucking or blowing on the stump. But, today, it was purring away as happy as Larry which suggested to him what he had long suspected: everyone should fuck at least twice a day and, in the absence of that, wank often. A pox on what the doctor said.

Those marvellous nipples floated through the clouds of his consciousness again like a couple of sexual flying saucers. Ah me. And that appendicitis scar, as fat as a clap of thunder ...

As the bus pulled into Bont he could see that men were moving about in the surrounding countryside in the rain, which was unusual on a Sunday morning, even in fine weather. But he thought no more of it as he leaped off the bus and ran down to Aunty Phyllis' house.

'Everyone's been looking for you,' she told him sharply, standing in the doorway. 'There's been mischief there's been.'

'Oh aye. Well they can't blame me for once. Are you going to let me in out of the rain or what?'

'Your Huw has gone missing he has. Emlyn has got men out searching for him.'

'Where's Maggie?' he asked, his good humour draining away as those flying saucers went whirring off to another galaxy.

'Home. Waiting to see if Huw will be coming home I expect.'

He ran down the terrace and, pushing open the front door, walked inside calling out Maggie's name. The living-room was cold, and there was no fire. He turned when he heard someone in the hallway. It was Mrs Pritchard from next door but one. 'Huw's gone missing Glynmor,' she said quietly, with no hint of reproach.

Glynmor just stood there, the raindrops hanging in his black curls as he wiped his nose with the inside of his palm. He kept staring at Mrs Pritchard but said nothing.

'He didn't get to the dance and he's been gone all night.

The miners have started a general search of the Valley.'

'Where's Maggie?'

'She's at Emlyn's. Emlyn is organising the search from the Hall. She sent word for me to keep an eye on the house in case Huw came back of his own accord.'

Glynmor ran down to Emlyn's in Richard Street, knocking on the door hard and surprised that Maggie opened it almost immediately. She was ghostly pale. 'Have you seen Huw?' she asked without asking him in.

'Where would I see him? I've been over in Aberdare.'

'Oh had a good rub with that fat cow did you?'

'I went over with a few of the boys and found this wine bar that stayed open all night.' He wasn't sure why he was lying to a woman who was on the verge of divorcing him but there you are. 'Where could Huw have got to?'

'What do you care? Get back to that fat cow of yours. Go on.'

'I told you. I was with the boys.'

She slammed the door shut and he knocked on it again. 'Come on Maggie. We can both get on out and look for him.'

'What do you care about him? Go on. Piss off back to that fat cow of yours.'

'Come on Maggie.'

'Go on. Piss off out of it.'

He ran back to the Hall finding Emlyn talking with Billy Discordant and Morgan Moses in the Rainbow Room. 'Come home have we?' Emlyn asked with a faint censorious sneer as he walked towards Glynmor. 'Have you any idea at all where Huw might have got to?'

'None. Maggie just asked me that. What do you think I might have done with him? You think I'd run away with my own son?'

'Just asking Glynmor. Just asking. You'd both gone missing at the same time. We put two and two together ...'

'And made six. Aye well I didn't. So what are you doing now? Have the police been called?'

'Not so far. They were told last night but we've got far more men than they have. Miners are always best looking after their own.'

'The police, Emlyn mun, have got dogs and helicopters. They've got frogmen for dragging the reservoir. They've go

314

communications with the other Valleys. If Huw's been found in some other Valley he's been reported to the police. This is not one of your underground rescues. Let's get the police in.'

Emlyn's eyebrows raised in the face of such unanswerable logic. He was bound to agree.

'Where are you searching?'

'A general box and sweep of the Valley first. The pit, the res., the tip, the river.'

'Right, well that's a start,' said Glynmor. 'Morgan, I want you and Billy to send out a general call to the village. Knock on every door and tell them to do the same. We want everyone here at one o'clock and we'll cover every square inch of the Valley by nightfall. Just send out the word that Huw Bungalow has gone missing and his father needs all the help he can get.'

Morgan and Billy glanced at Emlyn who nodded. Glynmor had now taken effective charge, just as Emlyn had always wanted. He had, in Emlyn's view, a most unusual combination of brains and courage. When properly motivated, there was no telling where he would lead the men. There was never any better motive than the protection of your own blood. Emlyn was happy to hand over the torch for other reasons too. He had always wanted Glynmor to get a taste for leadership. He still longed for a new leader to emerge in the Valleys and was perhaps alone in believing that Glynmor might be the one.

Emlyn and Glynmor were deep in conversation in front of the blackboard when Maggie walked into the Rainbow Room. 'So what are we going to do next?' she asked, walking over to them, her hands thrust down into her raincoat pockets.

'We're going to get the village together,' said Glynmor without turning around. 'Then we're going to turn this bastard Valley inside out. That's what we're going to do.'

Emlyn's blood surged hot and, slightly overcome, he had to turn away. It had been a long time since he had heard any fighting talk around the place and what sweet music it was to his tired old ears.

The general box and sweep search of the Valley produced nothing but the general call to the village produced the largest public meeting that anyone could remember. The Rainbow Room had been filling up long before one o'clock but, just on one o'clock, the room was packed to the point of suffocation

315

with the people standing on the chairs at the back, others sitting on the floor at the front and yet more trying to push in through the swing doors. Huw Bungalow had brought everyone together.

Among the first to arrive were a gang of skinheads from Giro City, all chewing gum and twitching a bit at the outrage which had befallen Huw. Then there were many of the miners' wives, who had always taken a back seat in times of emergency, grim-faced and talking to one another. Schoolchildren milled everywhere, a few with their dogs who, they said, would spot Huw for miles. The committee chairman, Max Million and his wife, were among the earliest arrivals too – already in oilskins and with walking sticks – as were Bits and Pieces, Idris and Curly from the bus shelter.

The more Glynmor studied their faces the greater his surprise. The two Pryce sisters from the big house on the corner had both come and they hadn't been seen outdoors for years. Billy Smiles had come from his farm down at the other end of the Valley. Even more interestingly, two of the Prosser brothers – who, not many weeks ago, had rolled Glynmor and his new car into the river – were sitting there too. Old Guto had come out from under his stone as well, the crowds making a big space for him and his smell as he just stood there, apparently uninterested in everything, and just glaring at Glynmor.

No one could remember when the Rev. Mordecai had last been seen in the Hall – or indeed at any public meeting anywhere – but there the mystic nitwit was, large as life and twice as puzzling, looking positively buoyant in his duffel coat and brandishing a furled multi-coloured golf umbrella. It was the way he was forever nodding and smiling at everyone as if they were in chapel that got up Emlyn's nose. Just where did he think he was?

Emlyn was even more surprised at the turnout than Glynmor and just sat there on a chair on the stage with his fingers interlaced and his thumbs circling one another. He had never understood why his maddening people so often managed to fill him with such pride. Most of the time they just drove him crackers but, boy, could they be there when you needed them. Such a motley crowd was a sign of their concern that one of their children had gone missing and had to be found. You could reach out with both hands and shape the anxiety in the air. Bu it was their concern and sense of purpose that was the most real; the love for Huw Bungalow that had made them as one.

'We have but three hours of daylight left so I want groups of you to fan out in different directions and search the whole Valley,' Glynmor said from the stage. 'We've already done a general search so now I want every inch covered. I won't give each of you a precise area but, if you come close to anyone, just move away. Just keep fanning out and looking for any holes; anything at all down which Huw might have slipped. He really could be anywhere.'

Maggie just stood next to him staring down at her feet as Glynmor continued, pausing only occasionally to think out his next words. 'If we have no luck by the time it gets dark come back here to the Hall and we'll already have got the miners' helmets up out of the lamp room. They'll be good for searching through the night. We'll keep going for as long as it takes till he's found.'

Emlyn was mildly surprised by the raid on the pit's lamp room since he had not been consulted but gave no sign of this surprise. If John Walsh, pit manager wouldn't allow the use of his precious lamps, they would just take them.

'The great likelihood is that Huw is in some house or building,' Glynmor went on. 'And we've not yet found his dog either. So, if we're still out of luck after dark, we'll start in Richard Street down near the river and work up through every house and building in the village. Check any sheds and garages. Look in any rooms you haven't looked in lately. Most of all, use your commonsense. If you see anything or anywhere that Huw might be, then check it out. The more thorough the search, the sooner we'll find him.'

Glynmor stepped down off the stage and there was an outburst of clapping with cries of 'We'll find him' and 'Don't you worry now.'

He stepped back up onto the stage again. 'Maggie and me thank you for your help,' he said, humbled and embarrassed. 'You will know that we have had our problems but today we are together. The whole village is together. We are all anxious to find our beloved son.'

Everyone clapped again and Emlyn smiled with a quiet admiration. Glynmor had tapped the emotion of the meeting and mobilised it with an instinctive political skill. If only the

317

lad cared to he could certainly become the leader the Valleys were waiting for.

A police inspector in full uniform stepped out of a car outside the Hall and asked for whoever was in charge of the search as the crowds filed out and peeled off into the rain. Even as they reached the outskirts of the village they broke up into smaller groups, fanning out on the Valley walls as they climbed higher and yet higher.

The one searcher who had moved faster than almost anyone was Guto, rope coiled around shoulder and old Davy lamp in his hand. Even when the others stopped to prod around the tip or under the huge iron sewage pipes, Guto strode on resolutely until he had gone well past the Banana Tip and the bend in the Valley, fording the river and coming to a stream bounding out of a gulley.

He followed the narrow shale bank of the stream and squeezed through a narrow opening before coming to the old mining cavern with its forecourt still strewn with rusty rails and drams. He lit the Davy lamp and stepped over a pile of old pit props, pausing only briefly to look at the scene of his emergence from a hallucinating hell. Just near the huge stone he hoisted his lamp up into the air and took in two deep breaths of air. If Huw was anywhere he was in here, Guto decided as he stepped into the darkness of that fearful, dripping tunnel.

The police inspector was in the Rainbow Room talking with Maggie, Glynmor and Emlyn when a skinhead burst in through the swing doors, holding a small dog in his hands. His eyes were red with running tears and his nose was dribbling too as he carried the dog over to the group. He was crying because – as he knew and Maggie had seen immediately – it was Huw's dog and it was as dead as mutton.

'He's had his neck pulled,' the police inspector said holding its head up by one of its ears. 'This dog's been killed.'

'Oh Glynmor!' Maggie bawled, her arms reaching out for him as her vision swam and all the strength began draining out of her legs. 'What's happening to us? I can't take this any more I can't.'

The discovery of the dog in a backyard next to the Hall sent

318

spasm of dry fear through the community and even more joined in the search, with Emlyn himself going up into the Hall's rafters and searching through all the Lodge banners which were stored there. The huge red and gold tapestries – honouring such as Horner and Ablett, the great trade union leaders of old, as well as extolling the virtues of brotherhood, unity and strength were now brought out once a year for the Miners' Gala Day in Cardiff.

But, just that minute, they seemed very sad indeed to Emlyn as he stood with his head bowed to avoid the beams, wondering quite what it was that had got loose in their small village. The creeping dereliction and loss of pride were bad enough, but murder too? He took out his fob watch and looked at it and could just feel the ghosts of Ablett and Horner standing there next to him, their spirits crying along with the rain that was still pattering on the grey slate roof.

Maggie had been put to bed but it was not long before, refusing all offers of any sedatives, she was back in the Rainbow Room again. So many people were now moving in and out, past the glittering one-armed bandits in the corridor that some of the women had set up a silver tea urn, dispensing hot tea and corned beef sandwiches off a trestle table. Clearly, the news of the disappearance had now travelled further than anyone had ever imagined. Dan O'Neill from the *South Wales Echo* had turned up. And he was sober too. 'Yes but I'm still not quite sure what was so special about this Huw Bungalow,' he kept saying as, notebook in hand, he went from tired, blistered group to tired, hungry group.

Down in the square, the rain had stopped as Abdabs and his butties were handing out the miners' helmets with the silver batteries and, quite soon, the dark Valley was scoured with hundreds of shafts of light; not just from the miners' helmets but from the myriad torches, flares and hurricane lamps that were now travelling in floating processions everywhere, criss-crossing one another as they moved up and down the Valley walls.

'It was much like the funeral of a Ming emperor,' O'Neill was later to write in the *Echo*. 'Everywhere there were flickering lights as far as the eye could see. It was almost as if the whole world was out and sorrowing for the loss of its king.'

Lights winked through the black needles of the pine

forests and glazed the still cold depths of the reservoir. Orbs of light moved around the high pyramids of the tips, like floating, magical glow-worms. Golden funnels of light waved along the dark gulleys and danced on the hurrying waters of the river. The Valley had become a vibrant symphony of moving golds on a black velvet, with half-formed, shouted words or the cry of disturbed sheep carrying through the damp air as the people, frightened by this awful glimpse of hell where love had gone, tramped the slopes in their search for their lost king.

Guto stumbled and cussed softly as he emerged from the old mine-working, holding up his flickering Davy lamp and staring up at the huge boulder. He had found nothing but flooding water in the cave. There had been no sweet whistling in the air. The song of the cave had fallen silent. Huw Bungalow had gone. The king had risen.

Chapter Twenty

Maggie was sitting on the stage, sipping at a mug of tea next to Glynmor when Rev. Mordecai went up to her and said that he was sure that Huw would be found soon. 'That which has been lost will always be found,' he added.

Maggie, in no mood to get provocative, merely nodded and Glynmor looked away.

'It comes to something when you have to search the houses doesn't it?' the Rev. went on. 'When are you going to start all that?'

'I'm not sure,' said Glynmor, vague. 'I should think they'll be starting in Richard Street now. Tony Chef is in charge of that side of it.'

By now, so many were coming in and out of the Hall a committee man had been posted on the door to keep out outsiders and, unusually, the bar had not been opened either. 'We'll drink our fill when Huw has been found,' the committee chairman had decreed. 'But not till he is found.'

Rev. Mordecai left and Maggie just sat there asking herself the same single unanswerable question. Who would want to kill a dog? But Glynmor was holding up well under it all, she was relieved to see. It was that unpredictable side of his personality with which she had first fallen in love with, she guessed. No matter how regular the play, you were never quite sure how he was going to play the part. Just now he was coming through as strong as a brick.

It was Oboe Parry who came in and told Maggie that there was a man out in the bus shelter who wanted to see her.

'Can't he come in here?'

'The committee is stopping everyone. He seems a bit of a strange one but he says it's important.'

321

She looked at Glynmor who nodded. 'It might be something. Better go.'

Oddly, in the circumstances, she had a presentiment that something valuable might be breaking out of the gloom. Even as she walked across the road she knew who her visitor was. And she had not seen him for fourteen years either. 'Hello John,' she said, her spirits singing sudden. 'Can't you come over the road for a cup of tea?'

His head turned and a smile broke out in his bushy beard. Even in the light of the street lamp she could see the intelligence in his big brown eyes. A police car went speeding past with its blue light flashing and they both turned to look at it.

'These are bad times Maggie,' he said. His voice had lost none of its warm and consoling power either. He was still the only man she had ever met who, despite his appearance, was immediately trustworthy. 'There are evil shadows everywhere and your people are under fierce attack but I just came up to tell you that joy will return to your breaking heart. You must trust that.'

'Trust what though John? Trust what? And where's my Huw? Just tell me that will you? I can't live without him John, don't want to live without him.'

'I can't tell you just yet, Maggie. But your heart will be full again. Joy will return to your household. Believe that and you must still pray.'

'But I do. Oh John I do.'

Angry shouts came from the end of Bont Terrace. It might have been a scene from some scabrous nightmare of end times as the house search party, some holding hurricane lamps out in the street, entered each home, whether the householder was a'willing or not. People were screaming their outrage at not being trusted but Tony Chef kept shouting that every house – without exception – had to be searched from top to toe. *Without exception now, boys.*

'I shiver when I think of all the evil that has come to our homes, Maggie,' said John, turning back to her. 'Even that which was once good has gone rotten. The people are ill, they are physically breaking down, they are crying out in pain. But keep praying to God now. He needs every single prayer He can get, since He is alone and embattled, fighting hard to hold onto

322

his power and authority. He does not work like tyrants and despots, murdering to have and hold. He just works through love and prayer. Those are his only weapons. He is suffering the most enormous pain. But be glad. Your Huw is important to Him.'

'I can't be glad though John. You see there's this enormous pain with me too. It's a mother's pain it is. There's only one thing I want to know. When will I see Huw again?'

'I cannot say Maggie. I cannot say because I do not know. But what I do know is that God needs Huw for the struggle that's coming to this Valley. Your very home is going to become a battleground between good and evil when God himself will be fighting for His own life. So remember your prayers. There are but a few faithful left and even a second of prayer is important to Him.'

'Oh John, I don't like any of this. I'm just a mother who wants her son back.'

'God wants His Son back too, Maggie. That's why there's so much death and pain in the Valley. The people have lost His Son and God is desperate to find Him again. He's searching far and near. Huw is important to Him.'

'I don't understand any of this. Why don't you come over and have a cup of tea with us?'

'Not tonight Maggie. Not tonight.'

After the wind had shunted away the rain clouds, moonlight broke over the whole length of the Valley. But still the searchers' lights kept travelling its length and breadth. Huge arc lamps had been set up on the dam wall of the reservoir, where the eerie silence was broken only by the soft splash of police frogmen as they toppled backwards off their boats, to sink deeper and yet deeper into the still, cold water. On occasion a flicker of light appeared beneath the surface, breaking into a small golden pond with the black-masked head of the diver bobbing in the middle of it.

'What happens when we find him Uncle Billy?' asked a watching child.

'That depends. If he's fine, we'll be happy. If he's not, the Valley will die of a broken heart.'

'But we will find him, won't we?'

'We'll find him all right son. If he's anywhere on this earth at all. We'll not rest till we've found him. Have no fear of that.'

'What's so special about Huw Bungalow, Uncle Billy? I mean everyone seems to be concerned about him don't they? Why's that then?'

'It's terrible hard to explain. Huw has become special to us 'cos we find it easy to love him. Love is never easy but Huw makes it easy for us 'cos he's without blemish or sin. Love has always been important in the valleys. We built our homes on love we did. We had everything we did, with this love. It kept our babies safe an' warm, it brought us close to our brothers, made us honour our parents. But there's too much hate now and we've lost what we had. Huw is all we've got left now. He's all of the past that we've got left so that's why everyone is up and out looking for him. They're scared. Everyone is that scared.'

A single, dusty 40 watt bulb dangled from a rafter in the cellar of the Libanus Chapel as Rev. Mordecai sat face to face with Huw Bungalow. He had been gagged with a cravat and his hands and feet were tied up with a thick rope.

Huw just sat there in an old chair looking directly at his captor but there was no fear in his wide, innocent eyes and neither did he make any sound when the Rev. took off his gag. Even despite the dirty stains and scuffs on his new canary-yellow jacket there was an immense dignity about him as he sat, slack-mouthed and uncomprehending, staring unflinchingly at old Mordecai. His black eyes looked down at the bread that Mordecai was breaking and now holding out with a trembling hand. But his mouth did not open to receive it and the accusing stare continued.

'Not hungry then, my boy? That is a pity. Everyone should eat well. Food is one of the very greatest blessings, as is water. You must allow me to baptise you Huw, before we do what we have to. I am very sorry about this Huw but the times demand that there must be a sacrifice. And you were the only possible one. You do understand that, don't you? You were the only possible one.'

Huw looked down at the bread in Mordecai's hand and then back at the minister's tired old eyes.

'It's no good looking at me in that tone of voice Huw. I had to do this. And I was left with no alternative but to kill

324

your dog. He would have led the people here to you now wouldn't he? He knew where you were. And with us the stakes are too high to worry about a mere dog. Since we are in the business of saving people's souls, Huw, making them well for eternity.' He picked a small lump off the bread and chewed it slowly. 'You see, Huw, when you study the pattern of Welsh revivals, you begin to understand that the Welsh only ever react to an emergency. Look at the Cholera Revival of 1849 – noted largely for the fierceness with which it grew at first and suddenness with which it disappeared again when the disease lifted. Look at the great 1904 revival and, when you dig around in the roots of that, you find that there was a train crash next to the village where it started, the Welsh lost to England at rugby, then the great Evan Roberts stepped in and tapped the general mood.

'The general mood, Huw. That's the key to Revival in the Welsh history. Get the right general mood, followed by an alarming emergency and there is almost always a return to the chapel. Well, today, the mood is right. Everyone is guilty and depressed about something or other. So what I've now done is create an emergency. I've taken you off them, Huw. Your disappearance is going to make the whole of the Valleys get up and look for its soul again. That which has been lost will be found. It *will* be found, Huw.

'That's why I've done this, as I'm sure even you, my broken, handicapped angel, will understand. I want to see if there's anything that's decent left in this Valley home of ours. I want to galvanise and goad it into life, make it a force to be reckoned with. I'm the new Evan Roberts you see, Huw. One day the people will give thanks to me for making them come awake again.'

He stood up and climbed the cellar stairs which came out into the vestry. Then, standing in the chapel doors, he looked down the hill, noting that the house search party had come to the end of Bont Terrace. He climbed back down into the cellar again.

'I'm going to have to put the gag back on you, Huw. They will be coming to search the chapel soon so I will have to move you somewhere else for the moment. Do not be uncharitable in your thoughts to me. If there has to be a sacrifice for the soul of the people it could only be you.'

Later that evening, Mordecai took three men down into

325

the chapel cellar and then through the manse. They found nothing, of course. It was nearly four o'clock in the morning before every house and building in Bont had been searched. A few stayed out on the moon-grazed slopes but most were grateful for at least a few hours shut-eye. But not Glynmor and Maggie. Fortified by tea and some hot bowls of cawl from Mrs Pritchard, they stayed the long night through sitting on the chairs of the Rainbow Room, smoking cigarettes and chatting about this and that in the casual way that well-established married couples do.

It was Maggie, mostly, who was fond of sentimental reminiscences, even going back to the night they had got married and he had taken a shower fully-clothed in that hotel in Barry Island. Then, do you remember, that time when you came home pissed out of your brain with that parrot on your shoulder claiming that you were Long John Silver? Aye and there was all that white shit over my best suit. And do you remember when you thought there were fleas in the bedroom and you bought all that sulphur stuff in the ironmongers? Aye an' it didn't get the fleas but all but finished us off.

Neither of them mentioned the landmines of infidelity and jealousy that had blown up so many marriages, including their own. With so many other real problems to cope with there seemed no point in adding to them and, anyway, their past problems seemed to have floated away just now, like dead leaves coracling down a stream. Just now they needed one another badly. They needed that long experience of one another — that collective, yet individual, memory of joy and laughter of a long marriage — to sustain and nourish one another in this time of anxiety and pain.

'You've been reading Jack London, I heard,' she said.

'Who told you that?'

'You know this place. I know more about you than you'd think. I've been reading him too. Aye. All that passion and honesty. It's almost heart-breaking.'

'Aye, he gets to you like that, don't he? *Duw* he makes you care. I can just feel my insides changing as I turn the pages. Needless to say Emlyn thinks he's marvellous. He says I should read some of Shaw's earlier stuff. Shaw was a good, hot radical, Em says.'

*

Dawn, the next morning, was so ravishing and so full of clear, ebullient sunshine that the people already milling around outside the Hall had to shade their eyes to look up at the sky.

But they were also shading their eyes to look at something else since, just where the light was breaking over the rims of the volcano, there were also hundreds of people swarming over the rocks and coming down the cliff paths. News of the search had carried into every Valley and they were coming from everywhere; a motley collection of odds and sods, many wearing walking boots and others daps; some with cameras and others with sticks; children with dogs and a gypsy with a horse; skinheads in Doc Marten boots and girls in school uniforms; a priest mumbling his rosary and many, many old-timers with their flat caps and shonny scarves.

Some were wandering up the main road and yet more were coming from the road leading up to the reservoir. But mostly they were trickling steadily over the volcano walls like blobs of wet paint falling off the outside of a tin; a dozen here, a pair there, one over there, a few coming up here ...

Who would have guessed that so many had heard of the disappearance of Huw Bungalow? Even more unfathomably who could have guessed that so many people cared enough about him to get up at the crack of dawn and tramp miles over these ancient hills of coal? The way the village streets were filling up it was as if almost every community in the whole of the South Wales Valleys had come, if not to find Huw, then to pay their respects to a boy everyone had loved.

The Hall could only hold a fraction of the massing crowd so Glynmor stood on the back of a beer lorry in the square to address them. 'We know Huw is here somewhere,' he shouted. 'We all want him home. Even if harm has come to him we must have him home. We've already searched the Valley and the houses. We didn't find him. So today we are going to have to do it all over again. I want men to go down the pit and look everywhere, even the old workings — particularly the old workings. By nightfall I want every single inch of this Valley to have been looked at and scratched and poked until we ... we ...'

He stopped speaking suddenly. 'Well kiss my aunty's cat's arse,' he muttered to himself. It looked as if the whole south

327

western corner of the Valley had blackened and was crumbling before his very eyes. Virtually the whole of Penrhos – which over the years had expanded to become one of the largest council estates in Europe – was pouring down on Bont like some medieval army come to lay siege.

'If that lot come to search our houses,' a warning voice shouted, 'we'll be lucky to have any chimney pots left by the time they've finished.'

'They once took the whole garage down in Ferndale,' someone added.

As the Penrhos army approached, a police helicopter came chattering overhead, its rotor blades chopping up the air into the finest slices, its fat body swerving one way and another above the approaching mob before lifting off up over the reservoir.

Glynmor drew himself up to full height like Adolf Hitler gazing down on his least-loved stormtrooper. It was Dan Bag O'Shit, former drinking butty of Tom Jones' bodyguard, former market gardener until the police examined his plants and locked him up, even a former Bont miner until he was caught stealing scrap from the pit and sent packing. Later sent to the new council estate of Penrhos – together with most of the other problem families of the Valleys – he was probably responsible for most of the trouble on that crime-ravaged estate.

So he had come back, his ratting cap set at a jaunty angle and a broad smile which suggested that he had never once told the truth or, if he had, it had been accidental. Glynmor had always been very fond of Bag O'Shit even if he was less sure of all the dole artists and ne'er do wells he had brought with him. You could even hear them all belching and farting when they were still half a mile away.

'Well, Bag O'Shit, it's been a few years since you honoured us with your presence in Bont.'

'Too long Glynmor. I came to your wedding, remember?'

'I remember all right. You haven't brought those bastard wooden spoons with you have you?'

'Left 'em home, Glynmor. But I've always loved Bont an I never pinched that iron down the pit either.'

'Thousands would believe you Bag O'Shit,' a voice shouted. 'An' millions wouldn't.'

'I know who stole that scrap,' Bag O'Shit bellowed back. 'An' it wasn't me. I was framed for that job I was. A year in the nick I did for that. An' I lost my job down the pit.'

'All right, boys, we're not here to debate Bag O'Shit's innocence,' Glynmor shouted out. 'But I say he done it.'

'Guilty as hell, Abdabs shouted above the cheers. 'They said he was going to pinch the pit wheel next.'

'Pity he didn't.'

'I never done this ... '

'All right, all right,' Glynmor chimed in again. 'Well, Bag O'Shit, I suggest you take you and your lot up to the pine forest on the west slope. People here wouldn't be happy with you lot searching their houses.'

'No, they fucking wouldn't,' shouted another voice.

'Your fucking language mun,' Bag O'Shit protested. 'There are women around aren't there?'

The search continued throughout the day, the pine trees resounding to the farts of Bag O'Shit's army, as yet more searchers came in from other valleys, kicking over stones and nosing into dustbins, peering and prodding down holes that had been peered down and prodded a hundred times before, opening doors uninvited and getting shooed away by irate housewives.

There were just too many enthusiastic volunteers to organise anything properly. When a search party of four miners tramped two miles underground just to check out the face of the old Trelewis Seam – abandoned as clapped out three years earlier – they met another group walking back.

'No sign of the boy there then?'

'Nothing except a load of good coal we could still get out if they let us.'

By midday many came drifting down the slopes to the Hall in search of a pint of beer. But soon they were wandering off again, thirsty and disappointed, since the committee chairman was still insisting that the bar remained closed until Huw had been found. One itinerant hot dog van was doing a brisk trade in the square and, in the chip shop, there was a long queue for fish and chips, bowls of curry and faggots and peas.

Glynmor and Maggie walked up to the reservoir and watched, with arms linked, as the frogmen continued diving into the cold lake. 'I saw the body of Stan Hughes pulled out of there once,' Glynmor said. 'Well, it wasn't a body really. It was a skeleton an' I'll never forget – his knee-cap fell off when they lifted him out of the water. A baker he was.'

'Oh I remember. I went to school with his sister. She was always falling asleep in the class she was. They used to call her Rip Van Winkle.'

'They say they're going to stop diving soon 'cos they've covered the whole of the reservoir.'

'I think I'd prefer not to see him again if he is, you know, dead,' she replied hesitantly. 'I'd like to remember him as he was. Always laughing. He always had some sort of smile on his lips didn't he? Even in his sleep he had that silly smile. I just couldn't look at that face if his smile wasn't there. Oh Glynmor.'

They had never once discussed that, at the root of their break-up, was Glynmor's wish to put Huw into a home. This conflict had floated away and disappeared like a long-forgotten argument. All they both wanted now was to have Huw back home again. That went without saying.

Neither had Maggie said anything about her visit from John. She wouldn't have known how to start explaining him to Glynmor. Anyway his visit now seemed more and more like a dream. The more she thought about it, the less sense it all made. But she was still praying, albeit secretly. She was still doing that. But Glynmor wouldn't understand, so she kept quiet.

For his part, Glynmor had been astonished at how forcefully his view of his son had changed over the past few days, how really desperate he was to find him again. Perhaps this reconstruction had come from the realisation that Huw was loved so completely by so many and perhaps the ideas of Jack London had begun to gnaw away at the inviolable citadel of his traditional selfishness. Perhaps it was merely the relief – and it was an immense relief – to be able to hold Maggie's body again, and perhaps it was because of other factors that he had not even thought of, but the sheer desperation of his desire to find Huw was something at total odds with all the previously-known features of Glynmor Jones. The shadows of deep-rooted personality change were falling everywhere.

They turned and walked back to the village again, the air

330